The Tempests of Time
Praise Page

Jeffries creates **another story that is on fire. A vivid time-ripping experience**...to unexpected new heights. Proves even more **confounding, brilliant, and astounding** (if this were possible). A stark, vivid, contemplative series...nearly **impossible to put down. A top pick** for libraries interested in the **cream of the crop** of Christian sci-fi and religious fantasy. An astonishingly vibrant read.

— DIANE DONOVAN, MIDWEST BOOK REVIEW

Not for the faint of heart. This story doesn't do half-measures. If you enjoy **apocalyptic thrillers with theological depth, visceral horror, and rapid-fire action**, this book is for you.

— LITERARY TITAN

Jeffries creates **a never-want-to-stop read** with fantastical, biblical, and immortal characters...**extraordinary**.

— LEX ALLEN, READERS' FAVORITE

The **beautiful writing and surprising twists** keep readers excited. Blockbuster scenes...dramatic dialogue...I **couldn't stop reading**. I didn't want the book to end.

— K.C. FINN, READERS' FAVORITE

Absolutely amazing...the drama, the chaos, and the intrigue were at their peak and I found myself hanging onto every page...**a masterpiece. Jeffries truly outdid himself with this book.**

— MICHE ARENDSE, READERS' FAVORITE

Gold Award, Feathered Quill
Silver Award, Feathered Quill
Bronze Award, Reader Views

Finalist, The Wishing Shelf Book Awards
Finalist, Chanticleer Int'l Book Awards

Semi-finalist, BookLife Prize
by Publisher's Weekly

BookLife Elite Author

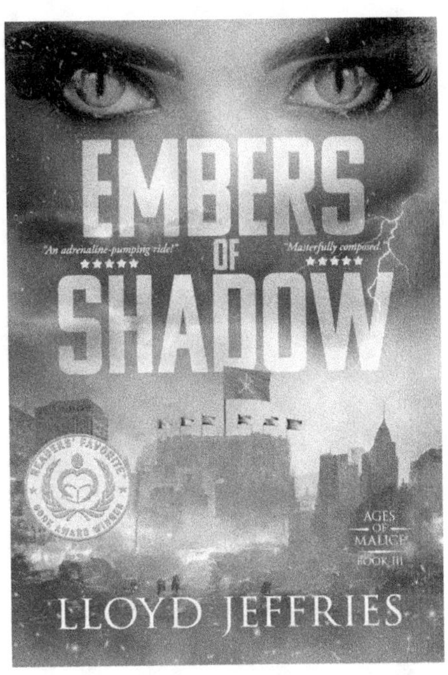

Gold Award, Literary Titan
Bronze Award, Readers' Favorite

Finalist, Feathered Quill Awards
Finalist, Reader Views
Finalist, Eric Hoffer, da Vinci Eye

"Jeffries creates another story that is on fire.
A vivid **time-ripping experience**…to unexpected new heights. Proves even **more confounding, brilliant, and astounding (if this were possible)** than its predecessors in the series. A stark, vivid, contemplative series that readers will find **nearly impossible to put down.** A **top pick** for libraries interested in the **cream of the crop of Christian sci-fi and religious fantasy.** An astonishingly vibrant read."
- Diane Donovan, Midwest Book Review

Follow Lloyd at https://lloydjeffries.com

THE TEMPESTS OF TIME

AGES OF MALICE, BOOK IV

LLOYD JEFFRIES

Copyright © 2024
The Tempests of Time
Lloyd Jeffries
First Edition
All rights reserved.

Library of Congress Control Number: 2025902615
ISBN 979-8-9906209-1-9 (paperback)
ISBN 979-8-9906209-0-2 (ebook)
ISBN 979-8-9906209-2-6 (hardcover)

Cover design by Design for Writers
Inkslinger Editing

For permissions, contact
Buckminster Publishing
Info@lloydjeffries.com

For the survivors.

Thoughts from the Verge

By Emery Merrick

Will anyone ever read this?

A common thought for word brokers, but one that looms as I ponder this volume and the events within.

Mysterious ways, indeed.

If you dare this twisted path, a word of advice: Venture at your own risk. The chasms are deep. The waters, foul and endless. The abyss, too cosmic.

This tome was written in scrawled words, jagged, streaked with blood. Ink forged from innocence, from deceit, from destiny and suffering. Turns out, this theater isn't for the faint.

What lies ahead is singularly unique. I've tried to capture all I endured with precision and agility. The full, spectacular, soul scorching truths of humanity, religion, God, Satan and the hells that plague us all. As I've mentioned, fate is a tortured mistress. A lass over whom I hold no sway and for whose actions I take no responsibility. My apologies if this changes your paradigms as it changed mine. But alas, you've been warned.

God help us all.
Emery

PROLOGUE

Flickering scarlet. Deep ebony. Stretching toward me. Thick, chunky, gripping, dragging.

The shriek of billions, a grating cacophony like all the Earth's raptors.

Agony sizzles, overwhelms my body, my mind, my soul. Smoke rolls from my being; astonished eyes bulge. My scream strangles in my throat. My skin blisters, melts, hits the floor and sizzles. The drops pulse with heat and anguish.

My mind shreds. Great, winged *things* circle, then descend in a black mass I can't possibly deflect. I raise my arms in horror. Barbed talons, then razor teeth, strip them to the bone. Blood vaporizes in a mist, becomes sticky, instantly congeals to new skin and muscle that covers my limbs.

They swarm again.

I lash, struggle, punch and scream. They tear me to shreds, these squawking beasts. Pointed claws rend an eyeball from my socket with a crunch that resonates through my skull. Two beasts fight for the morsel.

I'm fully aware, fully involved, no thought given to how I got here, the how's and why's made moot by ravenous furies and the decimation of all I am.

I'm overwhelmed, outmatched, helpless. Claws plunge and fangs shred, talons filet my torso, shred my neck and my face.

I wail, strangle. My mouth fills with ash.

Then a tooth's torn free. A bloody nerve dangles from jagged enamel as blood drips to sanguine vapor.

A beast delights, dances, holds its prize high before downing it in a gulp.

Another demon pounces, then another, then ten more.

Their weight crushes me to blistered, molten stone. My mouth's wrenched open, held fast by muscled arms.

My jaw cracks, then dangles like a windless flag.

They rip out all my teeth.

The anguish never ends. It coats me, defines primality in wrath and rage. It's complete and utter despair, an indefensible torrent.

They crush, flap, writhe, rend in ravenous delight.

A tempest of black drops—my own blood— burns to steam before my eyes. Flames wash over. New skin appears in the next instant, and I watch as blisters spread, congeal, and burst a serous rain that sizzles and steams.

I clamp my mouth shut, press my jaw with both hands.

Then they're back, prying my jaw, stealing my teeth, munching my bones to splinters.

Apologies fly from my shredded face.

A monster yanks my tongue and devours, shrieks at other beasts to keep their distance.

The torture's otherworldly, unbearable, molten, as demons dance in embers of shadow.

Then, I see the monster who possessed me, the one Cain exorcised. Somehow, its name floods my memory. Acedia, the demon of addiction.

I raise a hand, hear my own shriek as a powerful jaw rips it from my arm then spits it to sizzle in flames. I watch through a single remaining eye as a thousand demons leap after. Then, eight beastly arms, stronger than any twenty men, enwrap my torso and lift me high.

Demons gouge my back, gnaw at my head, tear my groin.

I'm an endless buffet.

My heart boils as it's ripped from my chest to coat my vision in clotted crimson.

The demon grins vicious teeth, chomps into it as more blood surges, as other beasts leap in.

A great howl sends them streaking away, leaves the first to feast on its prize.

Slobber drips neon green as the creature enjoys its meal.

The misery is unquenchable. I struggle, reach for my heart, try to reclaim it.

Above, a thousand furies swirl before swooping down and claiming the leftovers.

Hope's fled.

Mercy's unknown.

There's only torment.

There's only suffering.

Only ash-filled lungs and twisted eons.

I wish for death, cling desperate to finality.

But I'm struck. I shall not die.

I'm the main course. For any and everything that dwells here.

I raise new arms, try to fight, to defend, but they're ripped from my torso at first twitch.

Fetid mists rise as blood clots my throat, then mixes with a spiraling ash to become demonic clouds.

Arms regrow. My mouth fills again with teeth.

The demon drops my beating heart like a half-eaten apple. It sizzles like raw meat even as I grab it up, blow on it to clear the soot, then attempt to stuff it back in my chest.

Great blisters form, ripple, bubble, then burst in an explosion of crimson goo.

I hear my own anguish, feel my tongue like a swollen slug, choking my breath.

Then, a great winged dragon, larger by leagues than any other, absorbing wretched colors as smoke and hate and bile flow from scales in gleaming crimson.

Cracks spread on boiling stone. Geysers of vapor rise to mingle with the shriek of billions.

Demons cackle, howl, speed beyond the dark haze, away from the massive winged beast.

I crumple, trembling, weeping. An agony of burnt skin and renewed flesh.

The dragon looms.

My terror reflects in its eyes.

My mind fills with images of what it will do.

Nothing good dwells here.

Nothing good *can* dwell here.

Visions assault: Rhyme, nude, spitted, roasting above a bed of flaming lava and sizzling coal. Auburn locks singe to blistered scalp. Her face chars to black leather, leaves only gleaming emeralds that don't release my gaze.

She fades to ash, drifts to the hopeless mist.

Then my mother: chased by ravenous beasts, consumed again and again, her screams drenched in endless despair.

I cower, squeeze my arms close, pour tears, beg for mercy.

My skin renews, reblisters.

Then, Cain, framed in smoke, sharp eyebrows angled to acute points. His mark glows, throbs, flows everywhere to irradiate the horrible expanse.

Blood drips from his mouth. "Dearest Emery, welcome to immortality."

CHAPTER 1

JERUSALEM, ISRAEL

Rhyme's fingers are white. Hell, her entire hand blanches as she grips the steering. "Watch our six!"

I look at my watch. "Our what?"

"Our six. Behind us."

I crane my neck, press Houdini down, try to hold the big Doberman in place.

The truck shudders, then pushes me to the passenger's door as she squeals through a hard left.

"There," she cries. "More coming!"

I look up the street, a blur of roadside onlookers, then farther up, a blockade of Imperium vehicles.

"Hold on!" she screams, wrenching the wheel, lips quivering.

Houdini crashes into me as we spin through a U-turn to speed back the way we came.

A helicopter roars above, then circles and bears down.

"If you don't stop, they're going to shoot!"

"Good. I'd rather die, Emery."

I'm flabbergasted she'd ever think it. "And leave me alone?"

Her emeralds are calming. "Sorry. I forgot."

"Well, don't forget…" I start, but she bounces through another turn to streak down a city street. Residents gawk in blurred bewilderment.

She speaks to herself. "South is dead. North and west, equally useless." She hammers the gas, and we zip like lightning down the street. "You can't die, and I wish I was dead," she mumbles. "I won't go back," she says. "Never, never, never."

I look left, see the helicopter directly next to us, low, keeping pace.

Then the side door opens, and an Imperium soldier levels the biggest gun I've ever seen.

"They're going to shoot!" I squeeze Houdini with one hand, the holy shit bar with the other.

Then, from the back seat: "You dudes better chill. This is getting legit."

"Thanks for the news flash, Bill!" Rhyme yells, doesn't slow.

I stare at the helicopter as smoke flows from the huge gun. I hear reckless chatter as shrapnel shreds the vehicle's tires.

The world upends. A blazing blur of street, sky, buildings, and gawking pedestrians. I feel a sense of weightlessness, then the crash and wind-stealing grind as we hammer the asphalt. Sparks cascade through the smashed windshield, then mix with a tsunami of broken glass that peppers my face as we slide on our roof down the street.

There's a sickening grating sound, metal against concrete, then a decrescendo as we slide to a stop. Rotor wash rages, makes the interior of the crushed cab a gale force wind that threatens to sweep us away if we dare unbuckle or exit.

I reach for Rhyme, squeeze her arm. "You okay?"

Her head lolls, fists still clenched on the wheel.

Houdini wriggles from my grasp, appears upside down as he scampers across the vehicle's roof to lick her face. A small trickle of blood rolls up her forehead, then slides down auburn locks to drip on the ceiling.

"Rhyme?"

"She'll be alright," Bill says from the back.

Glass crunches on the road beside me. I see designer shoes, black and glossed. Then the grinning face of the elegant version of Longinus. "You shouldn't have run."

CHAPTER 2

JERUSALEM, ISRAEL

And here we sit, captured fugitives. Our crime: treason against Imperium.

Rhyme picks crumbs of glass from my face as she presses an ice pack to her head.

"We should've brought Crispy," I say.

Her head wags. "I doubt he could've helped. And why bring him into this? He's done enough. For both of us."

I examine my bumps and scrapes, pull an inch-long piece of glass from my forearm. "Have to admit, it was a hell of a ride."

She gives me a look, something akin to the stupid questions look Cain likes to give. "Yeah," she says, "together 'til the bitter end."

"You don't sound so happy about that."

"About what? The bitter end, or us being together?"

"The together part."

"Emery, don't be high maintenance right now. I'm with you no matter what. Do you still doubt that?"

My mind swims, tries to arrange the internal narrative into something sensible. I interlace my fingers between my knees. "I don't," I say. "It's just everything's moving so fast, like a nightmare from which I can't wake."

She sighs, sits back. "It'll only get worse. Especially if we stay."

I read her mind. When Cain gets here, if he comes at all, it's going to be bad. I've betrayed him, tried to run, with his wife, no less, and despite having very good reasons, I doubt he'll be in a forgiving mood.

The unfairness of everything strikes me. I'm a third grader cut in the lunch line, bawling my slight to an uninterested teacher.

Cain has everything. Can murder, steal, usurp, whatever he wants and without consequence. All serve at the pleasure of the gloved man.

Bill sits sucking a hard candy, probably something packed with THC. He seems no worse for wear. Not a mark on him, same hippie hair in dishwater blond, same far away gaze, same useless platitudes rolling from his mouth.

Houdini sits up, scratches his ear in a flurry of paw and nail. He yawns, then nudges close to Rhyme.

Since our mad dash for safety, we've been kept together, given food, examined by a doctor, even provided a comfortable place to wait with armchairs and a fruit bowl.

Waiting for what? I know Cain well enough to know he likes to soften up his victims before dropping the deadly anvil.

Then, I realize he can't kill me. I remember my immortality.

I'm going to say that again, this time more slowly, to concentrate on each word.

My. Meaning mine, solely me, the infinite I. *I* am immortal. *My.* Immortality. I roll the word, taste it, play with it, try to find the courage to discern all it means, subtle to glaring.

I am immortal. *I* will live forever. I've joined this league of madmen and now share their fate. I wonder if they have membership cards. Emery Merrick, Immortal, X'chasei Life Member.

"How am I immortal?" I ask my truest love. "How *specifically* was that accomplished, and why?"

Emeralds shine, then fade. A shadow of pity clouds her face.

She inhales, blows out, leans forward elbows on knees. "I don't know," she says. "It's not like Cain has the power to do that. I've wracked my brain as much as I can but continue to come up with nothing. Doesn't make sense," she says. "Maybe he's lying. Maybe he just said that to mess with your head."

"Mission accomplished. My head's a proper mess."

She moves close and lays her head on my shoulder. "The only way we'll know for sure is to test it, and I'm not about to shoot you in your handsome face to find out."

My stomach churns as I think of collecting Cain at the morgue after he was assassinated. I remember the tunnel through his head, the googly eye, the sight of my own crinkled reflection on the cupboard beyond.

I chuckle. "Yeah, let's not do that. From the way we've been living, I'm sure that experiment will happen on its own." I hold her eyes. "When it happens, I hope you're there holding my hand, waiting for me to return. I hope, when that happens, that I open my eyes to you."

Perhaps it's the recent stressors, weathered without the crutch of my fix to dull them. Perhaps it's the rigors of rolling down a littered street in a toppled, bullet pocked truck. Perhaps even, it's Bill, Longinus, Laslo, Igneus, Sebastian, Jonas. The fire fight over the spear, the harrowing ride to the airport, the abrupt and bumpy jet ride as we raced away from falling nukes. Perhaps it's the nukes themselves. Again, I examine the word. Nukes. Nuclear warheads. Nukes that murdered my country and all its citizens. Perhaps it's all of those things. Perhaps it's none of those things, but I feel emotional. And not at the thought of the hundreds of millions murdered. And not really at the thought of my own immortality. I feel drained in a way I can't quite put my finger on, like a sponge squeezed of every drop. Perhaps it's all the conundrums. I want to die but can't die. I want to run but can't leave Rhyme. I want to stay but don't want to be consumed by madness or madmen.

My eyes well with tears and I will them away. Rhyme's been so stoic, a bad ass really, and I don't want her to see me cry. Man up, I think, then Lenny's best impression of Crispy floats through my thoughts. "Grow a pair, FNG!"

"Right you are, Len!"

Rhyme gives me a comforting look, emeralds sparkling, then kisses the tip of my nose. "You've been through a lot, Emery. But know this, when the time comes, I'll be there come hell or high water."

I squeeze her close, inhale her fragrance, her essence. I've no doubt about her sincerity or her commitment to me, and that provides a soothing balm for my savaged soul.

Moments like these are cathartic, I think. Sometimes it's nice to reflect. To give myself a break and try to process all I've endured. Not to have a pity party or anything, but, I think, Freudian as I am, that sometimes one needs to give themselves credit for the blows they've suffered.

Still, had I allowed Sig to do his job, none of this would be happening.

> *If indeed you find me dead,*
> *you'll know I finally pulled the thread,*
> *and decompressed my raging head,*
> *with a hunk of heartless lead.*
> *I finally know there is no balm,*
> *for a soul deceived with such aplomb.*
> *Now even death subdued for me,*
> *no gun or cord can do the deed.*
> *—The ruddy plot's abandoned me.*

I chuckle as the new poem imprints. I hold her eyes, see her love in slick emerald. "And what about you? Could you be immortal too?"

"Not a chance."

"How do you know?"

"I just do."

"But how?"

"I don't know."

I lean close and squeeze her tight. Houdini moves closer. "We should find out how and you can join me."

"Not a chance."

"Why not? We'd be together—"

"Emery, there's not a chance I'll willingly do that."

I stare at her as Bill stands, stretches, his face twisted in a yawn. He looks like an alley cat, mangy and sinewed, comfortable in any environment, prepping to nap in the summer sun. "You dudes worry too much," he says. "Everything will be the way it's supposed to be."

"Thank you, Bill," I say, voice dripping with solemnity, "for that stunning commentary and amazing advice. All my worries have evaporated."

"Don't mention it," he says, entirely missing the sarcasm.

He sits, crosses his legs tight at the knees, then pulls a Ziplock and pack of Zig-Zags from his trousers. Deft fingers spin and before I know it, he holds a perfectly rolled, plump joint. "Got a light?" he says.

I shake my head both in answer to his question and in amazement that *this* is where his thoughts are.

"Never mind," he says. A pack of matches appears from his pocket. "I think this still has one or two."

"You know there's such a thing as lighters," I say.

"Yeah, but they seem dangerous. Newfangled contraptions can go south in a variety of ways." He strikes a match and rests the joint in the flame.

The bitter odor of weed wafts over us.

I lean back, suppress a chuckle. There's something about him that cracks me up, and I mean that in a good way.

He inhales deep, speaks through held breath as he offers the joint. "You should try this. It's really good."

Rhyme reaches. "I'll have a go."

I'm amazed as she takes the joint and draws deep. I've never seen her do anything close to this. Never seen her imbibe on anything except an occasional merlot or the very seldom Old Fashion.

A stream of smoke flows from her mouth. "Reminds me of college."

I grin, remember how little I know about this woman whom I adore so completely. "Just who are you again?"

She giggles and passes the joint.

An odd feeling comes over me just then, a weird memory about a favored pipe and a blood-filled hypodermic. "I used to be a junkie." It sounds like a question.

"Used to be?" she says.

"Yes, remember?"

"Oh, I remember. It's the *used to be* that has me confused."

"Cain healed me, removed a demon. I watched the whole thing. He pulled this thing from my chest, from my heart, it seems. Slobbering, writhing, muscles bulging, fangs dripping. It was horrifying." I reel in my own astonishment. "You know I haven't thought about a drug since then. I don't even know where my stash is."

A hint of a smile appears on her face, as if what I'm saying is some sort of joke. When no punchline comes, she becomes more serious, then smiles broadly. "Emery, I think that's the best news I've ever heard."

"You know he's evil," Bill says.

We both look at him. Seems potheads are always a few seconds behind. I act shocked, place a hand to my cheek. "You know, now that you mention it, he does seem a bit jaded."

Rhyme jabs me with her elbow. "Don't make fun."

Bill doesn't notice. "You'd better sit pretty because he's going to be here any second."

And a single second later, we hear keys scratch the locked door. Cain enters with Stuart, the hulking African bodyguard, standing behind, scowling.

"Why, my dear wife." His smile lights the room. "What sordid company you keep. Seems you've fallen in with a naughty crowd."

CHAPTER 3

JERUSALEM, ISRAEL

"Behold, I give you every herb bearing seed on the Earth." Bill stares at the smoldering joint. "God said that to Adam."

We all stare at him. "What?"

"The Bible, Genesis 1:29."

"Really? What's it say about heroin?"

Rhyme gives another sharp jab. "Emery," she scolds.

"Ever notice how *everything* starts with nothing?" Bill says, joint hanging from his lips, eyes glazed and bloodshot. He pulls a red scrunchie from his pocket and twists his hair in a ponytail.

Cain claps a single time. "Bill, you are *such* a delight!" He sounds giddy. "And, I see, no worse for wear from this morning's little adventure."

Bill ignores him. He's on a roll. "My point is that through the entirety of time, *everything* began from nothing. Whether you believe in the big bang theory or the concept of a world created in seven days. All of it, every instance, every single time, begat from nothing.

"Take Emery, an artist with the written word who stares at the nothingness of a blank page. Then consider the nothingness of the words jumbled in his head. He joins them to create something. See? He starts with nothing but primordial soup, so to speak. Like any artist, Degas, Sting, Picasso, all started with nothing."

"Thank you for that interesting…" I start, as the rest look with expressions from humor to amazement.

Bill continues undaunted, the words flowing from the nothingness in his head. "Pink Floyd, Donald Fagen, Beethoven, Stevie Ray. All started with nothing. Then consider the buildings around us, the jets we fly, the TV we watch. All products of nothing. Made entirely from dreams and vapor." He chuckles, eyes glazed and shining. An expression that says he's exploring the depths of his own blown mind. I'm familiar with the look, the earth-shattering insights. When awash in the high, the mind becomes a mighty magnet. Whether that be to draw a symphony to the blank page, or to smear oils in a perfect way, or to join bricks, wire and conduit in perfectly precise fashion. It all comes from nothing.

I snicker. "We get it, Bill."

"I don't think you do," he says. "It's as if—" he stops here, like the thought's run away. "As if— Oh yes. As if every care, worry, trial, hardship, is born from nothing, and thusly," he raises a finger, "means nothing. Yet we cloud our minds—and our judgment—with all these nothing cares."

I wonder how Bill knew what I did for a living. I don't remember ever telling him I'm a journalist. "Even the United States," his voice catches, "started from nothing." He looks down, wipes a tear. "And has returned to nothing." He suddenly becomes the hippie college professor, a Berkley academic exploring the mystical compounds of LSD. Rising to stand, he says, "Can anyone tell me what conclusions can be drawn?"

I expect a piece of chalk to appear from his endless pocket, for a chalkboard to pop up. He casts his gaze between us, waiting.

"Ah," he grins. "I've stumped you, haven't I? Well, I guess that's today's homework for all the guys and dolls." He winks, wears an expression of all-encompassing mystery.

The joint flares as he draws and holds his breath.

Cain chuckles, then claps his hands a single time. "Such a delight!

Truly, coming along wonderfully! I'm so thrilled I created you. You exceed all expectations."

"Created me from nothing," Bill notes. "As you were created."

Cain considers this for a moment, white hair brightening like the proverbial cartoon light bulb. "Right," he says, placing a hand on Bill's shoulder. He redirects his gaze to us. "Shall we proceed?"

Rhyme stands. "With?"

"Why, with getting you home, my love. With tending to your wounds and getting you fed, watered and rested."

Rhyme and I trade glances. Bill returns to his seat. Houdini stands, stretches, bristles, but at Cain or Stuart I can't discern.

Cain squats and takes the Doberman's massive jaws in his hands. He seems undaunted by the fact that this animal can rip his face off in a flat second.

Houdini calms, circles once then resumes the floor.

Without chemicals on board, my mind operates like newly greased. Drawing to my feet, I consider my question before asking. "I have to ask. Does something unsavory await us?"

Cain waves a hand, gives me the stupid questions look. "Nonsense. You were merely reacting to all that's occurred. Quite normal, really, for the mortal mind to be overwhelmed by such things. Frankly, I'm surprised it didn't happen sooner."

He looks to the white drop ceiling, then at Houdini. "Like training a dog, now that I think about it. A dog's first instinct, when taken in hand, is to run away. You and my wife aren't so different. You've both endured a lot, and it's only natural that during your training you'd try to escape. Quite normal, predictable even. Expected." He wears the air of a grin like a mother on a paper towel commercial. "You were easier to catch than I expected, especially considering my wife's singular talents. Alas, though, no harm done— a vehicle wrecked, some pavement damage, a few bumps and bruises that will soon be only memories. Come, let's go home and rest, shall we?"

Rhyme steps past him and into the hall. Houdini pads after, sticking close to her knee.

I wave Bill forward, wait the obligatory seconds for the motion to register in his head.

"Thank you, good sir," he says as he steps past.

I follow him down the sterile corridor as Cain and Stuart bring up the rear.

We are men of action, I think. Lies do not become us. I remember the line from *The Princess Bride*, remember saying it to someone at some point when my head was besieged by chemical demons and my body beleaguered for want of nutrition and sleep. I battle my logic. Cain isn't a man to forgive so easily. Yet he's shown wondrous patience and restraint regarding me and Rhyme.

"Where's Longinus?" I ask. The thought occurs that the huge Roman still has an ax to grind, probably on my head. Or sword, to be more appropriate to the centurion and his favored weapon. Or a spear. *The* Spear, now that I think of it.

Cain must notice the worry on my face. "Have no fear, dear Emery. Our Longinus has bigger fish to fry currently. I also believe he's calmed a bit and at this point will probably cause you no harm. And even if he does, it's not like he can kill you."

The statement prods my memory, the simple fact of my predicament.

I am immortal.

Or so I'm told.

I walk a bit faster. "Great," I sigh. "Big day for me."

CHAPTER 4

JERUSALEM, ISRAEL

<Ahem>

Well, so, I got the old recorder back from Cain and just listened to my last musings. My first suicide note, as it were. And one for the ages, if you ask me. Jesus, what a sad sack. But back then, thinking I'd gone through it all, not knowing it was all just starting. I mean, ridiculous right? But when the sums are tallied, it all adds up to too much.

I have to admit, I'm a bit abashed by my little sortie into misery and self-contempt. So, let's have a redo. A new beginning, as a fella once said. A one-take mixtape. We'll call it "Emery's Big Adventure."

Okay, calm down everyone. I'll keep the gloom to a minimum. Or try. After all I've seen, that may be a tall order. But, alas, it's all about the journey, no?

Anyway, am I blabbing? Probably. And here's what's funny: I don't even miss Macallan and haven't even thought about my fix. So, a step in the right direction and chalk one up for ole Emery.

Despite all that, I should mention how completely exhausted I am. Like a crusted sponge completely wrung of all soul, emotion, or energy. It's a bit surreal, the way this has fallen upon me. But maybe it's the…the…well, everything.

But fear not, brave adventurers. I shall endeavor to present this summary with as much precision as possible. I'll even avoid cliches, if that's even possible these days.

Is everyone ready? I'm a bit smoked, so bear with me and together we'll try to put this old recorder to better use.

<Yawn>

Here we go.

As a young reporter I had a habit of failing to *ground my audience*, as my editor constantly said. By that she meant, orient them to the particulars of place, time, and information needed to process the story.

Alas, here I am again, with the words of my first news chief ringing in my head, waving my story like a flag as she shouts. "Merrick! Where the hell are we? What are we doing when this story starts? The world runs on details, kid. Try to include them from time to time."

So, in sweet Catherine's honor, include them I shall. Consider this your orientation to all that's occurred from the second I pushed Mr. Sig to my head, to the day Cain collected us from that sterile room in the detention center. Amended for brevity of course, which, I'm told, is the soul of wit.

So, first, I'm immortal, or so I'm told. Made that way by some force unknown. Again, or so I'm told.

My pal Cain is the Antichrist and has taken over the Middle East and used his considerable gifts and talents to destroy both Russia and the United States. It seems they'd displeased him, so he'd swept them aside with a nuclear strike, timing the attacks perfectly so they coincided with his coronation as the Emperor of Imperium, a new kingdom of his own creation that comprises all countries in the Middle East. His first decree as emperor had been to usurp any sort of democracy and promote all heads of state to kings.

I know, sounds impossible, but Cain is the bearer of the gifts of charisma and diplomacy, and wields those intangibles with the deftness of a master samurai with a razor katana.

In any event, his timing was perfect. As the Spear of Destiny spun against a backdrop of crystal skies, he summoned it to him, and from it came a burst of white-hot energy that blazed into the heavens.

Turns out this was by design as well, because the resulting balefire destroyed any incoming nukes he wanted destroyed and left alone those he didn't. A spin on Israel's Iron Dome, except this one worked flawlessly.

So, as far as I know, the United States and Russia, perhaps China, are completely destroyed. Smitten in a stroke by the formerly gloved, currently silver-haired, crystal-eyed man.

I witnessed the fall of the U.S. from a plane I shared with Rhyme, my ex-wife and current love; Crispy, a dogged ex-soldier both capable and scarred beyond belief; Bill, a dope-smoking hippie clone; and Houdini, a massive black Doberman that Rhyme acquired at some point in her adventures in the northeastern U.S.

Sitting here thinking about it, I thought Houdini was dead multiple times during our rush to get to the only aircraft capable of saving us from the annihilation to come. But through some miracle, the dog's right as rain. Unharmed, unscarred, fully animated and alive as if it was never injured to begin with. Perhaps Sebastian stumbled upon it. Perhaps Cain healed it, although I don't know if his powers extend to the healing variety. Suffice it to say, Rhyme is overjoyed that the dog she's adopted is unharmed and well.

It does make one think though.

Then there's Igneus, Sebastian, Jonas, Longinus, Sima, Pappy, President Carpenter, et al. The rest of the cast in this picture show of shocky horrors.

Okay, so, Igneus and Sebastian. You see, Igneus is a frail Jew with the roaring heart of a lion. His story is that of the unlikely hero. Made immortal, like Longinus, at the crucifixion of Jesus, only to find that this punishment had a purpose—which, he thought, was to stop Cain from entering the newly rebuilt Temple in Jerusalem. At some point he found his true heart and now wields a crooked stick that has supernatural power rivaling the spear Longinus wields, the Spear of Destiny.

So, Igneus was instrumental in stopping an attack on Jerusalem brought on by a coalition of armies led by Russia. He used his staff to thwart a trojan horse type ground attack and infiltration, then laid Cain low when Cain tried to confront him. A story in and of itself. And already written down.

These days Igneus hangs out with Sebastian, a child who lived in a sterile environment constructed by Cain in order to produce the ancient Children of the Rocks, or priest cleansers, so that Cain could be cleansed and enter the Temple. Sebastian's a good kid, possesses some of the same powers as Igneus but in a different way. Seems Sebastian's powers are defensive: healing, protection and the like; whereas Igneus's powers are offensive: sizzling chain lightning that leaps from his staff and lays enemies low. Together they are a force of their own and have become a balance against Longinus and his Spear of Destiny.

They also hang out with an Israeli named Jonas, a former officer in the Israeli special forces. As adept at combat as Longinus himself, Jonas even rendered the Roman unconscious during a battle for the Spear of Destiny at the Church of the Transfiguration up on Mount Tabor.

Jonas has a tough story. But in typical soldier fashion, he, well, soldiers on despite the heartbreak he's endured. I don't know much more about him other than to say his heart's in the right place.

Then there's Crispy, Rhyme's old friend and mentor and also a mercenary of sorts. Again, I don't know a lot about the man except his face and arms are scarred like melted wax and he's a handy guy to have around if things get sticky. In fact, I believe him to be the sole reason Rhyme and I escaped the falling nukes with just seconds to spare. I know Rhyme loves him like a father, and they have a special relationship that I don't really understand but seems to give them both joy.

<stretch, yawn, sigh>

Jesus guys. Again, sorry. Just so smoked. C'mon, Em, dig deep.

<sigh>

Now, on to Rhyme, my ex-wife. The pure shit this lady has suffered from me alone, if stacked in piles, would probably be the first dung heap to reach space. That is, unless you count the piles Houdini produces. I mean, yeesh!

Anyway, in large part, Rhyme was responsible for the day I pressed a pistol to my skull determined to end it all. You see, I thought she was dead, that she had just died in fact. In my drug and alcohol induced state, coupled with my ruined reputation and completely empty bank account, I'd had enough. Then Longinus came knocking and, long story cut off, I found myself working as Cain's biographer, all the while trying to grieve for Rhyme while still angry at her for divorcing me.

But turns out she wasn't dead. Also turns out she'd married the monster Cain, the Antichrist, to protect me from him. Seems at some point her and Cain had "battled to a stalemate". Their words, not mine, and had come to some sort of agreement regarding something Rhyme possessed that Cain wanted. In any event, and like most instances where I become involved, I managed to fuck it all up. Then the adventure started.

The good news, though, is that Rhyme still loves me despite the dumbass I am. A special thing, really, that quality women possess. The ability to see into you, and right through you. To nurture the good and always, always, dream, hope, pray, that somehow you become the man only she can see. A man with attributes so grand, none of us can really live up to them. Call it intuition or whatever, but it's a sort of magic. In any event, and to my great fortune, fate chose her for me and we're finally together again. And for that I am the better, albeit confused.

It seems, there's much about her I don't know. Her past is scarred and jaded, and she's mum on the events that brought her to me. However, I did see her in action once where she killed a handful of men, after being tortured no less, and yet managed to retain the capacity to be nurturing to Houdini and to me.

What a wonder is woman, created from Adam's rib, as imagined on the storyboard. Although, if I compare qualities between genders, I'm willing to bet it was the other way around.

From my perspective, very little that's pure is born from man.

Alas, though, I digress.

So, Rhyme's married to Cain, who really seems to love her, if such a thing can be said about the Antichrist and all his evil. The good news, they've both told me of her preference for me, which remains something Cain believes will change in time. To that end, there's really nothing he won't indulge her, and he seems caring and affectionate during their interactions.

But too bad for him. Rhyme prefers me and does not equivocate as to her preference.

Will wonders never cease.

Let's see. Who's left? President Carpenter of course, the former President of the United States of America, or should I say, the president of the former United States of America.

Oh, here I go. Give me a second to shake this off. I watched my country die in a hailstorm of falling nukes and seeing that sort of thing tends to brand the soul.

So surreal, that memory, the grief and agony so deep, I haven't really processed it. It's as if my mind can't handle the full weight, the full realization, that America the beautiful is no more. It's suppressed, repressed. Like a movie I can't rewind or restart. It is horror in its purest form. A broken heart that endlessly bleeds but never dies. I don't know if you can hear the tears, but trust me when I say they're there, and that this entire story is drenched with them.

Excuse me, I need a minute.

Okay, I'm back. Please accept my apologies. I'd like to talk about something happier, but it seems *that* emotion is in short supply, not just in my own heart but in the hearts and minds of the entire world at this point. A product of the Antichrist and his reign, his subterfuge, his complete and total evil. It wasn't like Pappy didn't warn me.

<suppressed yawn>

Now, as to Pappy, he's a friar who heads the Franciscan order up at the Church of the Transfiguration. He was present as Longinus and I stood atop the church, Israel yawning before us, struggling with the Spear of Destiny, trying to repel and, turns out, completely annihilate, the attacking Russian coalition. What happened up there was truly awesome and not in the cliched way people use that word today, but in the genuine, factual way of inspiring pure and complete *awe*. A million bolts of lightning striking at the same instant, laying the army low in a single second. The briefest of sparks, a continental sizzle.

Pappy witnessed all of that, then afterwards, while Longinus rested and shook off the sheer power of the Spear, the friar and I had a chance to talk.

He told me he believed Cain to be the Antichrist. You see, Pappy reeks intelligence and is an expert on biblical prophecy. Couple that with a rapid brain and incredible memory, he put together signs and events in extraordinary ways. Ways that still prompt my favored cliches about these events. Preposterous, impossible, uncanny, pure farce. I was fixed up when he leveled his conclusions and, despite everything I've seen, my mouth still stretches as my favored phrase floats through. *Bullshit.* Can't be. Just no way.

Yet, here I am, happily droning, unhappily robbed of the drugs that numbed and the booze that buoyed. At this moment, I don't know what's become of Pappy. Does he remain on the mountain tending his flock, or has he been usurped, replaced, cast out, killed? I do hope I see him again, God willing.

Then we come to Longinus. The centurion who ran a spear through Christ's side during the crucifixion. Well known in folklore and myth, he's revered without even a smidgeon of irony by the Catholic church as a saint. He even has a statue in St. Peter's Basilica.

I assure you, though, a saint he is not. He's probably the most brutal, blood thirsty, nasty character one could ever encounter, and generally, after his encounters, coroners make their rounds to collect the dead. He's Cain's right-hand man and trusted ally. He also wields the Spear of Destiny, a relic created before my very eyes when Cain smeared his own blood on the spear's tip. Prior to that and for centuries, the spear "twasn't worth a frog's fart," to use the vernacular of my old centurion pal.

It seems Longinus and I are frenemies. He's offered to kill me a few times and almost succeeded when he ran his sword through my abdomen after I pissed him off. Even now, I fear he remains pissed.

Believe me when I say, of all shit lists on which to find yourself, his is the one best avoided.

<sigh>

In any event, the big Roman seems to have found true love in the form of a slight girl named Sima. A former world-class pianist, she's also mean as a stomped snake. It's the wonder of wonders that the Roman even has the capacity for love, but their individual evil, murderous intent and capability, combine them to a match made in heaven. At this point in our tumultuous relationship, Longinus has it in for me because I knocked Sima unconscious while she was trying to attack Sebastian. The fact that she stabbed me in the chest and I almost died doesn't seem to matter, so thankfully I haven't seen the Roman since that incident. Unless, of course, you count when he retrieved me from the overturned vehicle during our escape. It's odd, but he was in his elegant form then, and when he's like that, he's not much for words. Perhaps the elegant Longinus doesn't share the memories of the brutal Longinus. Either way, he'd turned us over to Imperium forces without a word, then stalked off to a waiting limo and disappeared. So, I have no idea if he's gunning for me. If he is, I fear I'll be treated to a buffet of agony never before visited on a wayward, ex-junkie like myself.

Anyway, that should do it, consider yourselves properly grounded. And thank God, now I can sleep a bit.

Oops, wait a sec, I forgot Laslo Slabav and his son, Israel. Laslo was the Prime Minister of Israel until Cain saw fit to replace him. A silent coup, now that I think about it, but, thinking about it, Laslo never really had a chance. When he was finally deposed, he was thrown in prison and tortured. He managed to escape and, last I knew, was part of Igneus's entourage, which includes, Sebastian and Jonas.

Israel is Laslo's son, and a kid who couldn't be more loved by his father. Unfortunately, and the details are a bit hazy due to how high I was when I met the lad, he's now a ward of Cain's and a blessed "Prince of Imperium." But Laslo is desperate to free him, and I'm sure he and the rest of the gang are hatching plans even now to do just that.

I can't imagine a peak so high or ocean so vast that Laslo wouldn't attempt traversal to get to his son.

God be with them all.

<stifled yawn>

Excuse me for yawning, the events of the last couple of days must be catching up to me and I feel the need to sleep as if I've never slept before. I'll try to knock out the next few paragraphs with precision and speed.

I believe all who remains is John the Apostle, current whereabouts unknown. Personally, I like to think he's in heaven, taken up after the events at the Temple that seem to have happened so long ago. The Apostle had been made immortal by Christ before the crucifixion and given some special task to perform. Of all the things that are interesting about that man, the fact that he was the same guy who wrote Revelation while imprisoned on the Isle of Patmos, is the most salient. "Modern scholars" disagree with that story, stating John the Apostle was too old to be on Patmos to write Revelation and, therefore, it was written by a different guy also named John.

But I know the truth, told to me from John's own mouth. He received the vision and wrote it down, not really knowing what he was writing or why. He told me that the writing was taken by Cain, acting then as Emperor Constantine, who commandeered the text and decreed Christianity as the empire's official religion. To think, Cain himself convened a council to create the Bible we have today.

But here's the joke for our Home Audience. Cain changed things for his own use—to control and direct the actions and thoughts of the believers. He did this as Cain does most things, using subterfuge, working behind the scenes, and then just stepping in and taking over before anyone knows what hit them.

Looking back, and forward, it seems this one particular move, long ago, was essential to all that's occurred: that commandeering of Revelation. I don't know what John's special task was or even if it was fulfilled, because he wasn't released from immortality when he set down his stylus. I don't know if he still walks the Earth and have only seen him in dreams and visions. I hope he's well, wherever he is.

Now, back to Cain, the eldest son of Adam and Eve and the world's first murderer. Made immortal and cast out after slaying his brother, Abel, in a fit of jealous rage.

Cain's done it all and nothing stops him. I'll try to list his antics from the top of my head as I'm too exhausted to review my notes: Let's see. Rebuilt Temple in Jerusalem. Created a one-world currency. Cleansed himself as a priest and entered the Temple. Was shot in the head at point-blank range and lived. Brought peace to the Middle East. Destroyed both the United States and Russia. United the Middle East under the single banner of Imperium. Repelled nuclear warheads. Created the Spear of Destiny. Fulfilled the prophecies of Revelation to usher in the end times where he plans on offering humanity as sacrifice to God. Marked by God and cast out, still has the mark on his right hand. Assassinated only to return on Easter Sunday with bristling white hair and sterling blue eyes, a distinct change from the dark hair and eyes he had when I met him. Anyway, the list goes on and on and much to everyone's detriment.

And that's it, I think, and just in time, it seems exhaustion has the best of me.

At this point I *must* sleep, the choice is no longer mine.

I've never been so tired.

I'll be back after catching some Z's. See you soon.

CHAPTER 5

JERUSALEM, ISRAEL

A normal reaction to an abnormal situation.

Rhyme Carter stares at the ceiling, watches a squeaky fan spin. Cain's left their bed. An early riser, he's generally gone before dawn. That's if he ever came home. She doesn't know, doesn't care. A pang of nausea grips as she thinks of her predicament, then slides from the bed, and moves from the room.

The Antichrist's pattern: late to bed, early to rise. If he sleeps at all.

Antichrist. She rolls the word through her head, the embodiment of all evil and iniquity.

And you married it.

A normally metronomic pulse flutters as fear seeps in. She swoons briefly, leans on a wall of cold marble, takes a second to collect herself as the problem crushes.

She's complicit.

Guilty.

Of everything.

As guilty as all Cain's henchmen, all of X'chasei, President Carpenter, every other madman in history.

If only Carpenter had listened, had given the benefit of the doubt, perhaps things would be different. Perhaps the U.S. and its hundreds of millions would still be alive.

She considers what she knows about nuclear fallout. Scant facts, the rest assumptions. The phrase *wind patterns* pops in and makes her think the devastation will be less for some, more for others.

She thinks of Carter's Glen and its simple inhabitants. The laundry mat, the pizza joint. The lonely kid playing on her phone before cold ovens. The people in the laundromat, watching cloth rainbows spin behind glass portals.

Her former home is death now.

Tears fall as she slides down the wall, hand pressed to an aching heart.

It's all gone. Thousands of towns just like Carter's Glen, vaporized in an instant. All the pizza joints and laundromats in all the little bergs throughout America, gone in a flash, turned to smoke and ash by her own husband.

Wiping her face, she wills the thought away as others flood in.

Houdini's cold nose presses her hand. His fur feels soft, soothing, as he licks a stray teardrop from her face. She pulls him close, squeezes tight, sobs into dense fur.

They'd barely escaped: her, Emery, Crispy, Bill and the dog. Had left America to its fate of fire and clouded mushrooms.

"Such a good boy," she whispers, nuzzling. "Such a handsome boy." Houdini presses close, gives another kiss. Rhyme inhales a stuttered breath, then rises. "Let's see if we can find some coffee."

Houdini stays close, moves easily, shows no wound or scar after being shot by that toad Jenkins.

Another oddity.

Houdini was mortally wounded during the firefight, but now appears as healthy and spry as ever. She kneels, runs her hands over his broad frame and huge black snout. Dark eyes return a gaze both steady and trusting. "What happened?" she says. "How is it that you're so well?"

A cold nose nudges her face, then he spins so she can rub his butt. "Just add it to the pile of things that don't make sense. You should be dead. Even Emery thought so. But there's not a mark on you. Doesn't add up."

Morning sun lays strips of light across Houdini's dense fur. "C'mon," she says, "let's find you some chow."

They pad down the stairs, past the wall of windows that frame Jerusalem's landscape. Outside, stone bastions crawl like lichen, over hills that mix sunlight and chase shadows.

Things are always better in daylight. Seems her life's been a never-ending struggle to survive each night. Staring at ceilings, ceiling fans, tent flaps, whatever; counting the ticks of an imaginary watch, hoping for sleep, mind clouded, invaded, tortured.

So much death, starting with her parents, then her first love. Flowing through others to her unborn child, then the millions who died in Russia and America, maybe China.

At the bottom of the stairs, she passes Emery's room, thinks of their reunion, longs to enter and spoon like the old days. To feel his warmth, the steady pulse of his breath, the little sounds he makes as he snoozes. She remembers Longinus's sword pressed to his throat. Remembers the icy grip of panic, of pure desperation, then flying down the stairs shrieking, begging Cain to stay the Roman's hand.

The familiar rises, clings, moldy yet vivid. Ever-present. Night and day. For weeks, months, years. Guilt. A spiked hand that pierces her soul, her thoughts, her psyche. Joe Bonamassa lyrics float through.

> *Blood on my hands and*
> *there's holes in my jeans.*
> *You scrub all day*
> *but you never get them clean.*

The stains, too deep.
The memories, too vivid.
The holes, too broad.
The dead. Well, just too dead.
The living, too occupied, too self-centered, too drenched in horror to lift their heads above the throbbing morass that is life.

That idiot Carpenter! He should've listened! If he had, perhaps Cain would be in custody. She and Emery off to parts tailor-made for disappearing. Maybe the millions would be alive. Maybe she and Emery could have a chance at happiness, contentment.

The spiked hand closes, makes her stomach ache, her face ugly.

Perhaps Emery would still be mortal.

If only she'd seen things clearly, had listened instead of punching out his lights and embarking on her lone crusade to finish Octavio and its leader.

So naïve.

Even if she'd known the truth of Cain and his immortality, his Godly punishment, nothing would be different.

The Antichrist has it well in hand. Plays on a chess board only he can see.

She's been outmaneuvered, outflanked, out thought, out planned, out strategized. Cain bided his time, used centuries of trial and error to attain his objectives, spinning silk like a brown recluse, thousands of threads, dark, sticky, invisible, diabolical.

He'd kept Emery close then used him to max effect. All the while making her think her struggle, her screaming vengeance, were enough to overcome the madman he is.

But it's never been enough. Not against this devil, this immortal, the everlasting, Cain.

The kitchen glares in white marble as sunlight streams from stainless steel. The coffee pot hisses, then glugs steaming liquid into a mug adorned with smiley faces.

As if, she thinks, staring at the emojis, leaning against the counter. Smiles are on backorder.

She thinks of death, of immortality, of her small role in such a vast production. A colossal failure, her efforts not close to being enough, all her plans and machinations twisted, used against her.

Even now, there must be a way. *The only time hope's gone is when you quit.* I'm not beaten. Not yet. I'm just confused, overwhelmed, plagued by guilt, regret, longing. Heartbreak.

So, what else is new?

"Seems God works in mysterious ways." Cain's words when he'd informed them of his little experiment. When he'd informed them of Emery's immortality.

Probably a lie, she thinks, hopes, as guilt rises like acid in her gullet.

The coffee is hot and bitter, provides a small measure of comfort.

Emery immortal? Another piece that doesn't fit.

Has to be a lie.

The thought melds with the spiked hand, adds crystals of terror, icy and sharp.

What if *I'm* immortal? What if Cain just hasn't told me? What if me and Emery have to endure the centuries together, yet apart. Centuries under the Antichrist's demon eyes and serpent tongue.

Houdini circles then curls on the floor. Rhyme shudders and shakes the thought away.

She's playing *his* game not hers, moving down twisted paths that lead only to confusion, deceit, manipulation.

Joe Bonamassa comes again, Joey B, Crispy's favorite. A smooth voice wails as he hammers his chords. *The hard rock bottom, ain't nothin' down there but the blues.*

What-ifs roll, gain speed, tumble down ragged mountains, fueled by grief, despair, confusion. *Blues at the bottom.*

Cain has her exactly where he wants her. Struggling, kicking, cocooned in silk threads, suspended, inverted, inert. He's winning without even trying.

Lies.

All of it.

Has to be.

Hasn't been tested.

The Antichrist's a liar.

A ruse meant to scramble her head. Why would Cain want Emery immortal? If anything, Cain's plans would be better accomplished if *she* were immortal, forced to share a never-ending life with a man she abhors and despises. That tacks better with the image of the Antichrist.

Has to be bullshit.

Who can grant immortality, anyway? So far, the only contender is God Himself.

Yet here I am spinning in the middle with no way to know, or stop, any of my husband's plans.

And with that comes complicity. Fuel for the guilt that more than sustains itself, that plagues and robs the good. Her baby, Crispy, America, Emery, the list goes on and on. B-movie credits with names no one knows or cares about.

But *I* care, she thinks, does that mean so little? Suffering for those you love, never giving up, struggling to stand after each trouncing.

A pointed spur prods. The burr in the saddle. The sand in the oyster.

She has to rend control, go on the offensive.

But how?

Longinus's spear, perhaps.

Maybe she can trap her husband somewhere, in some way. Perhaps, she can subdue, control, neutralize, change the equation.

Let's see; need a bulldozer, an empty field, superhuman speed and strength, maybe an army or two.

Thoughts fly away on wings of inanity then swirl into oblivion's gray ether. She's trapped. Knows it as sure as the insect in the web.

And the spider's coming, she knows that beyond doubt.

And where is Crispy?

When they landed in Jerusalem, she'd been in such a hurry to confront her husband she gave no thought to her mentor. A strange concept, that. Someone looking out for Crispy when he does exceedingly well taking care of himself.

She thinks of the worst. He's probably alone, somewhere, living on the street. Struggling for resources in a land where resources are scarce.

She reconsiders, then chuckles. Perhaps normal people would have a hard time on the streets, but Crispy eats hardship. Another staple of the scarred man's menu. Spam and eggs, tough times, tougher attitude. He'll appear when he's ready.

Until then, there's meatier bones to pick. There's too much

clouding my mind. I haven't slept well since who knows when, and with all that's occurred, it doesn't look like that's changing anytime soon.

When you get down to it, there's only one thing left. A single, desperate choice. A choice to forsake and take a giant leap of faith. A choice to trust her own counsel. A choice from which there's no turning back.

The coffee raises her energy as she stares over the stone silhouette of Jerusalem's skyline. She wonders at the city's tenacity. Thinks how centuries of sunrises have come and gone. With the city's history, she's willing to bet these golden morning rays have done little to buoy the spirits of this place and its past populous. But, someone here has been like her. Has spent their time thinking of the audacity, the barbarity, the inhumanity of the events through which they lived. Someone, through the bloody fumes of this land, the seething violent past of this country, someone has chosen to fight on. Someone has clung to hope as a buoy against depravity and madness. *Someone* has lived, died, have done their very best to survive the atrocities, the destruction, the malice. God's chosen land, she thinks. A land of silent stories. Stories of bravery, courage, and triumph.

All evidence says to live in Jerusalem is to die a horrible death. As if the city's heart oozes malice, thick, black and sordid. Noxious arteries spreading death, pumping hate. And blood. And war. And survival. In the name of God, history's curse.

But *someone* has overcome. *Someone* has done it before her.

God prefers blood. Cain's words in her head.

One desperate, crazy chance.

Crispy will *not* approve.

When Emery wakes, she'll discuss it with him. Make him see there's no other choice.

Her inner voice whispers things she doesn't want to hear. Encourages leaving Emery and saving herself. *He'll only slow you down.*

She glances at Houdini, a black outline on stark white marble. She'd be leaving Emery to the wolves.

They'll *not* be separated again. Come what may and despite everything else, they'll see this through together.

She stares at Jerusalem's ancient rock. Watches the sun brighten as shadowed clouds float above. *We'll not be separated again. At least until we're dead. Get yourself together, Rhyme. Raise your game. Be smart. Be worthy.*

Joey B flashes a warning, a klaxon of wariness and caution.

Ain't nothin' down there but the blues.

Think too hard and your head will ignite. Another of Crispy's axioms, the comic sage with a topographical face.

Rhyme wipes her eyes, then breathes deep and cleansing. A muted sun paints the stainless steel and the spotless marble a dead gray. Feet slap hollow as she pads into the hall.

I could be happy, even gleeful, living in such a place, priceless art on every wall, priceless furniture around every corner. If this place was robbed, someone would make a fortune.

She chuckles, half grimaces, remembers her husband and pals have no natural predators. Anyone with a mind to rob the place would be making the biggest mistake of their short life.

Hot coffee slides down her throat as she moves through the long corridor and tries to calm jumbled thoughts. In the main living area, windows rise to the second story, looming over stairs in glass and steel. Emery's door tempts, she feels her face flush. Noon. Why isn't he up?

She shivers, pulls her robe tight, stares at the door, fights the urge to burst in. The most dangerous room in the mansion.

If she enters, she'll be alone with the man she loves.

Cheeks flush. The cartoon princess appears in a resplendent gown and glittering tiara, sings of true love's kiss. In her mind, the melody rises, hypnotizes, beckons. Gooseflesh erupts with a shiver. It's a song of loyalty, of togetherness, of insurmountable odds, faced and overcome, buoyed by slim slices of fragile hope, slender dreams that hero and heroine will reunite, provided their courage holds.

She smiles. Together again, she and he, two halves joined to a wondrous whole.

The good life, it's coming. The princess sings, spins as birds flutter to her shoulders, as mice croon the backup like a seasoned chorale. Squirrels scamper through open windows as pastels flood the walls. The sun beams joyous, golden rays in broad bars as trees sprout verdant leaf to a thick, inviting canopy. A bed of moss appears by a trickling stream. The prince grasps her hand, and they dance the big finale voices stretched, joy flowing on wings of harmony. *The good life, it's coming,* prancing, whirling, exalted, triumphant.

CHAPTER 6

JERUSALEM, ISRAEL

Hackles rise. A giant paw scratches Emery's door. Houdini spins, whimpers in a high pitch, circles, paws the door again.

"Shh, let the man rest."

The dog nudges her hand, tries to warn of something.

She presses an ear to the door. Muffled moans seep through.

Her own hackles rise. She turns the knob and tiptoes in. Her prince's shadowed form is sleeping, vulnerable.

Passion devours. Her breath comes fast and shallow. She throbs, fights the urge to join him, to wake him with a special surprise, a flash of deadly desire. If he wakes, she doubts the resolve stretched over her feelings will do much to counter her passion.

She considers the consequences, considers what Cain will do to them if they get caught. Bound by marriage. Bound to the Antichrist.

Does pure evil absolve one of a promise? Does the fact of her husband's treacherous nature erase the vows she'd made? Worry deserts as a beckoning tickle centers in her tummy, then flows to her groin. She inhales a stuttered breath.

"Emery?" She suppresses thoughts like "feeble excuse" and "convenient need".

The room's a large rectangle. To her left stands Emery's bed. Past that, windows, broad and draped, block the muted light. How long's it been? Twelve hours, fifteen? He's never slept that long unless bent on drugs and alcohol.

Shivers trace her spine. He'd said he was cured, said Cain cured him. What if he lied? Or was tricked? What if he doesn't know and just took Cain's word for it? What if he's addicted still and sleeps so long because of the chemicals he ingested or injected?

He moans; arms twitch.

"Emery?"

Eyes adjust to the darkness as instinct nips her neck. Something isn't right.

"Emery?" A singsong voice, like the old days. "Time to get up."

She crosses to the windows, throws the drapes wide, giggles at the thought of his reaction to the sudden burst of gray light.

Then, her jaw drops.

Smoke rises from his body, from skin, head, arms. Thin wisps curl lazy, seem magnified by the gray light. Clad only in a pair of blue Tommy John's, he writhes, moans, small blisters bursting in real time over his torso.

"Emery!" She races forward, grasps his shoulders, shakes. "Emery! Wake up!"

Arms lift, then swat at invisible things. A muted wail rises. Hands tremble, clamp to his jaw.

"Emery!"

Houdini jumps on the bed, yelps, leaps away.

Emery's eyes flutter but remain closed, hand firmly pressed to his chin.

Houdini backs away, hackles raised, crouched. A low rumble rolls from his throat. He gives a look that says, "Um, you coming?"

The familiar returns, instinctual, a warning on full alert, sirens blaring as lights strobe. She feels it but can't define it. An inflammation of sense, of primal instinct.

She races to the bathroom, throws a handful of plush towels in the sink, then turns the water on full. Once saturated, she hurries back, drapes the drenched towels over scalded, blistered skin as thick smoke coils on the ceiling.

Emery whimpers, says something unintelligible as eyes flutter like a kite in a storm.

"Is everything okay?"

She whirls, finds Cain in the doorway, sardonic smile cemented on his lips.

She spits the words. "You know goddamn well everything's *not* okay. What did you do?"

He steps close, peers down at Emery. "Is he ill?"

She stammers, steps forward, blocks his path. "I don't know. Is he?" Great transparent pockets grow on Emery's body, threaten to burst a rush of sanguine fluid as blisters spread, thicken, become grotesque. His hand remains pressed to his jaw, locked there as if granite.

Cain looks puzzled. "Odd," he says, "illness shouldn't befall him. He's immortal."

Rhyme feels the rage, an acid that burns cartoon princess and fluttering birds to pastel ash. "Don't give me that. What did you do?"

Steely blue eyes return her gaze. "I did nothing save attend to pressing matters. I returned so we could talk about a task I need you to perform."

A feeling of calm smears her concern as she stares at icy orbs. She turns her back on him, sits on the bed, places a hand on Emery's forehead. "I'm busy."

Cain tuts. "Emery will be fine, my dear. I'm certain of it. Perhaps he's just experiencing the completion of his transformation from mortal to immortal."

Visions of vampires rise. Emery, pale and white, sallow. Long, yellow fingernails grow to crusted talons; teeth become fangs. "Nonsense," she says. "You're up to something and making Emery suffer."

"My dear," he says, placing a hand on her shoulder. "He cannot die. Anything that's struck him is quite independent of me. Perhaps he's suffering the rigors of casting off his addiction, eh? Withdrawal, perhaps?"

"Do we have any Doritos?" Bill stands in the door, dishwater locks bunched in a huge man bun.

"Bill, get in here," she says. "Something's wrong with Emery. I can't wake him. And…and his skin…it looks like it's burning. Look at the blisters, the smoke."

The joint burns red as he inhales, holds his breath, paces beside Cain. "Yeah, dude. He doesn't look good."

Cain chuckles and the blisters disappear. Wafting vapors hang stale, mix with exhaled dope smoke, then swirl and drift to nothing.

She levels a finger at Cain's shaking head. "You did something."

"I assure you, my dear, I did not." He sighs, smooths his suit. Anger flashes on his features, but fades just as fast. "In any event, he appears quite well currently. In fact, I can't say for certain what we saw was anything more than a trick of light. Floating dust combined with sunbeams. I'm certain he's fine." His smile dazzles, brightens the room by degrees. "I'm afraid I must leave soon, but was wondering if you'd be so kind as to spare a few seconds for your poor accused," he raises a finger, "but long-suffering, husband? Emery needs his rest and I'll only be a minute."

Bill's expression is vacant and glassed.

"Bill, can you keep an eye on him until I return? I shouldn't be long." She turns to Cain. "And I don't believe for a second that he's *fine.*" She exaggerates the last word, eyes locked on her husband.

Bill presses the weed to his lips and takes a long drag. "Uh, sure, dude," he says, smoke flowing. "Don't be long though, Gibran's *Prophet* awaits." His smile is boyish, innocent. He scratches a scruffy beard, then the butt of faded paisley pajamas.

She follows Cain into the hallway, stares at his back, wishes for a knife, or the twin Sigs hanging in the bedroom closet. "What?"

His smile disarms her. He steps close, places both hands on her hips. "Your country needs you, my dear." He looks like a snake basking on a warm rock. "This afternoon I've arranged for you to take the oath of Imperium. As empress you need to be beloved. An example of faith and loyalty. The most beautiful woman in all the realm, much adored by all our subjects. I've taken the liberty of arranging a wardrobe to be delivered. Not that anything could detract from your radiance, but an empress must be especially ravishing. As *my* empress, you need to reflect my power and glory."

She pushes his hands away and steps back. "I won't do it."

Cain looks surprised, shakes his head almost imperceptibly. "Indeed, my dear, you will. It's your duty both as my wife and to your country."

"My country?" she says, flummoxed. "*My country!* What a stupid thing to say. Perhaps you haven't heard, but *my* country was erased by some power hungry asshole."

Cain's head jolts like she just slapped his smug face. "Of course, of course," he says. "Still grieving. And not incorrect, incidentally. In fact, I'm happy to take the blame. An example had to be made."

"Is that what you're doing with Emery? Making an example? Of what happens when one tries to run away?"

Crystal eyes flicker toward the ceiling as he sighs. "My dearest Rhyme, if only you'd place the smallest amount of trust in your emperor. All I do, I do for us, for you. You're the light of my life. A blessed beacon in treacherous waters. What purpose does harming Emery serve me or Imperium? I need no such tricks and took no such measure." He motions to Houdini. "Like your new hound, Emery serves me well. I've no wish to harm him, only to train him."

"He's not a dog!"

"Isn't he?" A smile shines from a chiseled face, silver hair dances above. He waves a hand. "Let's not quibble, my dear. I must go. I'll see you this afternoon, at two o'clock."

No! The word rattles, scrawls bold lines and thick curls. Instinct says he's lying. Says he has *everything* to do with Emery's distress. *Go to hell,* she thinks. *I'm not taking any oath! Not wearing your stupid gown. Not going to be Imperium's shining fucking empress.*

Bill pokes his head out, clears his throat, drags on the joint. "You guys almost finished?" He peers down at worn slippers shaped like Easter bunnies. Button eyes stare back, looking as stoned as the man who wears them. "Doritos?" he mutters.

Another thought hits her. She's had enough of this, her husband, this evil, this crazy game and all its trappings. *Be smart, Rhyme. Be bold. Keep your own counsel.* "I'll be there," she says in a pleasant tone. "Send a car, won't you?"

Cain showers the room with sparkled elegance and effortless tranquility. A single clap reveals his joy and puckered, inert mark. "Excellent," he says, then gives a peck on the cheek. "Tonight, we celebrate in the grandest of style. I'll see you soon." She glares at his back as he steps away. Then he stops and turns. "If it helps, I'll send a nurse to stay with Emery until we return next week."

Rhyme stutters. "Next week?"

His smile holds her, binds her in a comforting, chilling embrace. "A grand tour awaits, my dear. Imperium's empress, the most radiant beauty the world has ever seen, *must* be displayed. There are rounds to make, uses for your grace and beauty to gain the world's confidence." He chuckles, presses a fist to his mouth. "It's probably hard to believe, but sometimes world politics distills to simple, gracious relationships." The Hollywood smile glares, grips, deceives. "You, my dear Empress, are my secret weapon."

CHAPTER 7

Stone sizzles as my skin erupts in flame. Something seizes my spine, searches, then plucks each nerve like taut guitar strings.

I grasp this reality, realize this can only be death. My throat seizes. My legs go numb, then shoot out, locked in agonized spasms.

The smell's horrific; molten flesh, charred, flaming. Thick dribbles that vent to filthy steam.

I wail, plead for mercy, grovel, beg.

Cain stands above me, a GQ model with dripping fangs.

Clawed nails, black and filthy, rocket forth and grip my throat.

Then, a blinding light.

All pain ceases.

Then a perfect white tablecloth.

I feel calm. Subdued. A bit sedate, even, detached.

Cain sits across from me, raises a porcelain cup painted with pink flowers.

To my right, an elderly man sits regal. His features give the impression of lengthy sickness. Gaunt, sullen like a vast and spreading cancer.

I swoon. The chair tips as gravity presses.

Then, I'm upright.

The man next to me snickers into his fist. "That was unpleasant. Eh, my boy?"

I'm afraid to take him in. There's something, a klaxon in my brain, flashing red. There's danger here. The feel of a knife plunging, of demons wrenching my tongue, then raising my beating heart before me.

I tremble as the warmth of urine soaks my pants.

The man leans forward, caresses my cheek with fingers like slimy fish. He whispers a single word, eyes half shut. "Serenity."

Something blinks. I inhale a fragrance, vanilla and lilac, think of my Rhyme, her hair burnt, her face charred, spitted above roasting flames.

From somewhere far off, I hear a discussion.

"You must be more careful with your servants."

"How was I to know?" This is Cain.

"Of course, of course. How does one know anything at first?"

Then, "Emery, my boy. Emery, come back to us." The voice is smooth and aged, like a somber trombone. "You are sound, my boy. The horrors are gone." A thin hand grips my shoulder. "Open your eyes, Emery. Look around. Breathe. Breathe. That's it. That's it. Now drink this, it will prop you up."

Porcelain rattles on its fragile saucer.

Trembling hands fumble, then raise it to my lips. The saucer falls to smash on the floor.

Then, a tuxedo. A waiter with broom and dustpan sweeping up shattered fragments.

"There, there, my boy. You see? Not all bad. Yes?" Before I can respond, he says. "Drink, drink. That's it. Now inhale again. Deeper. Good. Now, deeper still. Hold it in. Feel it cleanse. Search your mind, Emery. Reach for peace."

A moment passes.

"There we are," he says. "Almost good as new. That was quite a snootful, was it not?"

The man looks healthier, less elderly. He catches the cup as it drops from my fingers, then places it on the table.

"You really must be more careful with your servants," he says.

"Are they not mine to do with as I wish?" Cain says.

The man chortles, then presses a ghastly fist to his mouth. "Of course, they are. But within reason. You've yet to realize your true power. Temperance must rule, at least for a time. Now, now, don't look so glum. Am I incorrect in the assumption that Emery is your biographer?"

Cain pushes his plate away. "He is."

"Well, then, what's the harm in showing him everything?"

Cain remains silent.

The man snickers again, the sound of a strangled bunny. "I must apologize, Emery. You see, this is all new to us."

I muster my strength, aided by the tasteless liquid I choked down, then look the man right in the eyes.

My mind fills with scenes of blood and murder, of molestation and anguish, of hope banished, dreams crushed. Howling faces—

He averts his gaze as I inhale sharply. A tremor returns to my digits.

"Never look me in the eyes," he says, "for there, you'll find the unimaginable."

I reach for the cup but knock it from the table with a shaky hand.

"Oops," he says. "Here we go again." He snicker-squeals. "Breathe, lad. Deep. Slow. That's it." Then to Cain. "You may have been a tad overzealous. I'm not sure our Emery will recover."

Something inside me grows, demands self-control. His words inspire spite. I'll recover if it's the last thing I do.

I concentrate on Rhyme's fragrance, inhale, suppress visions of her torture.

Emerald eyes smile as she reaches, then wraps me up. My head falls on her chest where I weep like no tomorrow. "It's okay," she breathes in my thoughts, "you're made of bigger things, *for* bigger things." Feminine hands glide through my hair, then squeeze me tight, just enough.

I look up. Force my breath calm.

The man hands me another cup and I down what's in it. "Where am I?"

His snicker pops, echoes. "Where are you? Such a direct, succinct query. A supreme query, as one thinks about it. But I'm afraid the answer isn't gained so simply." Thin fingers tug a tie of silken blue, perfectly knotted. "Currently, you're in a sort of limbo. You possess space, but do not define it in the way of a sitting chair or a tossed ball. I suppose the best answer isn't really the best, if you catch my meaning. Let's say that you're in between. A shadow of sorts, but not a ghost or apparition—I mean, you yet retain form and mass—but rather a notion, a cobweb adrift on tempests of time." He props his chin on a pale palm. "Are you familiar with Dickens?"

I swallow hard, try to avert my eyes from that kittenish pose.

"Of course, you are, silly question," he says. "All writers know their Dickens." He clears his throat and suppresses a chuckle. "Are you familiar with his tale of Christmas ghosts?"

I nod as I continue to battle the rigors.

"Well, it's not like that at all. But then, it *is* kind of like that. The difference being that no one cares to change your beliefs or attitudes. No one here cares really, and let's do be honest, about anything you think or feel. I could go so far as to say that no one here really cares about your comforts, pleasures, sufferings, or thoughts." A bony finger rises, wags twice. "But don't mistake my meaning. This isn't singular to you. The same applies for Cain and myself. Where you are now is sort of an unreality, if such a thing makes sense. Had I not intervened, I'm afraid my servant may have done irreparable harm."

Cain speaks up. "I believe my servant—"

"You're dismissed." He speaks without even a glance. I hear a shush, like corduroy rubbed together, and by the time I look, Cain's gone. I peer around as tremors return to my limbs.

He focuses on me with an expression like he gives a damn. "But there now, I've changed your clothes and soothed your mind. I mean, as much as I can effect *that* organ. And I think, as you regain your sanity, you'll have a better understanding of just where you are. You see—"

"Hell!"

Feline eyes flash red for an instant, then chill to aqua blue. "Tsk, tsk, we mustn't blurt, my boy," he says. "Hell is from where I retrieved you mere moments ago. Or at least, the version of Hell most solid in your mind. I feel a bit abashed, if I'm being honest, to have usurped my servant's servant for my own purposes. I'm sure he has plans for you, which most exactly explains why you still live. And he tells me you're immortal, so let me be the first to welcome you to such an exclusive society. Unfortunately, your immortality means nothing here. Nor does mine. Or Cain's." A gaunt waiter appears, golden drink balanced on a serving tray.

The man takes the glass and sips, then waives the waiter away. "Thank you, my boy."

Dark orbs flicker. "It seems I digress. You see, it's hard to tell this tale a bit at a time. But I suppose that's my challenge, and I shall give it my best and explain to you exactly why I intervened.

"I was thinking about Cain's new testament, the one on which you currently endeavor. I was thinking of history, and the bad rap I've truly gotten throughout. It was then I realized I had no chronicle, no *record*, of my own exploits. Certainly, humans have attempted to pen unholy books in my name. But the fact is, they've failed to a person.

"It's clear now I was a bit short sighted throughout my long existence. Telling any one person my full story feels beneath a being like me."

He sips again and sets the glass before him. "In that ilk, I'd like to formerly introduce myself, then show you the story about the true nature of that place from which I pulled you." He focuses on where Cain sat, then continues. "I'd like to show you those things you don't know," he says, "and to borrow you such that Cain's biography is made even greater, not because of my exploits, but despite them. Consider what you'll endure as a bit of extra spice in the pot. Eh? Some extra zest for the sauce. See? Some pepper for the stew."

I surprise myself. "You can fuck right off."

He startles, blinks twice, then cackles like a broken harpsichord. "My boy! Language, language! If you'd like to refuse, I suppose it's your right, but no need for the profane. We have quite enough of that here and I find it distasteful. I mean, I certainly can't compel you to perform such a task if you don't wish to."

He stands, seems to creak like an antique chair, then paces a step and turns. "I accept your refusal," he announces to the room. "I mean, what's existence without free will?"

I nod and lift a newly placed porcelain cup to my lips. "Thank you."

"Oh, don't mention it." He steps forward, hands on his chair. "Then again, I'm reminded of that place from whence I retrieved you and think it advisable to remind you of that singular love of your life. Rhyme. Cain's wife, if I'm not mistaken. Yes, yes, Rhyme. Cain's wife. He's been exceedingly patient with both of you. Extremely out of character for one of his station and talents." A thin hand grips the glass. He sips, eyes turned upward, thinking. "I'm reminded of the old adage." His smile warms, his face appears more elderly, more trusting, a loving father with sober advice. "Love is blind. Do temper your choices with wisdom."

Then a burst in my mind, a single-second migraine: Rhyme spitted, roasting, her emeralds holding me as she shrieks.

"I'll do it." The words come before I even notice.

He doesn't miss a beat. "Excellent!" he says, then presses his fist to his mouth. "This will be a grand undertaking, and a story even you won't believe."

I sip and try not to think about whatever trick they're playing.

The old feeling returns. The rock pressing me to the hard place. The age-old damned if you do, damned if you don't. Seems a constant theme: fucked no matter what. "I'll need my phone and a notebook," I say.

"Tut, tut," he says. "That won't be necessary. You'll remember everything quite well."

I set my eyes on the shimmering white tablecloth. "As you wish," I sigh. "Let's be on with it. I generally start with name and occupation. Do you mind sharing yours?"

He appears suddenly spry, blooming mischief as he radiates power. His suit becomes fire red. A top hat appears, as does a stout cane like ebony granite.

With a doff of the hat, he bows with a flourish. "I am Iblis, Lord of the Jinn."

CHAPTER 8

A pleasant wind stirs the leaves of broad trees I can't identify. Branches, straight and strong, climb to the clouds and reach for a sunlight both glowing and cool. This place is verdant, leafy, lush. Warmth fills me, a sense of serenity, of joy. Then fragrances: jasmine, juniper, lively, fresh.

I look down, see nothing, not even my feet.

I reach forward. My hands don't appear.

Stepping, I move with fluid grace to glide over a grassy field that blazes the dewy mists of morning. An eagle soars overhead, floats lazy on rising currents. Sheep appear, start to graze, peaceful, unwary.

I shudder, look around, stoop a bit, wait for a blade to fall. At any moment now, some horror will visit.

Then, a being appears. Tall, golden, radiant, with features cherubic and sharp, casting rays of spun silver that nourish tree and leaf and seem to enhance the perfect serenity of this oasis. The herd's wool reflects the sun with molten intensity as the being glides forward, seems unaware of my presence, moving with an inhuman grace that is yet not foreign. It hovers, grasps an armful of dirt and raises it to the heavens.

Clouds swirl. Blistering rays surge over the clay the being holds.

The angel lifts the clump skyward, his blond curls tickled by a lilting breeze. Heavenly rays scan like a supermarket checkout thingy.

"Michael?" I say, before realizing this is some other angel, every bit as grand and beautiful as the archangel I confronted in the Temple.

"Gabriel."

A voice in my ear makes me jump.

I see no one.

Trees whisper as light crawls over the herd to coat the forest in shimmering hues—pink, crimson, spruce—that sprinkle leaves in a golden radiance. A warmth that possesses, that rises from forest, pasture and sky.

Gabriel lays the clump on the ground, and it turns from inert gray to creamy gelatin, seems to set, to solidify, then jiggles with a rush of great wings as Gabriel leaps for the sky.

In a flash he's gone, too fast to follow, too fast to see.

I move close. Hover above the gelatinous mass, reach out to feel it before realizing I can't.

I'm an apparition, reaching without hands, stepping without feet.

I feel no pain, no worry, possessed by an unshakeable peace that bonds my form, oozes through every cell, forces off thoughts of fear, despair, hopelessness.

A fine place, this one. I chuckle, feel a bit giddy. Sweet air fills my lungs and I inhale, holding as much as possible, stretching invisible arms to bask in a radiance that soothes both thought and soul.

A tiger strides from the depths of a glaring wood. It stops briefly, sits, licks a giant paw. Then it moves through the grazing herd, yawns, huge white fangs glistening, before it settles in a spot teeming with sunlight. Great yellow eyes fade, then drift closed as the sheep continue to graze.

Is this heaven? Have the horrors of hell sent me to my grave?

I glide forward and regard the twinkling gelatin. Man-shaped, it appears a waxy mold, a template of a statue yet to be.

Then, someone's next to me, a being a foot or so taller, skin flowing in dark maroon and splayed ebony. It's beautiful, sexy, chiseled lines and granite angles that radiate intensity, safety, protection. Obsidian wings curl to tuck neatly against its back, seeming to grab the morning's rays and fuse them into its form. It dazzles in darkness, hypnotizes with the most gorgeous display of thick, deep scarlet and rolling, sliding velvet. Colors cascade as ebony and maroon intertwine to frolic on the edge of light and shadow.

"What's this?" It bends toward the mass.

"Iblis? What is it?" Another being has joined the first. I realize they're unaware of my presence.

I stare, examine. They're amazing. Like nothing I've ever seen. Massive, muscled, dark angels with features that reflect both joy and savagery. Flickering skin glistens like armor, reflects flame as if plucked from the hearth of darkest night. I lose myself as colors dance, leaping like a campfire to reflect on a canopy of leaf. Shadows appear, congeal, burn away, race to deepest black, bleed to rippling maroon. Sparkling crimson mingles with shade, the thinnest whisp of light, the twinkle of moonbeams on a starlit ocean.

They consider the mass as shadows race, frolic, lead my eye over features sharp and pointed, flaming red subdued in smoldering, smoky charcoal.

I blink, stand dumbstruck, awed by majesty, by pure power.

They are confidence. They are rage. They are peace and wrath, simultaneously. They are a conundrum, a cosmic riddle in dancing hues and bold angles. They are a 3D special effect, an enigmatic fusion of fire and darkness.

Tucked wings smolder as heat rises to crinkle the distance beyond. They are the essence of flame; the very image of ferocity, of calm, of confidence.

A hint of scorn twists Iblis's face. He stoops and becomes a serpent.

My mouth falls open as I watch him enter the gelatinous figure, wriggle through glimmering wax as he examines every possible space like a worm pulled through lemon Jell-O.

With a squish and a pop, Iblis returns, stands next to his kin, dark hand rubbing a square jaw. "This is goo," he says. "Filled with jelly. It's nothing but muck. It can be no threat."

The words no sooner escape his mouth when he suddenly freezes, eyes focused on the distance. I realize everything's stopped. I cast a look to his mate and see he's frozen as well. I look around, see the herd no longer moving, bleating, grazing. Above, around, no leaf stirs on the peaceful breeze. No birds soar, no blade bends upon the field.

"A difficult concept for mortals, is time."

Behind me, a voice like a bumpy road. "And dare I say, one with which they should become better acquainted, for it is their master."

A shuffling step carries on breezeless air. I turn to see a man with a plain face and mediocre features. Twinkling eyes regard me and indeed, those eyes may be the only part of his countenance one would consider distinguishable. "If only I'd known then, what I know now," he says, "but it seems, I *am* time's fool, so unlike Shakespeare's idea of love."

Eyes change to cola black as he steps forward and waves a hand.

My feet and arms and body become apparent.

"After those things that I command took their liberties with you, I thought it'd be refreshing if we came here." A thin hand rises, motions around the glade. "Welcome to paradise." He sputters a chuckle. "Or at least what *was* paradise, back when everything started."

I swallow sand, harsh and prickly. Feel wariness jangle my nerves. My tongue glides over dried lips, and I revel in the moisture even as I remember I'm solid once more.

"Paradise," I say, "lucky me." I'm expecting the proverbial other shoe. In fact, I expect it to blaze from the heavens like a meteor and split my skull as demons fight for my heart and teeth. "This is a trick," I say. "Some manipulation with a sinister purpose."

I'm frozen, mid-sentence, watching in impotence as he draws near. I brace for what's next, unable to move but fully able to feel.

He pries my mouth open, stretches my cheeks to examine, lifts each eyelid in turn and peers underneath. Fingers both strong and thin glide over my ears, through my hair, across my neck, down my back, my ass, my legs. "What a piece of work is man," he mutters, lifting my arms, letting them drop, watching intently as they slap to my side. "How noble, without reason! How finite in faculty! In form and function, neither impressive nor admirable! In action, how like a field ass, in apprehension, how like a beast! So savage, so fragile, so stupid."

I unfreeze, take a step back, look to the surrounding woods and measure its distance against my own speed.

He steps forward and gives the mass a hearty kick. "What a waste."

I drop beside it, reach to feel the waxy, shimmering Jell-O.

"Don't touch!" He screams, snaps his fingers twice, three times. "Follow!"

Fuck off, I think, reaching just the same.

Then, I'm racing through the air to float beside him as we move down a wide path and into the forest.

"You prove my point, dear boy. My twist on *Hamlet.* But here's a measure of rhyme from my own pen." He effects a stance like a master thespian, then booms:

> *"O'er twisted paths doth fettered feet fumble!*
> *O'er tortured stones doth knotted knees quake!*
> *O'er barren ground, e'er-doomed to stumble,*
> *Oh, what twisted trails doth crooked limbs make?"*

He grins, bows. "Tortured paths, eh boy?"

"Doth," I say. "Nice touch. Very Shakespearean."

"Uh-thank ya." He takes another bow, then strides along in silence.

My arms and legs dangle, swaying lazy as we move. I flow through tree and branch like they're only vapor. I feel like one of those kids on a leash, the ones you see at the park. The ones who want to scamper away but lack the resolve or capacity to break their tether.

"You inspire in me a feeling I've not had for eons," he says.

I swing at his side, certain his next words will be horrible. "And what feeling is that?"

"Pity," he says. "Pure pity, I think, for the one chosen as the Antichrist's servant. The one chosen for such greatness, the one destined for such lofty heights. I pity you and the fact that you're bound to him forever." He peers at the canopy above us. "I'd be remiss if I didn't mention my complete disappointment in his choice." A thin fist presses as he mumbles. "Not my first choice, on that you can count. What he sees in you is beyond me. Perhaps his view is veiled by love's trappings."

I guffaw despite myself.

"You don't share that sentiment?" he says. "Perhaps you can enlighten me as to your thoughts."

"Can you put me down?"

"You see, dear boy, right there. Even after all these eons, I still can't grasp the inclinations of man. Are you not content floating? Exerting no effort? Nothing could be easier, I'm doing all the work and saving you the trouble. Even a sloth would cackle at such an arrangement." Done scolding, he swats the air. "Alas, though, as you wish."

I fall from ten feet, hit the ground with a thud that rattles my teeth.

And for that I'm thankful. Thankful I retain teeth to rattle after the horror of having them ripped from my shrieking face.

I stand, rubbing my neck. Wondering why I slid through trees like they weren't present yet slammed to an Earth that was very present.

"Come, come," he says, "much to do, much to see. I don't have all day." His chuckle squeals like a snared pig. "Actually, not true on the face of it. I *do* have all day. And the day after that, and after that, and so on, and so forth. Like you, I don't fear death, I rule it."

I chase after, stumbling over a thin branch rooted in the path. "Where are we?"

He stands at a bifurcation, puzzling. One trail heads left, dark and treacherous. The other leads right, wide and pleasant.

He mumbles, chuckles, mutters. "Duality. Darkness and light. Trickery. But what trick? What path? It's inverse, I think. Yes. Inverse. Light leads to dark and dark to light. Is that right?"

Black eyes take me in, wait for an answer.

I shrug. "How would I know?"

"Exactly," he says. "You wouldn't. Couldn't. Can't. Won't. Shan't. Shouldn't." A closed fist suppresses his delighted squeal. "Right is right. Right? Oh, never mind. This way, I think. Come, come. It's been a long time since I've been here."

I follow him down the dark path. "And just where is here?"

"Courage and tenacity you possess in great quantities, yet the obvious escapes your every effort. Come, lad, you'll see. I'm certain this is it. The beginning. The path to the start. You'll see."

He moves like a sprite, darts this way and that, disappears ahead to reappear behind.

I feel like Carroll's Alice fresh through the looking glass, as if I've been freshly ejected from the back of Lewis's wardrobe. I expect to see the Hare and Mad Hatter, Aslan the lion.

I realize I've no control of anything here, but instead of dismay, I feel a sense of wonder, of freshness. A replenishment that resounds even as it mutes anything that's come prior.

A clump of verbena catches my eye. Blooming in perfect purple, it beckons with a delicate fragrance that pleases my senses. I stuff my face in the petals and inhale.

With a kick in my ass, I'm sprawled among them.

"Come, come," he says. "Time waits." He chuckles at my outrage, grin stretched ear to ear. The squeal is one of bad brakes as he laughs himself silly, then suddenly becomes serious. "Time," he says, "waits for no man."

CHAPTER 9

"Now, during this time I was Honcho Johnson. That's to say, the head honcho with the biggest johnson. I ruled these parts, these people." He points to a clearing at the end of the path. "You see? Humans were here and people existed. Albeit primitive, but they forged what was to come." He looks into the canopy as three squirrels chase over a long branch. "The beginning, my boy, straight ahead."

"So, what was that other place? What was that mass shaped like a man? Who were those beings? One was called Iblis? Is that the Iblis I met at that restaurant? The Iblis who pulled me from hell?"

His expression reveals frustration. The look Cain gives to stupid questions. "You're not too bright, are you?" he says. "*I* am Iblis. *I* am Lord of the Jinn. It was *me* who pulled you from that pit, and *I* with whom you imbibed at that restaurant." Dark eyes bore into me. "You know, I'm starting not to like you. You're a rather rude fellow. You haven't even thanked me for pulling you from that pit."

Thunder rolls as a tempest blooms. The sky turns black, bathes me in darkness as foliage disappears. Then, a flickering hellscape with jagged rocks, rising, looming, bursting into the atmosphere to send showers of flaming rubble across the sky. The cackles start. Gleaming, festering eyes peer from dark, cragged ridges. Flames leap, as lava sends plumes of molten rock to splash against the mountain's craggy thighs.

I hear their approach—flapping wings, a legion of beasts blazing toward me. Wings of charred leather flutter, suck up all the light as the legion dives, gains speed, blazes over lava and crag to deftly touch down with a ravenous gaze in their eyes.

Knees tremble as I cower, trying to read their intent, watching as slender, forked tongues pop from razor teeth and crinkled jaws. It's feeding time.

"Thank you, thank you, thank you!" I blurt through clenched teeth. Talons scratch on blistered stone as they wade toward me. Claws clasp, rip my skin. My terrified reflection stares back at me from a thousand ghastly orbs.

Then, I'm back in the glade, still cowering, shaking my fear onto the verbena as squirrels eye in a way that says they're trying to figure out what the hell's wrong with me.

"You're quite welcome," he says. "I mean, was that so hard?"

"Not with the proper motivation," I manage.

"Tsk, tsk, lad. Always have to make it difficult. But suit yourself, I can't be bothered with nonsense like that. Come." He steps forward, and I follow like a lap hound brought to heel, padding close, insides quivering.

"Where was I anyway?" he says. "Let's see, dark is light. Did that. Go to the beginning. Ah yes! The beginning. Straight ahead, lad, just through there."

I follow the path another fifty feet, then step onto a ledge that overlooks a vast oasis. A beautiful forest gorges on beaming sunlight. It's an infusion, a sense of shielding luminance that warms and protects. Massive trees bunch together, join a chorus of stretched limbs that stretch for nourishment. Great white-tipped eagles glide above the forest, drifting lazy on unseen currents.

Tranquility. The very picture of the word spreads before me.

Iblis steps beside. "Nice, huh?"

I nod.

"Paradise," he says, then, "leap."

I look down, easily a thousand-foot fall to the valley below. "Not on your—"

A thin hand shoves and I plummet toward the verdant earth. Fear flows as I howl, gain speed, rocket to the valley floor.

But just before I smash into the ground, a sudden surge of wind lifts, then eases me down where I stand and shake. I fall to my knees and gasp.

Feet appear in front of me, the screech of his chuckle echoes over the valley.

"Do we have to do things like that?" I say. "You're being an asshole."

Nonplussed, he regards me. Eyes roll up in his head as he considers the term.

"Dear boy, I can't help but be an asshole, as you say. Once you know the story, you'll understand my nature, my plight. My endless battle with a cocky and ferocious foe.

"And for your information, I am *the original* asshole. The," he cups his chin, "the *quintessential* asshole. The asshole eternal? The asshole to end all assholes?" He winks, holds my eyes, waits, so pleased.

"Got it," I say, wishing he'd stop.

"Come. You need to see when it all changed."

Two minutes later, through a fairy tale wood, we enter a grassy glade. Tall trees stand sentinel over a gathering mass of dark angels like the ones I saw near the man-shaped gelatin.

He sweeps an arm, bows in grand style. "The Jinn. My people. Spawned by fire. Given dominion of the lower heavens and Earth."

We move through them like they're ghosts. Thousands are present, their combined aura giving the impression of fear and safety simultaneously. A barely balanced scale that will tip with the slightest provocation.

"Oh," he says, "here I come now."

I follow his finger to the sky. A dark angel blazes past like a jet fighter glimmering in deep maroon, flickering shadow yielding to deep crimson. Great, flaming wings streak toward us, then the angel alights so softly that I wonder if he's even bent a blade of grass.

Stepping forward, he gives the mass a kick. "My subjects! My kin!" he cries. "My Jinn! Hear me!"

The throng presses, seems to push forward as one. Shouts rise. "Are we replaced?" "Is this our doom?"

With a flap of wings, Iblis hovers, voice booming to the day. "For forty years have we wondered. For forty years have we considered, marveled, probed, suffered this stinking lump before us. For forty years have we endured this, this, thing. This pile of goop. This lump of festering decay. For forty years has this trembling, lifeless mold plagued our thoughts and our hearts. For forty years have we suffered the unknown and the unwelcome." He goes higher, gathers broad rays which fuse and flow over wing and body. "Today, we suffer no more!"

A cheer rises. Other Jinn lift on massive wings to spin and flip and swoop.

Iblis's teeth are a handsome contrast to his dark countenance. Gleaming, perfect, blinding white rays that surge from a shadowed face.

"Today!" his voice booms, "is the last day we suffer this insult! As I alone am lord of this realm, and, as I alone have become god of this realm, so will I banish that which causes such grief so that we might focus on our subjects and rule with justice and stern ferocity. Today, will I lift this thing to the heavens and fling it deep into the abyss."

Cheers ignite like flames through dry wheat.

"My Jinn, am I not the greatest among you? The wisest? The most glorified? The most honored? My decree is instant banishment and woe to any who usurp my order."

With that, he flutters low, scoops the mass up. Then, with a great rustling of dark feather, rises to the sky.

His kin cheer, leap to the air, spinning, swirling, as howls become cacophonous, fuse to a distinct harmony, something tuned, something pulsing, something heavenly.

A pleasant wind bears him high. An expression of triumph blooms.

Then, a crack of thunder.

A golden bolt shreds a cloudless blue sky.

Iblis shudders midair. His body drops to the ground as smoke trails behind.

A dusty plume erupts as he strikes the earth.

The Jinn go quiet. Some peer into the sky, some at their leader.

Then the gelatinous mass floats to settle softly within the glade and onto its original spot.

Iblis crawls from the crater. Wrath glares on a face both beautiful and dark. "Who dares!"

Jinn step back, lower their heads, those in the air flutter to the ground and stand quietly staring.

The man nudges me with his elbow. "This is the good part," he says. "The part that changed everything."

Not understanding, I turn back to the enraged dark angel who stands with fists clenched up at the heavens, wings angled in a stance of power and readiness.

To my shock, the gelatinous mass jiggles, sits erect, looks left and right, then sneezes.

The Jinn leap away, struck terrified in a single second, as if afraid the thing is contagious.

"What filth is this!" Iblis screams.

The tiniest breeze stirs. A spoken voice barely heard but clear to all. "This is Man," it says. "Created by My own hand."

Iblis looks gut punched, ventures a step as lips curl around blazing teeth. *"I am lord here!"* he cries. *"I am ruler and god of this place. I alone* say what transpires. What stays, what doesn't."

The breeze tickles, makes my eyelids droop as it speaks. "The time of the Jinn has passed, Lucifer. To Man, do I give dominion. To Man, do I bequeath this realm."

Murmurs rise. Wing tips loom above dark faces, angry faces.

"Bow," the breeze says. "Submit yourselves to Adam."

Iblis rises on angry wings, pulses with light and shadow as his voice rages. "Bow to this? Bow to dirt? To an oozing bag of water? To this fetid bag of filth?" He turns to his people. "Never shall Jinn lower themselves!"

"It is My command."

"Never!" Iblis rises high, fists raised, wings poised like a scorpion. "No Jinn will ever bow before a mud-filled sack! *We* are masters here! *We alone* have subdued, protected, nurtured and nourished. Are we to be thrown aside like refuse, usurped by a pus-packed paragon?"

A foul tempest blooms through a sanguine sky, then spreads to envelop in absolute darkness.

I see flashes, crackling lightning, followed by howls and pops. Then, the crash of timber, of great trees torn asunder and swept aside. Wind howls like wolves in a deep, dark cave.

A blink later, sunlight beams down as I stand with my guide, the form of a man, Iblis, Lord of the Jinn.

For a single second, shadows crease his aged features. For a single second, he flickers, becomes Iblis, the dark angel of moments prior. Dark orbs stare at nothing, shift back and forth, reflect eons. His expression becomes acceptance, then dismay, then a certain type of grief, an expression of loss, of disbelief, of precious things wasted.

He turns and plods off.

The oasis disappears.

Fiery mountains again bloom as demons race forward, press close, teeth flashing, dripping.

They shriek with delight as they surround me.

Then all goes black, soundless, endless.

CHAPTER 10

"For many years I watched this usurper of my throne, this Adam. This ouster of that which I was given and had made my very own." Dark, gorgeous lips crease to a snarl.

"I'd been betrayed. Abandoned by a God, who incidentally, abandons everyone at some point."

He snickers here, a squeal like a broken axle. "His followers say it's so you can grow, build character, experience the joy of trying to live without His help. But that argument's flawed." He tsks. "Only mortals dream up such nonsense as faith. Knowing without knowing." He scoffs. "Without evidence or proof. Even God chuckles at the concept, although it's served my purposes well. Better than I could've expected actually. But see, I get ahead of myself. What do you think so far, Mr. Merrick?"

I hear something percolate like an old coffee pot. Then, a spark flares in my head and I'm standing in a room of blistering white, devoid of sound or art, facing a middle-aged man, clean shaven with bright eyes and a sharp nose. "Iblis?"

"None other."

"Why do you keep changing forms?"

"Because that's what we do, Mr. Merrick. Jinn are shapeshifters. It's our nature. Like scratching an itch to you. Think nothing of it."

"Um, okay," I say. "Nice suit, by the way."

He looks down, realizes he wears a suit of navy adorned with thick gold stripes. A power suit, if ever there was one. "Why, thank you," he says. "I used to put much more thought into wardrobe but it seems to happen less and less these days. In any event, I was asking what your thoughts are?"

I chuckle. After the rigors of my visit to Hell, I think good feelings are akin to electroshock therapy. Like hitting oneself in the head with a hammer; it feels good once you stop. "You pose an interesting question," I say. "I guess my first thought is that I'm dreaming, and this can't possibly be real. Then, I think that this *is* real, and I've been imbued with the power to see visions. Then, I think asylum inmates probably follow the same line of reasoning. Then, I think I must be in an asylum, that all this is playing in my head while I drool and get antipsychotics stuffed in my mouth."

"All of that, eh?"

"Oh, there's more."

"I don't doubt it. I'm sorry I asked."

I shrug and close my mouth.

Cola eyes bore as he strokes a cufflink with X'chasei's symbol etched on it. "I guess you'll not believe me if I tell you that this *isn't* a dream. That you *aren't* in an insane asylum?"

"That's what I'd expect you to say. You are the father of lies, Mr. Iblis. Am I to take you at face value? Shouldn't we be making a deal for my soul or something?"

He laughs loud and long. Brilliant white teeth flash above a perfectly knotted double Windsor. "Those are tales, my boy, legends. I'd never wager for a soul. Why go to the effort when they're so readily offered?"

"Exactly what a con man would say."

He laughs again and adjusts his tie. "Let's change the subject. I assure you that you're not insane and, if your feeble brain withstood that pit, you probably never will be. At this very moment you're being attended to by the woman you love. Cain's wife, as I recall."

"Just couldn't resist, could you? Rubbing that in?"

"I am the master of evil. Please forgive my trespass."

"Even as you forgive those who trespass against you."

"Are you quoting scripture?"

"I don't know. Was that scripture?"

"Psalm 23."

"Well, if I was, I didn't know it. Probably just heard it somewhere."

"Ah yes, the Bible like Shakespeare. Hear a clever turn of phrase, then repeat it endlessly and appear intelligent."

"Something like that," I say. "In Sunday school, they always said Lucifer knows the Bible better than anyone. Is that true?"

He thinks here, eyes shifting. "Probably, haven't really thought about it. But if one listens to the same song long enough, one eventually sings along."

"So, you're a holy man…Er, a holy Satan?"

"Well, I know the platitudes and all that malarkey, I just don't buy off on them. Too much coincidence. Too much unanswered."

"Like?"

"Well, free will for one. Original sin, for two. I mean, an apple causes the fall of man? Only a mortal would believe that. Then, there's religion as both concept and institution, warped by mortals to greedy and nefarious ends." Sharp eyebrows crinkle with his next words. "Yet the blame falls at *my* feet? I was the grandest of angels. The most beautiful, the wisest, the most revered, the most loyal. It was *He* who turned on *me*, not the other way around." He circles as he speaks, arms moving in time with his words. I think Italian blood must flow in those veins.

"You know winners write the history books, right?"

I nod.

"Well, the masses only get God's take. A take where He's the heavenly good, and I'm the eternal patsy. I never thought it'd come to this, yet here we are. I get blamed for everything. And when blame falls like a summer rain, guess what happens? One stops caring. One rises, or descends, as one is regarded. None of this was my fault. I was happy with the deal I had: lord of paradise, ruler of the lower heaven and Earth. Then, I get accused of vanity, of thinking I'm God's equal, which, by the way, I've found, isn't so far off the mark."

"Says the father of lies."

"Would you stop saying that?"

"Or you'll throw me in the pit of Hell?"

He nods slowly. "Point taken. How about if I say, 'No more pit of Hell for you'? Will that ease your mind and allow you to concentrate on the task at hand?"

"It's an awesome first step."

"Okay, then, no more pit of Hell. No more physical pain."

"Says the father of…"

"Don't say it."

Though I close my mouth, I grin.

"There are many types of Hell, my boy, many flavors. You think Hell's just flame and torture, just demons and frustration. That's because of what you were taught as a youngster, but it's also by my own designs. My own manipulations.

"When I was ejected from paradise, I found myself with plenty of time. Not so unlike Cain, time yawned before me and I hadn't much else to do but ponder my downfall. Ponder the true nature of a God who can cast aside his creation so easily. You've seen it. Man's propensity to cast away what's truly important for the chase of trifle or feeling.

"Plucked from God's very image, the lot of you, but without God's qualities. I've often wondered if that was in His design. If He, Himself, planned for man to rise to such glorious heights only to bring them crashing back to the deepest depths.

"I guess one could say Hell represents those depths. And, as always, I'm to blame. The straw man in the closet. The thing in the shadows, the monster under the bed. And while everyone's checking their closets with trembling hands, or peering under beds with widened eyes, no one sees the real culprit, the real boogey man."

"And that is?"

"Fear, my boy. Simple fear. Probably the most powerful emotion of them all. Certainly, one that's effective in driving certain outcomes. Hell, even the hint of fear, its very notion, will make a human change their course entirely and on a whim. I wish I could feel it, really. I'd have so much more control if I knew what it actually felt like."

"You can't be scared?"

"Apparently, Jinn don't have that bone. We also lack the ability to love, although some have reported feelings of fondness toward your species. Take AeSma for example, she's a real demon, yet seems to genuinely love that other immortal barbarian."

"Longinus, you mean?"

"Precisely."

"Sima's a demon?"

"Well, not a demon, but possessed by one. Like you and Acedia, your addiction demon. Although AeSma is much more powerful, the demon of lust with unquenchable appetites." He raises a hand here like taking an oath. "And I warned your friend about her before he took her on. Thought it was the least I could do."

"What a sweet gesture."

"You mock when you should applaud. Your friend Longinus will be heartbroken by the time it's all done."

"As if," I say with a chuckle. "Like you, I don't think Longinus has that bone."

Dark eyes flick toward me, then into the distance. He speaks absently. "Poor fellow, lacking the capacity for something that doesn't exist? Hmm, of that, we'll wait and see."

"Wait. Love doesn't exist?"

"Endorphins, my boy."

"Bullshit."

"True."

"I love Rhyme."

"And she thinks she loves you. And maybe that's love. The thought alone, the belief that you truly care about another. Maybe that's what inspires action, motivates like a kick in the ass." He chuckles. "My God, these people and their choices!" His lips curl as he speaks. "She's as close to a superhero as Earth holds, yet she chooses you. I assure you, it's all a facade."

"Love, or Rhyme loving me?"

"Both, sucker." He watches my crest fall. "Now, don't look so glum. It's not unique to you two. The entire world is plagued by that concept, wandering around like morose puppies, pining for love, embracing love, discarding love, writing poetry. Gloss-eyed sheep who stare at the stars, wishing to be astronauts and not, well, sheep." He chuckles like a squeaky chair. "A great distractor for me, though. A mighty tool for heartbreak, deceit, murder. Sins of all kinds."

"I don't buy it."

"No one ever does." He turns abruptly and places a thin hand on my shoulder. "We've dallied long enough, Mr. Merrick. I have to admit though, it was nice talking to you. And for what it's worth, I have some regrets about your role in all of this and would like to apologize in advance for what's to come."

I hold his eyes, considering. "You can tell the future?"

A small squeal squeezes from his fist. "No, my boy, just the obvious. I was pretty confident where all this was headed. With the advent of your immortality, I'm certain. Nothing magical, just following breadcrumbs to obvious destinations."

"Care to share?"

"And ruin the fun? Where's your sense of sport? Your sense of adventure? Where's that pioneering spirit that inspired humans to explore everything in their environment and beyond?"

"God didn't give me that bone."

He chuckles, purses his lips like thinking. "Perhaps you'll grow one. Perhaps your discomfort will be so great, it will bloom spontaneously, like an extra appendix." He paces two steps, turns back, adjusts a cufflink. "I'll give you a hint though. Your path is chosen by your allegiances."

"Says the father of lies."

The corner of his mouth twitches. "Just couldn't resist?"

CHAPTER 11

JERUSALEM, ISRAEL

Hours later, Emery remains comatose.

At least the blisters have gone. At least he doesn't seem in pain.

"Lolo," Emery mutters, sounds dazed, talks in his sleep.

Rhyme presses a wet washcloth to his forehead as Bill sits munching Doritos from an open blue bag. "Thanks for getting these, dude. What's the plan now?"

Rhyme, taking him in, wonders if he remembers Cain's visit, when he'd ordered her to come, take some oath, go on a world tour.

Ain't happening, dude, she thinks as Bill stuffs another handful, Houdini curled at his feet.

What's the plan? What would Crispy do? Where is Crispy?

At two o'clock the car will be here; by three she needs to be a ghost —Emery and Houdini in tow. Can Bill keep a secret? Should she confide? Leave him here? He probably isn't hard to trick due to the fact he's always orbiting just above the stratosphere. Hell, he even thinks I refilled his Doritos.

What's Cain want with him anyway? Why would her husband take such measures to preserve a dope-smoking hippie, providing everything he asks?

She watches him munch, crumbs stuck to a short beard, eyes glassed, small grin bobbing as he chews. "Where'd you get the wine?"

Bill raises the cup and the chips, a hippie salute. "The wine I get from this glass. The chips I get from this bag."

"Oh," she says. "Thanks."

"Anytime."

The wardrobe Cain spoke of arrived shortly after he departed. A long, wheeled, reflective rack positively stuffed with gowns in every color. Below, an assortment of twenty different pairs of heels surrounding a wooden box packed with jewelry of all sorts.

One o'clock. Have an hour to figure this out. Car should be here in thirty and then off to who knows where, while Emery lies obtunded in this mansion.

Not on your life.

"Bill," she says, "would you mind getting me a glass of water?"

The hippie stops chewing as Rhyme waits for the words to pierce his high.

I shouldn't have so much experience with dependents of modern chemistry, she thinks. Seems Emery trained me well. Trained me too well, now I think about it. Taught me the ins and outs of addiction. The soul-crushing, dream-stomping horrors for those who bob in its wake.

Bill rises, adjusts the man-bun with a single hand, then turns to the door. "Water?"

"If it's not too much bother."

He grins, itches his ass. "No bother, dude. Happy to help."

That should keep him busy. If she's quick, she may be able to pull this off. With a glance at Emery, she creeps across the room, peers out the door and looks both ways. All clear. Bill should be in the kitchen trying to remember what he's doing. A master's degree in the care and feeding of junkies has taught her, first, junkies never remember what the hell they're doing. Sure, they have an idea when they start, but with them it's *completely* about the journey. Anything can happen along the way, and often does.

And that's addiction's seduction. For a junkie, everything's a trek of discovery, of having adventures and solving mysteries.

And what mysteries? Well, it doesn't seem to matter. Bill could be staring at wallpaper right now. Could be arranging forks in a precise and idiosyncratic order. He could be cooking breakfast, clipping his toenails, even staring at a loaf of bread and frigid toaster trying to remember how to combine them.

She takes the stairs two at a time, anxious to be on the second story and out of Bill's sight. In the bedroom, she doffs her robe and PJs, then rustles through the closet. Five minutes later, she darts into the bathroom and checks her appearance.

All black. Steel toe combat boots, black tactical pants, black T-shirt, twin Sigs strapped under her arms, black tactical jacket. She checks the knife strapped to her belt, clips the fabric strap that holds it in place. She pulls her hair in a bun, places a black ball cap over top. Sunglasses slide into the jacket's inner pocket. Sigs slide from their holsters and she checks the load, the slide, the action. Perfect, easy, sleek. Or, as Crispy would say, clean, dry, and serviceable.

Now what? What's the plan? Certainly, I'm leaving but can't leave Emery.

Emerald eyes stare back as she speaks to her reflection. "Car's coming. Okay. Options: Take out the driver, load Emery, steal the car? Or: Capture the driver, use him as a hostage, load Emery, steal the car? Or: Use Bill as a hostage, take out the driver, load Emery, take the car?"

Her sigh fogs the glass. She can't load Emery alone, too much dead weight. She can't trust the hippie or the driver. She has to be quick, precise, has to get away before Cain knows, before Longinus comes, before the driver or Bill can raise an alarm.

Easy, she thinks, sighs again. *All while lugging around a comatose and helpless man.*

A hidden voice rises, nudges. *Leave him,* it says. *He'll be fine. If Cain wanted to harm him, he would've done it already.*

She shakes the absurd thought away. Cain's *already* harmed him. What do you think the smoke and blisters are about? Why do you think he's still comatose? Withdrawal my ass.

I'm not leaving him, no matter the risk. Just isn't happening.

The cartoon princess walks dainty through a field of daisies. Birds flit and chirp, as woodland creatures gather for the next song. Must be nice. I bet *she* doesn't have problems like this.

She wishes this was a fairy tale and she the lonely lass. Beautiful, helpless, waiting for the gallant prince to arrive and slay the horrible beast.

A frown darkens the mirror. *My fairy tale's all fucked up. Instead of a prince, I get a junkie, a hippie, and the Antichrist.*

Pros: Leaving. Sigs, vehicle, knife, Houdini.

Cons: Emery as dead weight. X'chasei operatives everywhere. Already ran once, they'll expect it again. Weather. Foreign country. No sign of Crispy.

Cons pile like rugby players. She closes her eyes, inhales deep, stares at herself in the mirror. "You've been through worse," she says. "With less. Did more. *You* can do this. You *can* do this." Her reflected smile provides little comfort as she grips the holstered Sigs. *Now that's comfort.*

If Emery winds up dead, she'll never forgive herself.

Not going to happen. Just won't let that happen.

Then another thought hits. *Emery's immortal.*

She shudders. This might be the part where they find out for sure.

Guilt rises; visions of her father, Branch, her lost baby, America, razed and smoldering.

The doorbell sounds as she ticks off the checklist in her head, examines options, none of them good. Typical, she thinks, Rhyme's big adventure. We'll call it, "Little Hope on the Prairie".

Like a junkie, it's all about the journey, right?

Sigs hug her form as she zips the jacket. Dressed for "ass kicking" (another Crispy-ism), she exits the bathroom and descends the stairs.

CHAPTER 12

The space is cavernous like a stadium. White, with the appearance of what used to be glaring. Now covered in rusty stains and cobwebs. Finely etched pillars rise to a massive arced ceiling, stretching arms like the branches of a mighty oak to span and support the massive stone above.

The air is clean, conditioned like laundered, sterile in the way of an operating room but with an odor that stifles and causes me a thin film of sweat.

I'm surprised by this, surprised that my pores function even as I step forward on legs that feel strong and assured. I crane my neck, follow the pillars down to a floor in gray-streaked marble, dusted in soot and plaster.

Art is everywhere. Spaced unevenly, zillions of frames rise in shattered rows and columns hundreds of feet toward the massive ceiling. Cobwebs cling to tarnished wood. Ash covers the floor.

"Hello?" My voice bounds away and doesn't return. I peer ahead, down a dingy marble corridor that seems endless. Sculptures stand in line for as far as I can see: various winged beasts, busts wearing masks of torment, stone hands reaching skyward from what seems a pit in the distance.

I print my presence on the dusty floor, hear the shuffle of my own feet bounce down the long corridor.

The place is well lit, but I see no fixtures. It's odd but each painting and sculpture seems to create their own beams and even as I watch, I'm aware of a slight clicking sound above me, ahead of me, all around.

I stand absolutely still, taking in the corridor, watching paintings change, one second a swirl of lines and strokes, the next a portrait of people, or a landscape, or a demon, or host of demons, even children's art. It seems all this art shares the same quality. One of suffering or demons. Torture, murder, mayhem. A pinwheel of horrors neatly appearing, rearranging, clacking, shifting.

Others appear and seem to join the rotation of slick switches of changing art.

Before me, a large statue, gilded gold, comes in focus. A giant angel, sword poised to strike a bested demon underfoot. A sign stands beside it: MICHAEL THE ARCHANGEL.

I trace its lines, follow wing and muscle to a spear inches from Satan's throat.

Then, movement to my left, a subtle flicker that causes my head to swivel. I confront a morbidly obese man painted in subdued oils.

It blooms as I approach, seems to stand out in shadow and dusky colors that match the odd museum around me. The painting's subject is grotesque, indeed, mouth stuffed with thick strands of noodles that droop to a flabby chest and impossibly fat breasts. Eyes show surprise, even as they give a hint of fulfilled desire, yet a longing for even more than what's stuffed in his mouth. A pendulous belly hangs, and from the folds of flesh, a smile appears, then fills with blunt square teeth as it spans the image's entire abdomen. A thick tongue juts, then swabs crinkled red lips.

I step back a pace, read the plaque stuck to the wall. "GLUTTONY" BY DAVID SEIDMAN.

The image disgusts but arouses hunger. My stomach growls as I imagine sitting before the man, watching as he devours, mouth so stuffed his body's spawned a new orifice in order to consume even more.

As if it follows my thoughts, the gut-grin smiles big, then yawns like a sinkhole. The belly elongates and twirls, becomes thick stone stairs that lead to a darkness reeking of spoiled food and baked goods.

Something foreboding dwells here, something necessary, something cunning.

Pleasant aromas rise from the dank darkness to tempt with scents of cinnamon and warmed apples. Something baked, something delicious, yet ruined by competing odors of the fetid.

I stand on the first step and hesitate. There's no possible way this staircase leads to hot apple pie.

My mind rouses me to rethink. But then, the choice becomes simple. The step disappears and the staircase becomes a slick slide.

I rocket down, through luscious cinnamon and fragrant apple, through other sweet aromas: cocoa, cotton candy, twisted taffy.

Gravity obviously applies here because my speed accelerates until I burst into a firelit room and crash through dented pots and thick crockery.

Finally still, dizzy from my tumbling descent, I stand. Looking around, I find I'm in a room, quaint with Victorian stylings. A broad, vivid carpet covers a wood-paneled floor. The room's stuffed with tables in the way of a hoarder. Every surface is overfull. Small paths wind through stacked boxes, littered refuse, broken crockery, dated, dented furniture.

Empty dishes abound, crumbs gelled to their surface. Beyond that, barrels labeled PICKLES, BEER, HONEY. Old wooden crates teem with tarts and biscuits. Then, fruits—cherries, grapes, apples— rise to press up against an abrupt square ceiling even as the slide I just flew down swirls into dense mist that become a stairway once again.

I slip on greasy stone, move between the stacks, the pungent fruit. A scurrying sound wafts, like the claws of rats, which makes me hasten my pace to peer up the broad tunnel. It's like a dark cave, rising forever, offering a grueling climb that gives the appearance of leading straight to heaven.

To my right, taking up an entire corner, a fire burns in a huge stone hearth. Etched in marble, dark like blood, faces of demons peek through flame, all of them eating, devouring muscle and bone as if malnourished for decades.

Before the fire, two armchairs are draped in fabric like grandma's nightgown, light pink, stained, covered in small petals and flitting purple butterflies. I hear wheezing from beyond the false garden. Exhausted grunts that mingle with the intermittent scrape of leather on rock.

I squint down paths carved through the piles, see a giant, corpulent slug crawling toward me on emaciated arms that appear too weak to hold its proportions.

"Don't run," it pants. "Please. Don't run. I'm in no mood to catch you."

The thing is bulbous, morbid, skin bunched and sagging like one of those wrinkly dogs. A waxy substance oozes from its pores. Its tongue lolls, waggles as it grunts slow inch after slow inch. All the fat makes me itch.

It could never catch me, I think, but fast realize the only possible exit lies up the unending stairs. How many years would it take the slug to take me? It's like a blob freshly sprung from a liposuction clinic, crawling closer, stopping to wipe a corpulent face with arms that swing with pendulous skin. "I was sent," it pants. "I was…" It raises a stubby finger on short, weak arms. Its entire body heaves with exertion.

"You were sent…" It wheezes. "Such a long way…" The stub waggles as a grotesque tongue swabs lips like inner tubes. "It's just…"

I cross my arms, amazed I can feel such amusement watching this thing.

"I was sent…" Pant. Wheeze. "To show…" It pokes the stub my direction.

"Me?" I say.

An enormous head nods, more wax drips.

"Sent to show me what?" I say.

It flicks a nubbed finger toward the hearth.

I don't turn. "I'm not going in there, if that's what you're getting at."

"You…" Cough. Gasp. Wheeze. "Just…" It sounds like a freight train low on coal. It waggles the nub once more, tries to get me to turn.

A sudden light stretches my shadow to sinister shapes. I swivel to an eruption of flame and smoke that projects images like a cinema of tendrils, a theater of inferno.

"I'm not falling for—"

From the hearth a voice comes. "Lolo! Lolo!"

The picture appears fast: A boy of twelve enters a room strewn with magazines. Trays teem with refuse and dirty dishes, picked clean. Heaps of clothes lie on the floor, press against a nightstand littered with medication, inhalers, used tissues, find-a-word books, empty chip bags.

The images stuff my head, and I spin like vacuumed dust. I'm a swirling vapor that enters the cluttered room, enters the boy.

Before me, a corpulent woman lies on a king-size bed.

Shame washes over me, ugly thoughts of laziness, of excess, as she lies propped on pillows, gasping for words as I stare.

Flames grow, then dissipate. My senses tune.

I am the child, hovering somewhere in his psyche, unable to move him in any physical way yet able to experience every sensation, every feeling. Smell, vision, perception, his purest, most concealed intent.

I'm in the boy's thoughts as surely as if I've become him.

Chapter 13

JERUSALEM, ISRAEL

Houdini by her side, Rhyme opens the door and levels the Sig at the driver's face. "Who's with you?"

The man is huge, almost as big as Longinus. He returns a stare that's calm and confident. "No one."

Rhyme motions him in. "Give me your weapons."

A huge hand slides into a bespoke suit stretched by a stallion's muscles. He produces a Walther PPK in stainless steel, such a pretty pistol, sets it on a marble entry table.

"And the other ones?" she says.

"There are no others."

Houdini growls, creeps forward, hackles raised. "Yeah, and I'm the Queen of England."

The massive man sighs, bends, pulls a small Ruger from an ankle holster, sets it on the table beside the Walther.

"Is that it?"

The man nods, bald scalp glistening raindrops.

"If it isn't, you'll be dead before you know it." She wishes she could pat him down and check for herself, but the move's too risky. The man is huge, brims muscle, seems unflappable. "What's your name?" she asks, steps back. Beside her, Houdini growls, white teeth bared.

"Stuart," he says. "Sent to pick you up."

"Uh huh," she says. "Well, Stuart, you've arrived just in time." She motions with the Sig. "This way."

They move under a broad chandelier muted by the day's overcast light. Jerusalem sprawls from giant windows framed with glistening steel stairs as Stuart enters the big living area.

She marvels at him, a mountain range with feet. Does Cain grow them all this big? Give them some special elixir to make them huge and menacing? She keeps her distance, gun leveled as Houdini grumbles.

A crinkling bag causes her to turn.

Bill stands, chips scattered at his feet, arms raised straight above his head. "Um, what's up, dudes?"

She waves the pistol, eyes locked on Stuart. "In here, Bill. Stand next to him. Hands where I can see them."

Glassy eyes stare as the words take seconds to penetrate. He bends, scoops some chips, retrieves the bag.

"Bill," she says. "Hands up please. Don't make me tell you again."

Bill frowns, raises the chip bag high, moves toward Stuart. "You're a bully."

When they enter the bedroom, Emery lies muttering, face twisted, horrified expressions that alternate with confusion and flashes of bemused exasperation. Rhyme points. "Get him dressed."

Houdini leaps on the bed, gives a startled whine, then leaps back down and moves to the door.

"This is Cain's guy, right?" Stuart says. "What's wrong with him?"

"Never mind. Just get him dressed."

Stuart returns her gaze in a familiar way. He's sizing her up, calculating distance, her demeanor, her stance. Gauging her speed, wondering if he can take a round and still reach her.

"I wouldn't," she says. "This isn't my first rodeo. Clothes are in the closet."

Stuart moves with a grace that defies his size, opens the closet, pulls a dress shirt, slacks, then a pair of brown loafers.

Bill moves to the dresser, pulls out socks and a T-shirt, then shakes his head eyes locked on the clothes Stuart holds. "Nope," he says, rubbing his chin. "Way too dressy for this weather." His eyes brighten a bit yet remain dim. "He needs something casual. Something that looks good but keeps him warm and dry." His eyes are shaded like screen doors. "Ooh," he says. "I've got the perfect thing in my room." He turns and finds himself staring down Mr. Sig's barrel.

"This will do, Bill," Rhyme says. "Get. Him. Dressed."

Bill frowns, reaches in the chip bag and stuffs a handful in his mouth. Then his eyes fill with worry and fear. Hands shoot to the sky, chips sway above a tilted man bun.

"C'mon, Bill," Stuart says. "The sooner we start…" He mutters the last, seems resigned to his task. No less dangerous though, Rhyme thinks. No less of a threat.

A white T-shirt slides over Emery's head. Socks get pushed on his feet. Then they struggle with his legs as they slide on the pants. They heft him to sitting, then push his arms through the blue button-down shirt.

Stuart steps back and eyes their work.

Bill, again, stretches his arms straight above his head.

Emery flops back on the bed.

"Don't forget the shoes," Rhyme says, nodding at brown loafers. "Don't want his feet getting wet."

Stuart sighs, rolls his eyes and runs a massive hand over a bald scalp. "Do you want us to wipe his ass, too?"

Rhyme ignores him. "You look a little gaunt," she says, "think you can lift him?"

Stuart rolls his eyes again, then hefts Emery easily over his shoulder as Bill chases swinging feet, then slides the loafers in place.

"Now. To the car. We're taking a ride."

"None of this is nec—" Stuart starts.

"Move."

Stuart stares for a second, then moves along, Emery draped on his shoulder. To Rhyme's surprise, the big man's careful not to bang Emery's head, or any other part, on the door jamb or walls as they pass into the hall.

Bill pauses, lights a joint, then follows Stuart. He extends his arms over his head, joint smoking in his right hand, chips swaying in the left.

"Bill, you can lower your arms."

"Ha!" he says. "So you can shoot me? I think not, young lady. I wasn't born yesterday." His eyes look scrambled, searching his thoughts. "In fact, I wasn't born at all."

Rhyme stares, exasperated, wonders if the hippie understands the big picture, if he realizes this isn't a joke. "I'm not going to shoot you, Bill. You can lower your arms."

"No, no, no," he says. "I'm not falling for that. I saw it in a movie once."

"Can we get going?" Stuart asks.

"Out the door and into the car," she says. "No funny stuff."

"You hurt my feelings, you know." Bill stands brooding, hands now on his hips, man bun crooked, joint smoldering between his lips. "I thought we were bros?"

The hippie's words penetrate, make her think about who she can trust. "I'm sorry, Bill. I just can't take the chance. We're leaving, and I don't know you enough to trust you."

"Is this guy sick?" Stuart asks. "Look, I don't mind you pointing the gun at me or even scaring me with that giant dog, but I'd rather not catch whatever he has."

"And I'm trying to guess how many rounds will kill you."

Stuart stands stoic, holding her eyes, Emery draped. Finally, he re-enters the room and tosses Emery on the bed. "Shoot me, big shot, and load him yourself. I'm not playing this game anymore. You and the doper can manage without me."

Rhyme sees the ploy, the standoff. *Could've thought this out better.*

The tin ring of a cell phone blares from Stuart's coat. He looks at

Rhyme and grins. "That's the boss. Said he'd call and tell me where to drop you off. Probably isn't too happy we aren't there yet."

Every time, Rhyme thinks. Every single time you think it's going to be easy, details pile. *Details: where the devil dwells.*

"Answer it," she says. "Make something up. But if you give us away, I'll take your head off, then take my chances with what's next."

"Hello?" Stuart stares with dark eyes. "No sir, everything's fine. Just waiting on your wife." Listening, then laughing. "No sir, I don't think it's in their DNA to always be late…Uh huh…Roger that." The hulking African lowers the phone and slides it back in his suit coat.

"Good boy," Rhyme says. "Now load him up."

"Nope." He says, pauses, stares at the pistol. "You don't have to do this. I'm willing to help without the gun in my face or the giant dog on my heels."

Rhyme steps forward, points the pistol at his head. "Are you now?" she says. "You'll forgive me for calling you a liar?"

Their eyes lock. His face is serious and solemn. He sits on the bed next to Emery and looks at the carpet. After a few seconds, he says, "I've had enough. Truly, too much. I had family in the States. *A lot of family.*" Eyes glisten with moisture. "I think they're dead," he says, his look focused on invisible ghosts, visions of the family he loved and lost. A family murdered by her husband.

He focuses on Emery, on Houdini, then on Bill who's arms are again stretched above him, PJs drooping, Fruit of the Loom waistband jutting.

"I saw a meme once," Stuart says. "It had two Stormtroopers. You know, from Star Wars?"

"Yes."

"One says to the other: 'Do you ever think maybe *we're* the bad guys?' The other says, 'No, never thought about it. Now, let's get back to the Death Star…er… the ship.'"

He looks up and searches her eyes. "I'm in too deep. Have a feeling whatever I know isn't a fraction of what's there. My brothers, sister, parents, cousins, aunts and uncles, all dead, all smoked right up, all murdered." A huge head ticks like a slow metronome. "That *cannot* be allowed to stand."

He paces to the draped window and peers through. "As scared as I am, I'll participate no further. *Can't* participate further. Seems I've been provided an option to escape and the only question you have to answer is: Am I lying or sincere?"

His look is earnest, his face stern, even angry. Dark eyes hold hers, deep, mahogany. He waits as she considers the question.

Trickery, logic squeals.

Trust, says her instinct.

Sig slides back in its holster. "Bill, please. Put your hands down."

Chapter 14

Dim sunlight squeezes through lengths of lace, stained and torn. Young faces grin and jostle on the window's other side.

Giggles drift, surprising sounds of astonishment and mockery. "Lolo." They tease with a singsong lilt. "Mommy's little Lolo."

I step close, try to ignore the big-as-a-cornfield belly and the taut pink nightgown, stained and stretched. Embarrassment heats my face. I look at my shoes, Chuck Taylors, dingy and white, my jeans cuffed above them.

"I'm too old for Lolo, Mother." The boy says. *We* say. "Can't you call me Laslo?"

"Oh ho, growing up, is he? Thinks he's too big for his mother."

I shuffle my feet, gaze out the window, ignore the muted laughter. "It's not that, Mom. It's just the other kids hear you and they make fun of me. Of you. Of us. They call you horrible names, sneak up and peek in the window, stare like you're a freak in a sideshow."

"Crawl up here," she says, "sit and talk with me."

Emotion sweeps through my chest as I imagine the ridicule I'll face if they see me pressed to my mother's side.

"I don't want to." My voice cracks with puberty.

She grunts and presses a wrist to her forehead. "I knew it'd come to this. I knew someday your shame would take you."

"No, Mom, it's not like that. It's just…"

"That you don't love me anymore."

Curtains of torn white lace, grungy from lack of care, flap with the breeze from an oscillating fan.

"We need new drapes," I say, feeling awkward, knowing every word's fuel for the monsters outside.

"Don't change the subject. You're ashamed. Admit it. Ashamed of your fat mother and what your little friends think.

"And to think how I suffered when you were born. The pain I endured. The agony! Someday you'll know. Someday you'll care."

"I care, Mom. I really do. But can't you see it from my side?"

"It's all about you, isn't it. Day after day I lay here, too sick to move, and my only son thinks of nothing but himself."

Boldness shoves shame and embarrassment away as it seizes my tongue. "You're only sick because you don't listen to the doctors." A small hand rises, fingers pop up with each sentence. "You don't take your medicine." Index finger. "You don't get out of bed." Middle finger. "You say you can't do anything." Ring finger. "But you don't even try." Pinky finger. "Can't you try, Mom. Just once. I'll help. We'll get you better."

She strains for a half-eaten bagel on the nightstand. "It's no use, Lolo," she sighs. "I'm too far gone, will probably die any day. Probably won't even make your bar mitzva." Her eyes search me, make me think of that obese demon-slug as they bore into me from a bulging, frowning face. "You'd probably like that, huh?" she says. "They'll need horses to get me out of here, you know. Probably a crane. You and your little friends will have quite the laugh when that happens."

"Let's get you up," I say, ignoring the bait. "Let's move, Mom. We'll go somewhere. I'll get your medicine and before you know it, you'll be just fine. No one will laugh then, let me tell you. You'll show them all. We can go to the park, then to the store. You can come to my bar mitzva. Can't you try? For me?" I feel the pain, the pleas, the intention, the love, the unyielding belief that his mother can heal herself, lose the weight, become whole.

A pendulous arm swings as she dismisses the notion with a wave. "It's too late, Lolo. I'm going to die in this bed any day. Probably with your little friends watching." Eyes roll as I stare at the floor. She's playing a scheme I can't quite parry with a twelve-year-old mind.

"At least it'll be over for you," she bawls. "You won't have to tolerate the teasing anymore and can go about your business without the worry of an inconvenient mother. You'll never have to be ashamed again."

Sighing, looking at the dingy Chuck's, I shuffle a step closer. "I'm not ashamed," I lie. "I just want you to do better."

Her eyes jolt toward me. "Then get me some cake," she says. "If you love me, you'll bring me some. Do we still have the cake from Rubenstein's?"

I shake my head, shuffle in place. "I ate it all."

Thin lips stretch, cause her cheeks to bulge as she pouts. She looks to the ceiling, stares at cobwebs, talks to the air. "And now he lies," she says. "I never thought the day would come when my only son would become a filthy liar."

Indignation fills me. I did lie, but it's her words that foul me. The accusation, the injustice of such accurate descriptions of my genuine feelings.

"Okay, I'll get the—" I suppress the word *damn*, can't risk worsening her mood or loosening her tongue—"cake." Another idea strikes, an appeal to the highest authority. "Father will be home soon, and he'll be sore mad at me for giving it to you."

"He doesn't love me anymore, either," she whines. "He doesn't care at all."

Impossible, she's totally impossible. "Nonsense, Mother. He takes good care of you, gives you everything you want."

"If only his son would do so well."

My mouth snaps closed as the Chuck's fumble. Confusion and exasperation claim my heart.

"Cake," she says.

"But…"

Children's laughter.

I give in. "I'll be right back."

Piled clothes are like traversing small mountains as I move past, picking some from the floor to toss atop an overfilled hamper. In the short hallway, family pictures give glimpses of the slow transition of my mother from normal, smiling homemaker to obese, bleating matriarch. Hustling past, I ignore them, wish I hadn't seen them at all. Cake, I think, the last thing she needs.

Past a kitchen table that's seen better days and into a small, but tidy, kitchen. Vacuum, mop, laundry, shop. I go through my list, consider my tasks for the day, feel worried I'll forget to do one and have to add it to tomorrow's list. My studies will be affected, I think as panic rises. My studies, my only hope out of this place.

Ridicule and laughter reach my ears from the back bedroom. If I was bigger, I'd go right out there and give them all the trouncing of their lives.

Then my dad's words emerge clear: *Grin and bear it.*

Words that piss me off. Words that dismiss the horror of my embarrassment and shame for her nonsense conditions. Perhaps she's right, perhaps Dad doesn't care. If she'd only try. Just one attempt to get up, to walk, to take her meds, to eat a little less.

Magnets cover the refrigerator—pizza joints, bakeries, deli's—easy referrals for anything she could want. I grasp the scuffed steel of the refrigerator door. As I throw it open, a few magnets hit the floor.

I'll get them later; for now, get the damn cake.

I grab a saucer from the cupboard—painted with grapes, hand painted in Italy—and place a slice on it.

"And don't short me!" Her voice from the bedroom is as clear as the riot of laughter that follows.

Shame, embarrassment, humiliation, I choke them down, cut another slice and add it to the first.

"And milk!" she shouts.

Frustration consumes as small hands grip the sideboard. My teeth grind, my Chuck's tap. This is madness. The impossibility of her habits and my outrage. She's fatter by the day. Doesn't seem to care. Doesn't care about us enough to even try.

My boy fingers turn white as they clamp the counter. *I wish she'd die,* I think, not for the first time. But this time I own it, follow it, hold it in my heart as a fond wish, an escape from the impossible, the last light of hope. She doesn't care. Doesn't give a flying fuck.

My face heats. Even thinking a cuss can get me in trouble. I stand erect. *Fuck* her. *Fuck* this place. *Fuck* this life.

"Lolo! Where are you?"

Laughter peals.

"Yes, Mother!" I stomp down the feelings, the anger, the unfairness.

Too damn lazy to rise, too damn lazy to care. I'll cuss if I want!

The house is a shamble, and my best efforts aren't close to enough to keep it clean, do all my chores, and still excel at school. Then there's Dad, imparting useless advice—*Avoid the clap boy!*—while detached and drinking himself silly. Someday it'll be different. Someday I won't have these thoughts. I'll have a family of my own and show them how much I care. Someday I'll show them all. Someday I'll walk out there and beat the kids at the window senseless. Then I'll leave here forever and make something of myself. Something worthwhile, something not obese, something without excuses. Then, they'll see. Boy oh boy, then they'll know what a family should be.

From a faded white drawer, I grab a fork. *I'll never be like her. Like them. Never!* This family's an embarrassment. Not just to me, but to the entire neighborhood. Circus freaks, all of us, luring gawkers from everywhere. Always something good to see at Laslo's! Always something to laugh at! To poke at!

First chance I get, I'm out of here, fast as I can.

Back up the hallway and into the room, I ignore the sounds from the window and hand her the only thing she cares about.

She scoops a giant bite, then stretches her mouth to stuff it in. Her skin looks like it'll split from the strain. "It's about time," she says around the mouthful. "I almost starved to death."

Anger flares. I blurt. "Fat chance!"

Our eyes meet.

The gasp is audible as she stutters, strains, stammers.

I cross my arms and stare in defiance. What's she gonna do, get out of bed and thrash me. *Fat! Chance!*

She quivers, stares, disbelief in her eyes.

Here it comes, more bawling.

But nothing comes. Nothing but grunting and a hasty hand clutching her throat. Eyes bulge as her face goes from raging red to violet blue.

She waves frantic, eyes watering, dark crumbs stuck to lips and cheeks.

The saucer drops among the piled clothes.

I rush to the window and throw it open, stick my head out. "She's choking!" I yell. "Get help! Go get help!"

Astonished eyes reflect humor and insincerity.

"Get help!" I wail.

CPR. She needs CPR.

I've seen it on TV, it doesn't look that hard.

I leap on the bed to straddle a mountainous body. Clasping my hands, I press hard on a pillowy chest.

The bed shakes, the headboard thuds on the wall. Eyes bulge from a face bloated like a carnation, staring like panes of glass. I'm doing it wrong, they say. Doing CPR wrong on purpose, they scream.

"Help!" I wail. "I need help!"

Boyish arms press into flesh. Tears add wet stains to the pink nightgown.

Her hand drops from her throat and dangles over the bed side.

"No! No! No!" I push hard, fast, howling for aid, wondering if it's coming.

After five minutes, I droop, too exhausted to continue.

After eight minutes, I crawl from her body, toward the riveted faces clustered at the open window.

"I've never seen a dead body," one of them says.

"Fatty choked to death on cake," says another.

I stare at them as rage floods my core. Then shock and the purest measures of disbelief and inadequacy.

The room spins.

My mother's voice echoes.

If only his son could do so well.

Sweat pours into my Chuck's. Arms and legs tingle, quiver, go numb.

The floor rushes to meet me.

CHAPTER 15

I fall to my knees as bitter dust fouls my mouth.

The slug heaves close, watching as I gasp, spit dribbling from my lips.

I'm surrounded by broken crockery, delicious aromas, fetid odors. The fire blazes and makes the room too hot. Sweat dribbles down my forehead as I wipe my mouth, then stand to face the obese mass.

A bulbous head shakes, another bloated extension of its corpulent body. An emaciated hand wipes waxy sweat from its brow. "How'd you like that? Pretty good, no?"

I look at the chairs before the fire, think how nice they appear, inviting. But I'm afraid they'll swallow me up. "Was that real?"

"Of course," it says. "One of my more succulent friends. Let's see, what was her name?"

A phrase floats through my mind, from Thackeray: *Mother is the name of God in the lips and hearts of little children.*

Drooping slits rise and I notice the thing's eyes. The head twists in an odd way. "Susan?" it says. "Or was that the one in Des Moines? Maybe Sara. Something with an S, I think."

Anger rises. "Why'd you show me that?"

It peers at me through rolls of fat. "So you'd know, of course. So you'd see."

I'm dumbfounded. "So I'd know? Are you fucking crazy? For what purpose?"

"Ah, I always forget, your kind needs a purpose for everything." Its breath seems to come easier, the waxy ooze subsides. "I'm afraid I can do no better than what I've said. You'd think you'd be appreciative after everything I went through just to get here." It sweeps a sickly arm over its body. *"This* isn't so easy to move."

I'm disgusted, coughing again, dark particles spewing with each spasm.

"What are you?" I finally manage.

"Oh, how tragic. In my utter and complete exhaustion, I neglected to introduce myself. I am Belphegor, prince of the realm."

"Really?" I say. "A prince?" I look at stained walls, shelves bursting with rotted abundance. In the fire, beings swoop and swirl through a distant, rancid mist. "Of course, you are. Okay. Let's see if I can figure this out. You're a prince of hell." Its head settles like cottage cheese. "And hell is known for demons, so you can only be a demon."

It looks astonished, even hurt. "I don't care for that label. Demons are associated with nightmares, and I'm certainly *not* a nightmare."

"Then what classification would you give yourself?"

"Why, I'm a giver of gifts. A provider of needs, of wants, of comfort, of respite. Just ask Sheila there, or whatever her name was. Did she seem unhappy?"

"Well, not until she choked to death."

"My point made. She had everything a person could want and more. Everything at her fingertips. And it should be known that she gave herself over quite easily. Didn't even try and resist. She wanted that, all of it. And I, in my kindness and generosity, granted all I could." It sighs a raspy breath. "It does my heart good to provide for you mortals, you ape people. You always seem so lost and hopeless. It's nice to help in some small way."

"And kill them all. Is that what you mean? You're trying to tell me you get no pleasure from their deaths; from the heartbreak they leave behind?"

"Of course not!" It seems offended. "I get extreme pleasure for my efforts. The pleasure of knowing I made one life just a little easier."

"Easier? That was misery. Disregard. Abandonment."

Its face puckers. "You're insensitive," it says. "That hurt my feelings."

"Feelings? A demon with feelings?"

"Yes." It raises many chins, sniffs haughtily. "At least *I* do. I really do care. So much so, I provide endless encouragement, endless opportunity for rest. Your people love it, too. They don't even try to resist my whispers. I say, 'Eat the cake,' and the cake they eat. I say, 'Don't get up,' and down they stay. Really, I just give them what they want."

"Uh huh," I say. "Do they all die in the end?"

Thin eyebrows crinkle, cause a wrinkled forehead to droop. "Well, that's a dumb question. You *all* die at the end. Don't you know that's the way it works?"

"I'm referring specifically to those you *help*. One could make the argument that *you* kill them."

It thinks some more. "I suppose you could say that, but it's hardly my doing. My intent is pure."

I stare at the thing, dark eyes glimmering in earnest. "I wonder if Laslo thinks that."

"Doesn't matter if he doesn't. I was concerned only with his mother. Her cravings led to me and I entered. It was a match made in heaven."

I look around. "How do I get out of here?"

It motions to endless stairs. "If only I knew. I could be so much more useful if it weren't for those infernal steps."

It hits me then. "You can't climb them," I say. "You're trapped here, forever surrounded by all this deliciousness?"

It either misses my sarcasm or ignores it. "Do you want to stay? I'm having a wonderful buffet prepared and it'd be a shame if you missed it."

My stomach turns at the thought of watching the thing eat. The words *glutton* and *sloth* drift across my thoughts. "I'd rather not," I say. "No offense."

It grunts as it turns, as thin arms strain to move its considerable mass. "None taken," it says. "I'll always be here though. The horrid stairs assure that. But if you need me, call my name. Whether here or elsewhere, I'll come running."

Like you can run, I think. But before the thought even finishes, the blob is gone. No theatrics, magician's smoke, or abracadabra. Just there one second, gone the next.

I glance at cracked pottery, stained chairs, endless stairs.

With a sigh, I start the climb.

CHAPTER 16

GEORGE WASHINGTON NATIONAL FOREST,
WEST VIRGINIA, UNITED STATES

Days earlier

Crispy chews granola but craves a cheroot.

"Bad for your health," the doctor said. Yeah, like granola's any better. Besides, get in line, health risks oblige a merc's life.

He squints into darkness, knows he's well concealed, watches the two idiots who watch Rhyme. Middle of the damn night, the time duty most often calls. Tracked her from the scrapyard to the library in Carter's Glen, then from the library along the circuitous route to this forest.

And why the hell did she waste time on a camper? How on Earth does that pile of rust benefit her, help her elude, escape, evade? Maybe she's slipping, rusty. Maybe with all those emotions, she's forgotten the lessons I taught, hard lessons too.

He pushes a cheroot between his lips but doesn't light it. Can't have those morons see the flame: a certain beacon on a dead night.

Have to help her but have to remain hidden. Be a ghost, a guardian angel.

The thought hits him like a falling tree. He scrambles into the back, grabs the clothes Rhyme left behind, lifted from a D.C. donation bin, then presses them to the dog's pointed snout.

"Here you go, buddy. Take it in, that's it. This is her. Go find her. Protect her. If nothing else, you'll be a great distraction, a wild card, something unexpected for the G-men and the X'chasei boys."

He remembers the shred out. Rhyme's image slowly appearing as he contemplated the heat in the small ops center beneath his house in the scrapyard. *Still need to change that vent.*

He slides to the passenger's side, flicks a look at the camper, at the two mercs who watch it. They won't wait forever, he knows. Time's short.

"Here you go, fella. Guess I shoulda named you at some point." The big Doberman sniffs the clothes, then whines a bit. He's ready to go, already on her scent. It's a shot in the dark, but the best we've got. Might even the odds a bit. Might make a difference.

It might also fuck things up.

A crack of the door and the dog leaps away to disappear in shadows.

He remembers the call and performs the calculus in his head. The FBI had sent the shred out, had employed merc's to gain their objectives. Then Cain called, said, "Protect her, but remain unseen. I'll call when it's time to extract her completely. Her ex-husband, Emery Merrick, is on an airplane bound for Washington. Be there to receive him, then do what you must to leave him behind while you get my wife out."

Agent Elroy should've handled that. He had the reporter in his sights and took the shot. Then, Emery saved by a ring? I'd never be that lucky. I'd have been shot in the chest and bled out in the hangar.

And Drake—Cain, now. What a dastardly bastard. A dastard?

What's his play? His ploy? And why leave Emery behind? A smart way to part the pair, if I have to bet.

What a dastard.

He watches the idiots exit the vehicle and move toward the camper.

The rifle's cold in his hands. He presses an eye to the scope, watches the two approach.

It's gonna get interesting fast. A complete ambush.

Hopefully, the dog will help.

Hopefully, she isn't too rusty.

CHAPTER 17

JERUSALEM, ISRAEL

Days following

The landing in Jerusalem is smooth. Rhyme storms from the jet, auburn hair glistening rain, emerald eyes filled with scorn and anger. "Hurry up!"

Emery and Bill don't hesitate. Then the dog scampers after, healthy, ready.

At a waiting SUV, Rhyme ejects the driver, enters, revs the engine, crinkles her eyebrows and departs without a second glance.

She's pretty pissed, and Crispy wonders how Drake—Cain—will handle her arrival. What words he'll use to soothe her wrath.

And what about the hound? A strange thing, that. On the verge of death yet, now, completely healthy. It bounded down the stairs, spry and strong, then leapt into the SUV without a sign of impairment or injury.

Mangy thing must be part cat, used up one of its lives.

He flashes to the flight from the U.S. The abrupt turns, the white-knuckle climb to the sky.

Using a taxi way to takeoff? Seriously? That pilot has big brass balls, probably polished just for the trip.

But the dog's the kicker. Words like supernatural, arcane, magical, float through his mind. But he'd seen it himself and can't find a way to refute what his eyes beheld.

As the jet tipped to float on silver wings, launching them from the Earth seconds before the cataclysm, he remembers dodging missiles. Remembers the mushrooms: blazing, giant orbs of fire, more vast, more unbelievable, when seen in person.

He'd watched, detached and numb, as multiple infernos swallowed the horizon. Then missiles from the mainland streaked toward targets of retaliation, and disappeared.

They'd all pressed their heads together: Emery, Bill, and Rhyme. They were despair, pure and utter sorrow. Tears dropped from their cheeks and plopped into a small puddle.

Then, the hound sat straight up, somehow, impossibly, healed.

Crispy thinks of the implications. The possibilities.

Nothing on Earth could've caused that. Nothing on this planet could've saved that dog from his wounds.

He'd seen the blood, the dog rasping its last. Had tried to think of the words he'd use to soothe Rhyme when the animal finally succumbed to its injuries.

No small tasks for Crispy. Let's see: watch your country get nuked, then your favorite person wracked with grief as she mourns a dying pooch.

Being a mentor ain't easy; requires lots of platitudes, witty axioms and clever words, filled with wisdom, most of the time falling short.

But the dog *had* risen, *was* fully healed. He'd watched Rhyme's face light up with confusion and joy. A weird side show of features flowed across her face, first twisted in sorrow, then glowing with delight. The animal stretched out, nudged her hand as if feeling her anguish. As if refusing to let her bear the horrors alone.

That dog is dark, hard and sharp, possessed with a soul more fully good than any human he's ever met. But how'd it live? Maybe luck?

Possible, but doubtful. Fate? Maybe, maybe not. Divine intervention? Absolutely crackpot.

The pilot pulls up in a dark blue van. "Need any help?" She's pretty, young, trusting.

"No thanks, lady. You did enough getting us here in one piece. Besides, I have some pressing business. You know, old man stuff."

"Suit yourself." She smiles. "See you around."

He watches her drive away, then boards the jet and retrieves the two Pelican cases they salvaged from the States.

This is getting stupid. I'm wrapped in too many things. Bound by too much. Too many players, so much happening.

I need info, need to know what plan's been hatched. The assets, the objectives. It's going to be tough to self-direct, especially while under Cain's thumb, but if that time hasn't come yet, it's racing toward me like a meteor.

A movie quote pops in, something inane. Jim Carrey, playing the Grinch. *"That's what these tests are for!"*

He chuckles at the scene, the Grinch as crash test dummy. Gripping the cases, he heads for the truck. Good luck? Fate? The cases and what they contain *are* going to come in handy after all. Somehow, during the narrow escape from nuclear bombs, he'd had a feeling, an itch, a tickle, not to leave them behind.

He throws them in the truck bed. A newer truck, shining with rain, recently detailed. Not me at all, he thinks as another song lyric intrudes. *"You can set my truck on fire, roll it down a hill, I still wouldn't trade it for a Coupe Deville."* Who was that? Joe Diffie, maybe. *Pickup Man.*

Get your head in the game!

Things are getting ridiculous and *some* plan trumps no plan. Rhyme's life may depend on it. Hell, all their lives might. He thinks of Rhyme now. "I love you, Emery," she'd said to the inept reporter. Surprising. Her with him. She's definitely out of his league, but what a lucky guy. Hope he realizes Rhyme Carter's made from something else entirely, something special, something rare. He ponders a slate sky and wandering clouds. Doesn't make sense she'd choose him over everyone else; couldn't make sense if he pondered for a century. Then again, who can predict the seasons of women?

The truck smells good as he enters, smells of pine, a Christmas tree-shaped air freshener hanging from the mirror. Where do those come from? Someone must've made a fortune. So classic. Old school. Don't need nothing flashy, just pine and a pickup.

It hits him then, World Famous Crispy's Scrapyard. Now nothing more than melted lead and charred lumps. He sighs, feels a bit of relief and a simultaneous pang of sadness. The place was his life, an oasis in a world fraught with danger and deception. A place he'd made a fortress, a headquarters, a glimmering bastion of rusty piles and chain link.

Relief sets in, and he even laughs as he turns the key and drives from the airfield. Guess I don't have to worry about that vent anymore. But damn! All my arms up in smoke, a lifetime's collection, everything a growing assassin needs, gone in an epic flash of invisible particles.

There's Mitch, Julie, that picture lost. He presses the pedal, turns right down a road lined with parked cars and charred storefronts. Jerusalem's coming back in record time, rebounding from the attack like a phoenix from the ashes.

We can thank Cain for that. If nothing else, the guy gets it done. Wipers squeak as he drives, he taps a beat that recalls an Eddie Rabbit song: *I Love a Rainy Night.* Hope the safe house is still in one piece.

If I'm smart, I'll lay low, give the old bones some rest.

If I'm *intelligent,* I'll do what I came to do then make a decent plan for after.

Plans. Planning. Loads of work typically scrapped within seconds of enemy contact. The GI's way: seat of your pants flying, running, gunning, grinding, grunting. He thinks of the old motto, a motivator for a different time, more poignant by the hour. "Kill 'em all, let God sort 'em out." Seems Cain's bought that playbook, worn it dog-eared with study. Or perhaps he just has a knack for fucking up a lot of shit in a short time. Either way, things are getting hairy. It's getting tougher to dodge the questions, the events. To turn a blind eye for the sake of a paycheck, massive as it is.

Cleaner: a guy who cleans up. Got a problem? Call ole Crispy. Need someone wrecked? Call ole Crispy. A quiet intervention? Call ole Crispy. Maybe I'll open a new place, a better place, here in the land of prophets and endless sand in your crack. Ole Crispy's Bar and Grill. Drink myself silly every night, spend my days tossing drunks, loving the ladies. I'm sure if I throw some dough around, they'll look past the corrugated face.

He turns left through a blinking red light. A military vehicle passes loaded with troops, bearing a strange emblem.

Not Israeli, something else, something unidentifiable as any other country. The men in the truck wear black, hold guns propped in their arms and elbows, have the strange symbol sewn on to their sleeves.

He passes them, makes another quick turn, then another.

Things to keep low: speed and profile. The safe house isn't far. Get there and settle in, do your thing, no distractions.

Another turn and the road narrows, then a small dirt drive leads through sparse, overgrown vegetation. Guess the landscaping crew bailed during the attack and never returned. Who can blame them? And more the better, now that I think about it. Thick vegetation gives concealment, makes noise when someone approaches. A poor man's security system, rather perfect for this situation.

The house is gray, dirt-streaked plaster from steady rain down a slanted roof. The windows are dirty. It needs a paint job. Used to be white, or was it always this drab? Jesus, looks like a crack house now. Hope it wasn't raided. He chuckles, doubts Israel's authorities care much about drug trafficking right now.

Relax. It's probably just as you left it, good enough for safety, for concealment, for a lair.

He pulls up, exits the truck, moves to the bed and lowers the tailgate. Rain beads on the Pelican cases, makes him smile through wrinkled lips. This next part should be fun. Having a look at X'chasei's real intentions.

Voices, raised and rough, split the rain, echo over the brush, waft toward gray clouds.

When you've haunted all the world's shit holes, you develop an ear for the flush. The sounds of victim and perp. He freezes in place, listens intently.

All males, shouting, confused. Good. Let boys be boys. Local thugs probably, robbing, pillaging, on the lookout for easy victims. Or perhaps some men playing soccer, blowing off steam with sport. Either way, hope they don't come around here, I've had enough headaches for one day.

He grips the pistol in the small of his back. A Kimber Scorpius, .45. A gorgeous gun in black and steel, originally purchased because, well, it was just to pretty *not* to purchase. Turned out to be a hell of a sidearm, too. Seems Miss Kimber's alluring gaze has the ability to stun an enemy with beauty alone. In the past, her smile has certainly bought seconds when seconds were short.

Seems beauty, from a woman, a site, a weapon, seduces even in the throes of battle.

Beautiful and deadly, just like me, he thinks, chuckles, hefts a Pelican case to the ground. He plops the other atop the first, wipes the rain from his face. Inside he'll be high and dry. Fat, dumb and happy as the grunts say.

The vegetation breaks, crackles, rustles. It's harsh, harried: someone's panicked. Then, a man breaches at a speed best described as fair to middling. Not an athlete to be sure, certainly no soccer player.

Crispy watches him rush past and duck behind the truck's front bumper.

"Um, can I help you?" Crispy ambles around to confront. The man's obviously homeless, dressed in a garbage bag, cheap sandals. He's breathless, nervous, probably just stole something.

"Yes! Yes!" he says. "You *can* help me. I'm being chased and need aid. Would you be so kind?"

Crispy laughs. *Kindness, what a joke.* "You're not from around here, are you?"

The man hunkers down. "I'm a friar from Mount Tabor."

Crispy turns north as if looking at the mountain. "A long way from home, Padre."

With a shout and stomp of leaves, three men appear from the bushes. A smirk crosses the face of the first, the biggest. He draws a gun and points it at Crispy.

"Seems our luck's changed, boys." The man closes the gap, eyes locked, then his face twists with disgust. The expression isn't foreign, a look that assumes Crispy's only use is as a monster.

The man's laugh is comical, maniacal. "Oh, look, we found a toasted marshmallow."

"Very funny," Crispy says, "but you're too late. He went that way."

The man looks down a twisted goat path, barely visible in the overgrowth. Small, narrow, heading into the brush toward the city proper. He waggles the gun. "Doesn't matter, you seem more... *profitable.* What's in the boxes?"

Crispy steps before the cases as the other two move to his flanks. "Nothing that concerns you."

"If we can sell it, it concerns us."

Crispy pulls a cheroot from a back pocket, a zippo from the front, then sparks the smoke alight. Drawing deep, he blows vapor through a mist of rain. His eyes flare, lips twist as he speaks. "I'm not in the mood, kids. Please, move along before someone gets hurt."

The man steps three quick paces and presses the pistol to Crispy's forehead. "It'd be a shame to mess up such a pretty face."

Before the words hit air, Crispy snatches the gun and drives his knee into the man's groin.

The two others react, but before they can take a step, Miss Kimber appears. Crispy spreads both arms, trains both pistols on the now stunned and silent attackers. The first moans, clutches his balls, slops in the mud, crawls breathless toward the brush, all zest for robbery gone.

Crispy feels the rage, the madman pressing a thin screen.

Kill 'em! Let God sort 'em out!

Fingers twitch as both pistols bark.

But the men don't fall, just stand staring and stupefied.

Just before he fired, someone pushed his arms up and ruined his shot, his kills.

He spins, levels dual pistols at the astonished face of the homeless man.

The attackers waste no time, sprinting through the brush and toward the city. Seems softer targets are their forte. Branches crack, brush flutters as they race away. Young, he thinks, dumb. Not too brave though. They won't be back.

He stares into the homeless man's blue eyes, presses both pistols close as anger smears scars to a weird Picasso.

The friar shows no fear. Just serenity, an acceptance of death like an old friend, a release to a better, grander reality.

"Why'd you do that?"

"Don't you know?" Pappy says. "Thou shalt not kill."

Pistols lower. Astonishment floods. "Jesus H. Christ."

Chapter 18

Legs ache as I climb endless stairs. Beside me something flashes, and I blink at a wall dripping with grease and mold. Then a door appears.

I grip the knob, feel exhausted by the miles left to climb. Better than nothing, I think as I open the door and step through.

The air's rancid and I chortle, gag, try to channel calm to quivering, aching legs. A warm wind flows like days-old tapioca. I feel coated in oil, feathered in filth, peering to endless darkness.

The space gives a feeling of vastness as shadows rise. Ahead something percolates, makes sounds like a bubbling morass.

I step forward and almost fall. I'm on a ledge, thirty feet above something thick, clouded, black as night. It bubbles as I stare and think of Nietzsche and his abyss. The eternal riddle. What happens if one gazes into it?

Precise clicks bounce from stone walls, move through shadow to plop in my ears.

An outline appears, sharp, confident and poised. A man in silhouette. His face is sharp, seems fake. His eyes blaze a sense of fury, a whiteness like trapped in a blizzard. A sense of destruction, of hopelessness, of terror.

"Who are you?"

His countenance is restrained rage. "I am Asmodeus." A gouged voice, an uncaring voice. "I am wrath."

Gooseflesh erupts as I swallow, step back, and almost plunge from the thin ledge into the abyss below. His words hold no emotion, no sense of rhythm, just icy discomfort, the feeling of frigid misfortune. Fogged breath flows through his nostrils, small icicles appear on the tip of his nose and the lobes of his ears. He's a nomad frozen in place, a mysterious snow creature traipsing mountains too remote to be known. He is predator. He is apex.

He snaps his fingers.

⸻

Afghanistan

Helicopter blades spin to a stop as I step from the chopper.

"Sergeant Holcumb!" A private rushes forward, breathless. "The CO wants to see you ASAP. Said to send you the second you land."

"What about?"

"I'm not sure, Sergeant. He didn't say. Just made it my job to collect you as soon as you got back."

"Roger that." I sigh, feel my eyebrows raise as confusion wrinkles. I take in the dusty base, everything beige, everything dirty. "Let's go."

A five-minute drive later, I enter a hardback tent in khaki green, the major's office.

My hand pops a salute as I say, "Sergeant Holcumb reporting."

"Have a seat, Reggie," the Major says. "How was the mission?"

"Grueling but nothing some chow and sleep won't cure." I feel the fatigue, the numbness of my limbs, the thick blanket on my thoughts. I slide onto a scraped metal chair before the CO's desk.

The Major shuffles some papers, looks down, takes a breath. "Sergeant Holcumb, I'm afraid I've some bad news and there's no easy way to put this." He sighs, then frowns. "Your brother has passed away."

"What? Mitch?" Shock sends icicles straight up my neck. I focus, tamp down the emotion.

The Major frowns. "No. It's Tomlin. We just got notified this morning." He pauses, searches my face. "Wanted to tell you when you got back." He holds my eyes. "He took his own life, Sergeant. Left a note that said he couldn't stand living anymore."

I look to the floor. Sadness and dismay do a dance that's laborious and painful, singed with anguish, drenched in despair. Memories wash, lift, level me as I suddenly understand the history. Tomlin, Tommy, barely the youngest of three brothers, confined to a wheelchair after a collision with a semi-truck stole his legs. "Oh," I hear myself, us, stammer as Tommy's face blooms. The beaming smile, mischievous eyes glittering above a cleft chin. "Does Mitch know?" I, we, ask.

The CO's frown grows. "It gets worse, Sergeant. I told Mitch this morning and now he's AWOL."

A village appears in our thoughts, visions of dead kids. "I see."

"He took a bottle of bootleg hooch and headed out. We haven't been able to raise him on the radio and have no idea where he went." He leans forward and props elbows on his desk. "I know you're going through a lot, Sergeant. I know I'm asking a lot, but do you have any idea where he could've gone?"

The village rises bright in the recess of our mind. It snuffs in an instant. Then, we lie. "No idea, sir."

The CO's eyes are steely gray, pulling no punches in their earnestness as they hold ours. "Are you sure, Sergeant?"

"Yes, sir, I am." Lying again, without shame.

The pause is ripe. The CO's eyes don't flinch as we stare back.

He stands. "Very well, Sergeant Holcumb. You're relieved of your duties to prepare to return to CONUS and help your family with your brother's funeral. When we locate Mitch, we'll send him along. A chopper's leaving this afternoon. Be on it. And if there's anything we can do, don't hesitate."

We stand, salute again, feel anxious to leave. The village wavers, floats up in our mind. "Roger that, sir."

"Dismissed."

We take two steps before the CO stops us. "And, Sergeant, I suppose it goes without saying that you're confined to base until you leave. I know the urge, the need even, to go looking. You have to trust us. We'll find Mitch and get him back safe. Am I clear?"

"Yes, sir, very clear."

"Dismissed."

A burning afternoon sun squints our eyes as our mind races with questions.

Tommy. Dead. Took his own life.

Flagging down a private, we give instructions to find a vehicle and return ASAP. Then, we pull a tin and stuff our cheek with snuff.

Remorse knocks, then quietly enters. It wasn't easy lying to the CO, a man we respect. A man who, if told the truth, would've probably aided in any way he could. *Probably.* A key word with equal chance of becoming *probably not.*

Career ender, we think. Sixteen years down the drain. No pension, no retirement. Court martial. Humiliation.

We spit as boldness seizes, as we realize there's no choice. The village appears again, small, ramshackle, deserted. We know where Mitch is.

A toot of a horn reveals the private behind the wheel of a camouflaged pickup. We approach and hike our thumb over our shoulder. The private jumps out and we jump in.

"Um, Sergeant," the private says, "I signed for that vehicle. Have to return it today."

Gears grind as we engage the stick and drive off.

The village appears as a remote Inuit encampment without the snow: a handful of huts in stone and plywood, single story, mud roofs, nestled at the base of a broad, sweeping hill in the center of the ever-shifting desert.

At the village's perimeter, three corpses lie covered with a fluttering sheet.

This is the compound, the corpses, courtesy of Mitch, my brother.

From atop the hill, we peer through the scope of the sniper rifle. Our head becomes a map marked with possible routes and options.

Then a wailing shriek, blood curdling, muzzled, erupts from the village's far side.

"Emery? Emery can you hear me?" Rhyme's voice, sliding, far away. "Emery?" I lose my place in the soldier's mind, waver on a greased edge as if standing over a chasm between worlds.

"Rhyme!" I yell without a mouth, step forward without feet. The image shudders like a mirage, then shimmers, snaps, and I'm back with the soldier.

Has to be Mitch, we think as dusk's shadowy fingers creep over the desolate compound. Mitch always said he'd do it, and Tommy's unleashed his wrath.

We remember the mission, the children, buried in a shallow grave two clicks away. Mitch fought to get hold of their killers even as they kneeled in quiet terror, hands bound, waiting for transport.

Mitch is hard to hold back when fueled by outrage. He never forgets justice. Never forgets to complete a task undone.

Suddenly I know the story as if it's my own. Mitch heard of Tommy's death, got some bootleg and pickled himself. Soaked in alcohol, he smoldered, grieved his twin until the ghost children came, whispered, and helped him hatch a plan to go out on a high note, to avenge them and subsequently end his life as the right hand of Justice.

We imagine Mitch's pain. Imagine how Tommy's death shredded him. I know that, as twins, Mitch and Tommy were inseparable, a force magnified. Call it ESP or that sense twins share, but they spoke without words and always, always, thought the same things, did the same things. They moved according to an inseparable bond. Pure trouble visited upon the poor townsfolk of a Lake Erie hamlet. They were hell on wheels.

Our mind clouds, swirls with rancid jealousy. We could never break the bond they shared. Their love, as brothers, best friends, kindreds, had left us alone to be the responsible one. Had driven us to join the Army and find our own path, alone.

Then this, Tommy's accident, one of Mitch's dares gone horribly wrong. Mitch got lucky, had been thrown from the vehicle to suffer only a fractured arm.

But Tommy, well, he'd got the worst of it: lost his legs, mangled most of the vertebra in his spine, underwent seventeen surgeries to rid himself—impossible—of constant, agonizing pain.

But nothing worked.

Tommy's suffering continued, worsened even, until the day Mitch caught him slicing his own wrists.

Mitch rarely left his side after that, cared for him, cooked his meals, bathed him.

No man has a greater love than for a brother, and this was especially true for Mitch and Tommy.

Then, the day they came with the big news.

Mitch had joined the Army. Planned to make Tommy his dependent. Planned to leverage the service's free medical to pursue fresh surgeries that held little hope of correcting the defects from the semi-trailer.

They were giddy as they shared the plan, as if each had come to the conclusion that Army green was the safest bet for Tommy's recovery.

But things didn't go smooth. With Mitch gone, Tommy missed him terribly. He muddled through until the orders for a yearlong deployment: 365 days in the desert, combat ops.

When Tommy heard, he about lost his mind. When Mitch left, Tommy preserved himself with booze as Mitch's girlfriend, Julie, a beautiful, long-suffering farm lass, tried her best to care for him and keep him safe.

The letters she sent were bleak. On the phone, she described a settled depression in Tommy's heart.

Then the news that the Army reviewed Tommy's case. With dispassionate assessment, they decided the surgeries wouldn't be done. What had already been done was the most and best that could be done, the man on the follow-up call said. Then, he thanked us for our service.

Tommy started mixing opiates with bourbon as a way to "manage the pain." Julie's position became more tenuous. Tommy lashed out, threatened suicide, stopped eating for days at a time, refused to engage with anyone.

Seems their plan hadn't calculated the long deployments, the separations, and as things unraveled, Mitch became moody, morose, violent and unpredictable. He took wild risks during missions, had to be held back by his troops when he attempted to do something especially dangerous.

And that's the thing about war; it can kill you even when you're being as safe as possible.

But Mitch never cared and continued to the point of foolishness, rushing positions, bolting into the line of fire. Seems Tommy's anguish traversed both ocean and desert on the strings of magic juice cans connecting their hearts.

While Tommy, back home, was a wreck, here in the desert, Mitch was functionally insane. The phrase *don't fuck with Mitch* became a mantra around the base, words said with a shiver and a wink. And Mitch lived up to them, fearless, crazed.

And now we have it: the end of Regulation Reggie and his affair with the U.S. Army.

No one will care, we know, that all that will be left is a fluttering flag over at Paragon Park. In fact, many will be happy to no longer be chided about shined boots or tucked in blouses. Many others will be gleeful at the cancellation of Reggie's Risers, the early morning PT sessions loathed by the troops.

No other choice.

Emotions rise, bitter, gilded in glimmering steel. Commitment, duty, obligation.

Impatience pounds as we swallow hard our feelings of angst.

There's never time for haste, but always minutes for heartlessness, for icy calculation, for the reaping of souls.

CHAPTER 19

A good position. Sun at our back. We'll be concealed if we stay put.

I know these things because he knows these things. Our mind is uncluttered, yet crammed full of tactics, strategy, minute details about weapons, combat, movement, offense, defense, perimeters, call signs, regulations.

We have to move; I know it as surely as I know my name. We can't stay. We have to save Mitch. Have to trade our pension for our brother's life, to derelict duty and fulfill a sacred obligation. Family, brothers, kin. Enough to make me sick.

But some things are more precious. Some things, a man must do.

A voice in our earpiece shakes our thoughts. "Reaper two five, what's your location?"

They've been calling for hours.

When we saw the wrecked Army truck, its front buried in a thick sand dune, we knew we were on the right track. Deserting our own vehicle, we followed half-buried footprints for nearly ten miles, back aching under the weight of our gear as the desert branded us with its seared kiss.

This is a one-way trip, but what options remain? Desert our only living brother?

These are the times that build the character the Army's so proud of. Times to put aside self, rules and regulations. It's what she taught us, *Follow the right.* Despite the odds, the promise of certain death, the arrow remains fixed and unerring. There's no choice. If we die, we die doing what's right.

The radio squawks as we squint through the long scope at the desolate village.

"Stand down, Reaper two five." The CO's voice, a man we respect. A man who knows we've no other choice. "Reaper two five, return to base immediately. Confirm position, but do not engage. Repeat, do not engage. Copy?"

With a press of a button, we send our coordinates then twist the knob and end all discussion. They'll be coming now, should arrive too late to stop us.

We wish it was different, wish we had the option to wait for the force and raid the compound with them.

But it's too risky. If they come in numbers, Mitch will be killed before they even get close.

Simple math makes a simple day.

Can't take the chance of a firefight. Can't risk Mitch's life.

The troops call it going Captain America. Not a compliment but an epithet for those who aren't team players, for those who put themselves before the team, for those who act alone, good reason or not.

We sweep the rifle and plan our route through the village as a waning sun stretches broken shadows to a darkness that creates multiple places to conceal.

Here we go, Captain America. We promised Mom, promised Julie, soon to become a mother. "Keep him safe, Reggie," Julie pled. "Don't let our baby grow up without a dad."

Day flees with a final flash as we scrape a shallow hole and place the sniper rifle, canteen, uniform blouse, and rations inside. A camo sheet of mesh flutters, then covers the dugout.

A Glock 9mm raises, clicks apart, then clicks together again. We secure two extra clips in a pouch on our belt, then a yank of straps tightens our body armor. The big survival knife clicks into place on the left side of our chest.

We paint our face and arms in diagonal black and green. Essential for concealment, essential for stealth. Boot laces tug to tight knots as darkness envelopes.

We start down the hill.

The desert is still beyond a village eerily dark, seen only as smudges with broad angles.

It feels possessed, ghastly, ghostly, gripped by a quiet that hums to buzzing nothing.

At the first small hut we press against stone still heated from the sun. Eyes dilate to their fullest as vision adjusts. A moonless night, both help and hindrance.

The pistol feels hard, unforgiving, matches our soul as fumes of rage smolder. We consider the route, the plan. Stealth, concealment, silence.

Reaper. A deadly specter no one sees.

Shoot only if necessary. Find Mitch. Get clear.

The math clicks like an abacus.

Advantages: concealment, darkness, pistol, knife, surprise.

Disadvantages: darkness, alone, fatigue, hunger, emotion.

Unknowns: terrain, number of enemies, Mitch's location.

A shake of the head erases the calculus like an Etch-a-Sketch.

Doesn't matter. Doesn't change a thing.

This is personal.

Save Mitch or die.

We've seen no signs of habitation from the hilltop. Would've been easier engaging with the sniper rifle, but with luck, we'll find Mitch passed out, empty bottle of hooch cradled in his elbow, all the insurgents dead.

Luck. As if.

An agonized howl breaks the stillness. Could be a coyote. Do they have coyotes in this godforsaken desert?

Then we know luck isn't our ally.

The enemy's here, concealed among the wood and cinder, the bawling ghosts of murdered children.

If they're here, so is Mitch.

Blackest night obscures our vision as we move slow and smooth. In our hurry to leave the base, we'd neglected to bring our night vision. Rookie mistakes gonna get you killed, we think, stalking, ears strained for the slightest sound.

Goats bawl and jostle as we near the pen and feel along the rough wood to skirt its perimeter. The village center should be close now, a good place to wait, to listen, to react.

Another howl bounds over mud roofs, then flees down dusty paths.

The goats raise their cries as if responding to the agony.

Move faster! We chide ourselves. Accept more risk!

We step out and view the scene in shadow and angle like some wretched anime in black and white.

There's a small, square hovel twenty paces ahead.

We rush forward, skirt the building, then freeze solid when we hear a scratching sound.

Squatting, we try to pinpoint the source.

Then silence.

Move!

Instinct says wait.

We shudder and press close, choking on impatience.

Then it comes again, the scratching, just around the hut's corner.

Moving by increments, we peer around at a shadowed silhouette. A man leans against the wall scratching his balls.

Smart. Smart and smart.

They *do* have guards. Possibly patrols. We see the ploy; realize we've underestimated the force. They've kept their sentries hidden from the hill above. Kept them concealed behind the huts, out of view from anyone attempting to surveil from the most obvious vantage above the village. They've considered an attack, considered the possibility of hidden eyes, watching, planning.

Very smart.

The entire time we watched, the guards remained concealed. Standing, leaning, scratching, hidden and ready. Big trouble in capital letters. None of our calculations can be counted. None of our plan can be accurate.

Doesn't matter; it's a one-way trip.

The man props his rifle against the wall, stretches his arms and yawns.

He rubs his eyes, lights a cigarette then rounds the corner.

In a blink we're face to face.

The cigarette dangles, then drops. He starts to cry out.

Blood rushes over our hands, warm, dark, wet, as the knife appears in his throat.

We guide him to the ground, feel comfortable with our actions even as we retrieve the smoke and take a drag, then crush it under heel.

After a minute, listening, searching, we feel safe enough to move into the dwelling. A Turkish rug is set with four small pillows. In the corner, a pitted, wooden table holds a burning candle, strips of wire, short pieces of pipe, and a canister of ball bearings.

We drag the dead man in as quietly as possible. Then retrieve the rifle and check its load. Fifteen rounds, one chambered.

Better than nothing, we think, as we search the hut and find a pack of Marlboro's. Mitch's brand, a few left in the crinkled red package.

Wiping the blood on the dead man's shirt, we move to crouch by the wall.

One down. How many more?

Ears search the silence, strain for any sound, as we stalk silently across a rumpled trail and down a narrow dirt path that runs between two hut smudges.

A scream shatters the night, goads us to increase our speed, our risk of failure, to be quicker, more careless.

At the path's end, we peer into a sort of backyard, small, square, littered with garbage and old tires. Three men chat in Arabic, pass a cigarette between them, and exhale in smoky white splotches.

In his mind, I brace for the barbarity to come.

But we ease back, know the only way to take them is with the assault rifle, which will blow our position and our main advantage, surprise.

Turning left, we cross the front of the hut and hurry to the next.

At this door, we listen, watching our back trail in case the three we saw started a patrol. Beside the door, a small window reflects darkness. We peer through, see nothing but shadows and dirt.

Checking six, we slip twenty paces to another dwelling.

Voices rise, muffled, Arabic, harsh. Another scream explodes more intense than any prior.

We peep through a window half covered in plywood, half with a thick drape.

A shaft of light streams through a tiny slit.

Inside, a man holds a camera, takes pictures of Mitch, who's bound to a wall, spread eagled and shirtless, blood pouring from multiple wounds on his chest and arms.

Another man laughs, then poses with Mitch before punching him in the face.

Mitch's head lolls, his breath comes shallow as he fights for consciousness, as eyes roll into his head.

Wrath blisters in crinkled crystals as we grit our teeth and move our head in an effort to see what else the room holds. A couple of overturned crates, an old wooden box, most of Mitch's gear, a three-legged stool with a kerosene lantern propped on its top.

Mitch raises his head, stares at the tiny gap between drape and plywood. Does he sense our presence? A grin forms as insurgents continue their photo shoot, voices gleeful as they film.

We creep to the door and slide the big knife from the sheath, clenching our jaw, tightening our grip.

The latch feels of rust as we press upwards. It releases with a small *shnick* even as the night fills with another of Mitch's wails.

Cracking the door, we peer inside. Both terrorists face Mitch. One slides a knife across his chest, opens a gash, makes him squeal again.

Vision swirls to a long tunnel, Mitch shining at its end in vibrant golden hues.

We creep toward them, our thoughts calm, focused, Zen.

One turns, bearded, grinning, to pose next to Mitch.

We rise, a specter born of shadow, hate steaming like desert vapor.

Reap.

The poser's smile disappears as we slide the knife into the base of the photographer's skull. Then, that feeling: hot blood, sticky, thick.

The poser tries to scream but is a poor match for our speed and wrath.

With a lunge and twist, the knife guts his Adam's apple. He blinks, falls, knocks the lantern from the stool to plunge the room in darkness. The harsh odor of kerosene burns our nostrils as spreading flames cast the room in flickering orange and noxious cloud.

"Reg?" Mitch says through eyes swollen and black.

The knife flashes, slices bonds that hold his arms. "Stay quiet," we whisper. "Gonna get you out. How many are there?"

"You came. I knew you'd come. Why's it so dark?"

"It's night, Mitch. Your eyes are swollen. How many?"

Mitch's breathing sounds like a clogged drain. "I don't know. Lots. Maybe. I got three, injured two, I think. Don't know if they left or not. You shouldn't have come."

"Can you walk?" we ask, wrapping his arm over our shoulder. "Try, Mitch. Walk. You can do this."

Mitch groans. "What's burning?"

Flickering flames in the room's corner, spreading.

"We gotta go," we whisper, knowing the flames will cause others to come investigate. "Move your legs."

"You shouldn't have come. Mom's gonna be mad."

"Mitch. Move. You have to move." Hefting our brother, we shuffle slow steps toward the door.

Mitch gags, coughs blood on the dirt floor as smoke thickens to choke the air around us.

Voices squall through muted night, rise excited, draw close.

Our throat burns as we exit, hoist Mitch on our shoulder, cross a small dirt path to the corner of the opposite hut.

Sounds like twenty men, yelling, running, closer each second.

We prop Mitch against the hut's wall in the deepest darkness we can find.

"Where's Julie?" he says.

Checking the chamber on the old AK, we flip the safety off. "At home, Mitch. She's safe."

His smile grows, his head droops. "Thank God."

Voices flow past, racing to douse the flames.

Instantly, we know the sums. If we stay and fight, we'll have a decent chance, but Mitch will certainly die.

The realization comes with flat facts, precise as calculus. Only one option: draw them away, try to outrun and outgun in a field of our choosing.

We rise, level the rifle at silhouettes, fire three shots into the closest, then two into the one next to it.

Our war cry splits the night as we streak toward them, firing the pistol as we rocket past.

Confused tones solidify as they give chase.

We sprint blind, stumble on something hard, flail a few paces before catching our balance.

We turn hard left, press against the corner of a shanty and level the old AK at following voices.

Two shadows appear, and we gun them down.

Move!

Sniper training shoves everything else aside.

Shoot. Move. Repeat.

We turn, collide with a terrorist who circled in an attempt to flank.

He fires.

Our shoulder explodes.

The AK clatters away.

We slash, blind, fluid, desperate.

The insurgent jumps back, attempts to fire again.

The Glock spits two into his forehead, then we grimace through a blazing shoulder, ejecting the clip and slamming home a new one.

Goats bawl. Terrorists search, circle, shout.

The goat pen!

We sprint, dive headlong over a raggedy fence, roll a single time and pivot to one knee.

I feel the soldier's rage, the fumes of agony, of heartlessness. A high note in a frenzied chorus. *Reap!* Bloodlust, a slowing of time, a slowing of thought, the Asian principle of mind–no mind. Saliva gathers in our mouth, our motions are fluid, measured. We love this. Pain mutes to nothing but stilted lyrics.

More voices. Then, gunfire.

A goat falls.

Then another.

They're shooting blind, mowing down their own sustenance.

Shots crackle, the goats tromp and trample as sharp hoofs rain down.

Blood trickles from our shoulder, leaves a sleek smudge on desert sand.

Shadows approach, search, guns raised, shouting.

We're invisible, we realize. They don't know where we are.

We scramble under the fence, race to the wall of the next hut, circle behind, keep to the darkest shadows and away from searching voices.

Insurgents race past.

We don't fire, an attempt to reclaim the advantage of surprise.

We think about the hill, the sniper rifle concealed there.

Won't help now, even if we had it.

But there's still a chance to get Mitch and get clear.

We meld, become that shadow, that menace, that boogeyman, circling the compound, passing a couple sheds and a small pickup, moving closer to the burning building.

Flames leap and cackle, reach with spiked tongues to lap the night.

Mitch sits where we left him.

"Mitch," we whisper. "Stay quiet. We're getting out of here."

He says nothing as we heft, grinding through unbearable pain as the burning building telegraphs our location to the entire compound.

I feel his studied intent, his grim focus as we shuffle toward our original vantage point and concealed stash.

Spirits lift with each step. Searching voices recede.

Then a shout, one of warning, of excitement.

Someone's spotted us. How many are there?

Doubling our efforts, we rally speed, sacrificing silence for distance.

Shots ring, buzz past into the surrounding desert.

Resolve rises as I pour my support into the soldier. I will him strength, try to infuse whatever power I can. Try to heft, to help, to empower.

We veer behind a low boulder on the village's outer edge. Dropping Mitch, we crouch beside him.

Everything goes quiet. The pursuers are regrouping, collecting to coordinate their efforts.

We stare at the village, hard corners that flicker flame.

Mitch's shadowed face speaks without words. We'll die here. Be sent home in flag-draped coffins as Mom and Julie weep on the tarmac of the Delaware air base where the fallen return.

One-hundred thousand dollars.

A strange thought, the sum of money paid to the families of dead GI's. The death gratuity.

The value of a life lost in duty to country, probably assigned by some government pencil neck.

Reap!

Chances dwindle as we do the calculations. With the rifle gone, a single clip and a few rounds are all we have to feed the Glock. Add the knife and a wealth of gall, and it still doesn't add up to much.

One-hundred thousand dollars.

Death benefit. Times two.

Reap!

We rise, take two steps before a shot tears into our chest.

Our breathing dwindles, akin to sucking through a swizzle straw. The armor has done its job though, nothing penetrated, just have to catch our breath.

Horror is absent. There's no real pain.

We reel, fire blind. Dizzy, buzzing locusts invade our senses.

Shuffling feet approach as we crawl to Mitch and huddle behind the boulder.

"This is it," we say. "The last stand of the Holcumb boys."

Mitch gives the grin we love so much.

Voices rally, surround, close.

"Tell Julie to name our baby Lily," he says.

Locusts rise, their buzz deafening, warnings drifting on desert wind.

Ten men surround us, rifles poised.

A man steps forward, raises a portable camera.

Our thoughts solidify and accept our failure. We are serene, gave as good as we got.

Then, a blinding light shines from the heavens, tracing the landscape as it illuminates our pursuers.

We spring up, renewed, empty the Glock at the force even as they shoot at the source of the broad light.

Thoughts jumble, congeal, fuse.

Then it makes sense.

The locusts are helicopters.

Raining a hail of shrapnel.

Reaping the terrorists.

Then a clamor of footsteps, voices in English.

The Glock drops.

The calvary has come.

Mitch stares ahead, his breathing shallow and rapid, eyes focused on the blistering desert and its endless grains.

"Help!" We scream, waving our arms, ignoring the wounded shoulder, the harshness of drawing breath. "Over here! Medic! Medic!"

Mitch seems fused with light as we lean close, grasp his hand and squeeze tight. "Stay with me, Mitch! Help is here. We've done it. Hang on!"

That grin slides over his features. "Last ride of the Holcumb gang," he rasps. "I'll tell Tommy you love him. I'll tell him you came." His eyes lift, watching something only he can see. "Don't forget, Reg. Name her Lily. Don't forget."

Breathing fades, slows, then ceases. Open eyes stare at the unseen, the unknown.

Our trembling, bloody hand reaches forward and presses them shut.

I move to the background as Reggie slumps, presses his head to his brother's chest, then wails his pride, his wrath, his anguish, his failure, to the heartless sands of the eternal desert.

Palms press to granite as tears stream. My heart's cleaved. Torn edges with raw, dangling nerves. I'm on my knees, panting, numb, throbbing, disjointed.

The man watching doesn't give a single shit.

I stammer as the abyss percolates. "Awful. Just— Just—" I spit something black and foul.

Sharp features glow, hollow eyes like piss holes in a snowbank.

"Was that… Was it…"

A thin finger points to the mist.

A man sits in a faded Adirondack chair. Above him, an American flag mounted with drywall screws.

The picture he holds is wrinkled, aged.

Mitch and Julie. Joyous, full of life, full of love.

"Wish you were here," he says, then kisses the photo and raises his head.

A tear rolls over a face, horribly scarred.

He rises and opens a footlocker at the end of an Army cot dressed and pressed in olive drab.

With great care he places the picture in an envelope, then swipes the tears from his face.

Outside, a dog barks.

"Mangy hound." Crispy closes the footlocker, then inhales in a deep stutter.

He exits to the scrapyard.

Chapter 20

The scrapyard fades to flickering mist, the sounds of popping steam. I'm overwhelmed, over-awed, if one may indulge a brief spring to cliché. Before me the abyss oozes and bubbles. A thin mist swirls, then becomes a spiral tunnel a thousand feet high. It flickers, spits vapor over the granite ledge, churning, rising. I raise my eyes and trace its form. Then, it hovers, shimmies and spirals like a tornado before being sucked back like a slurped noodle.

The abyss calms, glimmers endless, a mirror impossible to look through.

"How was that?" A different man, but just as sharp and meticulous.

"Iblis?"

"They told me you weren't too bright."

"Who did?"

"They. We. Us. All of us. Belphegor, Acedia, Asmodeus." He waves a hand, presses a fist to his lips, steps to the very edge of the abyss, so close that the points of his wing tips hang over by three inches. "Hell comes in a variety of colors," he says, gazing over the glassed maw. "Many flavors here, too numerous to count." He turns and steps toward me. "Are they to your liking?"

I feel bold, wonder if I've been possessed by some other demon.

Just my luck, addiction replaced by something else, something worse. "This isn't real," I say. "There's no way this is anything but a dream. And if it's a dream, I can wake."

Her voice slices the mist, the darkness, soothing, calling me home. I look to the swirling clouds. Hear the long echo of rolling thunder, sonorous, like God forgot his CPAP.

"Rhyme!" I step away from the abyss and the man perched on the ledge. "I'm here!" I yell to shadow, realize there's no echo, just sounds thrown to ancient stone.

"She can't hear you." He looks at his fingernails, then bends to swipe soot from his shoes. "They never can. Another facet," he says. "More pepper for the pot. When you're here, you can hear the ones you love, feel their anguish, the longing of separation. But you can't speak to them. Can't see them, either." He cackles like a sandhill crane. "Simply brilliant when one considers it."

"I think you're lying."

He grins. "I've been accused of that."

"Then, I'll just step away. Wander until I find a way out."

"You make it sound easy."

"Listen, I'm not dead. You have no reason to keep me here."

He looks offended. "Indeed, I do. Like every other soul, you're here due to your choices. You promised to write my story and I promised—"

"You promised no more pain!" The words hiss, betray desperation as fear gouges my psyche with nails sharp as razors.

"P-shaw," he says, swatting the air. "I said nothing of the sort. Have you all your teeth? If you recall I promised no more *physical* pain. No more of your favorite version of Hell. Shredding demons, lapping flame, souls writhing." An interesting color flushes his face, somewhere between blood red and canary yellow. "Excuse me," he says. "When I put it like that it gets me a bit excited. I may have an erection."

Now I know I'm crazy. The devil with a boner. Only I'd have visions so sizzling and stupid.

He inhales, then sends a cloud of smoke over the mirrored liquid?

—solid? "Not too bright indeed. Allow me to explain." He motions me close. I look over my shoulder, see no escape from the ledge, then take a tentative step.

"Maybe this will help you figure it out. Like everything, Hell is what you make it."

"Great," I say, "because we're gonna need some ceiling fans and an icemaker."

"Ah, Merrick's classic defense: sarcasm." He snickers. "I see why you do that, and I'm impressed that you try while bathed in such depths. Do you have any idea how much worse I can make it?"

I'm tempted to say, "Do your best, Mr. Bigballs!" Instead, I look down and realize I don't have the clackers or the composure to experience what his best can conjure.

"Okay. Listen," he says. "Can we agree that the Earth is Hell?"

"I don't think so."

"Why not? The evidence is quite compelling."

"Because there's good. Good people, good things. Kindness, love, compassion."

"Uh huh," he says, "I've heard the same from others. Do you know you were created in God's image?" He says the last with thin fingers twitching outside invisible words.

"I guess so."

"Perfect. So, you understand God's flawed?"

"No. I can't agree with that."

He cups his chin and rubs. "Let's try a different way. Are you familiar with the Yin-Yang of the East?"

"I believe so. The circle with half a black swirl and half a white swirl."

"You got it. The one where the black has a bit of white, and the white has a bit of black." He searches my eyes as if expecting a realization.

"And?" I say.

"And? Jesus, that's the entire point. For anything to be perfect it has to be flawed. For every evil there's a sliver of good. For every good, a kernel of evil. That's the balance. The way. The Tao, as they say."

"So, the devil's a Taoist?"

He snickers. "The devil, my boy, is whatever suits his purpose."

Suddenly Rhyme stands before me, lips parted, face flushed. Blue sequins flow from shoulders wrapped in a sensuous evening gown. An X'chasei pendant dangles between her cleavage. "Emery," she says, voice sultry, hypnotic, dripping desire. "Come to me."

I float forward, mouth dry, fingers tingling, fully under her spell.

Then he's back. "Like that," he says. "Had to switch back before you kissed me. I saw the look in your eye. That wouldn't have ended well for you."

I shake my head in minute quivers like little spasms of my neck. "You're a dick."

"Granted," he says. "But I think we've been over this." He looks to the fuming sky, waves a hand as if dismissing noxious vapors. "I grow weary of your antics."

"Oh, I'm sorry," I say. "I didn't realize I was the one running the show here. You can let me go if I'm bothering you." Our eyes lock for a moment and in his I see a faint outline, an image of Rhyme spinning above smoldering embers.

I stammer for a couple syllables, "Um, um, you were saying how the perfect has flaws, and that's what makes it perfect."

"Yes," he says, stepping back to the ledge. "Occam's razor in reality."

"You mean the simplest path is generally the right path."

"Yes *and* no," he says. "One must consider parameters, multiple entities in a system. It's rather brilliant when one thinks about it and it's been used on Earth in all sorts of ways. But for our purposes, allow me to suggest, based on the yin-yang principle and with the application of so fine an instrument as Occam's razor, that perhaps the truth becomes more clear the closer one looks. As if, when we rid the system of all nonessential entities, reality appears and can be easily dealt with."

"Okay," I say, not feeling okay or even understanding of what hell this Satan speaks.

"I'll try to use this razor. To simplify, if you will."

"That would be nice." I've no reason to try and appear intelligent with this being. He knows my shortfalls, my short comings, my short hairs.

"If you take the concept of heaven, or perfection, and contrast it with the concept of hell, or complete chaos, certain things become clear. First, if a human allowed such devastation, they'd be branded the greatest monster of all time. Thus, it follows that, second, God *allows* all of this to happen and abides my dominion over it. We can argue if that's a mistake or not, or we can apply the religious principle that it's all a test, but, like the pebble on which you exist, spinning endlessly through an expanse too big for any human to grasp, you're limited by a finite brain. Thus, you accept the cage in which you're placed, feeling around the edges without really seeing anything *but* the edges. If you could see past that, stretch your puny mind to think outside your own limits, the truth of everything would be clear. You'd see that, third, God is Evil, and I am Good. I am the tester of limits, the zephyr that strains the tree and makes the trunk stronger. Do you see?"

"Not really."

A chair appears: red leather, high backed, puckered buttons on its exterior. "Sit," he points, "get comfortable."

"Comfortable in Hell," I say. "This is getting ridiculous."

"Precisely, child. That's the point. The whole thing's ridiculous. Testing creation, living well for rewards after death. Yet none of you knows what happens after you die. Like standing in a closet of pitch black, you can't see what's right before your eyes. Hell has to have some good in it, just as heaven must have its evil. Don't you see His true nature? His true evil nature? Remember when you were writhing and being torn apart by my pals down there?"

Shuddering, I slide forward in the chair and rub my face with both hands. "I'd rather forget."

"I know, pretty bad, but not as bad as it gets. What if I told you that when we're done here, I'm sending you back to be shredded a few dozen more times."

A dryness seizes my throat like I've just swallowed antifreeze. My knees start to tremble as I think of demons wrenching teeth from my skull, flaying my skin, fighting for my beating heart.

"Yes," he says. "Which is worse? The physical pain, or knowing the pain is coming again. And again. And again. Wouldn't matter if I kept you out of there for two minutes or two years, the horror of the knowledge that you're going back is another aspect of Hell. Of evil. Get it?"

"I think so."

Another chair appears identical to mine and he sits and crosses his legs. "I'm reminded of a joke that sums it up perfectly. A guy goes to Hell and is placed in a room where he's standing in sewage up to his knees. A demon appears and gives him a cup of tea. He takes the tea, looks around to notice that everyone else is also sipping tea. 'Not so bad,' he thinks, 'I thought Hell would be much worse.' Then, the demon says, 'Okay, breaks over! Everyone back on your heads!'"

I chuckle despite myself. Humor and horror aren't such distant cousins. "Good one."

"It's like that," he says. "The real horror isn't physical, it's about what that bulbous appendage stuck to your neck can process and what it can't. Ever wonder why God doesn't intervene on Earth to stop war, murder, pedophilia, genocide? It's because that's what makes Hell, Hell. The horrors of war. The inhumanity of everything. Parents losing a child and living with that. The slow descent of a loved one fighting their biology against a disease that will certainly take them. The disease itself. Why? What purpose? To test?" He stands. "Nonsense! Why would you be created only to be tested? Can there be another explanation? Why not be created to exist in harmony and live forever with those you love in a world without avarice, without vices, without evil, disease or death? Does that sound like the work of a loving God?"

"You sound like Cain."

He pauses, watches me as if he expects something more. "He and I are more attuned than you think."

"Yes, both evil as a witch's butthole."

His cackle jingles like Christmas bells. An ominous contrast to our surroundings. I peer up, squint through roiling clouds for as far as I can see.

"Are you looking for Heaven?" he says. "Looking for the Apostle, perhaps?"

"As a matter of fact, I am," I say, almost add, "and you can't stop me from looking where I want."

"Oh, he's up there. Or over there I should say. In these parts there really isn't anything like up or down or sideways. Most everything is spirals, vast beyond reckoning, can get you anywhere and everywhere. You'll see. As you fulfill your destiny, it'll become clear."

"Destiny?" I say. "I have a destiny?"

He tsks. "Dear boy, everyone has a destiny."

"Hopefully mine's to escape hell."

Her voice rises even as the abyss spews a thick mist from its gaping maw. "Emery, come back," she whispers. "I need you here. Come back."

I jump from the chair and move to the ledge, staring into a waterspout that instantly forms.

She fades, slips through my fingers without trace or outline.

"In time," he chuckles. "I think something interesting is going to happen. That's if Cain's little experiment pans out."

Chapter 21

Jerusalem, Israel

I must be crazy. My judgment, my decisions, bouncing along, no decent plan.

Allies: a hippie, a comatose man, and a hulking African who appears more ready for a body building competition than a getaway.

She sighs, looks at them, quick allies as they discuss their options.

Stuart strokes Houdini's head with a giant hand. "Okay, here's the play. We find a gown that's too big for you, dress you in it, take you to Cain, and when you see him, you put those double pistols to use." He flicks his gaze between them. "He won't see it coming, and he'll be done with. Super easy."

Rhyme laughs despite herself. She doesn't mean to insult but realizes Stuart has no idea of the truth of Cain.

When he starts to nod, her own head wags. "Won't work," she says. "He can't die."

Stuart stares for a long minute, as if he heard her wrong. "Of course, he can die. What are you talking about?"

"There's a lot you don't know about my husband, the emperor. First surprise: he's immortal, can't be killed. If someone tries, they burst into flames. He, however, lives on without a scratch."

"What?" The word comes in a wavered tone, elongated. "That's nonsense, who told you that?"

"He did. Also, Emery, Longinus, Igneus—everyone in his inner circle. It's really a long story and I can fill you in later but believe me when I tell you that your plan will just get me burned to a cinder."

"Immortal?" Stuart's mouth drops, eyes stare at the floor. "But..."

"We should go to the Temple." Bill munches with a grin, then shrugs and sips his wine. "It'll be cool to see the Temple."

They both stare. Does he think this a sightseeing tour? "Thanks, Bill," she says. "We'll go to the one place that's his shining achievement."

"They have healing there," Stuart says. "And food. A lot of people too. We can hide out, make a plan, maybe find some allies, some weapons."

Guilt rises in Rhyme's throat as she regards the giant man. He's a monster, an anatomy lesson on bulging muscle and fluid power. "You don't have to do this," she says. "You're risking your life. Cain will certainly make an example."

Stuart itches the dog's ear, considers the words, then whispers, *"And how can man die better than facing fearful odds, for the ashes of his fathers and the temples of his Gods?"* He regards her, eyes alight and ferocious. "Risk my life," he says. "The byline of my story." He stands, filling the room with his size. "No man knows when death will find him or how they'll face it when it comes. In the end, what's right is right, and I shall die—or live—with that as my guide. I think we *should* go to the Temple. I remember Cain being quite upset about some things happening there, some kid healing people, some other guy 'running his fat mouth'. If nothing else, we should find sanctuary. If nothing else, it'll buy some time."

Houdini pads close and nudges her hand. "A shitty plan," she sighs, "but the best we have. Although I'd feel better getting out of Israel altogether."

"Not as easy as it sounds. Imperium patrols the borders and with the vastness of this new country, it will take us days to even get there."

"By sea then?"

"Equally useless. Imperium's navy has it locked down. Seems the emperor guards against another attack. As soon as he realizes you're missing, he'll throw everything he's got." He paces to stare over Jerusalem's landscape. "Hiding out is the safe play. Our only chance, I think."

"But he'll most certainly find us at the Temple. Even if not quickly. Time isn't our friend."

A huge hand rubs an eye. "I can't think of a better plan, can you? Perhaps at the Temple we can rally people to our cause, raise a guerilla army? It's either that or run scared, without a plan or destination, fly by the seat of our pants. The emperor controls everything, there's just such slim chances of success if we run. Doesn't make sense to try."

There's a lot to consider. A lot she should've considered already. She feels overwhelmed, a bit hopeless, downtrodden. "You said a kid was healing people at the Temple?"

"Yep. Really pisses Cain off."

She smiles. "I don't need any more than that. If he's pissed, that means there's nothing he can do about it. If there's a healer, perhaps they can remove whatever afflicts Emery." She stands. "The Temple it is."

Emery's head rests against the window in the limo's back seat. Rhyme strokes his hair and wipes drool from his mouth, whispering, "Emery, come back to me. I need you. Come back."

"Alastor," Emery mutters, eyes fluttering, face changing expression by the second.

"He's in it now."

Rhyme whirls toward Bill. "What do you know?"

"Not much," he says. "Just have a feeling he's in a bad place." Another handful of chips gets crammed in his mouth. Everything the hippie says serves no purpose whatsoever, yet Cain thinks him a delight. Doesn't make sense.

Emery flails and she returns her attention to him, strokes his hair, squeezes his hand. She leans close, whispers again, "Emery. Come back."

They glide through Jerusalem's streets. The place looks better with each day. Streets are cleaner. Boarded up store fronts, less frequent. No visible corpses. Stuart speaks from the front. "The emperor conscripted all able-bodied men and women to help with cleanup and rebuilding. His progress is outstanding. It's amazing what people can accomplish when joined by a single mind."

Rhyme stares out the window, watches as groups haul debris, replace windows, sweep glass. They seem content, even happy in their labors. Cain's gifts at work, she thinks. Charisma and diplomacy, a deadly duo when wielded by the Antichrist.

"What news from the States?" she asks.

"Nothing much, seems it still burns. All the nukes created a giant gas cloud that hovers over the continent and blocks the view of any satellite. Countries have sent aircraft to fly over and survey the damage, but none have returned. They're wondering if so much radiation, so concentrated, is somehow damaging the planes and causing them to crash. It's like the Bermuda Triangle. Have you heard of that?"

"Yes."

"So, that's the score. No word from anyone, except their president, who's been taken in by the EU and is hiding out in some unknown location. He's been sending video messages to the world, decrying the act of war and seeking support to oust Cain."

"Any takers?"

"Not really. Seems the world thinks when the U.S. attacked a defenseless Israel, they sort of got what they asked for. Like a playground bully being knocked on his ass by the nerdy kid: poetic justice. His calls amount to nothing more than raging at the tempest. The EU's on lockdown. No comms out of Russia either. The Chinese occupied that country but got double-crossed when nukes rained down on both. Intel says there's not much left to occupy in either region. Like Chernobyl but on a much larger scale. Seems Imperium's the big boy on the block right now and in record time. Your husband's a real pip."

Rhyme frowns, returns to Emery, but thinks about the news. Cain's a global warlord, has subdued the superpowers and the world. Has used his enemy's traps against them and exploded them in their shocked faces. She thinks of Carpenter and feels good that she doesn't feel bad about his fate. She remembers the backhand, remembers pleading with him to stop Cain before it's too late. He deserves what he gets, and she doesn't have time to worry about what else awaits him.

"Cain's popularity soars," Stuart says. "He must've planned it to the letter. After the attack, resources poured into the country. Food, water, money, clothes. No one wants for anything. Even drugs and alcohol arrive by the boat load. When the EU tried to block them, their ships were summarily destroyed." Dark eyes flash in the rearview. "The world's cowed because of your husband."

Rhyme grimaces, then realizes she hates the word *husband*. Hates what it stands for, what it means: A glaring mistake that hangs around her neck with the largesse of an Easter Island stone man. She should've let him kill Emery. Should've denied his request of marriage and brought the fight back to him after she healed. Sure, she would've ended up dead, but is that so bad?

"The climate's all jacked up, too. Weird storms, hurricanes, crops dying, domestic animals attacking people. It's getting stupid everywhere. That's to say, everywhere but here."

Charred shops roll past, markets reset as music blares and people go about their business, building, cleaning, cooking, living. She watches them, expects drooped shoulders and sorrowed faces, instead she finds the light of life. The hopes and dreams for a prosperous future under the monster Cain.

Emery stirs, raises a hand as if blocking something. "Emery…" The rest catches in her throat. She swallows hard, stares out the limo's glass. Suddenly, she's lunging at the window.

"Stop the car!"

CHAPTER 22

I stand on a stage of granite, in a cavern that drips maroon from pillared walls like the ribs of an umbrella.

There's no light, yet I can easily see.

Her voice wafts on feathers of vanilla and lilac, but those are quickly replaced by another scent. Something cold and steely, palpable, coating my skin in blisters as the scent of Rhyme withers to a rancid stench.

"Emery," she calls, pleads. "Emery, I know you're—"

Horrors rattle my ears as chunky vapor rains a pulsing malice on the throng below me. Beneath giant, jagged stalactites, a wailing humanity. A blistering morass of fear, anguish, desperation.

Souls. At first the realization stirs wonders. I watch new ones appear in bright yellow, and that's when each one's screaming starts. The canary-fresh soul ignites to fiery red, then pulses to drenched maroon. Others throb, appear as if they'll explode and coat the place in bubbling horrors. The shrieks are endless, visible, circled beams through a sooty atmosphere.

Hands rise like that sculpture in Thailand, *Hands from Hell*. How apropos.

And on they rage, neither seeing their folly nor pausing to inhale.

The cavern oozes regret, injustice, the howls of the endlessly tormented. But I see no demons, no beings diving in to coax terror from the throbbing souls.

My heart beats for them.

But before I can follow the urge to somehow descend and offer a small measure of comfort, the cavern shakes. Hell's earthquake, as palpable as one on Earth. Stalactites shimmy as they cascade from the vast ceiling, raining pebbles and dust, threatening to break and crush the souls and writhing hands below.

But they're undaunted, these souls, ignorant of any danger, consumed with their longings, their grief. Dark, pulsing, bristling with intensity, they appear as kernels ready to pop.

I stand, puzzled, fully immune to the energy that fills them. Is it rage? Hatred? Misery? Some uncompleted task? Perhaps some task performed in life has placed them here where the walls bleed and the ground burns? Whatever it is, these billions, caught in human form, barefooted, on tipped toes, speared by endless need, cursed with rage. Their mouths stretch wide as spit throws mucous webs behind varied gaping guises.

Injustice. The word seizes and I know it's truth. These have been harmed. These have been corrupted.

"Vengeance is mine, sayeth the Lord."

The space rattles and sets the billions in a frenzy of shrieks that threaten to shake down the great stalactites. Arms shoot up, fuse to a sea of trembling hands like the sculpture. Fists rise, fingers writhe, creased and charred, as a shadow swoops from on high to race over them. Fire rains down, adds energy to spaces that simply cannot bear more.

I step forward, a rock star taking the stage before a disinterested audience.

The demon is sleek, the thinnest trace of a dark line as it swoops, then rises only to course through a lazy curve and bomb-dive into the accursed.

It's a bird/man fusion, a mother hen attending souls.

"The voice of my father calls from the grave!" it shouts, swoops again, causes the throng to pulse like bubbling lava and sizzle with a heat that makes my nerves tingle.

The shadow flashes too fast to follow, then I sense a presence behind me.

I crane my head, staring up at the being, at sinew stretched taut over skeleton. Thin skin pulled over ribs that appear as a canvas on a ship's bones. Eyes of fire stare from a face broad and triangular, resembling the great maw of a crow. Nose and jaws thrust forward in sharp angles, snap open to reveal nubbed teeth that seem only ornaments.

Pulsing like those tormented, it focuses only on the mass, seems to nurture, to feed and nourish, to fuel and make them glow a raging red that flares to bristling white then quickly snuffs until renewed again.

Great wings rise, torn sails with holes smoking and jagged.

It doesn't notice me; makes me think I'm invisible.

"Who are you?" I ask.

It twists its head as if annoyed by the distraction from its true task. Then, it thunders a tremendous shriek, causes the smoldering mass to pulse renewed. Below, some souls ignite as they fully absorb the power, then flash to a vivid white that smolders steam with a core of pulsing crimson.

"I am Alastor," the demon croaks, barely discernible over the shrieks and wails.

It rattles its head, squats, shakes like a duck ruffling feathers, then stretches forward. Massive, charred wings rise still higher as billowing fog pours from its mouth to hover over the mass.

The souls wail as if their view of this demented sideshow is suddenly blocked. They blink, remind me of Christmas lights in a snowbank. Pulsing red, white, yellow, flashing, popping, fading, then bursting with malice renewed.

A nudge at my back pushes me a step closer. Fog fills the cavern as images dance on its billows.

The scene's set.

A boy, in his room, fists clenched as tears drop on brown trousers.

Vengeance fills me. A murderous intent that pierces my heart to arrest all other thought.

Then calculation becomes a plan. How to kill and get away clean. How to take the first steps toward snuffing a life.

The room is sparse, a teenager's. Posters of various idols hang on the wall as an overfilled hamper bursts its contents beside an unmade bed covered in comics.

Then, a gun, something old, like a relic.

The boy raises it, puzzles it apart, then slowly back together. He's intelligent, fearless but nervous.

His plan forms to a soft gel.

We leave the room and race downstairs through an empty house.

A child's voice calls after. "Jonas, where are you going?"

Chapter 23

Beep.
 Ping.
Chaaaah.

A transparent mask squished over a face not that old.

The funeral's tomorrow. That's the day.

My small hand squirms into his, under the wrinkled blankets that entomb him.

Vengeance.

Beep. Ping. Chaaah.

It's musical, the machines doing their thing, forcing air past crusted lips in a tempo to which one could tap a foot. His eyes flutter open, then he speaks hollow and breathless. "Jonas?"

"I'm here, Dad." I squeeze his hand, try to reassure my words with action.

Eyes close as more air is forced. *Chaaah.* "I'm sorry it's come to this."

Rage clots my throat like hardened phlegm, presses against thin walls that bend from the pressure. "I'm going to fix it, Dad. I'll fix it."

"Where's your mother?"

A fist squeezes my heart. My chest aches. "She's fine, Dad. She's waiting for you," I lie.

There's a blood-stained bandage on his chest, a single tube running from inside his body to a chambered machine on the floor.

Beep. Ping. Chaaah. A tear glitters as it slides to his ear.

Lips quiver to a faint smile. "She's a good woman."

"I'm going to fix it, Dad."

His head wobbles. *Beep. Ping. Chaaah.* "Don't." He struggles, makes the machine's *chaaah* stretch to eternity. "No point," he rasps. "Too strong. I shouldn't have—" The words trail, the *chaaah* stretches. "Shouldn't have gotten mixed with him." The machine sounds like Darth Vader. "Got greedy." *Chaaah.* "Failed us all."

I lean forward. "You did what you had to, Dad. That's not greedy." Injustice scrapes like a swallowed briar. The unfairness of everything. We pay our debts. Silverman owed us, I think. Although I don't know the details of the arrangement, I know who Silverman is and what I have to do.

Beep. Ping. Chaaah. "We didn't need the money, Jonas. We were fine." *Chaaah.* "Greed, son, buries hooks you can't untangle."

I think of diamonds sparkling in his hand. His finger rolling through them, his face one of awe and admiration. His smile, a mix of glee and desire. "Plenty more where this came from boys," he'd said as Ishmael and I stared at the glistening crystals. "You can never have enough, and this will give us more."

Chaaah. "Don't make the same mistakes, Jonas." He hurries, his voice a whispered rasp, hard to understand. "You're the man of the house now. Take care of your brother. Tell him I love him." *Chaaah.* "Take care—" *Chaaah.* "Your mother. Be smart." *Chaaah.* "Be bold. I love—"

Beep. Ping.

Beep.

Beep. Beep. Beep...

Sorrow hangs like old drapes.

I approach two caskets. A small hand slides into mine.

It's Ishmael, dressed in brown plaid, eyes dripping as he stares at our dead parents.

Why is it so dark, as if turning up the lights would somehow disrespect the dead?

"Ishmael, sit here. I'll be right back," I say. We say.

Ishmael squeezes my hand tight. "Don't leave me, Jonas. I'll come with you." He looks afraid, beaten, terrorized.

"Stay here," I offer a smile I hope is reassuring. "I'll be back in a sec."

I pry my hand from his and walk swiftly up the aisle between endless rows of chairs. Pushing through the doors, I set my jaw and focus on my task, picking up the pace as I move down the darkened, musty hallway.

Morticians like it dark.

Makes it easier for me.

Then, Silverman's voice stops me in my tracks.

"The man's a gangster," my father said. "Everyone wants to kill him, but no one has the guts."

I have the guts, I think, fingering the Luger in my pocket.

I slip into the bathroom, two stalls, painted gray, flowers propped in the corner and by the sink.

From other funerals, I'll bet. Undertakers can't spring for new flowers all the time.

The door squeaks as I enter, step up on the toilet and stand.

The gun feels cold as it quivers in my hand, feels heartless as I look it over.

I'm pretty certain it will fire. Pretty sure I've done everything right.

Footsteps draw close, Silverman's voice. "Hold that thought. I have to take a whizz."

The door whooshes.

Then he's in the stall next to me.

I step down, stalk to his stall, then stare at his back while he pees.

The Luger trembles as I aim.

Do it! My mind howls. *The man of the house! Do it!*

I taste blood as I bite my lip. Tears slide as my heart throbs in my ears. My arms grow weak.

Do it!

I lower the gun, stand staring and seething.

He turns as I slide the Luger behind my back. He wears an expression as if trying to remind himself who I am. "Oh yes! Jonas, Jude's son." He kneels, then wipes a tear from my face with his thumb. "Me and your father were business partners." He grips my shoulders and searches my eyes. "I'm just beside myself."

I get the feeling he's wondering what I know, if I know.

A wad of cash appears and two fifties get stuffed in the breast pocket of my suit. "Take your brother for ice cream after. On me."

Do it!

He smiles, tousles my hair, then paces on expensive shoes back into the funeral home.

***

Mrs. Beacham. Mrs. Bitcham.

Chubby cheeks hold smudged glasses, framed in wire.

She sits like a cobra, back straight, neck curved like she's going to strike.

An elderly couple, ancient through kid's eyes, hands us an envelope, then nods in a way that says how sorry they feel. How much better they feel now that they've paid admission to this festival of heartbreak.

Silverman steps to the casket as cameras flash. Beacham rivets beady black eyes and watches his every move.

Adjusting an expensive suit, he smiles like a toad, wipes an eye, then turns and moves toward us.

Beacham straightens even more, cocks her head, sticks out her boobs.

"I'm sorry for your loss, boys." He speaks too loud for a funeral. With a flair and glance toward the cameras, he offers a fat envelope. "If you need *anything* come see me." He gives Beacham a smile like Dad gave Mom when asking if she'd like to join him for a nap.

Then he's gone, a crowd of goons following.

I hear laughter as they leave, then sit staring at my dead parents.

Mrs. Beacham's hand appears, palm up, fingers waggling as she offers a fake smile.

I hand over the envelope.

"Can't wait to get these brats to the orphanage." Her words, said outside when she thinks no one could hear.

I'm offended. *Brats!* I think to take Ishmael and try our luck on the streets.

More people gather, pay their respects, gaze at our parents, offer comments on the good people they were, pass us envelopes, hollow offerings of good tidings.

Mrs. Beacham holds out her hand after each then stuffs them in her purse, squeezing tight with grubby, chubby hands. "I'll keep these safe for you boys."

Realization settles. Like being underwater with no clue how to raise myself. The boy's too young to solidify his thoughts. Trying to be a man by suppressing his grief, his fear, his temptation to rise, to flee, to race away and try his hand with the gun and the streets.

Beside me, Ishmael weeps, stares at his shoes and says nothing. He doesn't care about Beacham. Doesn't seem to notice the funeral, the envelopes, the wishes and despair.

I know he cares only about what we've lost. Has the compunction to see our parents' demise as the bitter end to a good and happy life. He's special I realize, resonates with those who hold purity and kindness in their hearts.

I frown. He'll learn, I think. Someday he'll know what I have to do and the reasons for doing it.

I'll fix it all.

Beacham's car is a late model sedan with cloth seats. It smells like too many flowers, burns my nose and makes me nauseous as sweaty hands squeeze the wheel.

We're shuffled into a huge building of sullen gray stone. Three spires stare down as if wanting to gulp us up. We ascend the stairs and are guided to a dark, rectangular room stuffed with beds on both sides. "Yours are in the corner," Beacham says, squeezing her purse. "The empty ones. Sorry, we couldn't find two together."

Ishmael looks panicked, his eyes dart as we walk between beds pressed against looming walls on either side.

Heads pop from under sheets, watching as we pass, saying nothing.

"Help me with this." I grasp the cold frame of an empty bed and pull it into the aisle. Ishmael pushes from the other end and we drag it next to another empty bed.

"From this point forward, we'll always be together."

His eyes light up a bit, the smallest ember in a world gone sable.

In my pocket, I finger two envelopes slipped from Beacham's purse. They press against the Luger, crinkle a bit as I pet them.

"Lay down, Ishmael," I say. "Things will be better in the morning."

Ishmael crawls on the bed and flops sideways, knees drawn to his chest.

He won't stop crying, probably can't stop crying. I rub his back, try to calm and put him to sleep like Mom always did.

In time, the others get tired of staring and the room fills with the muted whooshes of sleeping children.

I should go without him, but I can't. "Come on," I whisper. "But be quiet. We're leaving."

He nods a single time, slips from the bed to follow me back down the stairs where we find the front entrance locked.

At a noise behind us, we bolt behind a loveseat in the small lobby.

A janitor passes, two bags of garbage held at his side.

Down the long corridor, I see an open door at the building's rear. We race to it as our shuffled sounds careen down darkened corridors.

When we're out, we race behind a car and huddle close, crouching.

The janitor appears, looks around, confused, then goes back in and shuts the door.

"Come on!"

Through the littered alley to a subdued street. Ishmael's hand slides into mine and I pull him along as he trots to keep up.

Fifteen minutes later we're huddled behind a hedge. Before us, the house is red brick with a wraparound porch and large windows.

"Ishmael, do you know what a secret is?"

"Yes."

"Do you know what happens if you tell a secret?"

"No. What?"

"We both go to jail where they feed you worms for breakfast, lunch and supper."

His face twists. "Yuck!"

"And that's not the worst of it. The worst is they tie you down and poke you with sticks and needles. Then, vampires come every night and suck your blood."

He looks pale. Says nothing, eyes shifting. "Yep," I say. "Keeping a secret is more important than anything in the world."

His eyes fill with the terrors of his imagination.

"We have to do something, Ishmael. And what we do needs to be a secret that's never told. A secret between us brothers that we keep forever."

Dark eyes hold mine, nod once, twice. "What are we doing?" he whispers.

"You'll see," I say. "But you need to be quiet."

He gulps. "Okay."

"I mean it Ishmael. If we get caught, we'll both go to jail."

He swallows hard and looks at the ground. "Okay," he whispers. "I'll be quiet."

A big man with a bulbous nose and cheesy moustache exits the house and lights a cigarette. He walks past our hiding place, gets into a new Cadillac, then backs out of the driveway and heads off.

"Hurry," I say. "Follow me."

We hustle past another car and across the yard, sticking close to the house as I pull Ishmael along.

About halfway up, we crouch beneath a window as light steals the darkness from a square strip of grass.

I press my finger to my lips, then rise a bit and peek inside.

Books wait on dark wooden shelves. Comfortable leather armchairs sit close to a broad marble table.

Lazy coils rise as Silverman sucks a stogie then hisses rolling plumes. Torn envelopes flood the table as he counts through a two-inch stack of bills, then wraps them around an already thick bankroll.

Heart racing, I grasp Ishmael's hand and lead him around back where we climb on the porch to press on either side of a fat white door.

I press my fingers to my lips again.

The handle turns easily and the door cracks open.

We creep inside.

As soon as we enter, a woman's voice startles. "Are you coming up?"

What's Mrs. Beacham doing here? I pull Ishmael close and remind him to stay quiet.

The response from the study is muted but lyrical. "Up in a minute."

Ishmael looks like I've just given him a slap as I pull the Luger from my pocket and examine it.

With a finger to my lips, I coax him to follow, then creep down the hall.

From the room papers shuffle, Silverman clears his throat. "Pretty smart, taking those envelopes. We made over a thou!" The odor of stale cigar wafts from the open door.

"That's great!" Beacham yells from upstairs. "Now come up! I have a surprise for you!"

It's now or never. I motion Ishmael to stay put, then step into the room, pistol raised like in the movies.

The cigar wafts tendrils toward the ceiling. Silverman sits with one leg propped on the knee of the other, the newspaper spread before him. He can't see me, the newspaper blocks his view. "I'll be up in a minute!" he yells.

I stare, gun trembling like in the bathroom at the funeral home. Fear fills me, the thought of the trouble I'll be in. The gun droops as my nerve flows away.

Then I see the headline. DOUBLE KILLING RULED HOMICIDE—NO SUSPECTS.

From the page, my parents smile at me.

Nerve returns in a gush.

The gun holds steady.

Singed holes appear as six shots tear through.

I jump, stand staring as the rapport shreds my ears.

A tuft of vapor rises from the Luger. Silverman stares with empty eyes. The cigar falls from his fingers. Bloody splotches appear through his shirt as a feeling of satisfaction, of accomplishment, of being a man, deadly, daring, bold, fearless, fills my small body. Images of cowboys, of superheroes, of secret agents, spin through my head, each wearing the grinning face of Jonas, clefted chin, square, stubbled jaw, intense smoldering eyes.

Then a vision of Dad, beaming, hand raised, thumb extended like he did at all our soccer games. He's proud. I know it. Can feel it flow from each strand of my hair all the way to my toes.

From upstairs: "Ronnie, honey, what was that?"

Beacham. Bitcham! She's next. *Do it!*

My heart beats so hard it makes my throat ache. Even Bitcham must hear it.

I race into the hall.

Ishmael's gone.

I freeze, mind running at speeds I've never experienced and can't handle.

Then steps on the stairs, chubby feet stomping their way down.

I race back to the study, slide behind the chair, behind Silverman's tilted body.

Where's Ishmael? I try to think, try to place myself in his shoes.

Bitcham's scream is as loud as the gun, makes my knees buck as I struggle to hold my position behind the chair.

Then, receding footsteps and excited chatter.

I peek down the hall and head for the door. My only hope is that Ishmael got scared and fled.

Instead, I find him at the door, crouched and trembling, head wrapped in both arms, eyes wide and distant.

Bitcham's chatter stops as her footsteps draw close.

I grab my brother. "Ishmael!" I hiss. "Come on!"

He doesn't move, only cowers as if forever rooted to this spot. "You killed him, Jonas." He whispers, trembles. "You killed Mr. Silverman!"

I cover his mouth with my hand, stare down the hall where her shadow grows.

I crouch beside him, both of us stooped and still as stone.

"Oh my god, oh my god, oh my god." Bitcham's voice, as panicked as Ishmael.

She appears in the hallway, trembling hands held to her head, a teddy slashing her frame with pink lace and black satin. "Oh my god, oh my god."

I hug Ishmael close, ease my hand from his mouth and raise the Luger. If she looks toward the door, we'll be caught for sure.

I won't let that happen.

"Oh my god, oh my god, oh my god."

Do it!

Relief washes me as she turns away and takes two steps. Then, she turns back to look at Silverman's body. "Oh my god, oh my god, oh my god."

The gun trembles as I point. My heart hammers like triple in size.

She drops to her knees, hands over her face, then sobs like a gasping radiator. Satin, stretched and useless, shakes as wails rise to pound the truth home.

She's beaten, broken, horrified, alone.

Ishmael's hand rises, then pushes the Luger to point at the floor.

Our eyes meet and he blinks.

You're the man of the house now.

I scoop him up, leaving Bitcham with her corpse, her god, and her cache of stolen envelopes.

Chapter 24

Jerusalem, Israel

Rhyme leaps from the limo and races to the emaciated man. "Igneus!" The Jew swivels his head, sharp cheek bones under bent eyebrows. "I'm so glad I found you!"

Igneus steps back a pace, fist wrapped around his walking stick, eyes flaring caution. "Well, well, if it isn't the empress," he says. "I see you've fully joined your husband."

"I haven't," she blurts, then lowers her voice. "I've run away, running away now, heading to the Temple." She motions to the limo. "Something's wrong with Emery. Stuart says there's healing at the Temple."

A blond boy steps forward, looks angelic and innocent. "I'm the healer," he announces. "And the Temple's been taken. It's not safe."

Rhyme reacts without thinking, grabbing the boy's wrists and pulling him to the limo. "Emery's in there. Doesn't look good. Like he's trapped in a dream."

Climbing into the limo, Sebastian notices Houdini, then kneels beside him. "I love dogs!" the boy says. "What's his name?"

Impatience rises. "Not important. Help Emery." She speaks loud, then pauses, gathers her composure. "Please," she adds.

His face flushes but his grin quickly overwhelms the color. "Sorry," he whispers to the dog. "I'll be right back." He slides next to Emery.

Small hands perform a quick exam, touching Emery's wrists, his forehead, even prying open an eyelid. "He's not injured," he says. "Maybe he's just sleeping."

"He's not," she says more forcefully than she'd like. "He had huge blisters all over, smoke rising from his skin. He's been muttering like he's out of his mind. I know him, something isn't right."

Sebastian regards her for another moment, then shrugs. "Okey dokey, let's see what we can do." He places his hands on Emery's chest, then withdraws them and shakes his head, staring for a second. His eyes light up, and he places his hands on either side of Emery's head. A blue aura appears like a sparked mist, rises to shroud Emery's head like an Easter bonnet. Sebastian's eyes roll upward. He turns solemn as if in a trance.

Igneus leans on a crooked walking stick. "Should only take a second," he says.

Then, a sour sound like fabric tearing. Sebastian jolts as a blanket of foul smoke coils around him and rolls from the limo in choking thickness.

"Sebastian!" Igneus screams.

Churning vapor pours from the boy's hands in clotted, fetid ribbons. The blue aura is gone, strangled by angry streams of barren black and clotted gray. Sebastian's eyes roll up so all she can see are the whites.

She leaps in, frantic, grasps the child and pulls. He doesn't budge, as if rooted to the seat.

Then Igneus is there, stick leveled, face stern with concentration. He mutters some words, but nothing happens. The stick falls with a clatter as he grasps the boy whose eyes are crazed, his face contorted in a silent scream.

Then a whoosh, a sickening crunch, and both Rhyme and Igneus crash to the limo's front. Igneus kicks, scrambles, pounces back to the child.

Sebastian's eyes are black coals, his face twisted in half a shriek.

Igneus pulls, heaves, flies back across the limo as smoke rolls from a frozen Sebastian, hands clamped on Emery's head.

———

The man is tall, gray, well dressed. A dark suit beneath eyes that flair red from shadow.

The girl, eighteen perhaps, wails, legs propped on a birthing table's stirrups.

She pants, cries out, bears down. Then the squeal of a newborn. Doctors hustle, dressed like prepped for nuclear war, thrust the baby in a large transparent box. Rubber gloves, yellow, hang limp attached to holes on either side of the box. Medics stick their hands in the gloves, start to attend to the baby.

"It's a boy," one says.

"I changed my mind!" Tears roll down her face, drip into her ears. "I've changed my mind!"

"Nonsense!" The man steps between the doctors and the girl. "Take him!" He turns to the girl, lowers his face, grips her hands. "It's all for the best, love. Someday you'll see."

Her shriek shatters the measured purpose of the medics. "I hate you!" She struggles to rise, leans up on her elbows as the man places a hand on her chest and pushes her flat. "This is hard, I know," he says, "but you have to trust me."

"I don't!" she screams. "I won't! I want my baby!"

He applies an even pressure as she struggles beneath. "Too late," he says. "They're already gone."

———

Darkness. Terror. Consequence.

Mr. Emery fades as the landscape takes shape. Fiery clouds spin atop jagged peaks. Lightning shreds a molten sky as thunder rumbles endless. Clotted mist parts to reveal belching smoke and raging flame. Souls howl, spasm, wail, wretch. Sebastian shivers as terror nips his psyche. Eyes dilate and take in the endless expanse of misery, mayhem and malice.

"No one loves you."

He whirls. Before him stands a man with kind eyes and a gentle face.

"Never have, never will." The man steps forward, holds both hands palms up.

Sebastian senses danger. Senses the absence of the great power like a switch thrown.

"I brought you here to show you some things." Compassion becomes concern. "Sadly, some of it is harsh, but I assure you, no less true."

Wails rise, cascade, peal through flames like dancing ghosts.

"Let's see," the man says. "What's next?"

Sebastian quivers and trembles; eyes widen to their fullest. Fear fills him, probes with a harshness like broken glass and razor blades. He bites his lip, tries to face the overwhelming terror, the blackness, the pervasive evil.

A mist churns, then congeals.

Images rise from the ether.

"That's your father," the man says. "Very rich now. Much older than your mother, who, I'm sorry to say, was a common whore with a nickel head."

Sebastian grits his teeth. "No, she wasn't."

The man returns a fatherly look. "I'm afraid she was, son. But to be fair, not at first. You see, she worked for your father, who owned a thriving commodities business. She was just a clerk, an errand girl. Then dear old dad spotted her and couldn't resist. Next thing you know, she's his personal assistant, assisting with…well…you know. They taught you that, what that is?"

"Shut your mouth!"

"I know it's hard, but truth is rarely easy. Like your mother, you'll soon see that I'm really just helping you. Oh look, here she is again."

Images flit, shift, become an alleyway dark and haunting. A woman squats by a dumpster, eyes wide, staring at her arm. The needle enters and she pushes the plunger. A few seconds later, her eyes glass over. She slides to sitting, riding the high.

"A shame really. She never got over losing you." He takes a step and raises a finger. "Although, when one thinks about it, one can conclude that she didn't love you enough to even look for you."

"You're lying!"

"Am I, prophet? Do you think I show you these things because they give me joy?" His nose turns up as he tsks. "They certainly don't. And if you must know, it's completely necessary for your journey. You see, in all the world, all the billions, I alone love you. I alone can save and restore you." His eyes glare sincerity. "Do you love your mother? Do you even remember her? Do you miss her? Want her back?" Great white teeth flicker reflected flame. "I can provide that, you know. Can give her back, if you wish."

Sebastian stares at the mist, watches his mother droop, head tilted, pressed against a greasy dumpster.

"She's racing toward death now, in real time, as we watch. Seems what she injected was a little stronger than her fragile, malnourished constitution can handle." He turns, beams, offers his hands again. "But *you can* save her, be the knight for which she always searched. Wouldn't that be something? Saved by the baby you abandoned?" He steps close as eyes simmer embers of shadow. "Just say the word and we'll go and pull her from that pit. Imagine her surprise, her profound love, when her long lost son appears to scrape her from the trash heap. A grand, symbolic gesture. One of humility, even love. Such forgiveness, such grace. The prodigal returns with love and compassion. You can reunite, live your lives together and, well, just exist like normal people."

Sebastian watches her droop. Saliva dangles from her chin, eyes closed, breathing diminished. "What about my dad?"

"Cares only for money."

"Not him! My real dad. Igneus."

Dark eyes flash hatred. The man scoffs, then spits on the floor. "The worst of the worst, that one. He doesn't care about you, just uses you for his own ends."

"You're lying! He loves me. He's the only one."

The man tsks again. A cathedral of wailing heartache pierces the mist from all sides. "Sadly, untrue." He steps forward and holds the boy's face with icy hands. "You're being harshly used. So like your mother, you don't even see it." His eyes are kind, hypnotic, as words drip in Sebastian's ears. He motions to the image. "All she needs is food and someone to care for her."

Sebastian's mind fills with visions: he and she in a faded minivan pulling up to a soccer field. Her shouting encouragement as he dives to make a spectacular save. Her beaming as he signs a professional contract. Sebastian. The finest goalkeeper who ever played.

Igneus strains, pulls his hands back and shakes them. "He's so hot. I can't hold him for long."

"Together then," Rhyme says.

Smoke rolls from the boy to fill the limo's interior and choke her breath.

"One, two…" Igneus says.

Rhyme grips. Hands sear like branded.

"Three!"

They pull with all their might, grunt with the struggle, exasperation mixed with clotted fumes. The pain's incredible. The burn, like picking coals from a campfire.

"Pull!" Igneus screams.

She bears down, teeth clenched, eyes watering, blinded by smoke, hands smoldering.

Another whoosh and they're shot across the limo.

From outside, Bill regards them, endless Doritos bag in hand.

Stuart stares open mouthed, head shaking like a reflex.

Then, Bill enters, sets the chips on the seat and a placid hand on Sebastian's shoulder.

CHAPTER 25

"You're lying!"

"Dear boy, why would I lie?"

Sebastian blinks at flame, cowers at the shriek of unknown voices. A red mist descends as his mother fades toward death.

"Only a few seconds now," the man says. "Then she will die, dear Sebastian. And you could've saved her."

The words echo, linger: *dear Sebastian.* Reminds the boy of Mr. Drake, the handsome gloved man. *Dear.* He never loved me either, Sebastian thinks. Then a vision comes of a charred street filled with corpses. Mr. Drake's approach, glaring smile etched, suit, crisp and shining.

"Before your very eyes shall I smite the boy, then I shall throw you asunder, in the light of day, for all the world to see." Feline eyes probe, eyebrows crease to a sharp point.

Sebastian remembers Drake's heat, feels it even now. Pure evil. An invitation to death.

"Get back!" he screams. "You're a liar!" He backs away, hands trembling, eyes searching for Igneus, for Jonas, for anyone.

"As you wish, witness." The man grins. "But I'll be seeing you

169

soon enough." Laughter cackles like the flames around them. Smoke and fire stretch, grow, lash, until sucked into a rolling whirlwind.

Flames flicker, then puff out.

The smoke clears, becomes the limousine. Igneus comes into focus, cheeks stained with tears, speaking fast, his words jumbled. Beside him, that woman, Rhyme, is shaking her head, eyebrows bent in concentration. Next to them, oblivious, is Mr. Emery, face pressed against the glass, eyes closed, lips quivering.

"Sebastian, dear, are you okay?" she says.

The boy gulps, rubs his eyes. He shivers at the *dear.* "I think so." He coughs, pitches forward. Igneus grabs him up in a bear hug and lifts him from the car. Outside, Stuart helps with the wide-eyed, trembling youth.

"Sebastian. My son. Thank God! Are you okay?"

The eyes that regard him brim with tears. The face is one of love, of joy, of home.

"Dad," he says, lips trembling. "It…It was the devil."

Chapter 26

Howls deafen like tinnitus. I press my hands to my ears as Alastor leaps from the stage to streak inches above raised hands and squirming forms. Lightning sizzles in his wake, pours into the crowded souls who glow more vibrant, pulsing, crammed with a hateful energy and the force of their curse.

"It's too bad really," Iblis says, suddenly beside me in the form of the wizened elderly gentleman. "That could've been so much better."

My body lifts, floats inches above the stage. Then we, Iblis and I, rush over the mass to streak miles per second as ghoulish fingers rise and pulse, attempt to grab, to escape.

Iblis arcs sharply, and we shoot through roiling clouds. We burst into a chamber of pallid marble walls that stretch to infinity. He drops me with a thud, touches lightly down beside me, then grasps my collar and hefts me to my feet. "You need to be stronger if you wish to endure."

He's speaking of my immortality, a flat fact to everyone but me. If I'm immortal does that mean just physically? Or does my soul live on through eternity? I reconsider the logic, realize souls are immortal without aid. Made in God's image, made from God's very breath, created to endure. Created to endure it all.

In reality, it's the physical realms that are the buggers. Like Cain, Longinus, Igneus, I wrestle with the realities of knowing I can't die. A reality that separates me from the writhing millions—I think. Immortals continue, souls intact, holding the knowledge we can't die, an inverse of the human condition, trapped on an Earth which is nothing more than a palpable hell from which the only escape is death.

"Ishmael never told," Iblis says. "He remained silent for the better part of a year, speaking only when coaxed by Jonas." He smacks his lips, tsks, seems to care. "Too young for all of that," he says. "As you know, children shouldn't endure those things without dilution."

"As if you care!" I'm fed up, tongue loosed by all this nonsense, this darkness, the needless and brutal levels to which I bear witness. "How much more?"

Laughter echoes hollow from broad arches in white plaster. Flakes chip away to flutter like falling leaves as artworks continue their steady shift. "There is as much as you can name," he says. "Like the universe, Hell is endless. You can't possibly understand all its nuances, its vastness, the things trapped here." He steps close, holds my eyes, then lowers his voice to a whisper. "I'll let you in on a secret most don't know and even less fathom," he says. "Most of my guests can free themselves at will."

"Bullshit."

"It's true, it's the genius of my creation. Take the souls who scream for vengeance. Perturbed at a lack of justice for some slight committed upon them, fueled constantly by Alastor who tends his flock with constant deliberation. He has one job you know, and that's to keep them inflamed. If a single one of them would let go of their slight, their need for recompence, their need for vengeance, they'd be transported to Heaven instantly, rushed to the pearly gates, which incidentally, are neither gates nor pearly. Do you see? Like most times, whether living, dead, immortal or mortal, the keys lie always within their grasp. A mere arm's stretch away. They may as well be dangling on a hook." He chuckles here like a gasping cricket. "Not a bad idea, actually," he says, beaming as he thinks. "Maybe I'll do that, conjure keys that remain always just out of reach. Distraction is a solid ally, a grand tool if wielded correctly. Why, your politicians use it daily to great effect. Don't like the economy? Get everyone focused on race or gender. Paint all facts in glossed coats of gray." He chuckles again as eyes gleam. "Like you said, it's all bullshit. But effective bullshit that causes the sheep to line at the trough and munch, munch, munch."

I step away. "Yeah, yeah, we all hold the keys. Um, if you don't mind my asking, could I have mine now?"

"Weary? Do you grow weary? Of what, if I may ask? Of evil? The lack of goodness? My boy, you need some conditioning. You still have many lifetimes ahead and should consider being fit for those challenges."

"Yeah, I'll take up yoga."

He laughs at this, head tilted in a flickering fusion of scarlet and shadow that glides across his features and infuses his suit. "Pearls before swine," he mutters. "The costs of every choice. Seems no one gets me, but just as well, I get them, if you catch my drift, eventually."

He motions me to follow and we step into the bright, plastered nothingness of this endless museum. "I'm beginning to think I'll be here forever," I say. "If this place has no end, at what point do you stop forcing these visions and allow me to return?"

Lips twist to a thick crinkle as he grins. "I've grown rather fond of you, Mr. Merrick. I see now why Cain chose you. Perhaps he's smarter than I give him credit. A worthy servant that one, but he has some surprises in store as well. Like you, he still can't put together the totality of the bigger picture, the endless fall from grace, the tempests of time raging over the present, the vastness of universal truth and destiny. Like a hurricane, you can't see the decimation until it's passed." An aged hand rises to tug the knot of his tie. "You two are tied together, I'm afraid, and even as Rhyme struggles to escape his clutches, you'll always be linked, no matter what happens. Good must have its evil. Evil must have its good. It's how She made it."

"She? Rhyme?"

He tsks. His brow furrows. "Limited thinking, lad. *She* as in God. After centuries of contemplation, I've decided, God has to be a woman. It's the only thing that makes sense."

"And why's that?"

"Because only a woman can make man this crazy." He slaps me on the back as he chortles. The sound runs away on thin curves and spirals.

"You're a real hoot," I say as sarcastically as I'm able.

He becomes solemn, wears a look of surprise for an instant, then glances at his watch.

"I thought you said time doesn't matter."

He holds up the watch, a swirling black pearl without number or hands. "It doesn't really, then yet it does. It's hard to explain with the limitations of language. One either grasps the concept or doesn't." He pauses as if waiting for a burst of realization from me.

I trace the dark angles of his face, try to truly fathom his features. They're blurred, giving more of a semblance, a hint of a face. Thin lips, pointed jaw, ashen goatee flickering to brazen eyes above sleek nose and cheeks. Like staring at a kaleidoscope, his features seem to change as if each second twists the dial another inch.

"The good news," he says, "is that we have time for a couple more."

I look down and groan out loud. "Really, you've been a wonderful host, but I've had enough."

"Yet you still miss the point."

"The point of hell?" I sigh. "I think I get it."

"I don't think you do. And since you're the student, and I, the master, the lessons must continue. I'd be abashed to leave such grand concepts untaught and unlearned. A worthwhile sage simply can't leave their students to their own devices. What mighty disasters would arise?"

I don't reply.

A pregnant pause ensues, broken finally by his words. "In any event, a couple more things and then we'll see what happens. Why, you may even want to stay when we're done. You might just beg me to keep you and teach you more. Wouldn't that be something?"

"Well, I've had a lovely time," I say. "But it's getting late and I still have a long drive. You probably have to work tomorrow too, and I'd be a rude guest to keep you longer."

There's a puff, and my hair stands on end. Brightness softens to broad rays, the pastel pinks of the rising sun.

Odors assault. The tang of corpses, of blood so thick I can taste it like chewing tin foil.

Then, loss, regret, deepest sorrow, quickly replaced by a sudden fear that seizes and burns like bowels ripped from my gut.

Air rushes from my lungs as if I've been punched. Then I'm kneeling, then floating, then speeding through a blurred tunnel of vapor and time.

The battle becomes apparent. Thousands, the screams, the dying, the crash of iron, the sharp thwack of bow strings, the squeal of killer and killed, slayer and slain.

I'm wrapped in a maelstrom of terror now, rising into a body not my own, then striking, driving, dodging blows, lashing out desperately.

I'm going to die. I know that more than I've ever known a single thing.

Yet on I fight, arms throbbing and weak. A single word lashes like a specter on a ghoulish warhorse.

"Gwenna."

CHAPTER 27

GERMANIA, 16 AD

The sword, heavy as a stone. The clang of metal, the thunder of battle, the wounded howling through morning mist.

I hear nothing and everything, a clamor punctuated with wails and shrieks, the heavy twang of catapults, the whistling shriek as chunks of stone rocket past to tear limbs and lay low entire groups.

I struggle to stand, then duck, dodge, run. My arms ache with each swing of the heavy sword, but youth and muscle push down the pain, and on I plod.

Hollowness glares, rises from my groin to clench with razor talons. Like ice water in my lungs, it squeezes air from my chest. A klaxon clangs in my head, a warning of preservation, a warning to flee, to desert.

Hide! It wails.

Run!

Thoughts cloud to vapor, mix with war's fog and wet mist. The symphony of battle, a crescendo turned elongated vibrato. The scene hums, thrums, warbles. We don't know the enemy, yet fight with abandon, thousands of us facing the Germanic tribes.

I know we're commanded by Germanicus, adopted son of the Emperor Tiberius. The memory conjures weeks on a boat, the heat, incessant boredom, an endless horizon rimmed by an inviting landscape too far away.

We wish we were there now. Wish we'd remained on that trireme and tried our hand as a sailor. We wish we could reverse time's traps and redo the actions that brought us here.

Gwenna. The woman I mourn.

The field is verdant, yet flecked crimson. Screams devour sounds of bird and cattle. Thought flees, a terror verging on insanity.

All I can do is dodge, leap, force my arms to stab, then run away and wish for the first time in my young life that I'm smaller.

Hills rise around us like the humps of a sea monster, silent observers that signal more carnage, crowned with clouds so very different than my home, so very different from the cones of Misthli.

The helmet is heavy, iron. Our neck strains with each movement even as the helmet holds the morning's heat and mutes the horrific clamor around us. Our armor, a breastplate, some gauntlets, heavy, too heavy, too ungainly for easy movement, yet doffing it only offers our body to the enemy's hammers and axes.

Hide!

A deft grace moves us. We leap the fallen like spooked deer drenched in sanguine raindrops; we sprint to the periphery, toward the rear, whipped by fear, by a will to survive, by a frenzy of instinctual flight that screams for only safety.

Home, that's where we're going, back home, back to what we know, back to mourn Gwenna, to sit at her grave and ponder our ruin.

The heavy sword's awkward, hard to control. We leap a corpse, then a massive hammer strikes our shoulder and sends us through a dewy moisture of blood-stained grass.

A giant strides forward and stands over us. A scarred face crinkled to a fiendish grin.

Avoid the veterans, boy. The only training I've received since joining the legion. *Avoid the veterans.*

"How will I know them?"

A coarse laugh. "Ye'll know, boy. Ye'll know."

And now I do.

He wears a fur cloak, the hide of a bear, and holds a hammer thick and broad, that captures morning rays and absorbs them into its iron.

A shaky sword rises as I gain my feet, wishing tremors didn't betray my fear. The helmet's heat doubles. Our knees quiver as sweat drips into my eyes, stings them red, dares them to blink.

The battle rages like a pulsing mass, fueled by its own energy. It's a wailing dervish with spinning blades, a reaper that trims men like weeds, that devours the weak, the young, the wounded. It's the very definition of brutality, of mercy lost, heartless, ferocious, tenacious, a whirlwind that snuffs life with brutal efficiency. Around us, a circle of men of both forces, pausing in the midst of the great battle. They are an island of observation in this ocean of barbarity.

I'm surprised by his size, have a feeling that it's odd to confront someone larger than me, than us. He steps forward as those around offer a wide berth. I don't understand why they're not fighting, why they don't aid me. Then I realize, I'm the chosen victim. That they've paused to watch the giant tear me to shreds. A matinee for the battle-hardened. This is one-on-one, me against he. A giant youth versus a giant German. I am today's lesson, the cautious instruction for any other rookie who survives the day.

The sword trembles in my huge hands, then with a clumsy slice, it slaps away the hammer as it arcs toward us and misses by a fraction.

Doubt fills us as we realize our slight advantage of youth and agility won't be enough to survive the onslaught of this foreign monster. Yet, our body follows every command, moves at the very instant trembling nerves bellow impulse to quaking limbs.

He rears, brings the hammer over his head like pounding a post.

We leap away, feel the earth quake from the force. The hands of both enemy and comrade shove us back toward him.

They'll have their blood, all of them. They'll watch my demise then use my tale to train new recruits.

My own comrades stand stoic, leaning on spears and swords, shoulder to shoulder with our enemy. All watch, weighing my worth, I realize, testing my limits, my resolve, my strength. With this initiation, the metal from which we're forged is tested.

If we win, we are transmuted, an alchemic transformation.

If we lose…

Thoughts race away as the man circles.

Behind him, a vulture lands, rips an eye from a corpse and downs it.

The hammer whistles. I stumble back and thrust the sword only to have it sent flying as another blow falls. He spins, hammer singing my death song, sizzling in a wide, broad arc, over his head like chopping a log.

I dodge, trip on something, roll headlong and off balance through the wet grass.

Move! My mind cries, prods. To be inert is to die.

I roll, feel the hammer impact the earth beside me, hear the man grunt with each blow as sod rises in clotted clumps of weed and dirt.

Desperation seizes. Certainly my comrades won't let him kill me, certainly they'll render aid. But as I roll, I see their faces, cold, uncaring, enjoying a brief rest and sideshow before renewing the battle proper.

I'm more afraid than I've ever been, manage to stay only a trace ahead of the raging barbarian and his huge hammer as he chops and I roll.

Then he's on me, using broad feet to block my path as he stands above as big as a mountain, as solid as a stone bastion.

His eyes showcase my future with a certain detachment. They say I'm one of many today. One of many he'll dispatch. Nothing personal, they say, just the wages of battle, the price of war, the dues of the legion and we legionnaires.

Wide eyes stare up at our doom.

Then a flood of peace accompanies the surge of death's serenity. A sense of relief, of knowing we'll soon meet Gwenna on the Elysian fields, the fortunate isles of fable.

And so, staring, we stare boldly.

And so, dying, we die with bright eyes and a heart that clings to lost love.

Then something hard presses into my side, then into my hand.

Something that's found its way to me through trampled field and horror's cacophony.

The hammer falls.

With a deftness of movement I've never experienced before, we thrust in a single fluid motion. The huge German's eyes bulge as the spear pierces bear hide. With a gasp, he drops to one knee, hammer falling beside him.

I hustle to my feet, yank the stifling helmet from my head as the cool morning celebrates with a basking caress.

We will not die today.

Let that be the lesson.

I yank the spear from his chest and stand regal. The vanquished tormenter prickles like a grizzly, then topples and struggles for breath.

Kill!

My mouth waters. Limbs fill with renewed strength. Breathing calms. My body ceases to tremble.

Kill!

The voice of a conqueror, the voice of carrion denied, of one who refuses to bloat dead beneath a burning sun as snack for bird and beast.

Victory is heartless.

Victory is cruel.

The giant stares at us from the killing field's bed. He makes no sound, even as his face contorts with pain. His expression begs mercy, but his mouth won't bawl the words.

A lesson, I think, on how to greet death. On how *we* die. How a *warrior* claims the only relief left, a gleeful surrender, an embrace of death's chilled trappings.

The look says much. To beg mercy is to fail life, an embarrassment that demeans the warriors we are and the way we live.

A second passes.

Our heart hammers as we lift the spear. His eyes broadcast calm serenity, whisper the truth of all warriors. *"This is how we die."*

I'm surprised how easy the spear impales.

I'm surprised as I watch light fade from his eyes, as if someone pulled the breaker on the conduit that animates the brave.

I'm surprised as his reflection turns to one of serene relaxation, an attainment of peace among the clamor of carnage and carrion, the shriek of crashing metal, the glare of shouted orders, the screams of the wounded, of the dying.

I turn, see the battle tumble through a valley to the east, furrowed fingers in an emerald blanket covered with wailing ants.

Glee fills me.

I lust for blood. My mouth waters, an erection throbs. I retrieve my sword as a roar flows from my throat.

Comrade's laugh as I howl above the clamor and race toward the enemy. I'm consumed with youth's fearlessness.

I *cannot die.*

I *will not die.*

I *will* avenge.

I *will not* allow my life to end until that task is done.

"Who's that?" I hear as I rush past, helmet left behind to ornament the ground.

"Using too much energy to be sure," another voice says.

"Cocksure boy," says another.

But I am boundless.

I am strong.

I am the match that sparks the fire and kindles it with blood.

I am the harvester, steel singing, body tuned, balanced, invincible.

I am Longinus, and I have come.

Fur cloaked enemies bear down as arrows whistle past.

The sun scorches swollen corpses as vultures bob in for their morning meal.

I am Longinus.

I am violence.

I wade in, arms fueled by infinite strength, mind tuned to every sound.

I am superhuman, awesome, fantastic, unstoppable.

Unleashed.

Voices rise to rally as others follow my lead, renewed by my onslaught, rushing forward as the enemy scatters.

I chase, dispatch two, skewer even more.

This is bliss!

We can't get enough.

Kill!

The spear rockets from my arm, covers twenty feet in a single second before plunging through an enemy's gut.

I'm a king! Burning bones for my fire.

Hands grasp my armor, four men, then ten. My comrades overpower me and pin me to the ground.

A centurion appears. He wears a smile that's long abandoned any semblance of joy or revelry. "Easy, lad. 'Tis over. Ye did well."

A solid jaw, eyes precisely wrinkled as if placed to brand the appearance of rugged will.

Comrades heft me to my feet as adrenaline makes my hands tremble. Nausea rises as we watch the army of Germania scatter.

"Ye did well." A veteran slaps my back.

"A brave one, that," another says.

I'm congratulated for my brutality, for quenching the seething rage of Gwenna's loss on our enemies. The spear juts from a dead man as I look for my sword.

A centurion confronts me. "What's ye'r name, lad?"

"Longinus," I say distracted, basking on the moans of the injured. "Longinus of Misthli."

The eyes that hold us say they know something; say they've forgotten more about killing than they remember. They are a solid period at paragraph's end. The definition of knowledge without boast. A certainty of performance, of bravery, of brotherhood.

"'Twas fate that saved ye, lad," he says, pulling the spear from the vanquished man. "Respect it, lest ye feel its bite." He hands me a sword and looks me over. "If I be catchin' ye without pike or blade agin, ye'be gettin' a hidin' ye won't soon forget."

I swallow hard and stare down at my feet. "Aye."

A rough hand grips my shoulder. I raise my head to a face weathered by the rigors of war, the ordeals of the legion, the trials of a warrior.

"Come, Longinus," he says. "Attendin' the wounded be our task now, then I'be teachin' ye to care for that pilum and gladius."

Saliva gathers and I swallow hard, clenching my fists, squeezing my eyes.

I've a taste for blood, sharp, acrid, acidic. I want more. Want again to feel my body move like an inhuman machine, unfeeling and merciless. I crave the flow of metal, the swish of arced steel. The cries of my enemies seduce and tantalize. A fuel for wicked intent that tempts a new lingering addiction.

I've never felt this way, never in my life wanted to kill anyone. Yet Longinus's feelings glaze my psyche to reveal my hidden flaws as subtleties ripe for exploitation.

Iblis appears. "That's a humdinger, eh boy?"

I lick my lips, swallow the collected spit.

"Bloodlust," he snickers. "Intoxicates and consumes. Maybe you're starting to get it." He winks and snaps his fingers. "A new Hell awaits. Let's not dally."

CHAPTER 28

JERUSALEM, ISRAEL

Bells jingle as Igneus enters Lee's Chinese. "Where's Laslo?"

Jonas shrugs, but his face betrays his thoughts.

"Did he go after Israel?"

"I fear so. He left early and I haven't seen him. So, who knows? Maybe he'll be back any second."

Rhyme stands. "What now?"

"We're going," Igneus says, frustration, even anger, etched on his face.

"To the Temple?" Jonas says. "That's a bad idea."

The Jew's jaw is set, his eyes on fire. "Don't care."

"Igneus, even if you had a thousand men, the Temple will be hard to take back."

"I don't need a thousand men. Just Sebastian."

Jonas's sigh is audible. "Okay then, I'm coming too."

"No, you're not."

"We've been over this. Try and stop me."

Rhyme interrupts. "You said Cain holds the Temple. Going there is suicide. I agree with Jonas. It's not strategic, not intelligent, not sane. I mean, what's there to accomplish? Getting us all killed?"

Igneus pauses, straightens, then takes Jonas's eyes. "I'm not sure but I feel driven to get there. Feel forced to recapture the place. I don't know what's next, but I know the Temple's vital. The Antichrist cannot be allowed a foothold there." He shrugs but seems unassured. "Rhyme, you and Emery should be safe here. Lay low until we return. Mr. Lee will take good care of you but don't poke your head out, too much risk."

Emery lies on a cot shaking and moaning, occasionally raising his hands, muttering. "Cain did this," Rhyme says.

"Without a doubt, but what is *it?*"

Rhyme glances at Sebastian who seems lost in thought, too riddled by life's questions to register anything. "No idea."

"Even Sebastian's power didn't work." Igneus's expression becomes fatherly, concerned.

"Will he be okay?" she asks.

"I hope so. He doesn't have any injuries, save of course to his mind." He moves to the boy, places a hand on his shoulder. "Sebastian, it's time to go. I need your help."

Sebastian, startled from his thoughts, looks into Igneus's eyes. He stands and manages a smile. "I'm ready."

Rhyme scoops rice in her mouth as she thinks about the ride here, the limo in the alley, covered in boxes and crates, flanked by dumpsters. Like a glaring orange balloon designed to get someone's attention. Igneus, Jonas, and Sebastian have been gone for hours and she worries for them. She considers advantages, the group she's with.

Mr. Lee watches a rerun of the old series, *Kung Fu,* laughing occasionally. "No. No." Turning to Rhyme. "They stupid on this show."

Rhyme laughs, looks at the screen, then moves to Emery and swabs his lips with a wet rag. His hair looks lighter, more silver, as if he's aged in the past hours.

In the corner, Stuart sits like a mountain on a too small chair. He stares at the floor, gives the appearance of a man used to waiting.

Houdini lies at his feet and seems to doze. "He must know we've run by now. Has to know you're not coming. The streets will be crawling with Imperium operatives." He focuses on Mr. Lee, glued to the small TV. With a subtle flick of his head, Rhyme understands what he's saying. *"Keep an eye on him. He could be one of them. Could've called and told them where to find us."*

Rhyme takes in the little man, considers the silent warning.

No way, she thinks. This man is kind and could never harm anyone. Besides, what choice is there? Where else is there to hide in all the city's ruins? Each Sig slides from its holster, gets rechecked for like the thousandth time. Stuart picks up on this, retrieves the Walther from inside his suit, checks it, slides it back. Then he does the same with the Ruger on his ankle. He sighs, watches Bill stuff chow mein in his face. He's skinny but eats like a lion.

Bill grins at the empty bowl, pushes it away, stands, clasps his hands together like praying and bows. He says something in Chinese.

Mr. Lee stays glued to the TV. "Welcome."

Bill disappears into the back of the restaurant, probably heading for the bathroom.

Weird. Just so weird. Did Bill save Sebastian? He'd entered the limo, carefully set his chips aside, then touched the lad's shoulder. That was it, no heroics, no words, nothing supernatural. Just a simple touch, just something normal. Perhaps a coincidence, but instinct says it isn't.

She recalls the scene. The limo filled with smoke, Sebastian frozen, horrified, hand clamped to Emery's head. Bill's a clone, she remembers, something created and raised by Cain. *How's such a thing possible?* Sebastian's attempt to help Emery had been useless, and judging by the way Igneus stood idly, stating "It'll only take a second," the task should've been an easy one. Add to that, the fact that Bill wouldn't even try and help Emery, stating simply "Dude's in too deep." What's that mean? Does the hippie clone have some supernatural power? You're being superstitious, she thinks. Perhaps Sebastian was able to free himself and it had nothing to do with Bill?

Either way, things had gotten out of hand and surprised all of them.

Frustration fuses with confusion. *I'm sick of these puzzles.* Nothing fits. Too much to digest, let alone think about. Longinus and his spear. The Antichrist. His minions. Bill. Stuart. Etcetera and etcetera. Her husband's manipulations, veiled so well they're imperceptible, impossible to put together in any logical way.

She forces away logic, focuses on intuition, comes up blank.

With the first task accomplished—getting away from the Antichrist —the math becomes simple. Hide, bide time, hope.

But what next? Wait for Igneus and the gang to return from the Temple? Confront Cain herself? Make plans to escape farther, closer to the border and possible freedom?

Questions rise, foamed mountains ringed with thunderous clouds. She glances to the back of the restaurant, at the door Bill went through. Should probably pee as well, she thinks. "Stuart, can you keep an eye on Emery while I use the restroom?"

"Shouldn't be too hard, doesn't look like he's going anywhere."

Rhyme rises, notices an image of her face on the small TV, words in red: EMPRESS KIDNAPPED. She pauses, listens to the reporter's outrage at the abduction of Cain's wife. Then, a reward for her safe return flashes across the screen: fifty million.

Typical, she thinks. Cain knows she's gone and uses it to his advantage. Who's he going to blame? The EU? Another unsuspecting country?

She moves through the door into the back storage area. Boxes are piled high, Chinese symbols running up the sides. Past them, the bathroom door stands open. "Bill?"

No answer.

She looks around, checks the corners, pokes her head through to the front to see if Bill returned while she watched the newscast. There's no sign of him.

Moving to the back exit, she feels a breeze, sees a rainy, gray day beyond.

Why would he go out there?

"Bill?"

"Over here, dude."

To her left, Bill stands by a tattered green dumpster sucking on a joint.

"Get in here! We can't be outside. It's dangerous."

"Why? No one's looking for me?"

She hurries twenty paces, grasps his wrist and pulls him to the door. "Come on. You can smoke later."

Bill rolls his eyes. "Buzz killer."

At the alley's entrance, a vehicle passes by, then flashes out of sight.

She pulls. "Come on!"

With the winding of gears, the vehicle appears in reverse, squeals into the alley, blue lights flashing.

"Uh oh."

Rhyme bursts in, Bill in tow. "They're out there! Coming in! Get ready!"

Houdini leaps to his feet and growls, hackles raised, senses tuned. Sigs appear in her hands as Stuart rises, Walther out and ready. "I'll cover the front," he says. "You get the back. Everyone else stay down."

Rhyme upends a table, huddles behind and calls Houdini. Then, she stands, grabs Bill and pulls him down next to her. "Stay here," she whispers. "Keep low. It's gonna get loud. If you move, you'll probably get shot."

Blood shot eyes regard her. He pulls a handful of chips, crunches them in his mouth.

Then, with a harsh whoosh and the clanging resonance of hanging pans, an explosion rocks the restaurant.

Stuart waves his gun toward the back. "They're coming in. Got three vehicles front. No idea how many back."

Rhyme shivers, swallows, feels comforted by the twin Sigs in her palms, thinks to check them again.

Six men enter in black uniforms, Imperium's crest sewed on their sleeves, rifles leveled.

Mr. Lee rushes at them. "You go!" he screeches. "No problem here. You go before restaurant get wrecked!"

The lead man levels a rifle at Mr. Lee as the others notice the hulking, bald African and the drawn Walther.

Stuart drops to a knee, reduces his size by only a fraction, fires twice. One of the soldiers hits the ground.

Then all hell breaks loose.

Rhyme rises, fires two rounds, catches the first man in the throat and chest.

Bill leaps up with a war cry, hurls the Doritos, screams something, perhaps an expletive. Houdini leaps, catches a man's arm in giant jaws and drags him to the floor. Then Lee's there, blocking Rhyme's shot.

"Lee!" she screams. "Get down!"

But the man wades in, moving in an odd way, gliding, pigeon-toed, sliding into the midst of the three remaining soldiers.

"Mr. Lee!"

The soldiers raise their weapons.

Lee's hands flash, his body moves the tiniest fraction as he pivots among the three Imperium soldiers. With a smack like dropped meat, his elbow smashes the first's throat. Twisting like lightning, his hand whistles past the second soldier's ear, almost imperceptible, then grips the back of his neck and pulls forward. The soldier's eyes go dead, expression erased, senses jangled, as an open hand pounds his throat and his rifle clatters to the linoleum.

Rhyme scoots left, levels to shoot the third, but there's no need. Lee pounds a flurry of blows up and down the soldier's body, moves so fast that the grunts come a second behind each strike. The soldier drops under the onslaught, struck in nose, throat, abdomen and groin in a single second. Lee sprints to Emery and shocks Rhyme when he hefts him like a fireman and carries him into the back storage area.

Rhyme chases as gunfire erupts from the front. The place explodes in a fury of wood chips, plaster, glass and shrapnel. The front door blows open, flies off its hinges to send glass in a razor shower that bites her back. She ducks, twirls, hears Stuart fire. Then shouted instructions from outside.

Rifles chatter as the plywood covering the windows fills with a hundred holes. How many men out there? What kind of fire power?

A soldier bursts in, gets caught by Stuart who slams him to the ground, puts two rounds in his head, then slides back to the door's left side. He winks at Rhyme, holds both Walther and Ruger ready.

More soldiers pour in, and Stuart rushes like a bull with its ass on fire. He collides with the first two, cracks their heads with his pistols then steps back and ends them with one bullet each. He's smart, agile, strong and deadly. Always moving, always a step ahead. A thinking fighter, Crispy'd say, someone immune to the fog of war, situational awareness off the charts.

A soldier enters, and Houdini takes him down, raging as he shreds. Then they come from everywhere at once: through smashed windows, front door, rear door. Rhyme turns to the back, sees two break the threshold, takes them both with the Sigs. *Got to get to Emery.*

Three more push through. Rhyme fires, hits one as Lee appears and does his pigeon-toed death dance, sweeping the first's legs, then plowing the second with an open palm stroke to the nose. Before that soldier even drops, Lee's back to the first, crushing his larynx then stepping away as quickly as he came. "Back here!" he calls.

Bill sits on the floor, legs crisscrossed, munching Doritos. "Bill! Go to Lee! Now! We'll be right behind you!" She pulls on his shirt, pushes him toward the back, suppresses the urge to assist with a foot on his backside.

From the front, soldiers enter.

Stuart fires, moves, fires again.

Rhyme drops to a knee, sees Houdini take a soldier by the throat and mangle.

Another enters, gets dropped by Stuart.

They pour through the door, smash splintered plywood to jump through broken windows.

Rhyme fires, drops one, then another. The hulking African's eyes are focused, pistols gone, replaced by a dropped rifle.

Houdini turns, jaws dripping blood, then leaps for another soldier.

Then, beyond the entrance, beyond the fog and debris and gunfire and clamor, Rhyme sees a man with a rocket launcher.

A thousand thoughts collide, press to come out as one. Surely, he won't risk his own men. Surely, he'll warn before he fires. Thoughts of her husband. His evil. Thoughts that *these* men are *Cain's* men. Thoughts of the value they put on life.

"Stuart! Get out!" she screams, turns, tackles Bill as she flies through the back door into the storage room. "Houdini! Come!"

Houdini leaps through just as the telltale whoosh, the blinding light, the breath stealing shock of the explosion crumbles around them.

Rhyme's rattled, head throbbing, covered in paper towels and wire, plaster and smoke. Houdini licks her face. The fire alarm wails as she rises and checks her Sigs. Lee moves behind some boxes to lift Emery again.

Rhyme moves to the door, levels her Sigs, peers toward the front of the restaurant. Soldiers lie, dead or dying. Smoke rolls as a gray rain falls through shattered windows. Past them, in the street, more lie inert and motionless.

But no Stuart.

No time!

She races through the storage room, past Bill and Lee, and peers into the alley. "Looks clear," she says, stepping out. "Keep your eyes open."

Lee steps forward, Emery limp on his back, still muttering. "Not safe here no more," he says. "We go. He heavy."

Rhyme steps farther into the alley, sees an Imperium vehicle idling, blue lights flashing.

Stuart appears at the alley's entrance, grand smile on his face, suit tattered and singed. *"That* was a close one! Whoo!"

"Everyone in!" Rhyme shouts.

A radio squawks. "Legion Twelve enroute. Kidnappers trapped. Empress inside. Awaiting orders. Copy?"

She stares at the alley's entrance, wonders what lies beyond.

Then, her husband's voice slices the airwaves. "Legion Twelve, kill them all."

Rhyme stands stupefied, rules suddenly changed. This isn't a challenge. This is for keeps. She looks at Emery, watches him twitch and mutter as Lee loads him in the truck.

Stuart steps next to her and frowns. "What's next?"

A grim determination grips her soul. "If he wants a fight, let's give him one." Ferocity glows from a snarling face. "We're going to the Temple."

CHAPTER 29

JERUSALEM, ISRAEL

The Temple strobes neon, alternates fire red, sun yellow, eerie blue. Bass thumps the pavement, resounds through his soles and up his legs.

"Well, that's interesting," Jonas says. "Looks like a nightclub."

"We have to get closer," Igneus says. "Have to see what they're doing."

"They have turrets on the outer walls. Armed guards. Wouldn't be surprised if a tank pulled up."

Igneus moves close to Sebastian. Jonas checks his pistol, then slides it in the holster on his hip. "I'll go. I look like one of them. Should be able to reconnoiter without much problem."

Igneus regards his friend, eyes the stolen uniform, an Imperium officer's. "Shouldn't you take a rifle?"

"Nope. Doesn't fit. Officers don't carry rifles. What I have will do." He squints at the flashing structure. "Looks like a party. Will probably be fun. You two stay put."

Igneus grips his staff as Jonas steps off, considers the fact that the plan is no plan at all. "Be careful. Don't take unnecessary risks."

"Roger that," Jonas says, "see you in a few."

He moves through a circle of Imperium vehicles, counting them as he walks. Twenty, all with mounted guns. He thinks of Igneus and his staff, the power the thin man wields. Questions invade: Does Igneus control it? Can he use it at will? He remembers the bale fire, the parking garage, now long gone. The PM's office, Cain sent sprawling. Then the attack by the Americans and the staff's power both offensive and defensive. An enigma to be sure. He thinks of the etchings. Frogs, virus, ice, others. He can't remember them all, yet Igneus stated he knew their purpose, perhaps the purpose of the staff as well.

He exhales a misty fog into the rainy evening. As he moves toward the vehicles, he's greeted by Imperium soldiers. "Good evening, sir," one says. Another turns, drops his cigarette and proffers a salute.

Jonas returns the salute. "Keep your eyes peeled, stay alert." He moves past without another word, confidence rising. The charade's working. Just another officer sent to check on the Temple and troops. Just looking around, checking supplies. Nothing to see here. Nothing to worry about.

A line of civilians stretch around the Temple's outer walls, ancient stone mixed with new brick makes the barrier broad and thick. They await access to the courtyard within. Beyond them, neon dances, painting the Temple, the surroundings, the lingering crowd, with muted tones that thump in time with a pounding rhythm.

Fifty, perhaps more, stand here, seemingly unbothered by the steady drizzle as dusk gives way to the envelope of night. Strobes flash as broad white beams trace the night sky, circling like buzzards, they're bright enough to illuminate bruised storm clouds above.

He skirts the line, head low but still taking in the people. Everyday folks dressed for a big night out as neon stripes the ancient stone on which they stand. He moves forward, thinks of the men who trod this ground before him. Prophets, kings, immortals.

"Sir!" A young soldier snaps to attention, offers a salute. Jonas returns the salutation. "Everything's in order?" Jonas asks, resisting the urge to crane his neck for signs of discovery.

"Affirmative. The band started about an hour ago." The soldier looks down, loses his train of thought for an instant, grasps an ancient wall for support. Then, his eyes brighten, and he continues. "Trucks arrived as planned. Delivered everything. Should be a hell of a party."

Jonas traces the line stretched behind them, then steps close. "You stink of alcohol. Have you been drinking?"

The soldier blinks but looks unabashed. A smile blooms on his young face. "Of course," he says. "There's no threat here and the standing order was to have a good time."

The scene clarifies like a blanket pulled back. He examines the line, sees three men huddled together. One injects a syringe. Past them, a girl with a dusting of white on her nose dips a fingernail in a small bottle, then holds it steady as another lady grasps her wrist and snorts.

Jonas's mouth falls open, snaps closed. He was about to chastise the soldier for dereliction but realizes the scene is perfectly set for his task. "Carry on," he says. "And do have a good time."

His grin grows as he enters the courtyard and pauses to take in the gathered thousands. Music thumps, pounds, pulses. The crowd is striped in neon, white teeth flashing, hips grinding, arms raised. None notice the rain as they splash, shout; stop only to snort, or inject, or make out.

An Imperium officer splits the crowd; a raven-haired beauty offers him a bottle. He takes it, notices Jonas, then beams as he pours liquor down his throat. Wiping his mouth with the back of his hand, he pulls the woman close and takes her in a probing kiss, one arm wrapped around her neck. She melts into him, pressing her pelvis as lips entwine, as music pounds a sleek rhythm.

Jonas steps into the crowd. His task grows easier with each second. The more inebriated the guards, the partiers, the easier to get the lay of the land.

At the checkpoint, the line's grown even in the few minutes he's been here. Music thumps like a sledgehammer, makes his head ache as hundreds cry out, wail, squeal, delighted, joyous. Revelers pack the grounds, a teeming mass that sways in unison. Fourteen feet above them, poised on the sacrificial altar, a three-man rock band shrieks and riffs. Below them, on a stretched sheet, pointed script glows like written in fresh blood. Seventh Sunday.

A shirtless singer steps up, glistens, strobes neon as long hair dangles, dripping rain. He looks stoic, mesmerizes, glows neon and glimmers moisture. Thin but well-muscled, sleek, sexy, he eyes the crowd as the music slows. Then, the piano rises and lilts dramatic.

Cheers go up as revelers slow the frantic pace of moments before to stare up at this god of showmanship. This Poseidon in aqua and crimson and gold. Hips sway as they press close to one another, lips and hands grasp, clamp, probe.

A guitar flickers black and red, reflects laser shards over the stage, the crowd, the surrounding darkness. The singer works the strings, briefly matches the piano's melody, then changes to a different one that fills any pauses the piano's left behind. They work in harmony, raising the pace by degrees as notes drift across, through, and over each other.

The effect's hypnotic, the crowd, mesmerized, swaying, sedate, as piano and guitar distract like a snake charmer.

The lead man steps up, shakes rain from drenched hair and grasps the mic as the melody rolls, sad yet unrestrained.

Eyes squeezed, he presses the mic to his lips then sings in a graveled baritone.

> *My heart is lit with fuses, each one a little blown.*
> *Cobwebs hang from barren walls and float from*
> *chamber's stone.*
> *The blood that's run has long been bled.*
> *The life that oozed is gone.*
> *As I in sorrow hang my head and pine salvation's dawn.*

The piano tinkles a gentle exclamation, then returns to its hypnosis, smooth, detached, alluring.

> *Each fuse is crusted, blown apart,*
> *shards upon the floor.*

As I alone seek grace's face and knock on heaven's
　　door.
Each fuse is crusted, blown apart,
　　dust upon the floor.
As I alone seek saving grace and pound on heaven's
　　door.

Fingers trace taut strings with effortless precision. The guitar gleams neon that paints the swaying crowd. The drums kick in, hammer a brief rhythm as the bass lopes in bursts and throbs.

Jonas pushes through, heads up the Temple's steps. Grand doors rise before him, burst with cherubs in throbbing neon. He steps over a passed out partier, then inside.

His breath catches at the scene.

The space is cavernous, formerly gorgeous, now strewn with discarded cups, syringes, beer and liquor bottles, clothing. People dance, press close, most half-dressed, some fully nude as various activities bloom in full view of everyone. Couple and triples openly fornicate, howling passions that echo from sacred pinnacles. Others lie on the floor, empty bottles tilted in their grasp. Others prop against walls, eyes half closed, glazed. Above them, various sayings and symbols spray-painted in lime green, neon orange, darkest black.

Dumbfounded, he wonders that the people have been allowed to do such damage. He steps over outstretched limbs, inert and motionless. A fair number of Imperium soldiers occupy the place, some dancing, or snorting, or openly having sex. Others lay comatose on white marble as oblivious to their surroundings as their surroundings are to them.

Jonas waves away an offered bottle, then watches his step to avoid the tangle of limbs and drunks.

A hand grasps his arm, and he spins to look into a woman's face. Her smile is gorgeous, alluring. Sandalwood and marijuana reach his nostrils. She offers a joint that Jonas waves away. "I was just saying how no one here is my type," she says, eyes glazed, smile gleaming through soft ruby lips, full and moist. She regards him for a second, dark eyes tracing his form. Her tongue glides over sensuous lips. "I think *you're* my type." She steps close enough that he smells the mint on her breath.

"I'm not interested, ma'am," he says. "Just here to do a job."

She presses closer, traces his chest with a sultry finger. "Like him," she says, glancing to the right. Jonas follows her eyes to another Imperium officer lying unconscious on white marble. "I'm free tonight," she says. Dark eyes lock as breasts struggle against a bustier of red leather. "By free, I mean complimentary. As in, free of charge. Everything's covered by the emperor."

Visions of his wife bloom. This woman has the same complexion, the same naughty smirk. "C'mon," she says, ignoring his protests, pushing close to whisper in his ear. "Don't be shy. We'll find a nice corner and I'll warm you up." Her lips tickle his neck. "Then, I'll cool you down."

Jonas gulps and follows as Seventh Sunday wafts through open clerestory windows. Emotion grips the Temple as the guitar pleads, holding each note long and rapturous. Fear, longing, desire, heartbreak, the singer croons a sultry voice as string and key duel melodies that intertwine, compliment, race away, rejoin.

> *Such brilliant bulbs—how long so dead?—turn*
> *   chambers rank and cold.*
> *As I embrace a wretched fate,*
> *and stare at walls of mold.*
> *Oh savaged heart, oh wasted dreams, now dry within*
> *   my breast.*
> *As I lament my wasted years,*
> *and lay the thing to rest.*
> *Each fuse is crusted, blown apart,*
> *fragments on the floor.*
> *As I alone seek grace's face and pound on heaven's*
> *   door.*
> *Each fuse is crusted, blown apart,*
> *crumbs upon the floor.*

*As I alone seek saving grace and plead at heaven's
door.*

She pulls him along. A good way to blend, he thinks. This woman may be able to answer some questions.

They pass a woman bent at the waist gripping the marbled base of a massive stone angel whose wings stretch to support the Temple's vast ceiling. A man stands behind her, thrusting, eyes half-shut, rolled upward. Her moans are muted by another man who steps forward and guides her head to his crotch.

"Anything goes tonight," the woman walking next to him says, eyes glazed. "And I have to say, until you walked in, I didn't think I'd find anyone to suit me." She giggles. "But you'll do just fine. You see, when I'm free of charge, I'm free to choose. And *you* will do just fine." A syringe appears and she twirls it before her eyes, hypnotized by the amber liquid within. "I'm happy to share, too," she says. "Might put you in a better mood…one that's more fun." She leans against a wall of white marble scrawled with graffiti, then tightens a rubber tourniquet around her arm. "You do me. Then, I'll do you." Her smile is mischievous, so close to that of his wife.

He looks for the exit. In the near distance, there's a doorway covered by a thick drape. "Not interested," he says, stepping toward the thick fabric. "Have a nice evening."

She stops him with a firm grip, spins him toward her. "Not in there." She flicks her eyes to a sign taped to the wall. "No one goes in there." The sign resembles the one he'd seen on the altar, scrawled letters in blood red. ENTER AND DIE.

Jonas examines the thick fabric, a trained eye looking for signs of traps or other dangers. "What's in there?"

Her face blanches for a second, then becomes relaxed and serene. She pushes the plunger, her words trail, slurred. "You don't want that. Any who go, don't come out." Dark eyes dim as the drug seeps. "We tied a rope to one guy, waited five minutes, tugged out a corpse." She moves close, presses hands to his chest, lips close to his ear. "We can do whatever you want," she whispers. "Right here. In the Temple. So naughty. No one minds. I'm free tonight. Get to choose. Who I want, who I don't." She laughs, purrs, cups Jonas's crotch. "This emperor is the shit."

CHAPTER 30

JERUSALEM, ISRAEL

Tires squeal, a smoked fog, an acrid scent of molten rubber.

"Buckle in! Hold on!" Rhyme yells, glancing in the rear where Mr. Lee attends to an obtunded Emery. "Is he hurt?"

Houdini pokes his head over the seat toward the front as Lee does a quick exam. "Don't look like it."

Stuart sits in the passenger's seat, gripping the holy shit bar as they fishtail out of the alley. Rhyme presses the accelerator to max as she squints into the night.

"There's a short cut," Stuart says. "Turn left. Here!"

Rhyme takes the truck through a turn so sharp it feels like they'll tip over. Strewn on the ground to their right, a chain link fence piled with coiled razor wire. "What happened there?"

"That's the prison. Wrecked during the attack. I think the PM escaped from there. According to your friends, anyway. Turn right at the next street."

Rhyme slows, checks the rearview, sees flashing blue light on city walls. "They're coming, but I don't think they've seen us."

Tires shrieking, she takes the turn, then straightens the truck with a jerk and stomps the pedal. "Buckle him in, Lee."

"You drive like crazy lady."

"I'll keep it straight! Get him buckled."

Stuart leans forward, peers through the windshield as bright light flashes the cabin. "Helicopter!" he yells. "Got us in their sights! You better go faster!"

Her mind fills with the sparks and ground metal of their last escape. This has to go better. Can't get caught. Cain's done forgiving.

She thinks of the newscast. EMPRESS KIDNAPPED. FIFTY MILLION REWARD. Thinks of her husband's command: *Kill them all.*

In the rearview, Emery's head bobs with each wiggle of the steering wheel.

What will he do to Emery? What's he already done to Emery?

"Right! Here!" Stuart yells.

They skid into an alley and send a dumpster spinning as she hammers the gas. Too much risk. Even if Emery's immortal, Cain will make him suffer, make him suffer more than he's done already.

"Look out!" Stuart shouts. At the alley's end, fifty feet, closing fast, cars cross in irregular intervals.

"Left or right?"

"Left!"

They explode onto the street, smash a small sedan and send it rolling to crash through a storefront.

"Sorry!" Rhyme yells, stomping the gas as the rearview fills with flashing blue. Two Imperium vehicles fall in behind them.

Stuart uses the side mirror to peer behind. "Those weapons are turret mounted! If they hit us, it's game over."

"Not gonna happen!" Fingers grip the wheel, steer the truck through loose zigzags. "How far to the Temple?"

"A few more blocks. Five minutes, maybe. Less, the way you're driving." His Walther rises. "Are you prepared to fight?" he asks. "To die?"

"It won't come to that. When we get to the Temple, Igneus will protect us. We just have to get there."

A shower of glass explodes from the rear. "What!" Lee cries, then brushes glass from Emery, unbuckles him and pulls him down. "They shoot at us!"

"I know!" Rhyme yells. "Stay down. We got this."

"Left!" Stuart yells.

She grips the wheel, pulls hard, sends Houdini, Lee and Emery to pile on one another.

"Easy!" Lee yells.

"Up there! Watch it!"

The view ahead is nothing but brake lights, nothing but stopped cars. Past that, a line of Imperium vehicles, mounted cannons all point at the speeding, stolen truck.

Kill them all.

Beyond, the Temple glows in neon. Search lights swerve through a clouded sky.

"Hold on!" Rhyme yells, lowering her head as far as possible. She twists the wheel, hears Stuart yell, "Oh! Oh! Oh!" Then they're on the sidewalk, blazing past stopped cars as blurred faces stare, as parking meters pummel the sides and spin behind.

A telltale flash warns—the muzzle flash of weapons.

There's a curt pop. Rhyme tenses. Bullets pock the metal as the truck whips back and forth.

Stuart leans forward, tries to compress his bulk into the smallest possible space. "They mean business," he says. "You better think of something."

The truck sways, not responding as well as it did even seconds ago. "They got a tire," she says. "But we're still moving. They'll have to do better."

Then she feels the heat.

"Fire!" Stuart yells, head craned toward the back. "Did they get the gas tank?"

"If they did, we'd be dead," she says. "Maybe—"

The helicopter appears before them, flames stream from a turret on its nose.

"You've got to be kidding."

"They mounted a flamethrower?"

Rhyme scans the road ahead. Imperium picked the perfect spot, a perfect bottleneck without road or alley. Ahead, the helicopter sweeps flames in a quick burst.

"They're letting you know they can get us," Stuart says. "That there's nowhere left to run."

"Then I guess we'll see how well this thing burns!" In the rearview, she can't see Emery or Lee, but imagines them both hunkered on the floor, piled on Houdini. She does the math. No apparent advantages, but disadvantages pile like Legos.

Maybe the truck can take the flame. Maybe it can handle a few seconds of intense heat.

They race toward the helo, an enraged hornet with a fiery snout.

The thought hits her like a blow to the stomach.

Will her husband fry them all? Will he kill her and cover it up? Do even worse to Emery? Blame it on someone else in order to achieve his goals?

Kill them all. The words bounce through every synapse. She's surprised by her own shock, surprised how little Cain cares for any of them.

Thoughts sizzle, too many to count, let alone consider.

Her right foot presses the gas, her left hovers above the brake. Only a few seconds left to decide: stop or go? It's that simple.

Is this where we see if Emery's immortal?

Is it worth the risk?

If we stop, what happens next?

Stuart will be killed. Lee too. After that, who's left? Cain will twist the narrative and ensnare them yet again.

Stuart grips the dash, his expression set to meet his fate.

Decision made, she stomps the gas. This is her last opportunity to rid her life of Cain, her last desperate attempt to escape. Flames bloom ahead, a roiling stream fifty meters long like a furious wave.

Rhyme drifts left, then right, testing what remains of the steering.

The stream is thin but focused. If she can get them guessing which way she's going to zig, she may be able to zag at the last second and avoid the worst of the blast.

Take the chance, she thinks as they rocket toward the stream, a single second away. "Get ready!" She braces for heat, braces for death.

Flames squish the truck's windows like car wash pads.

Lee screams as fiery fingers lap through the smashed rear window.

A second later, they're through, and Stuart's voice joins hers in a raucous whoop.

"Lee, you okay?"

"Singed," he replies, slapping flames from burning seats. "Okay though. Emery too, I think." Houdini pops up, apparently unharmed.

Take that, Cain. I'll die before I come back.

Then, the shooting starts.

***

The truck lurches and squeals. Metal scrapes.

Rounds shred the roof.

The steering worsens.

The helicopter returns, keeping pace, above and slightly behind.

Rhyme wrenches the wheel. Thoughts fill with Emery's death, his bullet riddled body. Then, Stuart's lifeless eyes gazing at nothing. She thinks of Lee's kindness. Then, the martial prowess he'd displayed at the restaurant.

Guilt fills in nauseating spasms.

Gas pedal slammed, they streak down the road, toward the Temple and the surrounding barricade.

A harsh pop says another tire's blown.

She's frantic, searching for something, anything. A place to hide, an alley, a store window, anything at all.

"Look out!" Stuart's eyes are locked ahead.

Igneus steps into the road. Before their eyes, he raises his stick. Behind him, the Temple strobes neon as giant spotlights sweep the sky.

Rhyme slams the brakes, skids sideways. Lee cries out as they all lurch forward.

The helicopter whistles past, then turns so abruptly, the rotors loom like a vertical saw blade about to slice them to death.

Then, an explosion of light; blinding, immense, intense, raging through Jerusalem.

Teeth rattle, eyes go wide as the helicopter becomes a rain of flaming debris.

Rhyme looks to Stuart. A small gash drips blood down his temple. "You okay?"

"Yep." He stares at the emaciated man in the road's center, watches as Igneus obliterates the chasing vehicles.

Fire yellow lights up Rhyme's face. She ducks instinctively, checks the mirror for what's left of their pursuers. "Lee, you okay? How's Emery? How's Houdini?"

Lee's head pops over the seat. "We okay. I think, we okay." He struggles, hefts Emery from the floorboard onto the back seat. "He don't look hurt," he says. "No burn."

Rhyme unbuckles, then notices her hands numb and trembling. She exits, moves to the back seat and examines Emery. "It's okay," she sighs. "He's okay."

Sebastian appears, looks somehow different from the boy he was before. Like he's aged. Like everything he's endured has finally caught up. Igneus appears next to him. "Anyone hurt?" the child asks.

"I don't think so," Rhyme says. "Unless you count the paper cut on Stuart's forehead."

Stuart grins as tension deflates. His hands visibly tremble, and he stuffs them in his pockets.

"Stay here," Igneus says. "All of you." He turns to the child. "Come, Sebastian."

"Don't leave," Rhyme blurts. Her voice rings with a desperation she can't disguise. The Jew's their only chance, their only hope. Without him, it's back to Cain's side. "Where are you going?"

Flames shade his face, harsh lines like canyons carved by raging waters. He pauses, flicks his eyes ahead. "It's time to cleanse this Temple."

CHAPTER 31

JERUSALEM, ISRAEL

She glimmers, shines, exotic, alluring. Moist lips part above a sensuous neck, then bulging cleavage. She leans close and brushes his lips.

Jonas pulls back, presses against the marble, tries to remember the last time he kissed a woman.

She grips his crotch and he is inflamed.

Just this once. Can't be so bad to have a little fun. He grows dazed, entranced by the crowd, their lack of inhibitions, as if he's shared their drugs and imbibed without thought to consequence.

She presses close, gives his crotch another squeeze. "Feels like I'm talking you into it."

Dark eyes stare back as awkwardness rises. He pushes away. "This isn't me," he says. "Not with a—." The words clog in his throat.

"What? A call girl?" she says. "A hooker?" She chuckles, seems undaunted, not insulted. "I'm not a hooker." She mews, presses, squeezes. "Not tonight."

Her eyes turn contemplative, as if considering some new idea. "Can't we just be two people tonight? Pretend fate pushed us together?" She turns those twinkling eyes back to him; her voice tempts. "Can we do that? Just for tonight? In the morning, we'll part with fond memories."

Her expression is curious. One of longing but melted like candle wax. She oozes desire, radiates like a furnace. But not for sex, he thinks, for something more, something real and valuable. A union, a longing for something that matters in a world where nothing does.

He pulls her close, and she presses against him. "Is this enough?"

She sobs quietly, the party girl gone. A call girl replaced by a living, pulsing human who craves nothing more than closeness, than emotion, the slightest brush of precarious attachment.

Jonas feels her racing heart, her breath in quivering spasms. Despite her choices, anything else she's done, in her heart she wants connection, perhaps some empathy, some compassion, the closeness of souls.

They sway as music drifts melancholy over graffiti and littered debris. Two strangers enwrapped as death lurks behind a curtain a few meters away.

Mascara streaks her cheeks when she raises her eyes, leans forward, gives a gentle, lingering kiss. "Thank you," she says, wiping her tears. "What I sought, you gave." She looks abashed. "Seems the best gifts are free."

His grin turns grim. He can feel it, unsure of her words' full meaning.

Before he can parse it out, voices rise from outside in a raucous cheer, excited, joyous, amped.

"The music stopped," he says. "What's going on?"

The answer comes in soothing tenor. "Welcome! Is everyone having fun!"

She pulls away, stares at the Temple door. "It's Longinus! They said he was coming but I didn't believe it." Her face flushes. She wipes her eyes, pulls a tissue from somewhere, dabs her makeup. "How do I look?"

Her face is streaked lines and powdered clumps. "A trip to the bathroom probably wouldn't hurt."

Her expression falls, and she looks a bit panicked. "There's no bathroom here." Frantic eyes scurry as if one will materialize. "Oh God, do I look *that* bad?" She smooths her bustier, runs a nervous hand over her abdomen. "I *can't* look *that* bad. This is horrible. He pays so well. I can't let him see me like this, can't miss this opportunity."

Longinus enters to the cheer of hundreds.

Jonas slides behind a massive statue, then peers around the base. If the Roman sees him, it'll be game on. A fight he can't allow. A fight for which he isn't prepared and probably can't win.

Then, like a torn off scab, a blistering animus fills his soul. Sima enters with sensual grace, on stilettos that lift her six inches. Pristine, white stockings climb lithe, muscular legs as crimson garters disappear beneath a plaid miniskirt. Her blouse is fishnet, her breasts barely visible. A braided leather collar circles her neck, appears to squeeze her throat as pigtails sway with each movement.

People surge forward, shouting, offering drugs, hands, bottles.

"Scotch!" Longinus bellows, then lifts a spear. Gleaming gold courses with soft aqua. The man is handsome, chiseled, slim and fit. A bottle rises from the back of the crowd, appears to levitate as it's passed to the front.

Longinus lifts it high. "Drink! And live among the good!"

Cheers erupt with a harshness that surprises.

Jonas slides back, lowers his head, struggles to control the murderous rage boiling in his heart.

Sima glances his direction, grips Longinus's hand.

Should've brought that rifle.

He thinks of Ishmael, his death at the hands of this witch. Thinks how Sebastian healed her. How she should be dead, was probably minutes from death when the child intervened.

A thought invades, blocks out the partiers, the yells, the harsh music that's restarted from the courtyard.

Even if the Roman can't die, she probably can.

An eye for an eye. Vengeance is mine. Words that gouge furrows in his heart.

Longinus takes a long pull of liquor, then taps the spear on the marble floor.

The relic rises, spins slowly on its axis as aqua rays fill the Temple.

The Roman's a superstar, an A-list celebrity surrounded by fans.

Jonas presses to the marble, fights to control a tsunami of rage. *Now's not the time. Don't be foolish. Pick your battle.* Words he'd said to Laslo, words he should heed himself.

A hushed voice whispers in his ear. "I'll be back," the woman says, then pushes into the mass and disappears.

Voices rise in a cacophony, male and female, hands popping like kids in a classroom. "Me!" they yell. "No, me!"

"You," Longinus points to a voluptuous blond. "And you." A freckled female with a gawky gait. "And you." A whoop goes up as the woman who just left Jonas sweeps behind Longinus to join the others.

Three men lug a massive round ottoman to the Temple's center. Jonas cranes, looks for a clear path to the exit. Longinus grins and motions Sima, who crawls on the cushion like a cat intent on a nap. Side tables appear, then thick rugs in swirling patterns. Then, dozens of pillows in all shapes and sizes. The Roman slides next to Sima and accepts a small bottle filled with white powder. He pops the lid with his thumb, tips back his head and sucks the contents into his nose with a loud snort.

Aqua eyes dilate. Eyebrows rise as lips part. He pulls Sima atop and motions the others close.

The throng closes around them, blocking Jonas's vision.

Time to go, he thinks, fighting the urge to attack. *Not the time. Pick your field.*

A guitar wails from the courtyard as he steps down from the marble base. Drums thrum a rhythm like striking every skin at once. The singer shrieks, high-pitched, unintelligible, rough and loud. Seventh Sunday's switched to pure metal.

Head low, Jonas pushes past the dozens, the hundreds, more who enter the Temple, seem crazed to be near the Roman and his entourage.

Sliding past a young couple, he's ten feet from the exit when a shout stops him. "Legionnaire! Halt!"

He freezes, turns. The crowd parts. Thick rays stripe them blue.

The Roman abandons the cushioned throne, stands stoic like the stone angels around him. "Dear Jonas, how nice of you to join us."

People press against the walls. The woman who was with Jonas huddles near Sima, tracing her lips with a delicate finger.

Jonas hopes he looks bold as he watches the Roman raise the Scotch and chug, liquor dripping from his chin. He wipes a perfect face with the back of his hand, then rattles the walls with a belch. "I'm glad ye came," he says. "'Tis a good chance to settle things."

Sima squirms on the ottoman. Holding Jonas's eyes, she smiles like a barfly on a tempting morsel. Her hand rubs the spot where she'd been skewered.

"'Tis for honor," Longinus says. "To the death." His grin's malicious, his eyes steaming with cinders of vengeance, with portions of malice.

Jonas watches as the woman takes Sima in a lingering kiss. "No spear," he says. "No sword. No guns. No knives. Just us."

Longinus's laughter is elegant, pleasing to the ears. "Where's the fun in that? Have you no sense of sport?" He grips the sword's pommel as eyes flick to the spear hovering eight feet above the crowd.

"Tell you what—" Longinus says, then motions almost imperceptibly. The spear drifts to spin a foot from Jonas's nose.

"What's a gladiator without a weapon?" the Roman says. "What's a fight without steel, eh?" He scratches his chin as if contemplating. A broad smile appears. He bows and sweeps an elegant arm. "Do me the honor of wielding the spear as I wield me sword. Then, we'll see what's anon and agin." Blue eyes flash. "After all, 'tis only sporting."

Jonas unbuttons his blouse and lets it drop. He unstraps the pistol and lets it fall too. He thinks of Ishmael dying in his arms, of his last words, the bitter loss. *See ya, hooligan.*

Before him the spear spins, a kaleidoscope of sizzling lines, crimson, gold, aqua. He reaches and grasps the relic. Then voltage like a live wire, a donkey kick to the chest, ripping straight through him.

Breath races away. His head spins, throbs, pulses. He tries to kneel, realizes he's no longer upright but crunched at the base of a cold marble wall. His abdomen aches, an electric current that makes his fingers tingle.

Visions swarm: a desert, some tents, a lad. He shudders, tries to focus, can't.

The sword rings hollow as Longinus pulls it from its scabbard, swings it as easily as if it's an appendage. He grins and takes another pull of scotch. "Perfect, lad. Just perfect."

Valley of Elah, Near Bethlehem,
Israel, 1020 BC

A harsh sun drips molten rays on tents of all colors: a makeshift city, born in a few days, erected on rock, verdant plain, spreading like lichen across the whole valley.

Two armies mass, yet neither attacks. For days, they stare, taunt, wait, face off.

A giant strides down an angled green slope, then lopes over a collection of smooth boulders. He moves to the center of the quarter mile that separates the armies. Sun glimmers from untarnished armor.

"Who will face me?" he shouts. "From your cowardly horde, who will stand as champion?"

Men cringe and lower their heads, disguising their fear. There's a shuffling sound as many step back. Before them, a king watches the colossus in silence.

He stands, breathes silent thanks that his legs yet have strength despite the rigors of age. "Is there no one?" the king asks. "Do we have no champion?"

Silent men stare at their feet, some step farther away.

An advisor speaks. "They possess an unfair advantage, Sire. Who among us can best that warrior?"

The king takes him in, small of stature, pointed nose crooked above fat lips that continue to flap.

"Might I suggest a different course?" the man says. "Send a

champion as a decoy, then attack with the full might of our army. The surprise will set them on their back foot, and if we're quick and decisive, our disadvantage becomes our advantage. Who among us is fleet of foot? Who can battle this giant and evade his might while we reposition our men? With all eyes locked on the duel, a small force will go unnoticed and can easily flank our enemy."

King Saul stares upon him. "Tell me counselor, how many will die? How many graves we will dig for our countrymen?"

The man lowers and bows slightly. "Some will die, my lord, but better than losing the entire battle."

A bellowing laugh rolls over them, whittling the combined fears of their army into pointed barbs.

The king looks at his men. "There must be one," he mutters. "Must be someone to take this challenge."

"I'll go." A lad pushes through, a boy not out of his teens.

Silence permeates as everyone stares, then laughter rises to a burning sky.

"You are not a warrior," King Saul says. "You look like a shepherd. Do you seek death or glory?"

The lad takes a knee and bows his head. "I seek only the health of our people and an end to this day. I seek only the will of God and His blessings on our land."

Saul snickers, then moves to the lad and places a hand on his shoulder. "No, lad. I can't allow it. Why…if you…" he sighs, averts his eyes for a second. "It will be a massacre. You cannot stand against this foe."

The lad keeps his head down, speaks softly. "Of course, Sire. Perhaps you'll find someone more suitable from the other volunteers?"

A quiet gasp erupts. The lad's stated the problem in a deft way. "Of course, of course," the king says, chuckling as he watches the pacing giant taunt from the broad valley. "Your words are jest yet shame my army and expose their cowardice." He scans those around him and looks disappointed. "Aye, your counsel is wise." He paces to the edge of the tent, leans against a pole, then watches the giant roar from the battlefield. "For ten days has he taunted. For ten days has he shamed."

The king turns and motions. "Rise, lad. Face me like a warrior. Let me favor you with some counsel." He looks the lad up and down. "Respect your life and know your limits." With a gentle hand he turns the lad to face the giant. "See how he moves. How he paces. That warrior will make quick work of you."

"Still, I'll go," the lad interrupts. "I do not fear him. He's a braggart and overconfident. But I am a servant of God and shall show this heathen the power of His might."

"You're a shepherd!" the king laughs. "A mere boy! Nothing more! How can you defeat such a foe? I admire your bravery, son. I do. But I can't let you waste your life on a fool's wager."

"Who else then?" The lad holds Saul's eyes with a boldness seldom seen.

The king blinks at the question, then returns to his throne and grasps a goblet from a small wooden table. He pauses for a long moment. "Very well," he sighs. "If God demands trust and obedience, then you will be my champion."

Murmurs of protest rise from the others, yet none step forward.

"Get him armor!" the king bellows. "And weapons!"

The advisor leans close, talks fast. "Sire you can't. He'll surely lose, then—"

"Silence, fool! My mind's set."

Armor bearers make haste and soon return with all that's asked.

"Dress him," the king says.

"Sire?" The lad stares at the heavy armor. "I can't bear that weight, nor am I trained in the art of sword or spear. I will go as I am."

"With only a staff? With only your tunic? Nonsense, lad. I can't send you like a lamb to the slaughter. You must have support."

"As I offer my life in your service, allow *me* to choose my own armaments."

From the battlefield a thundering bass. The giant taunts, paces, armor gleams broad rays that glisten invincible.

The king stares for moments, then finally waves a hand. "I might be daft, lad, but something about you prickles." He pauses, scans the lad's slim form. "I wish I believed as fervently. If you—" He stops, chuckles, becomes serious. *"When* you return, you'll be richly rewarded."

The lad bows. "My reward is service to God and king."

"Then drink! Share my cup as we toast your bravery."

The lad accepts, takes a sip, then returns it to the king who drinks as well. "Go," the king says. "Find your duty, in this life or the next."

The lad steps on the battlefield. The giant roars. *"This* is your champion! A boy! Is this a sign of the Jew's bravery? This, this *boy.* The best you can muster!" A riot of laughter as the giant slaps his knee and wipes his eyes.

David reaches into a pouch on his waist, pulls a strand of cord and ties it to a notch on the end of his staff. He eyes his opponent, looks for weakness where none can be found.

The giant shimmers as if his very skin is gilded metal. A broad helmet sits atop his head, conical, gleaming, spackled with rubies and sapphires. Broad strips run down either side to cover his massive face and jaw. He seems unaffected by the heat, stands huge, a statue twinkling beneath a blistering sun.

The lad reaches in his pouch, pulls a thin, smooth stone.

The giant's shout is as harsh as the steaming landscape of rock and dirt. "A sling! The tool of a shepherd!" Laughter rolls to the sky. "They send a shepherd when a warrior is called. Very well, boy. Come and die."

David places the stone, then runs the sling's untied end down the staff's length where he grips it tight to the rough wood. In a well-practiced motion, he rotates until it spins like a buzzsaw.

The giant's expression turns serious. Then, with a cry like thunder, he sprints, a raging behemoth, covering yards with each step.

David trembles but wills himself to stand firm, reaching to a God he knows is there.

The sling whistles, whirs.

The giant rages forward, as big as a chariot and just as fast.

A hundred feet gets halved, then quartered as the giant rushes, sword poised, face creased with fury and terror.

The stone flies.

The giant takes three jilted strides.

Then, a steaming dust rises.

No noise is heard, no clash of armor or wails of battle.

A breeze rushes dust into the desert.

The giant lies at David's feet, a stone crushed into his massive forehead.

The dust settles.

The breeze disappears.

The army roars delight.

CHAPTER 32

JERUSALEM, ISRAEL

Igneus's staff. Like the dream, the etchings. Jonas grins, has no idea why the images came and doesn't care. He feels emboldened, invincible.

"Whoo!" Longinus screams. "That's a hot one!" The Roman whoops and pours more scotch in his mouth. "She's a tad frisky at first. Take a tick and try again."

Jonas rises to trembling knees, tries to slide a foot in front and gain his feet.

Dizziness overwhelms as nausea rises. Vision glows in aqua and crimson, lines that sizzle with gold, blinding and powerful.

Around him, bystanders shimmy like rising heat.

Then she's there, helping him to his feet, propping him against the wall. "Quit," she whispers. "Leave. There's no shame."

Seventh Sunday continues to rail from the courtyard. The beat is frantic. Guitars wail as drums hammer to match his throbbing head like a hive of hornets.

He manages to stand, sees Longinus pacing, sword swishing, liquor held in his other hand.

Jonas steps, wavers. Vision returns to something close to normal.

Flames of rage cut through the fog. His temples throb, his feet feel numb and heavy.

"Yes, take a tick or two," the Roman says. "Get your wits, then see what's anon."

The spear hovers elegant, inches from his grasp. Crystal and crimson race, fuse, collide.

"Ye think a trade?" the Roman says. "I use the spear? You take me sword?"

Jonas reaches out, prepared this time. He's held the spear before. Had thrown it at Sima and pierced her chest. None of this occurred then. It was just a regular javelin.

Jonas raises a tentative hand, ignores the Roman's taunts, grasps the spear anew.

This time, there's no pain, no donkey kick.

"She's temperamental, lad. Takes a bit to warm her up."

Jonas turns to the woman. Her eyes betray fear, even concern. "Leave. Now," she whispers.

"Stay clear," he says. "And get out of here first chance."

She swallows hard and steps back. "Be careful."

Jonas chuckles, *great advice.* He holds the spear before him, tests its heft and balance, spins it once, twice, then levels it at the giant.

Longinus's grin is as elegant as his body.

He thinks I'm easy work, thinks this will be quick. Eyebrows crinkle as a snarl appears. *I've beat him once; I can do it again.* He glances at Sima, curled like a cat. Soon, he thinks, very soon will she taste my vengeance.

The crowd presses against the walls, bottles, syringes, lovers, held loosely as eyes pine for battle, for blood, for barbarity. This is the new coliseum, privy only to those who seek its vices. Drugs, alcohol, flesh, all easily grasped in this Temple.

Jonas steps forward. "Let's get on with it."

Longinus's grin grows wide. "Let's do."

Chapter 33

This place bristles; vibrant, opalescent. Red and yellow, subtle orange, pearl, onyx; shimmering, sliding.

I'm not numb, not unaware. Consciousness hovers, floats, teeters on the slick edge between reality and something else, something all-consuming, something awesome.

Then, fear. Terror with spiked intent. My skin prickles as all thought shatters.

The shimmering shaft goes dark, transparent, a tunnel without form or edge.

"Relax," a voice says, "you've seen His version, now let me show you mine."

A dark angel rises, beautiful, majestic. Glimmering wings fuse shadow with scarlet to slide down steely feathers and meld to the very notion of flame.

"Iblis?"

"Of course," he says, as we float down the fantastic tunnel.

Shadows speed past, a vapor that flings an icy chill to condense on my face. Then we dive, rocket downward as darkness becomes streaming, wailing haze.

"I've been here before," I say. "I saw a war in Heaven."

"Ah, yes, with the Apostle," he says. "Lies, lies, all of it lies. He made you think *we* were the aggressors, that we battled because of base desires. Vanity and pride."

We stream through a cavernous expanse, blaze past mountain peaks leaving a slick fog in our wake. Diving through chasms that seem bottomless, my shrieks rise above the flapping of wing and the guttural wails of grinning demons who watch from hidden perches. Terrific eyes pierce the gloom, watching as we streak past.

Exploding into an underground expanse, we stream over a sea of foaming, rolling liquid that puffs great smoky pillows into the atmosphere. Massive dark walls shimmy with flickering flame and dripping shadow as we stream inches above the decrepit ocean.

Iblis rises high, spins a single time then rockets straight into the roiling waters, plunging us through noxious waves that absorb our speed with no more than a ripple.

My mind floats on spiral tides, helixes of time and space.

My father holds my hand, helps me atop a pony. He turns and smiles. Then his face melts to flame and bone, becomes a grinning skeleton with hollow sockets.

I yelp and avert my gaze.

"Only the bold can abide these visions," Iblis says.

I've nothing to prove, I think. No need to see what horrors await.

Eyes burn as I squeeze them tight. We streak forward, downward, deeper into a thick canvas of bruised purple and aqua.

Sizzling terror assaults as burning eyes are forced open, as fists clench and teeth grind. I resist, staring boldly, foolishly, as children rise, then burst aflame on howls and squeals.

Great fiery clouds ravage distant cities and raze the landscape with horrific explosions. Rounded mushrooms rise, bloom, and spread death. The landscape goes barren, becomes cragged and harsh, as skyscrapers collapse in great plumes of dust and rubble.

People pour into the streets only to be vaporized. Their skin puckers, blisters, peels away in slow motion. Burning muscle turns to ash, is stripped from bone. They are skeletons, somehow still moving, still running, shrieks pealing from open mandibles that turn to dust and drift away on flaming winds.

I cry out, bite my tongue. Staring hard, forcing courage.

Flames rise, buildings smolder. Death rules a barren landscape once vital, once teeming with life. The stars and stripes flutters past like paper, its edges black and jagged.

Then, Carter's Glen, the shitty apartment, awash in flame.

The laundromat, demolished.

The pizza joint, a husk of embers.

A few humans drift past with zombie eyes. Their skin is molten, mottled from extreme heat, extreme radiation, plodding aimless, neither seeking nor showing recognition.

Some drop and flail, then lie still. Others amble toward some unknown goal.

A woman appears, kneels, starts to weep. She turns her face to the sky as tears stream in thick black lines.

"Rhyme!" I choke on the sight.

She cradles my head in her lap, wails her anguish to the annihilated town.

I'm horribly burnt. Clothes, melted, charred, as blackened flesh bubbles. My right arm is missing at the elbow, my face, frozen in death, twisted to an expression of unbridled horror and the menace of sheer terror.

From somewhere deep, I groan. "Yes," Iblis says, "don't give in. Only death awaits."

I squeeze my eyes, inhale something akin to rotted chicken and kitty litter. The odor overwhelms, assaults like I've devoured it whole. Visions become slim fragments, turn to ash as my stomach churns, as bile rises to burn my throat.

We slip through the bottom of the horrible ocean, then blaze across another dark cavern. Below us, the abyss stirs, flickers, opens its eyes to gaze upon us. I gaze back, see fire, desperation, heartlessness, malice. A steaming whirlpool of deceit, of avarice. I know these as emotions, conditions, but the images brand on my psyche and defy all other descriptors. I see them, know them, am them.

I screech as we rocket downward.

Iblis swoops down, pauses for a second before dropping me atop a rocky ledge.

I struggle to stand, to shake off the visions. "She's alright," I whisper to myself. "A dream, that's all. Not real, not real. Rhyme's alright."

Iblis regards me like a crimson messiah. Watches me tremble, cough, vomit as shadowed features flicker vicious intent. He points to the sky.

Above, a glistening ripple of cloud and vapor. Golden hues overwhelmed by deepest shadow. The bronze of dawn, the silver of stars, flaring for the briefest second, then foaming to abstract, to intangible. Angry clouds rage and roll, fight the light, reflect, refract, pollute, make barren.

I glance at him, then back to the sky.

"A few seconds more," he says. Then, "There I am."

Lucifer, the Archangel I'd witnessed, wages war on heaven, blazes through rippling clouds. Suddenly, with a flash and sizzle, he falls, unconscious, wings shivering, shuddering with the speed of descent.

"Is that—?"

"Keep watching."

I fix my gaze on the massive, gorgeous angel as he streams through bruised clouds.

He gleams gold, a brilliance that's consumed by increments.

Brows furl, become thick, as chiseled, radiant features turn blistered and red. Feathers gleam a kaleidoscope, then sparkle and become leathery like a pterodactyl.

He sizzles past, then disappears into the great chasm.

I look up to see another angel, and still another, until they're falling like hell's raindrops.

Gorgeous faces turn, become intense, insane, enraged. Features twist, deform. Brilliant eyes go dull, then blaze as if fire burns at their very heart. Wings, grand and gorgeous, get stripped of elegance to reflect only darkness, only death, as resplendent feather becomes oily scale.

Millions stream past, fall for endless minutes. Tendrils of smoke stream like tails from a kite, like vapor from a jet.

The sky blisters and crackles. Flames trace the face of blazing thunderheads, lightning sizzles in a sudden downpour.

Then, above the clouds, past the flaming stew, I see a reflection and movement.

Two men, hands joined, wondering, watching.

It's me and John, gazing through a strained veil of fused gold and raging darkness.

The apostle turns, says something, then we both disappear to a radiance beyond the gloom.

I remember, then. Waking in the hospital, the home audience, Vince and Lenny, the limo ride, Longinus's sword at my throat, Rhyme pleading for my life. Images that flicker and flip like a high speed slide show.

"You see?" Iblis says. "Cross God, and that's what happens. No discussion, no credit given for past works, just ejection, just banishment. Ejaculated into the depths. Spit from His mouth as lukewarm. You get the drift." He moves to the edge, peers into the blackness. "Cain and I are alike in that way. Punishments that don't fit the crimes. But still, there's more to the story. It seems I wasn't exactly helpless. Like Cain, I had limits to my prison. I'd been sacked on a heavenly scale, banned from Eden, from paradise, from the place I once ruled and protected. Humiliating, it was, and I the grandest, the strongest of all angels, discarded like dirty tissue." Features bloom as a fiendish smile stretches his cheeks. "But I had other plans. A vengeance meant to resonate through all time. To shake the pillars of His kingdom and turn it to rubble." He turns from the abyss, wears an expression of contempt. "Jinn are born of fire. You'd think God would remember that."

Great wings spread to their fullest measure. "What a slap in the face! To me, to my people. We sought only to serve. To be His pleasure, His right hand, was our purest desire. Yet we were cast aside for a bag of bulging poop. A pulsing, living, sac of unpotable pustulence.

"I'm punished for pride and vanity, yet God was so pleased with Himself and His creation, Adam, that He threw us all aside, then commanded us to bow." He sniffs, raises his head in a regal way. "Jinn don't bow. That's how God made us. He knew we wouldn't. He knew there'd be a war.

"And there was! But not much of one really. God's tough to beat, but His mistake rallied our convictions. Made us turn on that which He created and stymie their every move while visiting our wrath upon them."

He stares at the roiling heavens, pauses for a moment. "No man knows the mind of God." He scoffs, then hikes a thumb at his chest. "Except *this* angel. This *Satan*, this *genie*. Not everything goes God's way, you know. You'll soon see, soon understand how I gained the upper hand. Everything that's happening is because of me, proves my greatness, my resolve, my perfection. Soon, very soon," he says, "the time will come."

He steps back and squeals into his fist. "I sound deliciously evil, don't I?" He winks. "I'm not though. I remain only a quintessential victim of circumstance. The acceptable loss. Collateral damage, as they say. But I assure you, my intent was, and *is*, pure.

"You see, to us, nothing that befalls man is a sin or a tragedy. A benefit of immortality is that one gets to view everything through a different lens. You're newly immortal, someday you'll come to the same conclusion. Man is the ultimate selfish ass. Every thought, given only to comfort, to pleasure, to *needs*. A universal expectation really, an assumption that every being *thinks* just like them."

Stepping close, he leans in. "But *we* are Jinn. *Think* like Jinn. Exist on a level where death and misery doesn't affect us. The life of a man, seventy or eighty years, is nothing to us. But Man thinks it's the end all and be all and that, thusly, everyone functions to please only them, to serve only them, to mourn only them." He scoffs again, bright fangs burning through lips that snarl in shadow. "God wasted His dirt! I mean, goats would've been a better choice, or sheep, now that I think of it."

He stares over the bubbling abyss, eyes faraway. Then, that

squealing chuckle. "Look at me, going on," he says. "I do hope you'll gloss that over in your work."

I nod. "I'll do what I can, but again, I've been employed under duress and shown the most horrible visions. Do you think we can tone those down?"

Eyebrows raise as dark eyes brighten. "This is Hell, my boy. You're just starting to taste it."

CHAPTER 34

Jerusalem, Israel

Jonas closes his eyes, thinks of David and Goliath.

When he opens them, he sees Longinus, elegant and shirtless, sword held in one hand, bottle in the other, myriad scars across his torso.

The spear sizzles energy as Jonas wonders how to make it work.

Then, with a calm, deep breath, he steps forward.

They circle, begin to test as spear clangs on steel. Longinus's grin is immovable, stretched over supermodel features.

Jonas thinks of David, of impossible odds. At least Goliath was mortal.

He breathes a prayer, continues to circle, to test.

Then, Longinus leaps, sword sizzling through a razor arc as Jonas jolts back.

From outside Seventh Sunday's in full metal mode, screaming lyrics that stick and skewer.

All of us cry,
All of us die,
All of us cherish,
All of us perish,

All of us yield,
All of us wield,
All of us strike,
With pointed pikes.

A glint of steel as the sword presses. The elegant Roman is faster than his gigantic counterpart, bearing down, grin in place.

Jonas reacts, spins the spear low and sweeps his legs.

But the Roman leaps, lands like a ballerina, then lunges again with the sword.

Jonas cries out, feels a trickle of blood from his shoulder, a pain like shredded paper. He counters, spins the spear like a dervish while blocking out the raging riffs from the howling band.

Longinus is fast but small now.

Jonas considers his options, the threats around him. A plan forms.

He looks to the ottoman. Sima's gone. *Where?*

The odds skyrocket. Two to worry about now. He's not so foolish to think that she won't help Longinus if given the chance.

The Roman's fast, agile, gives Jonas the advantage of strength, *if* he can avoid the blows, *if* he can avoid injury.

Haven't done great, thus far. His shoulder warns, throbs, shrieks. He spins the spear to a streaming buzzsaw of aqua and crimson. It feels alive, fights his efforts, seems to writhe, to clunk like a bent fan.

Longinus angles, thrusts. Jonas spins through, slams the spear's blunt end into the Roman's gut, then pulls sharply with his lead hand to slam the Roman's chin.

Longinus reels, stutters back. Blood drips as Jonas presses the advantage, changing course, slapping aside a blow from the thrusted sword.

The Roman charges. His speed is off the charts. All Jonas can manage is evasion, avoidance, endless retreat from the vicious onslaught.

He presses his back to cold marble. He's distracted, not concentrating, thinking of Sima, trying to guess from where she'll attack.

The sword slides past, slices his forearm, his forehead, his right thigh. The spear clatters to the marble floor, clangs like a boxing bell.

Jonas bolts, trips, rolls, then rises and sprints for the exit.

There's a shadow, a blurred smudge. It's Sima, blocking his path, jeweled dagger drawn, delicate mouth pulled into a mischievous grin.

He hears the sword swoosh, ducks a single second before it parts his head from his neck. He rolls sideways, pops back up, faces the Roman and the spear lying behind him.

He's too fast, too accurate.

Longinus bellows a laugh. "I'm not wanting to kill an unarmed man, dear Jonas," he says. "'Tis more delicious to draw it out. No?" He tosses the sword to Jonas.

Jonas snatches the weapon from midair and sprints forward, blood flowing over his eyes, obscuring his vision, turning the world a crimson sheet. He leaps and strikes.

But Longinus is a step ahead, moves under Jonas as he flies, then heaves him upward, out of control.

A bloody smear streaks the marble as he lands to slide breathless.

A glimmer catches his eye, the spear lies inches away.

Jonas grabs it, stands, levels both sword and spear at the Roman.

Then his back sizzles, worse than before. He twists, swings wide and wild.

Sima dances away, untouched, gleeful.

Got to get out. Outnumbered, outgunned, outmatched. A no-win situation, sticking like hot tar.

He presses his back to the wall as bystanders part.

The move's instinctive and protective. If he keeps his back to the wall, it will minimize Sima's surprises and force both to attack from the front.

Longinus rubs his chin, lifts his hand, licks his own blood.

The spear hums, shivers with a scalding heat that makes it impossible to hold.

Jonas ignores the pain, grimaces as smoke rises from blanched fingers. *The giant's toying with me.*

He tries to focus, to see everything and nothing. If he concentrates on one thing for too long, he'll be blind to any other assault.

The spear trembles, jolts, singes, sears. Then, with a violent twist it breaks free and flies to Longinus.

The air sings, sizzles like hot grease, a blinding flash.

Longinus stands in his original form. The Legionnaire of old, every inch of seven feet, a Zentangle of scars puckered over a hairy rippling torso.

Glimmering teeth sparkle through a beard that wasn't there moments before.

The Roman rears as muscles ripple. Then the spear flies with the force of a missile.

Jonas dodges, feels it slice his scalp. Feels more blood trickle through his hair, further into his eyes.

Panic prods. Death looms. Cackling laughter rolls from the gathered crowd. These barbarians, these new Romans, this new coliseum.

Sima's near, he senses, knows she's lining up another blindside. He glances at the doorway and sees an open path. He sprints wild, crazed. His options have dwindled to nothing but escape. No choice. Have to sprint, have to risk another blow from the witch's dagger. A pound of flesh, the cost of escape.

The crowd parts as he rushes, screaming. Seventh Sunday rages like a gutted lion, drums like a Zulu tribe, screeches like a hunting hawk.

Jonas dives, gets a glimpse of Sima racing toward him, dagger held high, angled at his chest.

Then she slides across the floor, spread eagled, curses flowing.

Her foot stretched from the surrounding crowd, the call girl grabs everyone's attention.

Sima twists as she slides, lets the dagger fly.

Jonas's reaction is pure instinct. Lunging, he slaps the dagger a split second before it penetrates the woman's throat.

Laughter booms as the Roman stomps toward them.

Jonas thrusts her before him as they race for the door, as Sima pops up to fly after.

He wants to turn, to take the witch by surprise, end her atop the Temple's steps.

Anger flows, consumes, rises like an angry tornado, clangs through every cell, every synapse, streaks his body, flames his mind.

He grabs the girl, lifts as they sprint through the doors. They roll, entwined, a fury of arms and legs, marble stairs bruising with each bounce.

He's on his feet in an instant. From the altar, Seventh Sunday shreds.

> *To shove, to love,*
> *To wither, to fade,*
> *To feel, to rave,*
> *To try and be brave.*
> *To rest, to tarry,*
> *More burdens to carry.*
> *To live, to lie*
> *To plead, then die.*
> *To heaven? To hell?*
> *What toll? What bell?*

He feels dizzy. Can't tell if everything's red or if it's just blood. His eyes lock on the Temple doors. The crowd around him moshes, wails, grinds, ingests.

The woman struggles to her feet, stands gawking beside him.

Their hands clasp. A haze appears from within the Temple, brightens as it nears the door. Shadows flicker, become a golem's silhouette, a hulking darkness, impossibly muscled, perfect teeth glowing crimson, aqua, startling gold.

Seventh Sunday shrieks:

> *A thread so pulled.*
> *A head so filled.*

A mind so stretched.
A heart so wretched.
A world that's shattered,
for nothing that mattered.
To fawn, to flay,
To make it the day.
To rise anew,
And crow what's blue.
A God,
A cross,
Our greatest loss.
And on and on,
when comes the dawn?
And on and on,
when comes the dawn?

Jonas turns. "What's your name?"

"London," she says, eyes pasted on the Temple's entrance, the looming shadow.

"Okay, London. I have friends outside. Go there. Get them. Look for a man with a staff. Tell him Jonas needs help."

She pries her eyes from the door. "Okay," she says but doesn't move.

"Go!" Jonas says. "Be quick." She blinks, shudders, then moves into the crazed crowd.

His vision wavers as nausea and weakness pounce. His head spins. Did the spear steal my reserves? Have I lost too much blood? He wipes his face, leaves a bloody handprint on the altar's base.

Longinus saunters down the stairs, sword in scabbard, spear in hand.

Sima appears like a lingerie model.

Jonas reaches for rage, for vengeance. He remembers the gangster he killed as a lad and tries to embrace the same emotions.

Then, Ishmael's voice, loving, human. "Stand, hooligan. *Do not fall.*"

Jonas wipes blood from his eyes, then swoons and drops to a knee. He looks past the stomping giant at the real focus of his rage. Perhaps, he can play possum. When she gets close, he'll muster what strength remains and crush her larynx before the Roman finishes him.

Seventh Sunday wails:

What have you given?
What have you got?
When all your life,
has come to naught?
Join hands. Let's pray.
A waste of a day?
Then pass the plate,
to ease your fate.
A penny? A pound?
Buys nothing profound.
No joy, no zest.
You've done your best.
Let ring our cries,
while under God's eyes.
And on and on,
how far we've gone.
And on and on,
when comes the son?

The music dies, abruptly, with impact. Seventh Sunday, every single member stands on the altar above, staring at the massive Roman stomping down the stairs.

Jonas's head buzzes. Is it blood loss or a foolish attachment to consciousness?

A chill breeze rises like a zephyr. Those around him smile, observe, offer no assistance. The drip plop of his own blood can be heard as it falls to littered stone.

Longinus nears, slow and calm, grin etched. Behind him, Sima giggles.

One more step, Jonas thinks. One more step and I'll make my move. One more step and the witch will die.

Then Sima stops and props a hand on her hip.

Jonas raises his head.

Longinus fills his vision. The spear splays aqua and crimson, mingles with searching spotlights.

The new Romans cheer, wild for blood, by the drop, the stream, the gallon or ocean.

Jonas breathes a prayer, thinks of Ishmael, feels the joy of journey's end.

"I will lift up my eyes to the hills, from whence cometh my help," Ishmael whispers.

Jonas tastes blood, sways dizzy.

He lifts up his eyes.

<h1 align="center">CHAPTER 35</h1>

The cry is endless.

A red mist envelopes everything. Above, a domed ceiling with smooth faces staring in expectation as tongues dart from sensuous lips. All are waiting.

A scent commands my attention. Cedar and tea tree. Refreshing, it makes me wonder about this place, this hell.

Around me, round walls with etched angels, dark and beautiful. They are massive, permanent. Stone wings glimmer as stern, beautiful faces regard me with glassed eyes. Each holds a sword at waist level, clawed hands grip as muscled arms ripple with movement but appear inert.

I step forward to stand before taloned feet that pierce the stone. Beneath, a trough runs the room's perimeter and flickers light, elegant and subdued, over granite talons. I peer in. There's no fire; no smoke. I see no abyss.

The cry trails off, is replaced by music, something elegant, something soothing yet primal. Is this still hell? And what was that shriek? My skin crawls, it sounded like Rhyme.

I shiver and look for an exit as stone gargoyles raise powerful wings inches beneath the cavern's curved roof.

Scents haunt me. Although beautiful and pleasant, the tea tree burns my nostrils, the cedar makes my skin itch.

A mist forms as from a magician's whisper. Rose red swirls with candy white, foams over me, turns my skin a pale rouge, sticks to my hair, makes it damp yet crusty like hair gel.

Then the sound. *Click.*

Like water dripping in distant caverns.

Clock.

Something hollow, something slow. Perhaps Belphegor?

Vapor thickens as odors overpower. My groin tingles. My skin prickles.

Clock.

What is that?

Click.

"Emery, I'm so glad you came." The voice is feminine, sensual, hypnotic.

I stare into the mist, slowly spin, unable to tell from where the speaker speaks. "Hello?"

Click.

"So succulent," she says. "So masculine."

"What?"

Etched angels rise around me, seem to guard the periphery of this expanse.

Click.

Clock.

"I've long waited to have you alone." The voice is dusky, sexy. A lust of dripping vapor that churns and swirls with each syllable.

"Who are you?"

Mist rises from a stone floor. Elegant feet glisten in black stilettos.

Click.

"I'm anything you wish," she says. "Any desire you crave."

"Not interested," I say firmly, as massive sentinels raise great stone wings to stretch over the place.

Click.

Clock.

Mist rises, the outline of legs slowly appear, their form both elegant and strong, athletic, toned like a dancer. "Of course, you are," she teases. "No one can deny my pleasures, and many have paid the price for their insolence." Her chuckle bounces over great stone bastions. "Do not join them, Emery. Kingdoms have been betrayed for a single night in my arms. Great battles have been waged for but a taste of my lips."

Click.

"Don't be like them. Don't make that mistake." She steps closer as sugary fog raises inches more, reveals black panties wrapped on lithe hips, garters stretched to clasp fishnet stockings in gleaming, glaring white. Her abdomen ripples as she steps through sensuous shadow. *Click.* Elegant arms sway as the mist teases her approach.

A comic book heroine, I think. Something drawn in broad terms to fit every sexy cliché. Sleek, she steps forward, mist draped like a regal robe. Her face comes into view: raven hair cascades, foams over shoulders like a breaking wave, a sharp chin beneath sensual, seductive lips that part and glisten. She bites the corner of her mouth, appears coy as she gives a look that says, "I hope I meet your standards."

"Who are you?"

Her giggle's like a tinkling bell, like a single water drop oozing lazy to invade my mind, my psyche. Eyes like rubies peer at me. Her nose is pert, delicate on a face that could adorn the front page of any top-tier magazine.

"I am AeSma," she says. "I exist to inflame."

My chuckle rings hollow. "As if, demon. I'm no stranger to this place and its lies. Whatever Iblis set you to, you'd best forget it and be on your way."

A cloud floats around her as if bound to her. Drawing near, she places a hand on my chest, then whispers in my ear. "I'll show you much about love's craft. Show you *the best* ways to please a woman— or man, if that is your wish."

She steps back, presents herself beneath an umbrella of stone wing and flickering embers. Arms spread as ample breasts strain a gleaming white bustier.

Her form flickers, changes to a blond in the tradition of Marilyn Monroe, a girl next door with bombshell looks. "Does this please?" she mews, voice tinged with the smallest teasing lilt as eyes flick toward the surrounding sentinels.

"Or perhaps…" Light flickers. Tea tree makes my eyes water. I rub them, stare ahead. See her become conservative. A tight miniskirt wraps her waist and accentuates every curve. Above that, a sleek white shirt, crisp as if just pressed, buttons bulge as ample breasts press. Her hair is tied in a tight bun, and she wears spectacles with neat, smart frames that only enhance her appearance.

"Nope," I say, turning away, wondering at the huge, dark angels.

"Emery," she says.

The voice makes me turn before I know I've moved. So familiar, so attached to my psyche. Rhyme stands before me, auburn hair flowing over sleek collarbones. A thin film of sweat glistens over my favorite cleavage. She bites her lower lip, traces an elegant finger across her abdomen.

Click.

She steps in and presses her lips to my neck. "I can't wait any longer," she breathes. Her tongue traces my skin. Hands glide across my abdomen, toward my groin. "This is the place, Emery. The only place we can be alone." Emeralds invite with a mischievous gleam. "But we must hurry," she says. "Cain will be here any minute."

A grand, stone bed appears as sticky fog swirls. A granite headboard rises as massive wings lower to create a private canopy safe from prying eyes. "I've arranged everything," she says, grasping my hand, walking before me as I stare at her form, her legs, her delicious, soft skin. Vanilla and lilac numb my mind and engorge my manhood. I'm a drooling hound. A primal neanderthal.

Click. Clock. "Come."

She leads me to the bed, then delicate hands unbutton my shirt. She gives my neck a playful nip that sends a chill down my spine to tingle in my toes then course up trembling legs to settle on my erection.

My breathing is heavy, labored, longing. Thoughts swirl, pulse with emotion like the sweeping vapor around us. Endless denial, like a tickle you can't quite reach, massaging, needling.

Her hand reaches my belt, and the clasp comes undone. "I've waited so long for this," she slides my hands around her waist, then nudges them down to cover her butt. "This is *our* time, Emery. *This* is *our* chance."

Her tongue grazes my lips and juices fill my mouth. My eyes close as stone angels seem to avert their gaze and give us much desired privacy.

"Rhyme." I hear the word, not even aware I've spoken. She presses her breasts against my chest, feels amazing, strong, toned. Soft, yet hard, like iron wrapped in velvet.

Another playful nip as my zipper slides down, as she presses her lips close to my mouth.

"Now," she says. "This is *our* time."

Her lips seize like a pouncing lion. Then the taste of ash like chewed charcoal. My eyes pop open to see the demon's original form, raven hair, beautiful face, lithe, grinding, pulsing in my arms.

But not Rhyme.

I snap to, grasp her shoulders and shove her on the bed. "Get away, foul thing!" The words come instinctually, from somewhere deep, something subconscious, some semblance that remains untainted.

Dark eyes rage as she stands. Fangs appear like gleaming daggers. "You dare resist?" she says. "You dare assault?"

I stand defiant. This place and its rigors make me bold.

I'm tired of fear, exhausted by Iblis and his endless tricks, his endless manipulations. I calm my voice, try to sound soothing as I bargain. "I can't betray my love," I say softly, reasonable. A caring, trusted friend.

A grating sound assaults as stone angels lift their wings. Fire springs from the trough on the cavern's periphery as candied mists change to something foul and black.

"Love?" she hisses. A gorgeous face tilts to the ceiling. Breasts heave as she laughs. "You talk of love, foolish man?" she scoffs, takes two steps. *Click. Clock.* "Do you think Rhyme loves you? Do you think you're being noble rejecting my pleasures?"

I rub my eyes as odors like cordite, like burnt rubber, assault my nostrils. The rouge on my arms is now sticky and black, dripping to the floor as she paces across the room. *Click. Clock. Click. Clock.* "I've something to share, love. Something that may change your mind."

The shriek returns, bounds over rounded walls and muddy mist.

It's Rhyme. I know that now for certain.

Prior images flood my mind: Rhyme spitted, roasted on open coals.

I raise my hands, rush toward the demon. "No! Please..."

The word trickles, stretches, elongates like an echo through tunnels deep and dank.

Dark angels open their wings to a vast ceiling that shimmers and draws me in. I spin through raging foam, through blackened mist as grotesque fingers reach and claw.

Her shriek is endless. Her misery palpable.

The void takes me.

Something bumps us repeatedly.

This mind is different.

Transparent bubbles like a sea of balloons. Rising, floating, refracting light like a million dust particles. Images appear in each: a redhead girl, blue paint smudged on her nose. An old room lined with shelves, stuffed with books. A sky of stars looming overhead, inviting, serene.

In the other minds, those of Crispy, Jonas, Longinus, Laslo, I saw what they saw, felt what they felt, now I see only transparent bubbles floating on an endless background of muted black.

The shriek returns. A sense of helplessness, of invasion, of doing what one must.

Bubbles fade as the howl rises. As it subdues, they flicker back to life.

A Joe Bonamassa concert.

A lazy day beachside.

A hammock with a favorite novel.

I hover, find I'm able to move freely from bubble to bubble, to watch through transparent walls.

We're bumped again, this time harder.

Bubbles waggle, dim a bit, then return brighter than ever.

A trophy held high as teammates cheer.

A bubble bath, pink painted toes poking through foam.

I float in the spaces between, regard each image as it blooms and settles.

Then a bubble catches my attention in glowing red. Different than the millions, this one is radiant, warm, sends a feeling of safety, a feeling of permanence.

A man of twenty-something appears, tortoise shell glasses darken hazel eyes; a thick mop of dark hair lays parted to one side. He's ripe with youth and fitness, wears a comforting smile that radiates kindness and sincerity. His clothes are that of a janitor. A stitched oval shows the word BRANCH.

Then Rhyme's there, in a library sipping coffee, staring at the man like she stares at me. Emeralds gleam with pleasure, with serenity, with love.

The place flickers. The bubble dims, changes.

Gunshots permeate in muted pops. Branch runs, spins, fires behind as menacing men give chase. He runs toward Rhyme, and I see her face turn to horror as the bubble snuffs to nothing.

The shriek shreds my ears like death metal up full blast.

We get bumped again, bumped continuously now, like a metronome, thump, thump, thump. Each bubble flickers, jostles, threatens to fade to vapor.

Then they rouse anew, glow with increased ferocity as if suddenly plugged into a generator. Floating lazy, they spin in serenity, seem immune to the harsh bumps.

The howl fades.

The sweetest music starts.

A concert stage in a park, perched inside a little amphitheater.

On the stage, an orchestra plays Mozart as a crowd of two hundred look on from a quilt of blankets and towels set on a manicured lawn.

Long legs stretch to cross at the ankles. A feminine hand slips into a masculine one.

Then my own face, smiling, leaning forward to share a kiss.

Then I know: This is Rhyme's mind. Rhyme's hell.

Then, another thought, a punch in the gut. *I'm* her hell? *I'm* the one who causes such shrieks, as if each second in my presence shreds a new strip of her soul?

The howl returns. The bubbles flicker, wane.

Then a force of will, of redirection. The bubbles light full force.

We stand, she and I, gather our blanket, our plastic glasses, a half-bottle of Merlot, then weave our way through the crowd.

Bump. Bump. Bump. Thud. Thud. Thud.

The spasms increase as the image flickers, then rages fire red to rise above all others. I float beside, wonder how I'm the cause of so much of her pain.

For minutes we walk, hand in hand, talking quietly, happy. Not hell at all, I think. What sorcery is this? And what has AeSma planned to ruin it?

I remember the day. The setting sun tracing long lines of pink and purple beneath storm clouds clustered on a gleaming horizon.

I remember the glade, watch as Rhyme pulls me into a copse of trees, then spreads a blanket on the ground.

In the distance the orchestra plays as a countertenor rises sweet and clear. Handel, I think, remember. *Xerxes,* "Ombra mai fù," I think.

Lust floods her emeralds as she presses against me and joins her lips to mine.

Passion consumes. I remember as if reliving the moment. Frantic hands grip my head as we kiss. Then, she guides me to lie on the blanket as pinks, purples, subdued magenta, peer through shadowed branches. Night falls as Handel wafts.

Then she's atop me, sliding aside her sun dress to slip me inside.

Bump. Bump. Bump.

She grinds, writhes, holds my eyes as I hold hers. We are one, joined in the moment, grinding, panting, thrusting as passion flows like a freed flood. Delicate hands press my chest as she lifts, then slides down, as her lips part, as her emeralds draw me in to hold me breathless and gasping in their depths. Then her breath in my ear as we climax, the whispered words she's never before said to me. "I love you, Emery Merrick."

Thump. Thump. Thump. Thump.

The bumping stops.

I feel her relief as bubbles vaporize, as surrounding darkness brightens to a room both elegant and expensive.

A marble chandelier drips crystal as a man, nude, rises from the bed. He is masculine, powerful with a chiseled body like Laocoön in that sculpture, limp penis and all.

"I trust *that* gave you pleasure?" It's Cain, and suddenly I'm filled with joy and rage in equal parts. Rage at the thought that Rhyme's given up so much of herself to assure my safety. Has given her very essence, her body, her soul, to assure the Antichrist doesn't destroy me.

I think about immortality, about wisps of fate that stick like silken webs.

Then joy.

What a wonder is woman. What a wonder is my love, bearing the brunt of this madman's machinations, fulfilling her obligations while shrouding herself in memories of precious things. She ignores the shrieks, her own shrieks, suffers in silence to endure the foulness of Cain's touch, the furious thrusts of his passion, all the while shrieking to the core.

She's found a way to refocus though, to endure, to block him out.

Joy doubles to elation, triples as if cubed. AeSma's ploy has backfired. Where she sought to show me my truest love with another man, she'd miscalculated her measure of Rhyme, the armor she wears to save and soothe, to overcome, to devour all obstacles whether physical or mental.

AeSma doesn't know. Rhyme's more powerful than her, more

powerful than even Cain. She's playing chess like a Russian master and allowing them, Cain, to believe she's subdued.

I think of the sundress.

Think of Handel's weeping innocence, of love beginning, plaintive, moving. Think of her rapture as she shuddered and collapsed, breath ragged, overwhelmed with a love I can't possibly imagine but am starting to understand.

At that instant, my love for her doubles. The grandest sensation, experienced in the darkest, most tempting pit of all of hell's holes.

My Rhyme. *My* love. Neither the apocalypse, the Antichrist, the torture of separation, the demons of hell, nor the hosts of heaven, can break the bond that joins us.

"I found you." I remember her words, said on the day we met. "I knew I would."

A smile stretches my face as I think of my wife. Stand awed by her endurance, her strength, her tenacity in the midst of every dark thing.

I am the luckiest of treasure hunters, the most fortunate rogue to ever wander.

Doubt vaporizes as I stand beaming in hell's deepest pit surrounded by legions who claw and devour. Surrounded by misery in its purest form, by despair and desolation so soulless one can't even place a foot through the darkness. Every vice, every imaginable horror, congealed and distilled, sticking to rock walls, oozing over ancient stone, consuming souls in terror.

Yet, I feel a beauty that even hell's gates can't douse. The gorgeousness of unbreakable bonds.

I know nothing can break us. Not this smoldering pit, not these demonic legions, not Iblis, not even God.

We've found that storybook treasure and it's bound our souls with unbreakable cords.

We are joined, never to be parted.

I stand smiling, gawking at stone angels and charred mist as the simmering despair of billions echoes over ancient granite corridors.

AeSma approaches,—*Click. Clock.*—wrath etched on her face.

And as I watch, swallow my fear, mind trembling, I realize, in this simmering cesspool, this endless pit of terror and grief, that I alone am the one soul, perhaps the only soul in history, to stand amongst such horror, such despair, such mind-numbing agony, and feel true joy.

CHAPTER 36

I inhale deep and cleanse my psyche, hearing only the swishes and clacks of innumerable paintings swapping form and place around me. I look for AeSma, arms raised to block her wrath.

She's not here.

I close my eyes, shiver, reach for goodness, for the only thing I can conjure to soothe and ground. Her scent floats on sterile air. Lilac, vanilla, cleanse my mind, pull me from the remainder of Rhyme's psyche to touch down in my own.

I am Emery.

I am good.

I am *not* a madman.

"Emery, I'm here." Her voice soothes. "Come back to me."

I squint at the grand space before me. I'm somewhere in the middle of this vast museum. Somewhere in an alcove with many branches leading to other rooms.

I look to the floor, see only a layer of dust and soot. No footprints, no sign of others before me. I scuff a line with my shoe. See it smear to a blanched gray, proving that if someone were here prior, they'd have certainly left prints.

"Like the universe—" Iblis's words float through my brain. "You can't appreciate the scale of which I speak."

I consider the point, the vastness of the universe, the fragility and insignificance of being human. Of inhabiting a speck of dust whizzing around a sun that, in reality, is but a tiny particle of flotsam in an ocean of bigger things.

Then there's time, vast beyond comprehension, inescapable as Belphegor trapped in a Victorian pit. It flows, leaves us all in its wake to dry and blanch on the barren shores of wasted destiny.

And I think that's the point. The flowing nature of time, visible to mortals as only brief flashes. Seventy or eighty years—a cosmic blink, a flicker in the distance like sunlight from a mirror.

I think of Laslo. Of Crispy. Of these glimpses, of these secrets. Of Longinus and his fear, his want for revenge, his rise from shaking child to victorious legionnaire. Meteoric, I think, done in a single battle, his first battle.

And who's Gwenna? A question I'll ask if I ever see him again.

I look up as new paintings slide and shuffle on the vast walls around me.

What to do now?

Then, a memory: "If you hear the music, you might as well dance." My grandpa's line, used at almost every family function. "Grandpa, do you want some chicken?"

"Well, I hear the music, so might as well dance."

"Grandpa, is it time for bed?"

"Well, I hear the music, so might as well dance."

I wonder if I can find him here. Wonder if I wander long enough, or perhaps ask Iblis, I might be able to look. He was such a mean bastard. If Heaven accepted him, then there's hope for all of us.

Before me, the room is a small square with rounded corners, positively stuffed with shifting paintings that seem somehow bound to this particular vault. In the center, a large statue dominates in faded, cobwebbed bronze. Next to it, the sign reads: "Satan" Jean-Jacques Feuchère, 1833.

A contemplative Satan sits on a rock, wings partially wrapped against his back as his chin rests in his hand. The artist was certainly adept at capturing expression: eyes downcast and reflective, thin horns closely tracing a round skull to flow over his scalp to the back of his head. One leg is crossed over the other, and he seems to be hugging himself with his free arm.

"What could I have done?" the expression says, and I see its eyes shift back and forth as if thinking over all the questions retained in his fall from grace. "How could God have bested me?" it says. "What means have I to fight back?"

The word "humanity" floats through my head like a subtitle on Sesame Street.

"Good luck with all that," I say, then move on to other displays.

"DANTE AND VIRGIL IN THE UNDERWORLD" FILIPPO NAPOLETANO, 1622.

This painting changes to:

"INFERNO" DOMENICO BECCAFUMI, 1514.

Which changes to:

"THE GARDEN OF EARTHLY DELIGHTS" HEIRONYMUS BOSCH, 1490-1510.

I wonder how many artists reside here. A little treasure hunt for me and Grandpa: How many artists can we find? If I'm stuck here, perhaps a little aimless searching will help pass the time. I mean, I hear the music, right?

"INFERNO" ANON., 1520, appears before me and reminds me of a sort of mini-hell, perhaps a little side room of horrors. People boiled in cauldrons, hung upside down, stretched on racks, etc.

"Disgusting," I say, tracing the terrors.

Behind me, a shuffle of wings.

I turn as the contemplative Satan rises from his rock to hold me with stone eyes.

"What?" I say.

A harsh flap of wings lifts it to the air where it hovers, focused and unwavering.

I hear a swish and a clack behind me, then turn to look at what new painting has come.

"LA MAPPA DELL'INFERNO" BOTTICELLI, 1480-1490, the sign reads.

Before me, the painting shows a funnel of sorts, a cone, a wide top tapering to a flat, thin nipple that extends into a small arch in the painting's bottom center. It looks like a tornado, like some giant funnel cloud rising from the Earth to lay devastation in its wake.

The image starts to spin like a carnival ride. Wavers side to side, gains speed, becomes so fast I can almost hear amused howls from within.

I regard the stone Satan, wonder for a second if he serves as metaphor for heartlessness, for cruelty.

"Um, is Iblis around?" The words escape a single second before I'm lifted from my feet and thrown into the canvas.

The funnel howls, looms as a skyscraper. Screams rush over. Not screams of amusement as conjured in my imagination, but screams of the totality of Hell's inhabitants, amplified, tortured, glaring, crushing. Hands shoot to my ears as the thing spins awkward like a child's top.

I'm rising. The contraption spins closer, daggers flowing from concentric circles. A second later, I hover above it, stare into a mouth, the abyss, as big as an ocean. It beckons its hunger in boiling smears and bubbling lines, twists to spiral like a whirlpool of tar sprinkled with lilacs. A dizzying vortex, a massive blackhole, pulling me in as sounds of terror and agony float through to bypass my covered ears and ply their wares directly on my brain.

I howl. Emotions rush through me. Frustration, regret, remorse, fear, helplessness, betrayal. Abandonment.

I plummet like a stone dropped from great heights, streak toward the cesspool of misery, of despair, of utter separation from anything that's good.

"This is it, Emery." Iblis's voice. "Your final vision. Do enjoy. I'll see you on the other side."

Wind, like a zephyr, makes my clothes flap and cackle as I streak toward the gaping jaws of doom. Arms flap as the force of descent overcomes any effort to keep my hands pressed to my ears. I'm stretched to impossible proportions, my entire body enwrapped by the zephyr as a shriek claws my throat to join the howling billions tortured within.

It claims me.

I'm in a closet.

I hear the footsteps.

Then, a warning from my sister to stay quiet.

I wail to the confines of this mind, search without hands, move without feet, desperate to find a way to flee the terror of this memory.

"Emery! Come out!"

"Stay still," my sister whispers, hefting a knitted blanket over my head.

I'm seven years old, quaking, hiding, an impossible fear clawing my tiny breast.

"No!" I scream with everything my disembodied self can muster. "Not this!"

Through knitted holes I'm bathed with light as the closet door's ripped open. Then, my mother's chubby hand reaching in to enwrap my sister's hair and yank her into a clean bedroom with a made bed.

Her head swivels with force, blurs with speed as Mom grabs her hair, muttering expletives and shaking her like a wet rag. "Who left the glass in the sink?" she screams. "Tell me or I'll give you worse."

The hands of a girl grasp those of my mother, search for a place to ride the whiplash, perhaps even hoping to free herself from the iron grip.

"I don't know." The whimper of a ten-year-old.

Mom yanks like a beast as she says each word.

"Jesus—" My sister's head whips. "Told—" Her face is a blur; tears fly like drops from a pinwheel. "You—" Small hands hold for dear life. "Not—" Her feet leave the ground. "To—" Pink flip flops fly away, tumble into a corner. "Lie!"

A final beastly yank and she releases her own daughter, turns her eyes to the closet where I sit, peering through the blanket, knowing I'm next.

A sickening thud grabs my attention as my sister hits the door jamb. She falls and lies motionless.

Mom stalks toward me.

"Mom!" I say. "Look." I don't speak from a sense of worry for my sister but rather to distract my mother from my own beating.

On the door jamb, a trickle of blood oozes toward the floor.

Mom looks to the door, reaching blind as I dodge her cruel hands.

Then her attention returns, her face a mask of evil intent and focused rage. Her fists are hard. I cry out, beg her to stop. I scream sorrys, try to take my beating as stoically as my unconscious sister as hands like iron pummel my back, my face, my thighs.

Softened up, I'm dragged from the closet by my hair, then kicked in the ribs and ass for good measure.

Gayle lies still but whether truly unconscious or just playing possum I'm unsure. My seven-year-old mind must lack a sense of justice, of camaraderie, because I think, "My turn can't last forever."

And it doesn't.

"Help your sister!" Mom stomps from the room, muttering over the yellow carpet of the mobile home's single hall.

I move to her. "Gayle. Gayle, you alright?"

In the bathroom, I wash the blood from her face. We can't afford Band-Aids, so I wet some toilet paper and dab the laceration. She sits on the toilet, staring at her feet, lips quivering, breath catching with sobs restrained and muffled.

"Quiet," I whisper. "If she hears, we'll get more."

Gayle suppresses another sob.

I'm inside my seven-year-old body, weeping like a newborn, curled into a ball.

I know this hell. I know these scars, born from bruises, from lacerations, from broken bones, will never ever heal.

I weep, strive to tell this child, this earlier version of myself that they'll never heal. That he'll be ever a victim. That throughout what remains of his life, he'll not find those keys of which Iblis spoke, those keys just beyond arm's reach. I want to tell him that this will affect every single moment, every breath, every single action of his miniscule life.

I want to tell him the scars are medals for valor displayed. I want to tell him everything he feels is normal. That every emotion, hate, revenge, vengeance, self-destruction, is normal and inescapable. Like the abyss, the only hope he has, I have, is to stare nobly into it. To accept the licks and lashes, to recognize these flaws were not chosen, not gained organically, but were poisoned upon him by the person who should have loved him the most.

I want to tell him to be brave, that things change, that someday he'll find a way out and then spend the rest of his life searching for an equation to total the sums.

I realize I'm a liar. I realize then I've never found that path. I realize that this abuse, this abject hatred, clings to me like rancid garlic. That in reality, the best he can hope for, the most wonderful thing he can ever be called, is a survivor. One who suffers. One who endures.

I want to tell him nothing lasts forever. That if he can endure, that someday this monster, my mother, will die, probably racked with age because monsters live a long time. Probably alone and demented, stuffed in some tiny room of some wretched nursing home where the staff steals your stuff and shows you the true meaning of neglect.

More than she deserves, I think. Too good by far.

"Yet someone had loved him. Borne him in her arms and in her heart. But for her, the race of the world would have trampled him underfoot, a squashed, boneless snail." It's Iblis, skin rippling like black velvet, sleek, shiny, darkest red in black cascades. "James Joyce," he says. "Says a lot, eh?"

I'm in the same room from which I departed. The stone Satan sits again on his rock, chin in hand, contemplating where it all went wrong.

Humor gone, I take my shot and leap at the dark beast, raining punches as fast as my arms can move.

He becomes a blur, dodges every blow.

I've no chance against his speed but continue unabated, raining blows, growling with each miss.

Then I'm gripped from behind in iron hands, grasped just above each elbow. The force is gentle yet demanding, stronger than what even Longinus could muster but with a feel of empathy.

Iblis's grinning form recedes as I'm pulled through oceans of hate, through a maze of demons and tormented souls, through gelatinous vapors of malice and greed, through murder and revenge, past gluttony and vengeance, the flickering shapes of Belphegor, of Alastor, streak to colored smears of slug and bird.

Air sizzles, becomes opalescent as I streak backwards down a shimmering tunnel to a place that feels harsh and sounds horrendous.

The smell of gunfire.

The heat of flame.

A wet tongue on my face.

CHAPTER 37

JERUSALEM, ISRAEL

Emery continues to mutter as Igneus and Sebastian approach the Temple.

Soldiers' voices rise. "Halt!" "Don't take another step!"

Then night becomes day. The staff sizzles, strikes the nearest soldiers, then leaps from one to the next. Explosions shred the night. Vehicles fly, then roll away to smash on ancient brick and stone.

Then darkness, sprinkled with sounds of the wailing and maimed.

Igneus doesn't stutter in his steps, walks on as turret mounted guns boom and sizzle, unloading a wall of shrapnel and rain of steel.

Sebastian raises a hand. A slight haze surrounds them.

Then, another sizzling jolt shatters the night and the guns hang limp and melted.

They step through the checkpoint and into the courtyard.

Jonas lifts up his eyes as Igneus and Sebastian stride through the arch. Behind them, flames rage, rolling into a burnt sky. Men cry out, some crawling, all slapping flames from their bodies.

Igneus's eyes flair, focused, intent, angry. Sebastian shares the expression, a cherubic face bent in concentration and fury.

Longinus looks toward the commotion, seems confused for a second, then bellows another laugh.

Now's my chance, Jonas thinks, *end her while he's distracted.*

He twists his foot for leverage, keeps his eyes on the ground. *Can't telegraph my intent.*

He moves in a blur, dives past Longinus to land hard on empty stairs as lungs search for absent wind.

Where is she?

In the second he took for setup, she vanished.

Longinus raises the spear, flips the razor point toward him and slams it home.

Jonas gasps as the spear pierces his chest. He stumbles against the altar's base.

Igneus's cry splits the crowd. "It's gonna be a bad day, oaf!"

Surprise blooms in Longinus's eyes, then a look of purpose. "I'd say the same, dear Igneus. This will not be pleasant."

Igneus raises the staff but Longinus is quicker.

The spear jolts, an odor of cordite, of burnt flesh, a flaming bolt that takes Igneus in the chest and sends him sprawling.

Jonas musters what little strength remains, lunges at the Roman, gets slapped aside where he falls panting, bleeding, spent.

Then a shadow atop the wall, shrouded by the spear's glow and sweeping spotlights. Sima!

Her face is expectant, her eyes focused.

Focused on Sebastian.

Jonas, struggling, yells. He needs to warn the boy, but swoons, dizzy, spinning, weak.

Darkness takes him.

Rhyme's dazzled. The night, so bright, so sudden. She rubs her eyes. Sirens sound. Imperium vehicles appear from everywhere.

"Where's Bill?"

"No idea."

"Stuart, stay with Emery. I've got to help the others."

"No way," the African says, pistol up and ready. "I'm coming with."

She looks at Emery, knows she can't leave him alone, opens her mouth to say so, but the words choke. A sultry shadow crosses her vision. The form of a woman moving atop the wall with great agility.

Although they'd only met briefly, she knows the movement, knows the woman. It's Sima, stalking, up to no good, which means things have gone very wrong for Jonas.

Another glance at Emery, then a prayer for his safety.

"Let's go," she says.

"I go too." It's Mr. Lee.

"Stay with Emery."

The man's face shows defiance, perhaps anger. "No, no. He your man. You stay. I go. He safe here anyway. Fighting there."

Emery mutters, moans, waves his hands. A tear slides down his cheek, glints flame and shadow.

Sima leaps from the wall and disappears out of sight.

Then the piercing scream of a child.

"Sebastian!" she cries, jolts forward. Eyes narrow, her breast fills with rage, with purpose, with a sour need for vengeance.

"They want hell," she says. "Let's bring it to them."

A wet tongue, rough like sandpaper, licks my face.

I open my eyes, feel the bristled fur of Rhyme's Doberman. Dark eyes, razor white teeth. He leans in, continues to lick, to prod.

I'm in a truck, jagged glass and charred seats. The leather is hot, partially melted, thin fingers of smoke rising from torn fabric.

I step into the night, feel fit, strong. The dog bolts past, pauses, leaps in a circle, jolts ahead, then turns back again. I scan the landscape, wonder where I am, why I'm alone. Where's Rhyme? Where are we?

All around me are toppled vehicles and melted guns, smoldering, red hot. Flames rise from corpses in the street, mingle with screams, with shards of rock, with a panicked, fleeing crowd.

An explosion rocks me on my heels, turns my attention to the Temple. Lights strobe, aqua, crimson, as great smoldering beams sweep the sky. Smoke rises as lightning sizzles, streaks past at ground level, inflames an arched opening in a great stone wall.

People stream through as shadows paint my vision. Beyond, the Temple rises: a silhouette on a flashing neon backdrop. It's some skirmish, some battle. Are the Allies attacking again? Impossible. Russia? The EU? Is Igneus in there? Longinus? Where's Rhyme? Where's Cain?

Houdini barks, gives a look that says he's tired of waiting and sprints to the arched opening. Dark fur serves as perfect camouflage. He races through shadow, then blends and disappears. If anyone knows where to find Rhyme, it's him. I look for a weapon that, if found, I won't know how to use. A shiver grips my neck, warns to avoid the place, to stay put, to go the other way.

But I've never been accused of doing the smart thing.

I trot after the dog, bent over as I move. Another movie ploy, staying low. Behind me, Imperium vehicles pour in, thirty at least. Soldiers leap out and race toward the same entrance as me.

I'm enough ahead of them, though. Feel surprised as I break the threshold and enter the Temple's courtyard.

It's a madhouse.

People scamper, cower, run, drop. So many things are happening at once, I stand frozen for a second. The contrast between shadow and flame confuses my vision. I'm blind one second, plunged in darkness the next.

I step aside, hunker behind toppled stone next to a man with a purple mohawk and a woman with glassed eyes. "What's going on?"

The woman regards me, moves her mouth but no sound comes. The man's mohawk appears as a game rooster. "Everyone just went nuts," he says. "Started shooting, shooting fire. Like Dungeons and Dragons."

I peek over and try to make sense of the chaos. The Temple glows, seems singed but unharmed. Atop the altar, a shirtless man with long hair holds a guitar and stands watching, still as stone. Behind him a bass player and drummer peep. Below that, through the stream of screaming, terrified people, I see Jonas slumped against the altar's base. Blood streams from multiple wounds as a woman tries to drag him off. His eyes are closed, but I'm really too far away to see clearly and know only that he's not moving on his own.

A massive shadow appears, so huge, so monstrous, it can only be Longinus. "Have ye had enough?"

I follow his voice, see Igneus rise, stagger. Smoke pours from his body. His clothes are singed and tattered. He wavers slightly, then the staff emits a thundering bolt of white light.

Longinus raises the spear, absorbs the blow like it's nothing as he paces forward. "Time for cinders, little man."

I stand as Imperium soldiers stream past.

Then, beyond Longinus, a giant African rises, levels a rifle and fires. I hear the Roman grunt with the impact, see three soldiers fall as others scatter for cover. Longinus turns for the briefest second, then sends a sizzling bolt like casting a line.

The African's big, fast, though, somehow anticipating the attack and managing to sidestep just enough that the bolt impacts the Temple's wall instead.

Stone flies, flames sweep to the sky and quickly die. Then, people pour from the hole, tripping, trampling, eyes wide, mouths stretched, screaming, racing to the lone exit.

Longinus turns again to Igneus, who emits another sizzling bolt of white light. Longinus levels the spear and absorbs the impact, but here he slides back ten whole feet.

Then I hear the voice. Tuned to my memory, to my psyche. Rhyme, calling, screaming, voice stretched and high.

She flashes by, a brief outline lit only by explosions and gunfire. A delicate form chases her. The glint of steel, of smooth agility. It can be only Sima.

My mind does the sums.

Igneus and Longinus battle with crazy biblical relics as Sima and Rhyme fight. If Rhyme's running, she's lost the upper hand.

"Get moving dipshit!"

It's Lenny, shouting encouragement.

Then Vince. "What an idiot."

I step around the rocks, get ignored by soldiers as just another bystander.

Then I sprint. Past Longinus, past Igneus, who are so focused they don't notice or don't care. I streak past the altar, past the ceremonial basin.

What I see next is both impressive and awesome. A battle of titans, of elegance and grace, of agility, hostility, of focus and economy of movement.

Rhyme hits her knees to slide next to a small body. Then she turns, eyes crazed and squinted, twin pistols firing simultaneously.

The first round strikes Sima. But the next, what? like ten or twelve, miss the mark entirely.

Then Sima's on her, dagger flashing, moving so fast there's no possible way anything human can muster such speed. Her arms blur as Rhyme does her best to block, to dodge, to parry.

But Rhyme still has her wits about her, manages to protect the crumpled figure on the stone.

It's Sebastian, I realize. Rhyme doesn't fight for herself but for the boy.

But she's losing.

Sima's too fast, too good, powered by something otherworldly, moving not like a human, but like a super being. Like the demon she is. The dagger blazes, trailing flame and smoke. I think of Hell, think about AeSma's anger at failing to seduce me.

Rhyme blocks, cries out, steps back, holds her arm, seems to struggle for breath.

Sima grins, steps in and continues her dervish bullshit.

Then Mr. Lee's there. Blocking, parrying, driving Sima back. He's Bruce Lee. He's Jason Bourne. He's an action hero. Like the Green Hornet. Movements I've only ever seen in movies. Seen up close, a wonder to behold.

He stands in an odd, pigeon-toed way, knees bent inward, almost touching. His posture's spry, foreign, head back, eyes loosely focused as Sima attacks, dagger blazing.

Lee's hands are like a pinwheel, moving yet not moving. Striking with such economy, they appear to require very little effort to exert great power.

Sima slashes. Lee pivots, turns his right foot a single inch, a single centimeter, smashes her chest with an open hand.

Wind escapes like a whistling teapot. She slides, topples backwards, rolls, gains her feet, then stands rubbing her chest, staring at the awesome Asian.

Lee stands perfectly poised, perfectly still, perfectly serene like a Zen exercise.

Sima snarls, eyes blaze. She leaps with fantastic speed, doubles her efforts with the dagger as Lee blocks, moves, parries. Then, she steps back, a grin on her face, and for the first time I see Lee's composure break. He shakes his right hand. Blood flies into the aqua. The crimson mixes with the blazing gold from Longinus's spear.

I look to Igneus. See he and Longinus locked in supernatural battle. The staff against the spear, the Jew against the Roman, David against Goliath. They step close as each relic sizzles and tries to overpower the other. One blazes a rippling white stream, the other, red-hot balefire. Seems they're at an impasse, seems some other way will have to decide the contest.

I look to Rhyme, see her cradle Sebastian's head in her lap.

Then, I'm moving without thought. Sprinting to her, past a surprised Sima and shaken Lee.

I skid to a stop beside them, find her bleeding from multiple wounds. She doesn't notice them or me. "Sebastian, stay with us." Her whisper is barely discernable above the crescendo of gunfire, blazing relics, the screams of the injured, the panicked bystanders. She coughs, turns her head, spits blood.

"Rhyme?"

She stares for a long second, looks through me like I'm an apparition. "Em— Emery?" She blinks, tongue grazing her lips. "Emery?"

"Yes. It's me."

Rage fills her eyes, makes auburn hair roil above stormy emeralds. A ponytail bobs as she watches Sima and Lee. "Hold him," she says, coughing more blood, and thrusts the boy in my lap. "I'll be right back."

CHAPTER 38

JERUSALEM, ISRAEL

Sebastian mutters from my lap. "Dad? Where's Dad?" I look to Igneus, see him and the Roman locked in a stalemate, bristled with sizzling streams of energy.

The giant African steps forward and rains a few shots at a number of soldiers. As they back away, he turns the weapon again to Longinus.

The chatter deafens, rises above the chaos, the screams, the struggle of arms. Each bullet hits home, but they bounce right off the barbaric Roman. The African's expression is raw bafflement.

Longinus doesn't notice. "Ye thin' ye can match me, Jew?" Bulging muscle constricts, tightens, doesn't appear to struggle with the spear as he had on the roof up on Tabor. Stepping forward, he grins through wiry whiskers. "Always the wise one," he mocks. "Always terrorized, protected, weak." He thrusts the spear and sends Igneus back a pace. "The emperor will be happy when you're subdued."

Igneus retreats a step with each word. Past them both, I see Jonas crawling, striving to get close to the Roman as he resists the woman trying to drag him off. What his body won't do, he does with sheer will. I smooth Sebastian's hair, think of a way I can help Jonas, help Rhyme and Lee. But what? But how?

Lightning sizzles, mixes with the color, the sounds of spear and staff. I see great white teeth, a streak of shadow that leaps over Jonas.

And clamps Longinus's arm.

But not for long. The dog becomes a spinning cyclone that rockets against the Temple wall, where it falls and lies motionless.

Rhyme squeals as Longinus continues undaunted. Tipping the spear, holding it horizontal, his eyes roll up in his head, then turn as black as a well digger's ass. Words flow, something harsh, something like I heard when confined to hell with Iblis.

Thoughts hit me. Where am I? What am I doing? Then, where was I? How'd I get back? For some reason, I look for Cain.

Igneus rockets past, skipping like a rock on smooth water. He staggers, struggles a step, then flops to the stone.

Sebastian's eyes pop open. He somehow senses Igneus's fall despite the bleeding gash on his neck. He wrestles from my grasp to drag himself close to the Jew.

Longinus approaches. A black mass, that's all he is now. A giant shadow fuming chaos, malice, rage and death. "Three little mice," he snickers. "I wield a power ye can't imagine. A power that makes immortality moot." He speaks like Cain, yet like the giant Roman of old. Mixes his brogue as if a simmering duality lies just beneath the surface.

He raises the spear.

I close my eyes, hear Lenny say, "Uh oh."

"Immortal or not, this is going to suck."

Then, a calmness. The sound of singing angels, the light airiness of burdens cast off, of fear dissolved, of safety, of joy.

I take a peek as Longinus somehow slides away. Igneus and Sebastian have entwined their hands, which now grip the staff together.

I look to Rhyme. Then, Lee and Sima. The delicate one rockets away, dissolving before my eyes. Then I'm sliding, stretching for Rhyme's hand, grasping her middle two fingers as she grasps Lee.

We hover, float, drift away like butterflies on a strong breeze. The scene wavers, elongates. Igneus rises, face creased, shrouded in mist, bristling fury.

He raises the staff high, then slams it with the force of an A-bomb.

The explosion deafens as rock, statue, altar and basin, crumble, collapse, become debris like shrapnel.

I pull Rhyme close with one hand, Lee close with the other. "Houdini?" Rhyme calls, and I look to the spot where the dog crumpled, nothing now but huge piles of spiked marble.

And still we slide, surrounded by a flickering haze, a fogged mist without moisture. Pale like a cloud, fogged like a mirror. The sounds of heavenly voices fill my ears, my brain. Perfectly tuned, perfectly sung.

We settle to the ground outside the Temple's walls. The sounds cease.

I pop to my feet and stare at the spectacle before us.

Above the Temple, a shroud appears, shimmers, then radiates an aura that beckons and lures. It grows higher and higher, thousands of feet, until it fully envelopes the Temple and the nearby Dome of the Rock.

From behind me, I hear: "Get in there! Blow them up! Sever their limbs, their heads, every single part!"

Cain barks orders, teeth bared, eyes dead like a shark. If he's noticed us, he doesn't show it. He raises a hand, screams, "Fire!" and three tanks belch their payload at the shrouded Temple and Dome.

The rapport stuns, makes my ears tremble and my mind stutter. I drop low, pull Rhyme closer, cover both of our heads.

But it all comes to ripples.

Each shell strikes the shroud, then echoes away without so much as a puff or hint of debris.

"Get in there!" Cain screams, and Imperium soldiers, twenty or more, sprint toward the mist.

They race unimpeded, guns ready and raised. They strike the wall like a football team and explode to shards of dust that swirl languid before racing off on the wind.

Cain's face glows rage. Despite the god he thinks he is, this has surprised him. I glance around, know Longinus and Sima will surely return to exact payment from me and Rhyme and Lee. But I don't see them, have no idea where they've gone.

Then Igneus's voice, rising, thunderous, riding the wind.

Rhyme covers her ears; Lee cowers, covers his as well.

Around us, soldiers drop to their knees, hands pressed to ears.

His voice is a raging tempest. A cacophony, a million voices raised as one, timeless. Like a gong in a concrete bunker, it resonates, consumes, impossible to ignore, impossible not to hear.

"From the throne of Heaven hath I sent my servants.

"By the Hosts of Heaven is this soil blessed.

"Hear me, my people, for the time has come!

"My children! Lift up your hearts and cast away your fears. Rejoice, thy followers of goodness. Rejoice thou good and faithful servants. Come! If thou art pure. Step into my kingdom, if thou art worthy. Come! Come to my grace. Forever shine in the light of my glory.

"Hear me, my people, for time is short! If thou dost tarry, if thou dost hide, my wrath shall fall upon you as it shall the entire Earth. And lo, I will rain my vengeance upon you, the evil doer, the unholy, the blasphemer with treacherous tongues.

"The harvest is nigh! Dost thou not see? Can thou not hear? The harvest is ripe! Dost thou doubt thy Father's power? Dost thou fear the tremor of my voice?

"Fear not, you untainted. You who have kept my covenant. You who celebrate goodness in your hearts and hearths.

"If thine heart is true, come! Fear not, in purity! Fear not, in grace!

"Do not tarry! Come! Step through! Stand in glory, among the blessed Hosts of Heaven. Hast thou not heard? I've prepared a place by my side.

"Judge your heart as you have judged others. Time is short. Do not tarry. So sayeth the Father."

It ends like a radio transmission, a slight sizzle that arcs over the shroud with electric fingers.

It's become so thick, so fogged, any view of the Temple or the Dome is now obscured.

I stare at Rhyme. She blinks, bleeds, says, "Emery?" then drops to ancient stone.

More tanks appear, followed by trucks with huge cannons mounted to their tops.

I press my hands to her injuries. "Rhyme? Rhyme?" Her eyes are closed, then flicker a bit only to close again.

Behind us, an Imperium officer speaks into a radio, "Begin bombardment."

"Send everything," Cain says. "Everything short of nukes."

"Roger." The officer turns away, speaking rapidly.

"Where's Longinus?" Cain bellows. Then, he notices us. Our eyes meet and there's no sense of ever having been of use to him. Then: "Take them into custody but keep them close. They may be needed."

I'm shocked by the utter disregard for his wounded, unconscious wife. A snarl grips my face as I rise to confront the monster. Beside me, Lee tenses, assumes the pigeon-toed posture.

Then Rhyme sputters. "Emery, don't. Trust..." She drifts off, unconscious.

I look at Lee and shake my head. He deflates, then stands erect, and allows himself to be cuffed.

Cain smiles at me in an odd way, as if he's prepared a special buffet of just desserts. Then he beams gorgeous, white hair blinding, dancing on his head. Crystal eyes glare so bright they can be seen from space. His smile blooms molten, devastating, stretches his cheeks with the purity of undistilled joy. "At last," he says, breathing the words like just finishing a marathon. "At long last, dear Emery. I've won His attention."

CHAPTER 39

JERUSALEM, ISRAEL

I lift Rhyme as gently as possible while looking for somewhere safe from the coming bombardment. Long black rifles point at me and Mr. Lee. Then, Cain's hand falls on my shoulder. "Dear Emery, do stick around. I'd hate for you to miss anything." His tone tells me it isn't a request.

"Um, the bombardment," I say. "Seems reasonable to be farther away." I nod at Rhyme. "I mean…your wife?"

He waves a hand, then snickers into a clenched fist. "If my guess is correct, all my missiles will amount to nothing. Seems the Jew and the boy have cloaked themselves in cowardice." He snickers again, icy eyes twinkling. "We'll get to them soon enough. But, I assure you, dear Emery, we are quite safe."

As if on cue, five fighters streak past, missiles dropping from their underside.

I shudder, step back a pace as Cain's hand tightens on my shoulder. "Stay."

I feel like panting. Maybe he'll scratch me behind the ear, let me play in the park with the other dogs, chew on his slipper, sleep at his feet.

Missiles flow through a lazy spiral, sizzle in a squealing whoosh and race for the Temple.

I gaze at the shroud, white fog, thick, impenetrable to the human eye.

Perhaps Cain sees through it? Perhaps he knows what's going on— because I sure as hell don't.

I brace for the shock wave, the buzzing whine of shrapnel. But the missiles strike and disappear as if fully absorbed by the thick mist.

I think of Longinus, of our adventure up on Tabor, of the regal purple haze that formed to protect us and the structure.

"Just as I thought," Cain says. "Just as I imagined." He cranes his neck, seems to have a silent conversation with himself, perhaps with Iblis.

More fighters appear, shrieking like proverbial banshees. Then, more missiles.

The shroud absorbs them without so much as ripple or wave. The impacts are soundless, the shrapnel nonexistent. I wonder again why the Roman and Sima aren't here exacting their revenge.

A medic appears. Cain flicks his head to Rhyme. The man rushes to her, kneels beside and starts to examine. Not so worse for wear, I think. Probably just blood loss. He opens a bag and produces a bunch of bandages, then starts to tend her wounds.

Then, the Imperium officer is back, waiting to be noticed.

"Report," Cain says.

"Yes, Emperor. It seems the missiles had no effect, like the shroud protects in some fashion. If we can get close, we can attempt to examine it. Infrared shows two humans inside, no others. It sounds impossible but every living thing was…well…swept clear before the shroud fell. I've double-checked everything, there's just no other explanation."

Cain grins, holds his gaze on Rhyme.

"There's more, Sire," the officer continues. "We're getting reports from all over the world. From other religious sites. That state…that say…" He produces a small camouflage notebook.

"Let me guess," Cain interrupts. "They're all destroyed."

The officer wears an expression of dismay. "No sir. Not exactly. It's…well…" He sighs, seems to set his jaw for Cain's wrath. "It seems they've all developed the shroud. The exact same…fog…as here. We're talking thousands of locations, perhaps hundreds of thousands. Reports are still coming in, but it seems each location had similar things happen. People hovered, floated, slid. All were removed from the sites before the fog fell. They report being lifted, then gently expelled, such that no living thing remained within the shrouds at these sites." He pauses, wipes his mouth, eyes filled with wonder. "How on Earth could that happen all at once? At tens of thousands of sites? I mean, the coordination would be impossible. How could anyone coordinate an operation on such a scale? And down to the second? It's…well…"

"What?"

"It's simply not possible, sir. Even X'chasei couldn't pull it off. The scale's mind-boggling. The numbers, the math, just too much, too vast. And only religious sites. No other places reported these cloaks except religious sites. Churches, cathedrals, monasteries, mosques. Even Buddhist temples, shrines, abbeys. It seems anywhere that *anyone* goes to worship their specific deity has been enshrouded with this same fog."

Cain sighs like he just lost a bet. "Is there any good news?"

The officer flips through the notebook. "Well, sir, not much. Seems at all these locations, when people tried to re-enter, some could, others couldn't. Those who couldn't were…" he flips more pages, "quote, turned to dust, unquote." He lowers his notebook. "Sir, I can suggest some ways to handle this but there's just no rhyme or reason to any of it. It doesn't make sense, defies all logic." He pauses, briefly holds Cain's eyes, looks away. "I fear we don't know if this is a threat or not."

Cain grins, his hair dancing a hula, a mamba, a jig atop his head. He steps a pace closer to the fog. Then, he laughs like being tickled, like centuries of joy just burst the cork and are loosed on his face and countenance. Tears roll down a face red with hilarity. He breathes in quick gasps between repeated peals of laughter. Wiping his eyes, chortling, he becomes stoic for a second then bursts again into elated spasms.

I wonder, wish, he's finally lost his mind. That whatever happened was the proverbial straw that broke the beast's back. That now, maybe, he'll be easier to subdue. More will see the truth of his menace and his plans to scorch the Earth and all its denizens. I watch as the great Caesar, this Antichrist, guffaws, slaps his knee, wipes his eyes. Crazy people rarely know they're crazy.

It goes on for some minutes, his roaring laughter, his streaming tears, his complete and utter abandonment of decorum. He puffs to a stop like a train out of coal, turns, looks at the officer, wipes a stray tear. "Gather your troops, Major. It's time for a little experiment."

CHAPTER 40

JERUSALEM, ISRAEL

FNG, Crispy thinks, peering through the window at the so-called friar.

He'll die out there, has no idea what to do, doesn't have the sense to use the tarp I tossed him for a meaningful shelter, instead holds it like an umbrella. He's obviously never heard of hypothermia. Rain and wind wear you down, steal your energy, your will. Hell, not a bad way to go. At least you die happy.

Outside, the man shivers like a chihuahua. His feet must be freezing. Sandals ain't good for shit.

Gotta stop attracting them, like burdocks to corduroy. It's never served me once. Like Rhyme, like Branch, slowed me down, got me fucked up. Seems Rhyme has the same problem. Towing Bill around, that good for nothing hound. I bet Emery even started as a cling-on.

Not this time, goddammit! No more. Not my problem. He can freeze. If he ain't smart, he ain't needed. Look at him, standing there, gawking like manna will magically fall from the sky. Like a savior will appear to wipe his nose and powder his blistered ass.

Not doing it.

Nope.

No way.

Ten minutes later Pappy sips coffee and stares around at the lack of furnishings in the old house. "Again, my thanks. May all God's—"

"Stop! Don't start the God talk, padre. I ain't in the mood. If you've been through what I've been through, you'd see it the same. I was nice enough to let you in, don't make me suffer for it." He flicks his eyes from the screen. "Besides, I need to concentrate."

Scarred fingers type code into a keyboard. Beside him two open Pelican cases spill wires, electronics. Pappy snaps his mouth shut. The coffee's hot, good. Probably wouldn't have made it much longer out there. But, as always, God provided, sent a most unusual angel. Now what?

"Can I help with something? Tidy up, perhaps. Cook?"

"Ain't got no stove," Crispy says. "Got MRE's. Everything a growing boy needs." He nods to a box in the corner. "There's an open case over there if you're hungry."

Pappy sees labels: CHILI W/ BEANS, BEEF SHREDDED IN BARBECUE SAUCE, CHICKEN CHUNKS. The packaging is light brown, the letters MRE in a diagonal black stripe. Everything a growing boy needs, eh? He rises, walks to the window and peers at the relentless rain, the darkening puddles spreading wider, deeper.

Should be doing something. Should be out thwarting Cain and his plans. But things haven't gone exactly as planned. On his trip from Mount Tabor, he'd encountered more than he bargained for, had exposed the depths of his naiveté involving God and the things He'd tolerate on the planet.

No man can comprehend the mind of God, indeed.

He'd seen more dead than he could count, than he could ever imagine. He'd helped, hitched rides, wandered, realized his hasty retreat from Mount Tabor had served no purpose.

Nukes. The epiphany he'd had on Tabor, blazing visions in his head, billions dying. He'd stepped off in sandals, arms poked through a garbage bag, a small tote of possessions swinging by his side.

Then the days got long. The sandals, devices of torture. Not up to the trek or the task.

The rain kept coming, the dead, piling. Until eventually, while giving a side of the road eulogy for three fallen civilians, it hit him. He had no way to stop Cain. Would never arrive in time to prevent the inevitable launch of the nukes.

Doesn't God expect us to be smarter? Doesn't He expect us to follow His lead and things will work out?

He watches the typing man, scars illuminated in the laptop's faint glow. Badly injured at some point. Must be some story.

Suddenly, Crispy's eyes light up, his face twists, makes the scars crinkle like a broad range of rolling hills. "Amazing," Crispy says, typing faster. "Simply can't be. No one could manage this." Fingers fly as he types, then he reaches into one of the cases and pulls a black square box and plugs it into the laptop. He speaks to himself, seems oblivious to Pappy's presence. "Got to get this out, show the world. It's a smoking gun. Can't be ignored."

Pappy wonders if the man knows what's left of the world isn't much at all. Mostly smoking embers and radiation. If anyone remained alive in those countries, they won't be for long. "Who's left to tell?" he whispers, not realizing he's spoken aloud until he notices Crispy's eyes staring over the screen.

"What?"

Pappy looks at the floor, feels abashed. "Sorry to blurt," he says. "Didn't realize."

"No," Crispy says, "what was that you said?"

"I said: Who's left to tell? Perhaps you're unaware, but there's been a nuclear attack. Last I heard the U.S., Russia, possibly China, have become nuclear wastelands."

Crispy betrays nothing as he calculates the meaning of Pappy's words. "Good point," he says. "Who's left to tell? Who's left to care?" He mutters something, says, "I think we're all fucked."

Pappy grimaces. A life of ministry has shielded him from certain realities, certain crude expressions. "Indeed, my son, but God has a plan."

"Really? Is it to burn us all to a crisp?"

Pappy stares, not sure if the man is being serious or poking fun at his own deformity.

Crispy continues. "Have you ever seen Monty Python?"

"Not enough to know anything more than the name."

"Well, they did this comedy skit where a flock of parishioners were singing hymns in Sunday church."

"What's funny about that?"

Crispy holds his eyes, wears a look that says he has endless comments on the hilarity of singing hymns to God. "It's not the hymns, it's what they sang. A song like: *Please Lord don't burn us, don't boil or baste your flock. Don't fricassee or roast us or braise us in hot stock.* You know, like that. What made it funny is that they did it with complete reverence, as if it was the most normal thing to ask of God while living on this planet where death lurks at every turn. What else can a man do but sing songs asking not to be broiled or roasted? Fucking, *hi*-larious."

Pappy winces, thinks to tell the man of his preference for more subdued language. He thinks of the song, the humor that Crispy seems to appreciate so much. "I think I get it. What makes it funny is everything we're exposed to and our chances of being killed in a variety of ways. All the while an omnipotent God turns a blind eye."

Crispy's look is dubious. "Something like that. Although the way you say it sucks the funny right out of it."

Pappy looks down. "Sorry. My sense of humor isn't as developed as some."

"What I've just found seems to back all that up. Seems to take God out of the equation entirely."

Pappy chuckles. "One cannot simply remove God from the equation. God *is* the equation."

It's Crispy's turn to laugh. "Which makes the rest of us moot. Just characters without meaning. Just X's and Y's forging our way through a graphed chart of God's design." He holds Pappy's eyes. "Look, padre. I don't mean to offend, nor do I want to disparage your beliefs. Perhaps we should stay away from topics concerning religion."

Pappy glances at the robe, the soaked sandals beneath, says nothing as an awkward silence ensues.

Then, Crispy jolts forward, strikes a few of the laptop's keys and unplugs the square box. "For what it's worth, I got it all downloaded to this drive. Hopefully my hacking skills are good enough that no one notices I breached the server." His grin is mischievous and crinkled. "It's been awhile, and you know us old guys, never too good with computers anyway."

Pappy grins. "On that we can agree."

Crispy moves to the MRE's, withdraws a pack labeled BEEFSTEAK w/MUSHROOMS. On the desk next to the laptop, a phone starts to vibrate. He looks at the screen, sighs audibly, then thumbs a button. "Go."

"Dear Reginald, I hate to be a bother, but it seems I require your services once more. You see, I'm at the Temple and things have gotten a bit—how do you phrase it—sideways. In any event, I need you to locate a friar who wandered away from the Church of the Transfiguration and is thought to be near Jerusalem. He goes by the name of Pappy, short for Papadopoulos. If it isn't too much bother, I'd like you to locate him and bring him to the Temple, unharmed, of course."

Crispy listens, flicks a glance at the monk. "How much for delivery?"

"Oh, the usual. But if you do it quickly, add twenty percent."

"That's very generous."

"A trifle for such excellent work. Do remember though, unharmed."

"Roger. I'll poke around and see what turns up." With a press of a button, the call ends. Crispy peels open the MRE, grabs his canteen, adds a bit of water to a rectangular pouch in transparent green, then places another package inside. In seconds steam rises as the food heats.

He watches smoky wisps, wonders what Cain would want with this friar. Wonders at his luck and the money he'll make by delivering him.

Unharmed. Cain made a point of that. Unharmed. Crispy thinks it over, a first really, the first contract from X'chasei where the subject is to be unharmed. Generally, it's the other way around, in spades.

He watches the water bubble in the pouch, an apt metaphor for his problems which seem to ripple from some endless invisible fountain.

No man can serve two masters. He doesn't know where he heard that but knows all too well it hangs on him now like a massive stone.

The facade's harder and harder to maintain. His conscience, harder and harder to keep at bay. Nowhere left to go except to Cain and X'chasei.

And Rhyme married the fucker, plays a similar game, some sort of love triangle involving Emery. He sighs, I taught her better. She knows better.

But perhaps she's outsmarting him, out thinking him. Has learned the safest place, the best place to survive, is right next to the man who makes it all happen. I taught her to survive and surviving she is. Has even managed to keep Emery safe throughout the process.

Too much calculus. Too many X's and Y's, crossing, veering, multiplying by exponents. Sooner or later the sums will come due and when that happens, they'd better be ahead of it or instinct says they'll be crushed underfoot without a single second's thought.

CHAPTER 41

JERUSALEM, ISRAEL

Crispy places the phone on the desk and turns to Pappy. "Have you been to the Temple since they rebuilt it?"

"I'm afraid my duties to my congregation keep me busy. I'm ashamed to say, I haven't found the time. I usually visit Jerusalem twice a year and thought I'd see it on the next visit. But seems God has other plans."

"Of course, padre, makes perfect sense. It's really something though. You should see it with your own eyes."

Pappy takes a bite of something labeled COUNTRY CAPTAIN CHICKEN, wonders what it is and how it got its name. Still, not too bad. Indeed, everything a growing boy needs. "Thanks again for the clothes. They fit well and I'm in your debt."

Crispy moves to the window, peers through dust and grime at the rain outside. "Don't mention it. Least I could do. A damn sight better than the robe and sandals. Is that all you brought?"

"Oh, no. I brought a small bag, but the ruffians relieved me of it." He wears cargo pants in khaki and broad boots with thick laces. A green polo shirt and a thick belt used by, as Crispy said, "riggers." "Seems one should consider the elements before travel. But a head of steam overcame logical thought."

"Well, those should do ya. Just try and keep them clean. I ain't got no washer here. Where you headed anyway?"

Pappy considers the question, feels as lost as the tribes of Israel. "No idea," he says. "I'll probably go to the Temple and see if I can lend a hand there. Either way, God will direct my steps. I'm sure you want me out of the way as soon as possible."

"Nonsense. You're not a bad guest, despite all the God talk. But interesting you should mention the Temple, I have to make a delivery there today. Would you like to tag along?"

Pappy looks surprised, then pleased by the coincidence. "Sounds like a good way to spend a rainy day." He takes another bite, CAPTAIN'S CHICKEN is salty and warm. "You're a delivery man?"

Wrinkled scars make his face look like melted wax. "From time to time. Only certain things, though. I mean, it pays the bills."

Pappy thinks of Cain paying the bills for most of the church's expenses, most of the parishioner's needs. He thinks of Cain's job offer, Imperium's Minister of Religion. Thinks of Emery working for the Antichrist and how he uses that to convince himself he's not involved. "It'd be nice to take a drive," he says. "Nicer still to see the Temple. I think I will tag along."

Crispy moves to a closet, rustles inside, then tosses a yellow rain jacket. "You'll need this. Can't have you catching pneumonia."

Pappy accepts and slides it on.

"I'll need about ten minutes, padre. I can't meet my employer dressed like this."

"Of course, my son. Whenever you're ready. Gives me a chance to dine on this scrumptious meal."

"If you think that's scrumptious, wait 'til you try the meatloaf."

Twenty minutes later, Crispy appears. He wears a dark suit, almost black, a white dress shirt and black tie, crisp and thin. Glossed black oxfords peek from beneath the trousers' hem.

"Wow," Pappy says. "That's quite a transformation. You look like a movie hitman."

Crispy laughs. "Think so? Just the look I was going for." He moves to a small end table, reaches under, pulls a two-tone gun that twinkles in the room's light.

Pappy startles, blinks a few times, then nods at the gun. "Are you trying to complete the ensemble?"

Crispy ejects the clip, eyes it, slaps it back in. Then he slides something atop the weapon, peers inside. "No. Just being safe. I was in the military once and those lessons stick with you. With Jerusalem the way it is right now, one can't be too cautious." He steps forward, grinning through a scarred face. "Allow me to introduce Miss Kimber. She holds nine shots, is easy as hell to shoot, comes in handy in a pinch." He offers the gun. "Care to give her a tickle?"

Pappy holds the pistol gently as wariness blooms on his features.

"Careful, padre. She's loaded."

Pappy eyes the weapon, turns it slowly in his hand. "A lot of buttons and things."

"Yep. If you treat her right, she'll blossom."

"Have you ever shot it at anyone?"

Crispy gives a look, purses his lips. "A million times, padre, a million times. You ready to go?"

Pappy hands the gun back, stands and tugs his trousers. "Indeed, I am. I'm rather excited to see the place."

Crispy grins. "I'm certain it won't disappoint."

———

Jerusalem is coming to life. Reborn, as it were. Born again. Traffic lights blink above a mostly crowded street. Cars move, honk, pull to the curb to eject pedestrians toward their destinations. "Hell of a change, padre. I'm told only a week ago this place was nothing but morose faces and corpses. Now look. Streets are buzzing, electricity's back on, stores are restocked. It's quite marvelous really. The emperor has a real talent for getting things done."

Pappy eyes the man and thinks of the Emperor Cain. Thinks of the Antichrist, the crown prophecy. The fact that he's been correct on his predictions causes no happiness, just concern. What's next? What does Cain have planned? Or God for that matter? With each day a feeling rises, grips, sinks deep. In his heart, he feels like a man without purpose. Like he serves no role in God's designs. He shakes the thoughts away. Just a test of faith, a chance to show his worth, nothing more.

"You okay?" Crispy asks.

"I am, my son. How much farther to the Temple?"

Crispy eases the truck to a checkpoint, reaches into his suit jacket, hands a young guard a leather bifold. "Not too far. It's just up here. We'll be there in a minute."

Pappy smiles, looks ahead to see crumpled walls and slight tendrils of rising mist. Past that, a huge round dome absorbs scattered sunrays and looks like condensed fog.

Crispy thanks the guard, reclaims his bifold, and presses the accelerator. Pappy points at the dome. "I don't remember anything like that before."

Crispy peers through slapping wipers and dots of rain. "No idea, padre. I've never seen it either. Looks weird, eh? Foggy. Maybe some weather phenomenon." He veers the truck into an area cordoned with orange cones. "Let's go see?"

Rhyme opens her eyes, looks at me, emeralds dull. She gives a small smile, a weak smile.

I move close, grasp her hand, glance at the medic, then the IV in her arm. "How are you feeling?"

"Not great," she says. "Don't remember much except a fight. How'd we do?"

I move to the side so she can see Cain staring at the clouded dome. "Not too good, I'm afraid."

She frowns. Her emeralds dull a shade more. "Shit. That was our big chance to get away. Help me sit up."

I cradle her head as Stuart helps me heft her to lean against some crumbled rocks. "How's that?"

She doesn't respond, only looks past me with wide eyes.

"Rhyme," I say, "you feeling okay?"

Her eyes are locked on something beyond me, probably Cain, contemplating her hatred.

Then I hear, "Dear Reginald! Always the prompt one. Why, you've completed your task in record time." I turn to see Cain with a delighted expression on his face. "I continually underestimate you and you always deliver. I see you brought the priest."

I'm poleaxed when Pappy steps forward dressed like an off-duty GI. Yellow rain jacket, khaki cargo pants, green polo, thick boots. He looks a bit comical and a lot nervous. "I'm not a priest," he says.

Crispy is dressed in black like some Hollywood G-man. He stares at Cain, but doesn't venture a glance toward us. Beside me, I feel the heat. Perhaps it's instinct, but they say if you live with someone long enough, you can sense their moods, their emotions. Without looking, I feel Rhyme's steam. Can imagine her blazing emeralds, flickering flames that broadcast her rage. I feel her move, then struggle to stand.

I stand too, following her blistered gaze. She's locked on Crispy, mouth open, hands trembling at her side. She shuffles a step, seems to waiver as if off balance. The medic appears and she waves him off. I notice the empty holsters and thank the gods of luck she's been stripped of her pistols.

She's weak, her words shaky, betrayed, angry, seared. "Cr—Crispy?" she says. "Tell me you don't—That you aren't working for…" She trails off, looks away, disgusted.

Cain beams radiant. "Of course, he does, my dear. I've no room in my kingdom for the average or useless. Crispy's been a solid ally for years now. Since his unfortunate…accident. Why, if it wasn't for him, you'd be nothing more than a cinder." He gives Crispy a sidelong look. "Although he did manage to bring dear Emery back, even though I instructed him not to." He waves a hand. "But alas, forgive and forget, doesn't change my plans in the slightest." He turns away, grasps Pappy's arm and steps toward the fogged shroud. "There's a new wrinkle, dear Pappy, some new theatrics from our loving Father. I was wondering if through your research, through your long nights of study and contemplation, if perhaps you have a clue about what this is and why it's here." His hair starts to writhe, to brighten, and I wonder if it indicates rage, if it indicates he's about to do something awful. "I'm told they popped up all over the world. Hundreds of thousands of them. All at religious sites. I'm told that some people step through never to be seen again, while others attempt the same and end up piles of salt. Salt, mind you. I tasted it. We've tried everything here. Missiles, tanks, guns, troops. Nothing penetrates. Nothing can pass except for the occasional soldier." He motions to a line of men in Imperium uniforms. An Imperium officer steps to the front, discusses something with a soldier, then points him at the dome. I follow the line, see worry etched on their faces as if drawn in color. The kind of look someone wears when plunged unarmed into a raging battle. Some appear to search for an exit, a way to run off. The officer frowns, then nudges the first soldier toward the shroud.

The soldier steps tentative, shuffles forward, brows creased, fists balled at his side. Around the perimeter, I notice other soldiers, rifles ready, as if to say those who don't follow orders will be gunned down where they stand.

The soldier is young, perhaps twenty-three. He steps near the shroud, two feet away, then extends a hand as if testing the thing's energy. It's obvious this isn't what he wants to be doing.

Then something peculiar happens. The shroud wavers, swirls smoke like the vapors of hell. But these are different, like cotton candy spun in pastel pink, calming green, gentle—happy, if happiness applies.

The surface shifts into a mirror, clearly shows the soldier's face and the angst carved onto it. He presses his hand to the surface, seems to test its girth and sturdiness. Around him, the rest of the massive dome remains a fogged mist. The only part mirrored is directly in front of him.

The Imperium officer barks an order and another soldier steps beside the first. The two exchange words, obvious barracks buddies bucking up their courage before whatever comes next.

Cain speaks. "We've sent thirty-seven so far. Of those, one passed through. One. He had orders to return with a report but hasn't. All the rest, well..." He motions toward the shroud's base. "Piles of salt, I'm afraid. A shame really, but they gave their lives in the best interest of Imperium, and for that, they'll be celebrated as heroes."

Rhyme stares daggers at Crispy. She moves apart from me and stands without aid. For Crispy's part, he keeps his eyes on Cain, focused like hypnotized.

Cain continues. "Quite a conundrum, really. When you approach the mist, it becomes mirrored. If you press a hand to it, you feel nothing. You can walk away without ill effect. You can even sit and lean on it and it will remain quite solid." He rubs his chin here, face creased with confusion. "I know, sounds ludicrous, but it seems to know if one intends to step through or if you're just probing it, touching it, testing it." Eyes of aqua search Pappy. "We can't figure it out. But then I thought of you. If anyone can provide insight, certainly our dear Friar Papadopoulos is the man for the job."

Cain looks at the officer, at the soldier. "Do get on with it."

The young soldier looks at the line of his comrades, inhales a deep breath, moves his head as if stretching his neck, then steps forward.

I don't know what I expected the moment the soldier moved into the mirror, but what I got was entirely unsurprising. After all I'd seen to this point: Cain's mark in all its evil glory, Longinus transfigured before my very eyes, ancient relics laying entire armies asunder, massive archangels with voices like rolling thunder, the splendors of heaven, the horrors of hell. And while I'm on the topic of horror, the horrors of Earth: mushroom clouds, avarice, molestation, gluttony, vengeance, abuse of every kind. Add to that, John the Apostle, born to heaven by Jesus Himself, Cain getting his head blown off only to survive as if nothing happened. Iblis/Satan/Lucifer. Laslo's hell, Crispy's hell, Jonas's hell, Rhyme's hell, my own hell.

I realize then, that when the final sums are tallied, there shouldn't be much left that surprises me. But as I watch, the soldier steps forward and bumps into the mirror as if it's just, well, a regular mirror.

Cain frowns and stares at Pappy with crystal eyes. "One other thing," he says. "Some *can't* step through. Seems like there has to be some kind of intent. As if they have to *want* to step through. A metaphor brought to life: if the spirit isn't willing, then the flesh cannot pass." He crinkles his eyes. Above him, locks writhe like white flame. Then he says, "Fifty pounds of gold to the next man who steps through."

The soldier beside the first swallows hard, then sets his jaw and steps into the mirror.

There's a flash like a camera, then a billion granules in an abrupt cloud. Some float to the ground and thicken to clumps on wet stone. Others drift away to flutter through Jerusalem and into the Levant sky.

"Like that, dear Pappy. Most unusual. Have you any thoughts?"

I glance at the line of soldiers, see faces stretched with anxiety. Cain flashes that smile, turns to fully face Pappy. "Apparently dear Igneus and his sidekick created this fog, presumably to protect these holy sites. He even made a little speech, something akin to *the pure can pass but everyone else is doomed.*" He pauses, seems to search his mind to see if he's forgotten anything. "In any event," he says, "that's what we know. I'd consider it a tremendous service if you'd share your thoughts on the matter?"

The monk scratches his chin, stares at the fogged dome. "I'm not sure I'd tell you if I knew," he says. "Seems I'd be aiding the Antichrist, embracing evil."

Cain grins his movie star smile and I see a change possess the friar like he's hypnotized. Cain's gifts at work, no doubt. Rhyme stays locked on Crispy. If she had her guns, I'm afraid her valued mentor and close friend would feel the bite of her wrath. She blinks and places a hand on my shoulder for support.

Pappy grins like an imbecile, stutters a bit, then starts to speak.

"I think…" Pappy says. "It's only a hunch, mind you, but I think that it's… it's the…"

Cain's patience holds by a slender thread. "Please, dear friar, haste is appreciated."

Pappy blinks, smiles through quivering lips as if his entire being fights Cain's gifts.

"Well," he says, blinking again. "I think…" He licks his lips and swallows hard, gaze locked on Cain. "I think it's the rapture."

Chapter 42

Jerusalem, Israel

Cain's laughter feels hollow as it rolls over us: Rhyme, Lee, Crispy, Pappy, me, and Stuart. The gathered soldiers move closer, some distracted by the fogged dome.

I look for Houdini as Cain collects himself but retains a malicious grin. "Dear Pappy, I'm afraid the rapture isn't a thing. It's just something I added to your precious holy text to confound God's control and ensnare His believers. A powerful device really, hasn't failed a single time through all the centuries. Get people worried about what happens after they die. Change their focus from how they're living now to fictional rewards that await after death. A master stroke really, people will bear up to almost anything if they're convinced their suffering has purpose, that casting their bread upon the water will result in it rolling back on the crests of endless waves. In the end, their intent, all of them, is nothing more than self-service. Nothing more than veiled avarice."

He steps away, places his hands on his hips, then cranes to look at the towering shroud. "No, no. Simple nonsense, the rapture isn't a thing."

Pappy stands serene and I admire his boldness, the courage of his convictions. Perhaps there are things that will intimidate him, but the

Antichrist isn't one of them. "Doesn't mean it's false," he says. "Doesn't mean God didn't want you to make that change. The Bible's the divine word of God, inspired by God. Couldn't that mean, even though you made the changes, that those changes were guided by God?" He wags his head, looks like a professor tutoring a student. "I'm afraid, like it or not, and despite your efforts, God still has things well in hand. I believe he's placed this shroud, all these shrouds throughout the world, to call the faithful home."

Cain's eyes flash anger. "That can't be. If it was going to happen the way I added it, then all the faithful would disappear in an instant." Cain blinks rapidly, hair writhing on his head like wheat in a storm. He takes a cleansing breath, smooths his hands over an impeccable suit. "Dear Pappy, I'm afraid your theory can't be correct. It…it just can't be."

I know he's flustered now, even panicky. Cain is to eloquence like a thesaurus to synonyms. When he speaks it's precise and perfect, not hesitant, not unassured.

A feeling grips me, the feeling of going too far. The feeling of sitting in the front row of a roller coaster just as it tops the hill and starts to plummet. Bad things are coming, and to humanity's detriment.

Cain paces, mumbles, appears on the verge of lunacy. Then, I hear a grunt, something akin to a decision made. I glance up. Stuart smiles, winks, then walks directly to the fogged shroud. It mirrors as he nears, then, without sound or light, no theatrics of any kind, he passes through and is gone.

We all stand dumbstruck.

Cain stares, blinks, seems awed by the sudden disappearance of the hulking African. At the confidence of his gait, at his instant decision to march right through.

"What?" Rhyme says. "Where'd he go?"

Cain's hair brightens, his eyes turn the color of the steel sky above. "Like that," he says to Pappy. "No sense for any of it. If you're right, friar, then our dear Stuart just took the initiative and proved your point. A bit of a conundrum, as I'm sure you'll point out. That man worked for me, was a trusted bodyguard. If your theory's correct, if I'm as evil as you say, then how could anyone who works for me be pure of heart and pass through without a word or chuckle?"

Just then, there's a flash from the shroud, one that blinds and makes me shield my eyes until the radiance dies.

When I look up, I'm stunned.

It's Bill, a determined grin etched on his face.

Then, Houdini appears, strides to Crispy, nudges his hand and sits by his leg.

Rhyme's eyes fill with delight, then simmering rage.

Cain stands frozen.

My mouth hangs open.

Bill walks past dressed in jeans and a Rolling Stones T-shirt featuring great stretched lips, bulbous red with a languid tongue. He doesn't seem to notice any of us, just walks by like we're strangers on the street. His brow is focused, his eyes clear, not bloodshot and veiled by the effects of weed.

"Bill?" Cain says. "What are you doing?"

Bill says nothing as he strides past piles of rubble and stone, past astonished soldiers.

"Stop him!" the officer shouts.

"Wait!" Cain wears an expression of delight. "Inhibit him in no way."

The officer pauses. The soldiers await his command. "Belay that order," he says. "Let him pass."

I stare at the hippie, look for the ever-present joint. I find nothing. He moves with a purpose. Moves like someone who knows their objectives and how to get there. As the sun dips, it casts rays of pink and orange, like God's fingers gripping the horizon. Bill moves into shadow, into dusk, into those places hippie clones go when they've emerged from magical shrouds to stroll into the sunset like a B-movie cowboy.

We stare until his shadow stretches thin, then vanishes.

The dome is huge and clouded. Stars become apparent above, the first sparkling hints of orbs too far away to imagine or comprehend.

Why's God so interested in us when the universe is his playground?

Why does God dote so on what amounts to nothing more than a speck of sand on a vast beach. I'd read once that if you could count all the grains of sand on every beach on the planet, that the figure would be akin to the vastness of the universe and the number of planets that float through the void.

It's a random cosmic accident that we're even here, that we even exist. A riddle of staggering proportions that humanity's survived these centuries and that those centuries amount to nothing more than a few grains of dust in some universal hourglass.

It's mind numbing when one thinks about it, the sheer luck, the sheer fact we even exist. A miracle balanced on the slimmest edge of belief and fortune. At any moment, some asteroid, some slung stone, can impact our planet and turn us all to dust—or salt—in the way of the dinosaurs or any other mass extinction.

I think of the term in a new way. Mass extinction. The end of all life on the planet.

It's happened before, why not again? Why not this time? At the hands of an angry God?

The thought hits me, rises from myriad webs in my skull. I'm immortal. And, for posterity's sake, it'd be a shame not to add my constant qualifier, *Or so I'm told*. It hasn't been tested, hasn't been proved.

Confusion overwhelms. My mind fills with spinning orbs and clouded domes, with pillars of salt and the price we pay for an existence we didn't request.

I don't want to pay that price. A feeling that numbs me to my toes. Why love, if love is folly? Why care, if caring is pain? Why the stoicism? The endless quest to strive, fall, dust off, rise again, only for another kick in the clacks?

Turns out I was right all along. My existence is meaningless. The pills, Mr. Sig—hell, any rope with a noose, would've freed me from all of this. Instead, and due to my choices, my, what? Valiance? My good intentions? My love for Rhyme? Here I stand with half the world a smoking wasteland wondering why I didn't pull that trigger when I had the chance.

I've had this feeling before, of being completely and totally fucked. Completely and totally bound to these madmen and the prophecies they seek.

Absolutely defeated.

Absolutely destroyed.

Absolutely depressed.

Freed from my addictions, I have little barrier with which to shield myself.

I hear their voices as if through a crowd. Like someone whispering during a performance of Beethoven's Nineth, barely heard, barely registered.

"Major Vasili, you stated the infrared shows two individuals inside?"

"Yes sir, and that hasn't changed with the emergence of the man and the dog. The infrared still shows two people."

I hear Cain mumble something, then comes a pregnant pause as the symphony mutes.

I hear him say, "Dear Reginald, might I borrow your sidearm?"

The gunshot startles me to reality.

I spin to see Cain with a smoking gun. To see Crispy's scars crinkle to complete horror.

I see Pappy, mouth open, eyes wide.

Then there's Rhyme. Holding her chest, a bloody patch blooming as if in time lapse. "Emery?" she says, falling as emeralds disappear behind her eyelids.

My rage forms a mushroom cloud, fiery and boundless.

"Before you do anything rash, dear Emery," Cain says, "it seems Rhyme's been injured and needs aid." He grins a bit. "I'm told the lad Sebastian excels at healing." His white hair dazzles. "Unfortunately, the lad seems veiled in the dome." He steps close, smile blinding, hypnotic. "If it isn't too much bother—and time is of the essence— would you mind terribly going in there and asking if he'd be so kind as to ply his gifts for the woman you love?"

I lunge but get knocked to the ground by Crispy. Then Pappy's there, leaning over me, speaking fast. "Easy, Emery. Take a breath. Don't let anger guide you."

I move for Rhyme and feel some small relief when the medic nears and crouches.

There's another shot and the medic flops to lie unmoving.

"No one's to render aid." It's Cain, calm and content.

Rhyme's eyes are closed, her breath flutters. The blood stain spreads with each second.

Pappy helps me to my feet, holds my eyes and places both hands on my cheeks to assure my attention. "You can do this, Emery," he says, but his face betrays what he thinks: I *can't* do this. I'm fucked. And by extension, so is Rhyme. "Only the pure can enter," he says. "On which side of that line are you?"

I glare at Cain, glare at Crispy, glare at the goddamn dog.

Sweat blooms as I turn to the shroud, a swirling mist, a giant cloak over Temple and Dome. It looks as easy as walking through a spring fog, as easy as traversing a waterpark's mist.

I step close, see my mirrored reflection.

I sigh, change my gaze to Rhyme.

Cain approaches, stands behind me as I stare daggers. "Dear Emery, allow me to help."

"Fuc—" Before another syllable passes, his hands are on me.

My mind spins. Tempests of time flicker alight to become only smoke. Like turning the pages of a book on fire, they whirl, tumble, fade ash and dust. And then we're there. Back at the ghoulish table where I'd first met Iblis. Then, I hear:

> *"If indeed I find you dead,*
> *I'll see a life that's been misled.*
> *By all that's never taught or offered,*
> *a dead man's tale so often authored.*
> *A million dreams in space and frozen,*
> *just more morass within the ozone.*
> *Cry for you? Forget the thought.*
> *It seems you've found all that you sought.*

—Now, get to stuffin' that ruddy plot."

The fist presses. Iblis squeals. "Delightful, no? And my apologies, dear Emery, but I've one last thrill for you."

I snarl. My hands tremble. "No more, you said. I'm done. I have enough for your stupid biography."

He waves me away, stands then adjusts a smoking jacket in red velvet. "I understand your trepidation, I really do, but I assure you this vision is quite painless. More of an encore. A bit more pepper for the stew. If you'll indulge me."

The waiter appears, faceless, perfect tux as I remember. He struggles to set up a small screen, then places an old reel to reel movie projector on the table. He flips a switch and the machine whirs.

"This is ridiculous." My words fade to singed wind, to swirling desert sands, then to a lush oasis. "What's this?"

"Watch," Iblis says. "Learn."

Chapter 43

The serpent slides through the grass. Black scales glisten morning dew and sunbeams.

Beneath a tree, a woman sleeps, chest rising, falling. Eyelids flutter with restless dreams.

The serpent slithers between her feet, then coils around her leg.

She stirs as it caresses silken skin. Ruby lips part as a sigh escapes.

The serpent sets loose tingles, slides slippery over flesh soft and ripe, smooth, electric. Hands appear, then massage as slumbering thighs part. Arching her back, a warmth invades her loins.

"This is the good part," Iblis says. "Watch."

Gooseflesh appears, then spreads across her nakedness like wind over wheat. She quivers, inhales, basks as each caress lingers. A sleek abdomen rises, falls, faster and faster.

The serpent changes form. Hands like iron but soft as silk, probe, linger, arouse.

She bites her bottom lip, presses her pelvis to the sensation, grinds inflamed as breath flutters, as breasts heave.

Delicate folds part as he enters.

She gasps at this new intrusion. Then, overcome, passion rising, she thrusts against him, takes him fully inside as sweat shivers on skin that bristles. Never has she experienced such a feeling, such fulfillment. Her hands claw, press divots on his back, grasp his hips, pull him deep.

Panting, flushed, chin tilted, eyes squeezed tight, she grips his buttocks, grinds into him, gasping with each thrust, thirst growing on waves of ecstasy.

He becomes fevered, his body slick, a morning sun glowing a rapture of harmony. She writhes, wraps her legs around his form, holds him inside as he bucks and gasps.

A serpent tongue snaps, tickles her neck. A moan escapes, betrays her passion to glade and glen. She cries out, fully willing, enamored, pulsing, filled. Broad shoulders rise, and she grips them desperately, pulls him even deeper as he expels his passion into her womb.

Breathless, motionless, she lies on a mossy bed, beneath a tree whose branches envelope like a soft blanket. A soothing sun warms, spreads rays through the thick canopy to spill over them in stripes of light and shade. She grips his face, devours his mouth; tongues dance, drenched, playful.

He rises above her and gazes at her beauty: raven hair, eyes brown and deep, cheekbones high over sensuous lips. The first woman, the model for women to come. The mold from which all others are created. God's gift to man, more tempting than anything man could think to conjure.

Serpent eyes peer from Adam's face.

She squeals and pushes him away. "Who are you?" She pulls her legs close. "What have you done?"

A dark angel rises on mists of shimmering radiance. Morning rays fuse as simmering wings unfurl to lace the canopy above. "I showed you what God will not," Iblis says. "I showed the pleasures God keeps for Himself." Glistening of crimson and deepest black, broad wings rise to ruffle in a cooling breeze.

She stands, bites her lip, but can't stop herself from moving close and touching again his body, a hypnotic flicker of texture and color. This new sensation, like nothing before. This man? Sleek, muscled, gorgeous, exotic. Arms enwrap her, and he pulls her close, presses his hardness against her quivering flesh.

With a gasp, she jumps away. "No! I can't. I've done too much. I'll be punished!" She leaps for the tree, stretches lithe arms to rip a young bunch of thick leaves from perfect branch. Her face is flushed, cheeks stretched taut. Her head swivels as she looks around the glade then uses the leaves to cover her nakedness. "What have we done?" she pants. "What have we done?"

A finger slides up her spine, over a supple shoulder. Her flesh ripples, electrified. "'Tis only natural, my love. Do not be ashamed."

"Eve!"

She pulls away. "It's Adam!"

Iblis presses close. "Let's share this new pleasure."

She slaps his hand and backs away. "No. Tell no one," she whispers. "No one can know."

He grasps her chin, gazes into naïve eyes. "You can't fight this," he says. "Passion, desire, joy. All God hides cannot be easily subdued." Brilliant teeth flash through a rippling countenance. "What's known cannot be forgotten," he whispers. "It will grow. In your heart. Its flames will make you squirm, throb for more, crave the release." He steps away and snickers. "Rage against it, but it will serve you nothing. Always, the heat will rise. Always, will this knowledge tempt, harass, consume, damn."

"Eve, where are you?"

"Get away!" she hisses.

Dark wings spread their full breadth to cast the glade in velvet shadows of ebony and maroon. In a flash, he's gone.

"There you are," Adam says. "I've been looking for you."

Eve covers her breasts, holds a fistful of leaves over her crotch. She glances at his penis, then turns away as her face heats and her nipples harden.

"What's wrong?" he says. "Why do you hold those leaves?"

She feels exposed, ashamed, yet the leaves fall from her grasp.

Above, unseen, the serpent enwraps a thick branch, watches delighted as she fights her desire.

Now, it's just a matter of time.

"Thus, the curse fell." Iblis snickers, a fist pressed to features that ripple like crumpled velvet. "Rather romantic, don't you think? That was my first temptation. My first soiree into the depths of man's longing." He beams, steps close. "A huge hit, exposing man's frailty, his lack of will. Exposing the knowledge of need, want, and biology. Like a switch flipped, the knowledge of flesh, of avarice, of temptation, tied to humanity for all time." He looks up, pauses, then returns his gaze to me. "You see, I was so disgusted that I tainted God's perfection. Left Him a flawed remnant of what had been so glorious. And what better device than the flesh? You've heard Cain say it, God prefers blood, and what's better than boiling blood, throbbing blood, lusty blood."

"Sex?" I say.

He gives me the stupid questions look. "No, my boy, desire. Avarice. Wanton lust. It's easy to think it all just physical, but the genius is that this lust, this unquenchable thirst, extends to all things. Not physical at all when one thinks about it, but psychological. An endless itch. An itch that can't be scratched, only soothed, for a time. Like gluttony, it doesn't matter what the desire is, just that it's fulfilled. Thus, drugs, money, *objects*. Everything attended like a hound to its fleas. Appetite, thirst, bodily functions. More, more, more and never enough." His eyes flicker with mischief and malice. "It was glorious when God ejected them. Even now I giggle at the memory. The way I introduced man to sin, to need. Everything—and I do mean *everything* —flowed from that. Then, it got better and better.

"That's the start of the pain, you know. Also hunger, deceit, sickness, greed—any itch that needs scratched sprang from that. I took His perfection and perfected it."

"I thought she ate an apple?"

He scoffs. "Nonsense, you've been reading too much Milton." He paces away, turns abruptly. "As I think of it, though, the 'dangling fruit' may have been a sort of sick pun, referring to a man's, what's the words you use? Balls?"

I think of the haiku I blurted at the Apostle.

"It makes sense," he says as if considering it for the first time. "The tree as metaphor for an inflamed penis." A squeal erupts as eyes shine with delight. "Simply delicious," he says, "just so very, very perfect. Once I introduced Eve to the true *Tree* of Life, human desire took over. Was it there all along?" He snickers again, stops abruptly and points to the mist. "Oh, I forgot something. This was a bit later but watch."

The projector whirs, becomes images of Eve.

Her face contorts. Her shriek echoes over rocky soil and barren earth, a stark contrast to the foliage of Eden's perfection. Adam squeezes her hands, worry etched on his face.

Eve wails. A baby cries.

A look of astonishment spreads over their faces.

Adam beams at the child. "He's perfect."

He kneels and offers the boy to Eve.

Her face twists in disgust. "It's horrible," she says. "It's our ruin. Get it away!"

Adam stands, cradling the baby and pushing his face close. "I'll call you Cain," he whispers, kissing Cain's forehead. "And you'll know my joy with every gaze."

"But..." My mind whirls, thoughts and questions invade like army ants. My hand itches at my pant leg. I stand, start to pace. Questions rain through tempests of time. Iblis *is* Satan, Lucifer, the Devil. He seduced Eve in the garden and got her pregnant. Then, she bore Cain and was disgusted by his very sight, a constant reminder of her failure. Did Adam ever know? If he did, did it matter? And what about God? Did He know? A stupid question. Of course, He did. So, He must've abided such a thing. Must've known Iblis would seduce, was seducing, Eve. Must've known of the pregnancy, that the child of Iblis and Eve would someday become the Antichrist.

Does Cain know? Does he call Satan father?

But I leap forward beyond this, if it follows that this child will be the Antichrist, then so must the rest. I struggle with obvious conclusions, searching desperate for another answer.

God ordained man's fall. Not so unlike the fall of the Jinn.

In human terms, if you do nothing, then you're complicit. Thoughts swirl as I stand puzzling in disbelief. I'm blown away, rocked to my core.

"So that means…"

"Yes," he says. "Cain's my son."

I blink repeatedly, probably wear an expression that reflects the tsunami in my mind. Cain as Satan's son. The Antichrist, born of Satan to fulfill his destiny millennia later. The symbol of the Yin Yang flowers as I'm reminded of Iblis's words. Good *must* have evil, and evil *needs* good.

"You're lying," I blurt regardless of what I know.

He grins like Carroll's *Cheshire*. Teeth gleam from the dark silhouette of his countenance.

"This can't be right," I say.

"Why not? Because it doesn't match your paradigms?" He steps close, a grin etched on features both chiseled and nefarious. "Your ilk will never understand. Always something else to blame, always some other to take accountability." The next sentence is hissed like a serpent. "So self-absorbed. So concerned with living, dying, that you never truly explore these mysteries. Never see that truth isn't hidden as deep as one thinks." He steps back a pace. "As Adam was a son of God, so Cain is a son of Iblis. The good, my boy, must have its bad. The evil must have its foil." He chuckles, wings rising behind him. "There's no other balance that works. No other spin—on history, on tale, for commentary—that usurps that simple fact."

A fist presses to his mouth. "And that, my dear Emery, is the nature of God."

I stand staring, blinking, struck dumb by this revelation, mind riding the corkscrews of time and the spirals of history. Thousands of questions explode in my head. I'm speechless, can't possibly fathom the depths of what he's shown.

"Has to be a lie," I whisper. "The father of lies. Has to be a lie."

"One would think," he says. "But as your puny mind grasps the truth, you'll start to see things in a new light."

"God planned Cain?"

He nods.

"God planned the Antichrist?"

He nods again, holds my gaze, appears earnest, eyes shining as if he's just won the lottery.

"God planned the end of humanity?"

Another nod as he looks at me with a mix of expectation and pity.

I hear myself as if far away. "God prefers blood."

CHAPTER 44

JERUSALEM, ISRAEL

Cain unhands me, and I blink at my own reflection.

He stands stoic as I look into the mirror and see the full picture.

Cain's crystal eyes, unconcerned, almost indifferent, betray nothing about his birth, his role as Satan's son. Did that just happen?

Before, I could easily blame the chemicals. Now I've no such respite.

Our eyes meet. My lips part as I start to speak. But he flicks his eyes at Rhyme, and the reason I'm here rages through.

Rhyme lies obtunded, dripping blood on ancient stone. Stone that's probably heaped with layers and layers of blood cells. Her auburn locks shimmy in a slight breeze. Rain splashes her face and runs down her cheeks. A different type of black pearl, yet no less treacherous, no less heart wrenching.

Crispy wears an expression of horror and rage, barely contained. Then, there's Pappy with an expression that says I haven't a chance.

Cain clears his throat, nudges me. "As Alice had her looking glass, so Merrick has his mirror. One best hurry."

I focus on the mirror, then up at the thick fogged wall. I place my hand and push, but it doesn't give a millimeter.

I take a good look at myself, notice how gray I've become, how deep my wrinkles, my trials, the trenches on my face.

I close my eyes, think of Rhyme, shut out Cain, Iblis, the rest of this cast of horrors.

Doubt floods.

What the fuck am I doing here? How on Earth do I find myself so thoroughly drowned in tsunamis of shit?

I think of John reminding me not to cuss, then wonder if God will disallow entrance based on my mix of vowels and consonants.

Is any of this true? I've heard about it, wrote stories about it. The wide-eyed teenager after a fatal accident. Hostages held captive by some crazy person. People who witnessed murder and survived. All ask the same question: Did this really happen?

I try to merge facts, feel the clock tick like Rhyme's heartbeat, realize that so many things can run through one's mind in a single second.

I open my eyes and take a good look at myself. They still carry that dark luggage, but there's purity enough in their reflection. I should take heart, I think. If I'm killed, well then, wish granted. I've been trying to do that since everything went to shit anyway. I think of Sig. The apartment on Mulberry street. Then, I run my tongue over dried lips.

Misgivings grip, icy claws that shred my flesh. Every lie I've ever told. Every impure thought, impure action, floats like waste in a cesspool. I think of addiction, of invasion by that demon. I think of shortcomings, far too many. The times I knew what was right and still chose wrong. For money, for drugs, for fame, for a story. I think of our lost baby, wonder if perhaps, behind this fogged veil, if I can just muster the courage to step through, just perhaps, he'll be there to greet me.

My hands tremble, then comes a soothing thought. Stuart successfully stepped through. Stuart knew, knew his heart, his path. Even as a minion of the Antichrist, he'd passed right through. I mean, he must've participated in some of the great ghastly. He must've murdered, torched, destroyed. It's not like Cain's job duties include reading to school kids or arranging bake sales.

I wonder about taint. The degrees, the guilt by proximity. Am I tainted? Certainly. Does that make me bad? Probably. Have I any chance to save Rhyme? Probably not. I'm covered, shellacked, horrified, terrorized, staring at my reflection, mustering the courage to take a single step, those inches that start the journey of a thousand miles.

Is there a poem for this? It's not really suicide, but yet it is. I mean if you know that you're not worthy, stepping through is certain death.

I should be glad, I think staring, searching my soul. Instead, I know only one thing: I'm *not* worthy. Certainly, when I step forward, traipse blind into this mirrored mist, God waits to render a holy beat down. He does prefer blood. Right?

And then, with that thought, hope rises. Maybe it's true. God does prefer blood. Perhaps it's all backwards. Iblis is the righteous one, testing man, giving opportunities and guidance. While God is angry, raging, waiting to burn your skin and shred your bones.

If that's the case, then I'll probably be fine. And who says this is God anyway? Could be just Igneus's staff up to its tricks. Something supernatural, something cosmic, biblical, unexpected.

A part of me cries bullshit. And I say bullshit because if everything I've been taught is correct, I'll certainly be turned to salt. A sort of warning for others like me.

It's too late to change. I know that. The time has come and gone. Can't change my heart, nor my vowels and consonants. It's too late to change thought or action. I can't reverse the past and make amends for those I've wronged.

Regret fills me, a true, resonant sorrow. As I've matured, I've realized how many things I'm truly sorry for, how many people I've hurt and the impotence of not being able to make amends for that harm.

I blink at myself, think back to Sunday school, the cliches of heaven. *It's easier for a camel to pass through the eye of a needle, than for a rich man to enter God's kingdom.*

Well, got that going for me. I'm poor as mud.

But what about my heart? My intent, as Pappy said? Is there an amalgam of actions that make the difference? Through my time on this speck of dust, I can't say with any certainty that my true intent has been anything but self-service. Chasing the story, the fame, so many drugs. An endless cycle of self-fulfillment.

I think of Pappy and Cain's conversation. Think of their belief that intent somehow makes a difference. Maybe I'll step forward and bounce right off? I shake my head, realize I intend to enter, intend to find Sebastian, because I fully intend to get help for Rhyme.

But what other intent? Intent to do no harm, like the doctors say, which means intent not to aid Cain.

The mist swirls, then presents a vision born of my thumping heart and rapid breath. I'm hyperventilating. Maybe I'll pass out and miss this test.

Visions fill my head: downtown Las Vegas. Sin City. Swirling colors, whistling bells, fancy cars gleaming neon as they pass endless rivers of streaming, strobing lights. Then, beyond that turmoil, that cacophony, through the men passing escorts' calling cards, through the endless throng who seek their favorites of the seven deadly vices, spending as much, in money, in soul, in flesh, in blood, to search out their sins and wallow in the muck. Past all of that, through all of that, beyond all of that, I see a small sign atop a crooked, splintered post.

It's made of wood, aged, rough, unlit, not appealing in the least. It calls no attention to itself, certainly not within the glamour and clamor of this city. It doesn't beep, ping, or whistle. No lights blare, cascade, or flicker. It possesses neither an image of giant breasts restrained by stretched Lycra nor an advertisement of drugs, sex, or endless buffets. It promises neither riches, nor gifts; portends no pleasures of flesh or mind.

People spit on it, piss on it, make it a target for their fluids. Then, others come and lean against it, but still fail to see the single word printed upon it.

I squint through the throbbing throng, through the barely dressed, through people poking needles in their arms, through men and women who seek only what's quick, what feels good, what tantalizes, or numbs.

I squint, focus, strain to read.

Perhaps it's a vital clue, a key just out of reach.

Behind me, Rhyme lies dying.

Behind me, no one moves to her aid.

I think of love. I think of choices.

I think of my heart and the blemishes it holds, caused by my own action or inaction, by my selfishness, my own deceit. I've been sold a bill of goods. I've failed to notice that the metaphor of our planet as a dust speck swirling through the endless vacuum of space is also a mirror that reflects the true meaning, the true depths, of everything that's important. For on this speck, where envy rules and vengeance parades, where avarice is celebrated and goodness smeared, we have it all backwards. It's Superman's Bizarro World. Everything you're told that matters, really doesn't. Everything that's a trifle gets raised to dizzying levels of importance.

We've missed it, all of us. Or as they said in Sunday school, we've all sinned and fallen short of the glory of God.

We've missed the little crooked sign. This splintered wood, this unassuming, unlit, un-dazzling post that holds the key to everything, that tells of the simple, the true, that warns of paths strayed and the horrors that await at the hands of Iblis.

So simple when I think about it, yet so very, very difficult.

And so, I squint through the throng.

And so, the sign clears, a series of block letters either misted by distance or my own tears.

RIGHT.

Thoughts swirl. I stare at Rhyme's reflection, see her chest rise and fall more rapidly. Is this the cost of my choices, the cost of my excuses?

She hangs by a frayed cord.

I consider my reflection, my scars. The gray hair, the trenched lines. Is this what folly earns? Is this the sum of my actions and my heart's desires?

If this doesn't work, I'll get my wish and be dead at last.

And so will Rhyme.

I look at myself and inhale. Words bloom in fire red, typed in blood: *What price for salvation?*

Behind me, Cain clears his throat.

I turn my head and snarl. "Hold your horses." I no longer care what he thinks. No longer feel a compunction to play his games of madness. I think to the Temple. To the decision made.

I am not a madman. Cannot be a madman.

Yet, who but a madman would stand staring? Who but a madman would choose a path of bravery over one of absence?

It's just my job.

The thought does not buoy.

This is my big chance, to enter and pass through. God must wait on the other side and He made me, made us all, in His image. He *must* understand our nature, our perversions, the horrors we dole, rely on, live in, breathe, ingest and belch on each other.

Is the nature of man the nature of God? Man certainly prefers blood, all the while speaking like the thought's abhorrent. But look at the movies, the novels, the TV. We're enamored with violence, with endless coursing crimson pouring from wounds both gifted and gained.

I've always lived by evidence, and the evidence tells me that man prefers blood.

Then so must God. My mind leaps on the slide, swirls around the thoughts and imagery. From day one, every single one of us, bathed in blood, bathed in misery. Like God?

What's true? What isn't?

The vision disappears, the sign being the last to fade, and leaves me looking at a man who isn't as old as he appears.

Then, a thought hits me. Maybe I'm looking too close, another facet of Occam's razor. Certainly its about deeds and actions, about choices. But at the bottom of that, the lining in the cupboard, the sheet on the bed, the floor beneath our feet, the air we breathe. Past specks of dust that spin through the universal Hoover, I realize, all that's true is hidden. All that's said is really lies. No one knows that for which my soul yearns. No one can possibly know my thoughts, good or bad, pure or evil. No one but me can ever probe the depths of my mind to grasp the truth and raise it to new heights.

I realize then, staring at that mirror, terrified, beaten, that no one knows *my* intent, the song of my soul.

My heart rises, bruised and broken. I think of Seventh Sunday. *"My heart is lit with fuses, each one a little blown."* And I see those fuses, empty sockets, burnt and charred.

But there's light. And standing there, knowing myself, extremely cautious of myself, staring at my battered heart and all its empty slots, I realize then and there, beyond any doubt, beyond question of proof or knowledge, what my intent has always been.

A bead of sweat rolls down my forehead, follows a trench to the corner of my mouth. It's salty. I smile, almost laugh.

What a bunch of horseshit.

I *intend* to save Rhyme.

I *intend* to thwart Cain.

I *intend* to retain my sanity while all around me crumble.

I *intend* to go on, immortal or not, in this life or the next.

I *intend* to follow that sign, to hold that single word as a fuse replaced.

I hope I'm right.

I glance inward, at the bleeding beacon that's the purity of my heart. Only a shred remains. I hope it's enough.

I swallow, clench my fists, think about courage. Doing what one must despite the fear. Like stepping through this glassed fog.

A feeling fills me, makes me bold, perhaps stupid.

I *can* stand in the face of my creator.

I *can* explain my actions, my shortcomings, my errors, my regrets.

I *can* tell the full truth, explain my intent, boldly look my fate in the eye.

I am *not* a madman.

The mirror shines.

I stare into the abyss, my own face, my own bullshit.

The abyss stares back.

And into that, I step.

EPILOGUE

Desert sand drifts, floats, sticks.

He misses his books, endless pages like these sands, these rolling hills, ever changing, ever present, vast as an ocean but without water.

Sweat drips from dishwater locks; sand covers toes full of blisters. He looks to where he kicked off his sandals, miles away at this point.

Water.

Just a drop. Just need a kernel, small as these endless grains.

Swooning, skin red from a burning sun, he steps, stumbles, falls, feels the crunch of the sand in his mouth, on his tongue. Trees dot the landscape, seem to bloom in the valleys between endless dunes. A snake slithers past, seems uninterested in the man with the dirty jeans and Rolling Stones T-shirt.

He checks his pocket. The weed's gone. Smoked up?

He doesn't remember, doesn't care. Just need water, if only a drop.

He staggers upright, then spins from exhaustion, from dehydration. How long's it been? What's the destination?

Answers elude him, race from drifting fingers that fail to grasp.

Is this a test? Why the drive to come here? To leave that eternal palace, that place of serenity, of joy.

"Walk," a voice says.

His throat hurts like swallowing razors. There's no shade anywhere.

He stumbles, crests a hill, hopes for an oasis, even a single tree, a slim slice of shade.

Is this hell? This burning landscape, these shifting grains like a giant hourglass.

He thinks to his books, the joys of the page, the stories of survival, of greatness, of prophets, kings, boys with slings.

The sun doubles its intensity, burns thick, glazes his eyes. Vision wavers, blurs. Heat rises and ripples. The throes of death? Too much exposure, too much wandering.

Nausea erupts and he chokes back vomit, then squints at the kernels clumped on his feet.

Then, the people. They appear. An endless line, thousands long, trudging, complaining, emerging from the dunes like Herbert's worms.

He raises his hands and waves. The vision musters him forward. Then he trips, slides through a beige cloud as sharp grains invade every orifice, blinding his eyes, sticking to the sweat on his hair, on his face.

He'd read in a survival journal the three things every human required: water, shelter, food. He thinks of the Earth's elements. Wind, fire, water, dirt. How does one trump the other with such aplomb?

And what about shelter? What methods are available to protect oneself?

The juxtaposition isn't lost on him. The desert, so hot during the day, yet equally, inversely, cold at night.

He rises, brushes himself, shakes sand from his hair.

The traipsing folks are closer now. They *must* have water, simply *must* offer aid.

He musters his strength and sprints to the head of the approaching line.

And moves through them like mist. They're an apparition. Simple ghosts, an illusion, a dream.

Sand flies as he plops and accepts his fate.

Then, everything changes.

Skin prickles. The landscape turns raging crimson. Fire reaches for the sky, laps the feet of crushed buildings, consumes corpses as numerous as the surrounding sands.

From a dune a stone emerges. The words bellow: *On this rock shall I build my church.*

He tries to yell, but the call cracks in his throat. He needs water, just a drop, a single molecule.

Crawling, spreading sand with each movement, he manages to reach the stone and flop down.

Anger grows. He pounds his fist, expels what little energy remains to express his outrage.

Then he hears it. The trickle, babbling drops flowing from the rock's small crack.

He leaps on it, sticks his tongue in, laps what he can. Not a lot, but enough to soothe his parched throat, enough to swish and rid his mouth of crunchy sand. He laps like a cow at a salt lick, like a cat with milk.

Above him, two figures rise: a man above the form of a wide-eyed boy. A gray beard shivers in the breeze as sand flows away like a specter. A dagger rises, glistens in unforgiving sun, aimed at the boy's chest. The man's voice is a tempest. "To my God, I submit my son!"

The knife slams down, hits something solid just before piercing the boy's chest.

With a dusting of sand, they're gone.

The stream in the crack ceases.

Dunes bloom, catch fire, turn crimson, radiate malice and hate. For the Earth? Its inhabitants? A savior's needed. Who will rise?

He rises, steps from the rock and into the desert.

Caves appear, then animals, denizens of this wasteland. Scorpions, spiders, strange bugs with thick shells. He looks around, sees many things:

The tribes of Israel walk past, unseeing.

Then a boy, hiding from a king, the shepherd who slew the giant.

On the rock, the man reappears, cries his obedience, plunges the knife only to have it stopped again by some invisible force.

"To my God, I submit my son."

A fiery wind rolls, and he covers his face, waits to feel the searing energy, waits to feel his skin melt.

But it rolls past, over, through him, causes no harm.

He steps forward, feels a bit stronger. Clouds bloom, rolling so high they cover everything. They're angry. Bruised lightning streaks their faces and flashes to the ground.

Then, finally, rain.

He ventures further, tips his head to the sky, opens his mouth to catch the drops. Not nearly enough.

Then more wavering visions, mirages through the vast landscape of fire and corpse, of flowing blood and raging battles.

A beast rises on monstrous wings, glides through thunderclouds, then over vast, burning sands. Then, through the fire, the molten crimson dunes, a light appears, serene and welcoming.

He stretches his neck, rubs sand from his eyes, licks crusted lips with a dry tongue.

A man sits at a desk, inhabits the one safe place in this vast inferno.

Bill steps forward, falls again, struggles to raise his head.

The reporter types.

His brow is creased as tears roll down his cheeks. Beyond him, a light shines through the fire, streams over cragged rocks glowing with heat.

But the reporter's unphased, bent in concentration, looks hypnotized, focused. He doesn't notice the verdant landscape behind him, a tunnel of fire with a paradise beyond. Something unlike this place of heat and death and misery. This is something fresh, something renewed.

Bill tries to yell but his voice chokes again from thirst, from dryness.

The reporter types with speed and precision, brow furled and intent.

In a flash, he's gone.

Hopelessness overwhelms as Bill drops and cries out.

Another vision blooms.

A man walks toward him, oozing confidence and character, control and ease.

Must be Cain, come to collect him.

Bill raises his hand, then drops it and stares.

It isn't Cain.

The man offers an old wineskin. "Drink," he says. "We can't have you dying out here."

The liquid pours over his mouth, drips through his beard, darkens the sand as it falls.

"Jesus?"

The man chuckles through a clenched fist, then bursts into laughter.

Recovering, he rolls his eyes and gazes down on the hippie. "I am Iblis."

A hard rain starts. Lightning flashes as fireballs consume the leagues above them.

The man chuckles again, smooths a gray suit with an aged hand. "Dear Bill," he says. "I think we'll be fast friends."

END

Dear Reader

Thank you for reading *The Tempests of Time*,
Book IV of the epic series, *Ages of Malice.*

Please take a moment to leave a quick star review and spread the word
to your fellow readers. By sharing your opinion, you lend credibility to
me as an indie author and generate trust in others that this is a story
worthy of their time.

Follow Lloyd for updates and more at:
https://lloydjeffries.com

Turn the Page for an Excerpt

AGES OF MALICE, BOOK V

LLOYD JEFFRIES

Ages of Malice, Book V

Excerpt

Father O'Toole opens a door creased with deep gouges. Ancient wood groans with each centimeter, uncared for, neglected.

Then, they're in a long hall, spooky even by their standards.

A chill traces his spine as cold, dank air rushes past them. It smells funny, like aged iron and spoiled flowers.

"Signorelli should be here to greet us," Father O'Toole says.

"It sounds hollow, Father. Empty."

"Peculiar, indeed. It should be a hive of activity. Praying, cleaning, cooking. A host of nuns to welcome us." He peers into a long dark hallway. "Two sisters died here recently, which isn't so odd when one considers their decades of service. But eleven should be left. Add the Abbot, the priest in charge, and you've got an even dozen. I expect at least one or two would welcome us."

"Maybe they left."

"To where?" O'Toole's eyes focus down the long passage. "No, boy. There's something different here. Stay alert."

Father Steven flicks the switch and a long yellow beam leaps from the flashlight. The corridor is stone, consumed in shadow. Cobwebs float in feathered wisps as spiders scurry, then vanish to deeper dwellings.

"The walls are wet," Steven says. "Greasy."

O'Toole presses a hand, then cranes his neck to examine the roof and walls. "Stinks like petrol. Strong and foul. And up there, it's dripping."

Steven steps aside just as a greasy drop plops. "Is it dangerous?"

"Not sure," O'Toole says. "I mean, I wouldn't eat it or anything."

Steven grins. O'Toole's expression remains focused. Then the old priest bellows. "Hello! Sisters? Signorelli? Hello!"

His voice dissolves as if caught in stretched shadow and silken webs.

"Peculiar," O'Toole says. "There must be someone here."

From down the corridor, a sound rushes. Perhaps a sigh. Maybe a moan of pain. Steven stiffens. "Up there," O'Toole whispers. Then, with a deftness that defies his age, he disappears into the darkness.

Steven gulps, shudders in place, licks dry lips, then buoys his courage to follow. He joins the much older priest at another door, this with even more gouges creasing its dark lacquer.

A shaky hand grips the ancient knob, then the door opens with a ghastly croak.

Steven sweeps the flashlight. The room is long, rectangular, with twelve small beds; six pressed to one wall, six pressed to the other. Beside each is a small wooden night table. Under each, a pair of thick, black shoes. The floor shimmers with soot, seems to glisten with slime. A couple of rats regard them, then scamper away.

"Odd," O'Toole says. "They're all asleep."

Steven scans the flashlight, fights fear's growing grip.

All beds save one hold a nun, fully dressed, but barefoot. Uncovered, they hold the same position: on their backs, hands folded over tummies, each face serene as if enjoying a deep sleep.

"Are…are they dead?"

O'Toole steps to the nearest, bends close. "This one's breathing," he says. "But it doesn't strike me as sleep." He grips her shoulders, gives a rough shake as his voice booms. "Sister! Awaken! Much to do. Wake up."

The nun stays frozen as if entombed.

From the bed's foot, Steven sweeps the flashlight to the wall above the bunk. There, a crucifix hangs. "Father, look. It's upside down."

O'Toole's head snaps to the crucifix, then to Steven, whose voice holds a tremor. He stands, takes a deep breath, then speaks slow and clear. "Give me the holy water."

Steven's face heats. "It's in the car," he mumbles. "I have only the flashlight and spray paint. The rest is in the car."

O'Toole speaks softly, carefully, his words measured and trembling. "Go to the car. Get the water and bring it back. Run."

Steven sprints for the door, bathing his mentor in darkness.

Then, a sound like sheets on a line. The whoosh of fabric. The creak of old bed springs.

Steven freezes, sweeps the light. "F—Father?" A quivering yellow beam traces the room. Words strangle like a finger down his throat.

Above each bed, as if suspended by invisible strings, a nun levitates.

His own gasp echoes as the full picture manifests.

Each sister hangs midair, appears still asleep, hands folded, faces blank like drugged or dead. A foulness invades Steven's nostrils like burning tires and unwashed feet. Stone walls ooze grease, seem to cascade an oily soot.

O'Toole's next to him, sweat running, his tenor a quivering leaf in a vicious tempest. "Run, boy!" he shouts. "Get the water! Our very souls depend on it."

His look is raw, molten terror mixed with dread.

Just as Steven reaches the door, it slams in his face.

The flashlight snuffs.

Darkness plunges.

Then, a shuffling sound and an odor like an opened grave.

"Fresh batteries." Steven mutters, smacks the flashlight. Searching for O'Toole, his eyes refuse to see. "Just changed them. They can't be dead." Panic rises as he hits the light again and again, flicks the button on and off.

O'Toole's hand makes him jump. "Easy, son. Do not fear. You're a servant of God."

Steven lowers the flashlight.

From the darkness comes a voice slick and warm, bold, yet foul, stretched and grating like grinding gears.

The room glows sickly green.

They squint ahead, fear blooming from brows and armpits.

A man appears. A priest. Bald and wrinkled beyond recognition.

The bony fist grips a crucifix, inverted, hanging from a rusted chain. His robes are filthy above bare feet that dangle six inches above the floor.

O'Toole squints. "Signorelli?"

Its face splits like balsa. A cackled hiss slimes their ears.

"No more, Signelli," it hisses. "Signelli no more."

O'Toole races forward, footsteps snapping like sprung traps. "Here, Steven!" He spins in a circle. "Quickly!"

The ghoul's mouth stretches with a sound like aged leather. Then, a howl like a roaring zephyr squelches all thought or awareness.

"Steven! Here! Now!"

Steven leaps in, an iron grip on the spray paint. Around them, nuns hover over each bed. Sludge bleeds from stone walls as the apparition yawns its blood-curdling screech.

The sound is endless, growling, gripping, foul.

Steven drops, starts to spray in the apparition's dim light.

"The power of Christ rebukes thee!" O'Toole cries with a boldness that belies his size. "Release your hold, demon! Leave this body in the name of Christ!" Fiery gold splays as O'Toole lunges to press the crucifix to Signorelli's chest. "We do not fear you, demon! You are rebuked!" His voice is powerful, courageous, bravado born of deep conviction.

Steven slides on his knees, sprays and sprays more, until a wide green circle surrounds them both. Then, he slides to an edge, tries to ignore O'Toole and the horrific apparition.

"Name thyself!" O'Toole commands.

Eyes like venom, burn.

Signorelli's face becomes solemn, a serenity, cracked and aged, mouth twisted, lips crusted like chimney soot. The voice is feminine, a whispered breeze, gentle on the ears. Around them, nuns float like undead specters, mouths creased, hands rising, reaching.

"I am Lilith," it says. "Mother of every foul thing." Its laughter is a shredded sheet. "You are no match. Priest."

O'Toole flies, lands hard, then slides through the circle. Steven lunges, drops the spray paint, grasps the old priest's ankle and pulls him close.

O'Toole's expression is shock and revelation. Boldness fused with confidence. "Leave us!" he shouts, focused on the beast, striving to gain his feet. Then, "Steven, complete your task."

Steven dives for the spray can, manages to nab it just before it rolls from the circle. He focuses, blocks out all else, spraying, sliding, spraying, sliding. "Done!"

Lime green glows from the circle; inside, a design like long leaves merging in the center.

Lilith's cackle terrifies. The wrench of squealing brakes, hilarity and evil in equal measure.

O'Toole thrusts the crucifix and stomps to the circle's very edge. His gait is bold, a solid rock, unquenchable belief.

The grotesque aura bathes him as greasy oil fouls his robes. "You've no power here, demon! This is a fortress of God!"

The demon shudders, stretches ghastly fingers, is repelled by Steven's circle.

"Stay in the center, Steven."

Steven grips his own crucifix in trembling fingers. O'Toole stares past the young priest, eyes wide, mouth open.

Around them, the nuns move as one, scowling, dripping faces that bely the terror of demon's possession. Habits hang in shattered strips, black sludge drips from stretched mouths to ooze over crucifixes hanging by chains.

"There are too many. How can—?"

Lilith's scream is blood curdling, ravenous. With a speed born of flame, a wasted hand snaps forward, grasps O'Toole, and yanks him. Straight from the circle.

Steven dives, catches his mentor's foot, amends his progress but just a bit.

"You dare?" Lilith screams.

The crinkled, howling face of Signorelli sends ice through his countenance, through his soul, numbing, paralyzing. "Back demon. Away!"

A howling laugh becomes feminine lilt. "What's this?" Her voice teases. "A doubting priest?" Her cackle rises, rages, looms in his heart as fear and worry coalesce. "You shouldn't have brought him, O'Toole."

Steven yanks hard, pulls his mentor to the circle's center.

O'Toole's lips stretch. The pallid face seems more wrinkled, more aged than just moments ago. He reaches for nothing, seems unaware of his surroundings, hands trembling, trying to speak, legs kicking.

"It's okay," Steven says, "I've got you." Fear-soaked eyes stare past him, widening and widening further. O'Toole's lips quiver like trying to press too many words at once.

Steven's collar tightens. A clawed, decrepit hand clamps, then drags him from the circle, toward burning eyes and a crinkled mouth.

Nightmare visions fill his mind.

Greasy sludge coats the floor, drips from the ceiling, flows down the walls.

Floating nuns rise high, then leap on him like a single entity.

"The young are so delicious," Lilith teases. "So fresh. So tasty."

Fueled by panic, lashed by fear, by loathing, by a sense of invasion, a feral will to live, to survive, to cling to all that's good, Steven claws, punches, kicks, screams.

But he's completely outmatched, his crucifix, ten feet away, lies inert in the circle's center.

His next feeling is death. Cold, uncaring, iced like an arctic blizzard, slicing his soul, blinding his mind. His thoughts fuse, turn crimson, then all becomes ebony darkness void of life or reason.

From Lilith's chest, something blooms. A blinding nightmare with coarse wings and impossible fangs dripping soot. It tears through ancient flesh, then joins the nuns pressing Steven down.

O'Toole seems comatose. Eyes rolled up, showing only the whites through wrinkled lids.

With a shriek, another demon leaps from Lilith. This like a wolf dipped in oil, mucous dripping from teeth and nostrils, seething, coal-eyes blistering like embers of shadow.

And still more flow through.

A ten-armed goliath, muscles bulging as a thousand tiny eyes mirror his horrified face.

A scaled humanoid with tentacles and a razor back.

Then, a lion-eagle hybrid, a griffin, a raging muscled body, gray, scaled, razor talons a foot long.

"Father!" Steven's plea sounds like shouting from a great distance.

Demons pounce and press him to the floor.

Nuns drop to their knees, inverted crosses clutched like praying. His skin stretches as demons drool and sniff. Then the agony of claws cracking open his ribs. Nails slice open his heart.

His shriek is endless, breathless. His mind, his nerves, his convictions sizzle, rend, snuff as Hell's very landscape fills his vision with endless ragged mountains before a flaming horizon.

Strength flees.

All thought, all emotion, smash to pieces in his mind.

This is the edge, the limit. Of consciousness, of control. Of life and sanity. It is the complete absence of anything pure, anything holy.

Steven's voice comes from far off, barely heard through the tempests of misery and rapturous demons. "No."

Nails gouge sludge in a vain attempt to grip the greasy floor. It's the last light, the last edge of sanity, of goodness. Of life.

Then, another voice. Clear and strong. Anointed. A blinding light. An energy that stands hairs on end.

O'Toole rages, crucifix raised, hair slicked in oozing sludge. His voice is pure, confident, unshaken and unshakeable. He glows, a pulsing quasar streaming from the crucifix. He's an archangel, a prophet, powerful, unmatched, robust and raging. He is an oasis in a nefarious desert, a hearth in a raging blizzard.

His words are powerful and resonant. "You are rebuked!"

Nuns shriek, contort, howl, then collapse and seize in the floor's slick sludge.

A flash erupts, then the crinkled crust of Lilith's smile.

O'Toole stands bold, crucifix raised and gleaming, light streaming from his eyes, his hair. With a sudden drop, he's kneeling, then pressing the cross in Steven's hand.

Demons pour from Lilith's breast. Legions fill the room's every inch. A seething mass of dripping fangs and razor talons.

O'Toole holds Steven's eyes for a brief instant. "Remember."

Stephen tries to move, to rise, to think, to help, to believe.

O'Toole stands and opens his arms fully.

The room explodes. A flurry of fang and wing and ooze and filth. A rushing wind, an onslaught so severe Steven can neither draw breath nor scream prayer. Quivering hands clamp the crucifix as eyes stream with tears, with folly.

O'Toole's wail scorches his heart, squelches the din of convulsing nuns and seething demons, the grating rapture of Lilith's howling cackle.

Then, all is black.

Silence reigns.

Close to him, the muted whoosh of breath exhaled, then the sounds of movement and confused exasperation.

Steven rises on trembling legs.

Nuns sprawl around him, panting and pale. Others roam drunk as if just awakened from a nightmare sleep. Their eyes search the room for some semblance of balance, of reality.

The sludge is gone.

Above the beds, the crosses are again upright.

Light flows from hidden passages to cast the room in the sunny glow of afternoon.

A priest lies on the floor and Steven races to him.

It's Father Signorelli, his face serene, his life gone.

"No. No. No." Steven fights nausea, gags on his own weakness, on his own guilt. "It can't be." Panic seizes, as he leaps up and races around the room upending all the beds. Then, down the hall and into the courtyard, bawling the name "O'Toole! O'Toole!"

Anguish strangles. Rage crushes. He trembles, runs, his mentor's name gouging his throat.

Grief clots as horror smothers.

He flops to the ground, tears pouring, stunned by a truth he dare not believe.

O'Toole is gone.

About the Author

Lloyd Jeffries enjoys dark comedies, philosophy, clever turns of phrase, religious studies and thought experiments involving the esoteric and legendary. A decorated veteran of numerous conflicts, he served in the U.S. military and has practiced Emergency, Trauma and Wilderness medicine for more than twenty years. He hides out in Florida with his family and Buck the Wonder Dog.

Ages of Malice series in order:
A Portion of Malice, Book I
A Measure of Rhyme, Book II
Embers of Shadow, Book III
The Tempests of Time, Book IV

Join Lloyd to get news and more:
www.lloydjeffries.com

X x.com/LloydJeffries2